Mother Time

—for Ann Smith, in memoriam

Mother Time

ISBN: 978-1-943661-60-2

Sij Books
booksbysij@gmail.com

Printed in the USA

The rocky hillside that dropped into a vast valley suffered a brown landscape, victim of the acid rains from the eruption of Mt. Leki in Iceland, eight months prior. The ever-present fog of sulfur dioxide clouded the otherwise blue sky. Crops destroyed and refusing to grow, the people of Shondo Province, Ethiopia, had grown hungry and desperate, the vast people of planet Arth weeping and watching and responding with grain, medical workers, dump trucks, corrugated steel, vitamin biscuits, and medicine for malaria, worms, and fleas.

Emma Smith walked at an angle to the steep hillside, grasping at dusty scrub to keep her balance. She was out and about to visit the monk digging a church into the rock, the Abba Paulos. Her jeans' pocket held a five-birr bill to give as an offering, as the Abba relied on the generosity of others to sustain himself. Emma wiped at imaginary sweat, being parched. Her short, dirty-blonde hair bounced as she walked.

After a half hour's journey from the village of Gajjo, she would find a ladder on her right. She stopped for a moment to catch her breath, gave a delicious half-smile to the hot sun, and continued forward, seeming to hear vague rustling sounds ahead. And there was the ladder, ascending a vertical climb of some twelve feet to a ledge above, where were the hut of the Abba Paulos and the entrance to his rock-hewn church.

Suddenly, a figure, not the Abba, but the village administrator, the Vulture, and behind him two minions, slack-shouldering AK-47s. Emma froze, perhaps fifty feet between her and these goons. From the clinic and warehouse, which she supervised, they stole grain and edible oils. The Vulture had arrested her interpreter Afewerki twice, since she had dropped alone into this barren land. What to do? She put her hands on her hips and stared, then glanced at the rough ladder, thinking of Reece alone in the clinic.

At a bark from the Vulture, his two thugs broke into a run as he urinated onto the ground with a flashy smile.

Emma made for the ladder and leapt up three rungs, but her foot caught, and one of the goons yanked. She held tight, thrashing her leg and stomping her free foot, breaking a rung. With both legs contained, she felt herself falling, just a few feet, but it seemed an eternity, and she hit hard the dusty ground.

"Damn you!" Emma unleashed a fury of legs and arms, but was soon pinned face-first into the rocky dirt. "Let me go! Fuck you!"

They looked to the Vulture before laughing. One kneeled on her legs and the other on her shoulders. Emma gasped for breath, dirty brown saliva streaking her face.

"Let us look." The Vulture went to his knees beside her. Emma spat as best she could, but could muster no sound. He stroked her white, scuffed cheek and then parted her hair behind her ear. "Yes, yes, I see it. The Sons of God have raped the women of Arth, and you are the evidence. Bitch."

The vulture unholstered the Makarov. He walked so that he stood between Emma and the ladder. The gun hung from his thin wrist, and there was a loud crack. A fountain of blood and fluid spurted from Emma's head.

"Nah, let us go," said the Vulture. "We must drink."

The Organon Complex at Fort Knox, near Tobacco Leaf Lake, seemed none other than a modern one-story barracks of bricks and cement. There was no fence or barbed wire or even a sign, just a small parking lot shaded by oak trees and three connected buildings. The front door required an infrared pass, followed by a white and plain reception area with a secretary and a computer screen. Denise, the secretary, verified clearance, and then once more, the infrared pass opened the next door into the sanctum. The final challenge, a nurse inside the locked medical unit verified the visitor with a camera visual.

Dr. Clyde Markush hit the buzzer and looked up at the camera. The magnets released the door, and he entered the chilly unit, laid out like a horseshoe with square edges. Markush nodded to the guard, Shark, a beefy specimen, and grabbed the handle to enter the nursing station, but had to wait for Debbie to release the lock. Recent events overwhelmed him with puzzles that had no answers.

"How's the flock?" asked Markush.

Debbie looked up from a chart. "So far, so good, just waiting for a storm."

"How's Grayson?"

"He's awake and cursing the world as usual, ranting about Dahlia."

Markush grinned. He could not get enough of Dahlia, even if it were at the hands of the psychotic Helmut Grayson. Primarily, though, Markush needed to check on Reece Myers, or rather, the body of Reece Myers. His EEG had been flat for nearly two weeks, and then there was the biggest shock of all, his reappearance at 47 Asterion Lane, along with that of the daughter he had murdered, Mia, and three characters from what could only be another universe—a nurse named Emma, an Ethiopian fellow named Afewerki, and last but not least the very specimen of Arthur Schopenhauer. How to tie all of this together? What to make of it? How to get to Dahlia?

"Going to check on Myers," said Markush.

"Yeah, which one?" Debbie was privy.

Markush went to the back of the station, past a break room and supply room, and scanned his pass and looked up. The door buzzed as the magnets released. This unit, also with twelve beds, was even colder, with a single soul as caretaker. Markush paused at the station door and waved to Shelby, who sat inside eating a pumpkin muffin. There was only one patient on this unit, Reece Myers. For a month, he had been seizing, traveling to other dimensions in a quest to find his daughter, Mia. He had found her but had not returned to his lifeless body, although another Reece Myers had turned up at 47 Asterion Lane. A thrill ran through Markush.

In room three lay Myers, a feeding tube snaking from his belly, lying on his right side, supported by a blue foam wedge inside a pillowcase. He had been given up as dead but his heart had kicked in as he was being prepared for the morgue. Shelby turned him every two hours. Electrodes sprouted from Reece's shaved head like vines. The EEG monitor revealed a continuous flat line, but other vitals, such as heart rate and blood pressure, remained within normal limits.

From his blazer pocket, Markush produced two magnets that fit his hands. He placed one on each side of Meyer's head. There were momentary jiggles, but the flatline resumed, the alarm turned off. "One and the same," said Markush. There was much to do.

Kristen held Mia tight for a moment longer, then released her. Mia, laughing, ran up the carpeted stairs to Kristin's bedroom on the left, the very room from which she had been replaced just over two months ago. Kristen wanted Mia to sleep with her, but it was Mia who insisted that she sleep in her own bed. She liked the smell of plastic toys and the greeny glow of the dark stars on her ceiling.

"Coming in," said Kristen. Having lost so much weight from the ordeal of losing Mia and now having her back, she seemed but a shadow, her thin face framed in curls.

Mia lay prone, a green comforter pulled to her chin. "When can we see Daddy? He saved me from those little girls. They had knives, long knives, and they were singing."

Kristen shook her head, still lost in disbelief that such things could happen. "Daddy's safe with Dr. Markush, the nice man who visits."

"You kissed him on the lips." Mia laughed.

"No, well, maybe, but Dr. Markush needs Daddy for a while, to ask him some questions."

"He asked me a lot of questions, too." Mia seemed sad.

"Do you know why he's so curious?"

"Is it because of Dahlia? That's what he said, but I don't like Dahlia."

Kristin breathed out. There was so little she understood. "You remember that little girl who used to come over every day?"

"Oh, Charlotte. She was mean."

"Yeah, Charlotte. She's part of Dahlia, or that's what Dr. Markush says, and Daddy too."

"She looked like those girls who tried to kill us. Where was I?" asked Mia.

Kristin coughed and fought a nervous yawn. "Ethiopia."

"Yeah, Ethiopia, where the nice man took care of me, Mister Abba, but I didn't like the food. It burned my throat."

"Well, you're back in the land of chicken fingers and macaroni and cheese, thank the Lord."

"Daddy saved me from those girls."

"I'm glad he did." Kristin flashed to the early hours of a September morning. Mia had been sleepwalking, and she had taken Mia into the big bed, and Reece had gone to sleep on Mia's bed as usual. After the alarm woke her, Reece had come into their bedroom. Without warning, he had rushed the bed, straddled the impostor Mia, and strangled her to death.

After visiting with Reece Myers' nearly lifeless body, Markush exited the unit for the open living quarters where lived the newly arrived Reece Myers, a woman named Emma Smith, the Ethiopian guy Afewerki, and what appeared to be Arthur Schopenhauer in the flesh. He found the foursome sitting in the open dayroom furnished with sturdy vinyl furniture, suitable for a hospital waiting room. A lone ceiling fan whirled ever so slowly. All remained silent, each preoccupied with their own thoughts.

"Hey, guys," said Markush. "We'll have a group chat, then some one-on-one interviews with yours truly." He looked smart but casual in his paisley shirt and brown chinos. He reminded himself of the call he needed to make to Kristin.

Reece slouched in a brown chair, his receding hairline askew, his hair the color of chestnuts. He took one last sip from the grape juice cup with an impossibly tiny straw. "We gonna do this? Time's wasting."

"You bet," said Markush. "Let's really focus on details today, versus getting caught up in emotion. I know it was a harrowing experience, but we have to dissect this to get at...to get at Dahlia. But you know that."

Afewerki shook his head no. He was the least able to comprehend in terms of science, but was fully aware of the legends that partially explained this Dahlia, or so he thought. He sat with arms folded, only wishing to have a proper meal of enjera with wots, especially the fiery dorowot.

"Mind if I sit by you, Emma?" asked Markush. She nodded, elbows to knees, and he took his place. "So, Reece, get us started. Last time we talked, you had arrived in—"

"I daresay," said Arthur. "Dahlia seems the queen. It's quite a puzzle." He looked comical in his Organon scrubs. His outfit of breeches and ruffled shirt had come off worse for the wear and were being analyzed..

Markush's eyes twinkled. "A mystery, my dear man, but perhaps the answer is forthcoming. We are probing the depths of the unimaginable is all I can say."

"Quite curious nonetheless," said Arthur.

"I'm all for diving in." Emma flashed a half-smile that nearly knocked the wind from Reece.

"Me too," said Markush. "So, Reece, Gwar 1987, an alternate reality...or universe. Arthur beamed in. That's the best way I can put it, from Gadam 3975, I think. Arthur thought he'd found Mia there, but she was yet another impostor. You had found the real Mia in Gwar 1987, your Mia, who is home with your wife, umm, ex-wife, in Richmond."

"Before that, I was trapped in this place called Dogtown, where Dahlia strolls around like a queen," said Reece. "I walked, ran, for days, maybe years, until I fell into this kind of no-man's-land, the Cylinder that leads to the Pinch. Dahlia was there, trying to get the secret of her mother from me, but hell, I didn't really know...something to do with music. All I wanted was to find the real Mia, not the impostor I...well...had killed *her*. It had to be done."

Although familiar with the story, the group sat with rapt attention. Afewerki said, "Tsk, tsk, tsk."

"And then?" asked Markush.

"I was close to the Pinch, like beyond a horizon. I had seen it in an old book the Abba had shown me, the Cylinder, pinched in the middle. Dahlia was there, teasing me about Mia. I realized that the last Mia I had seen had been an impostor, and suddenly knew where the real Mia was, Gwar 1987. Dahlia had told me that I couldn't escape. Then I remembered and said it..."

"And what did you say?" asked Markush. His eyes glinted.

"I'm afraid to say it. Afraid I'll be sent hurtling into another universe. Arthur here knows all about it and is known for those words. 'The world is...' I'm sure you know the rest."

"I dare to conjecture," said Arthur, "that he is speaking of man's ability to create his own reality through the senses."

Reece nodded.

"And so you said it. Dahlia released you? From the Pinch?"

"Not the actual Pinch, but from inside the Cylinder." Reece sighed and crossed his legs, folded his arms, tapped his fingers on his chest. "I was thrown into Gwar 1987, and Mia was there with the Icelanders and Emma. They were taking care of her. I was stunned, unsure of how we would get back, back to this place." Reece glanced at Emma, one of three Emmas he had met in his "travels." It had been another Emma, all those years ago, who had saved his life after the Hyena shot him. He had been working as a nurse in a clinic in rural Ethiopia, falling for her hard, but had been engaged to Kristin. He had survived, married Kristin, who had given him Mia, but had never gotten over

Emma. She was right here, in the same room. He could reach out and touch her, but there was a problem. The original Emma lived in Hueytown, Alabama. She still existed. This Emma before him was from another time and place, younger, but looked the same, that killer half-smile. He groaned.

"You found Mia in Gwar 1987. Tell me again how you get back here." Markush resisted the urge to stand.

Emma glanced at Reece and spoke. "The village administrator, the Snake, came to our compound. We opened the gate. And in poured these perfect little girls, singing, but off key, all the same, perfect faces and bodies."

Afewerki coughed and raised his hand. "With the knives. They are having the knives."

Reece's wide eyes strained. "And then, boom, Arthur appears out of nowhere, sent by the Abba Paulos."

"It was quite a sight to behold," said Arthur. "I've never been more terrified—"

"The girls, the namesake of Dahlia, backed us into the dining hut. The Icelanders, Gudmunder, Eydis, and Svana went over the fence. I lost track of the other Reece. I grabbed a pistol from Gudmunder's tent and started firing, but there were too many. They just kept coming."

Arthur couldn't contain himself. "Inside the hut, we stood helpless, and Reece shouted. There was blue light and no sound, and then we found ourselves thrown upon quite a lovely but frosted lawn, greeted by a charming lass, young Reece's wife. A conundrum, no doubt."

"Yes," said Reece.

Markush, slumping in his chair, sat erect, electrified. Silence reigned for a full minute. He wondered where they would go from here, what would become of his relationship with Reece's wife, Kristin. She had captured his heart while the original Reece was on the medical unit at Organon, Markush having interviewed her on base at Fort Knox. Kristin had filed for divorce, unable to believe Clyde Markush when he told her that Reece had not killed Mia, but had rather strangled an impostor, a replacement. But Markush, being very convincing, slowly won her over. Kristin had so desperately wanted to believe that Mia, her Mia, was still alive, but hidden among infinite universes? Markush told her that Reece was "traveling" during his prolonged seizures on the unit, visiting other times and places, looking for Mia. Markush gained her trust but not her belief, and filled the loneliness in her life in the absence of Mia and Reece. But now Mia was back at 47 Asterion Lane. Reece was back, too. But still she did not understand, yet had, against her will, begun to believe the outlandish details.

"The people need us," said Afewerki. He remained unsure of his new reality. He had often dreamed of coming to the States to study. Emma had promised to help him, but this was not the way he had imagined.

"It was just you and Emma working in the clinic, right?" asked Markush.

Emma stretched her arms over her head and yawned. She had not slept well since face-planting into Reece's backyard just two days prior. "No, there was Reece, another Reece. I'm not sure what happened to him. I hope he's okay. Afewerki was our interpreter. We worked for the Baptist Mission. What will everyone think now that we've vanished? I'm shocked, not sure what to do. Do you somehow send us back? Do we belong here?"

"That's a brilliant question," said Markush. "Reece, what do you think?"

Before he could answer, Arthur spoke. "Yes, I was called into this grand adventure from my apartments to a queer place, Gadam, the year being 3981. There it was that I met young Reece and learned of his quest to find his daughter." He ran his fingers through his thick, white sideburns. "We discovered we could travel through the cosmos using the powers of the Abba Paulos and the holy Ark. Perhaps it will be necessary for Emma and Afewerki, both charming, to return to this same village in our present time and engage the Abba once more. I should like to return to my humble abode as well."

"I've thought of that," said Markush. "But I need you. We'll take care of you. We...there are powerful people and agencies looking after us who can integrate you into our society. Afewerki, we can enroll you in a college with an ESL program. Emma, we can find you work as a nurse. Arthur, well, surely some great university would be happy to offer you tenure as a professor. And Reece, but Reece, you are actually *home*..."

Emma spoke. "I need to be in my own time and place. The people back in Gwar need me. My family is in that universe. I can't believe I'm saying that."

Markush shook his head of long, graying hair. "I get you, but I can say that national security, in this universe, and perhaps others, is at stake. We need you for now."

Afewerki fiddled with his Exxon ballcap. He looked small sitting in the lounge chair, his dark skin contrasting with those around him. "If I study and to get my degree, perhaps I can return to my village in this place?"

Markush grinned. "That's the spirit, but you have to know that most likely there will be another you already there who has no idea you exist. Just like Emma here."

"And then there is the other me, locked up somewhere in this puzzle of a place," said Reece. "How can there be two of me if this is where we're both from?"

"I don't know," said Markush. "This other you is alive but has no brain function. Perhaps that's the key."

Reece laughed, but then got serious. "Who's saying that I'm the real me? It feels like me. I used to teach philosophy here, or rather in Richmond. The house was the same. But there's two of me. Will the other me die? Am I not free until that happens?"

"It's obvious that there are long-term consequences for everyone here, and that we're all still grappling with reality. We have to stay in the moment, though. You are now part of a team of experts dedicated to understanding who Dahlia is, what role she plays in this time and place, what she really wants, and to what lengths she'll go to get it. I'm afraid that's the bottom line, and I'm asking for patience. Please?"

That afternoon, Markush drove from Fort Knox to Richmond to check on Kristin and Mia. He recalled his interviews with Kristin, her utter reluctance to believe the insanity. He had wined and dined her during those three days at the Organon guest house, his appreciation for facts about Reece, as Reece lay seizing and traveling the multiverse, soon melding into a quest to win Kristin's attention. By now, the divorce of Reece and Kristin was final, and nothing was standing in the way of their romance.

And the other Reece Myers lay motionless on the long-term wing of Organon. Markush had somewhat given up on him, thinking that Reece had passed over some unknown chasm with no chance of retreat. Was he there, lying helpless in that bed, or was he alive elsewhere, still ferreting out the secrets of Dahlia? The alive-and-well Reece, and the one who was brain dead, if he regained consciousness, would learn of Markush's relationship with Kristin and might react in a manner that precluded the sharing of secrets.

Salted slush slung from the tires of Markush's trusty Volvo, not a day for the Jaguar. The end of his two-hour drive in the chill air, breeding clouds of dirty white, drew near, and he exited the interstate. He fought the urge to grab a burger and drove somewhat east of Richmond proper to 47 Asterion Lane. Kristin's Toyota sat in the driveway, and he pulled alongside, patting down his graying beard, a shade darker than his hair.

"Come in. Good to see you, Clyde," said Kristin. "I need

to know everything." She leaned in for a hug, and Clyde kissed her hair, curling and dark brown.

Clyde Markush, having stamped his shoes free of latent snow, took a deep breath of the house, the house where Reece Myers had strangled the impostor. He held Kristin at arm's length for a good look into her green eyes flecked with brown.

"You look great. I love that sweater," said Clyde.

"Well, the holidays are upon us, and it's Mia's favorite. I can't believe she's actually here to open presents. I was so dreading that."

"Where is the miracle girl?" He passed through the living room and into the kitchen, looking.

"You're just interested in Mia, I see. She's your little experiment. What about me?"

"Don't be so…" He wanted to say crass. "So reductionist. I'm thrilled to see you. It's been, well, three days since the grand reunion. Mia?" He peeked into the den, which dropped a step from the kitchen. There was nothing extraordinary about the house, a Cape Cod with two large bedrooms upstairs.

"Reduction what? Are you insulting me?"

Clyde sighed and turned back toward her, putting his arm around her waist. "You're gorgeous."

"But not smart?"

"No, no, it's just that I have a two-fold purpose here, and part of that is business, to figure out what the hell happened over the past month. Your daughter, Mia, we presumed dead. You buried her, or rather, her replacement. And now Mia's back, having traveled across barriers of space and time that I can't fathom. How? Why? The details, I need the details. You have to understand." He gave her a side hug.

"Okay, buster, she's in her room."

"Okay, in her room, but first let's talk about you, about your finances. How is that going?"

She led him into the den and motioned toward a lime-green loveseat facing a fireplace. "The money is coming in, direct deposit, so that's good. I'm still waiting to hear about paying off the house. I had planned to move, you know, because I couldn't stand the thought of being here. But that's changed since Mia's back. Maybe the house is good luck."

"Let's just say that Organon is well-funded and has friends in high places. You'll never have to worry about bills again, especially since Reece was the breadwinner."

"I worked too, dummy, but I quit. You know that." Their knees touched, each angled toward the other.

"Right, but our help means you can be a full-time mom without worrying, even without Reece." He loosened his tie and struggled out of his sports coat without standing.

"I appreciate that. I really do. Everything happened so fast. I'm still dizzy. I was so damned depressed, but now..."

"Looking up roses," said Clyde.

"You say that I can survive 'without Reece,' but there's a Reece Myers who walks and talks back at Organon. He's the Reece who *killed* Mia. Then there's the Reece, who is nothing more than a vegetable, but he killed Mia, too. You said he could come back, back to life, that is. What then?"

"Both are your Reece's. One is, as you might say, 'a vegetable,' but under circumstances that have yet to be understood. If he makes it back, he will be forever changed and of utmost importance to us." His face lost the animation of his speech. "Do you still love him?"

"Mommy! Hi, Clyde," said Mia with a big smile.

Both turned, having forgotten her briefly. Mia looked the part of a seven-year-old girl with light red hair, shoulder-length, freckles, and wearing gray corduroys with a long-sleeve t-shirt.

Clyde stood, his arms out. "Mia, aren't your feet cold?"

"No, my feet stay warm." Mia failed to rush into his arms as if they were best friends. She'd just met him three days ago. She knew he wanted her to come and visit him at his workplace, but she was afraid to leave the house, and Kristin had said, "No way."

Clyde saw that his enthusiasm was a bit overdone and let his arms relax. He glanced at Kristin, who seemed as if a favorite ring had been lost.

"Mia, what were you doing in your room? Still drawing?" asked Kristin.

"Yeah, but I ran out of red. I miss Shooting Star." Her smile left.

"Honey, come here." Mia sat beside her with Clyde standing behind the loveseat.

"I know you loved Shooting Star, but I gave him away when you...left. We'll get you another hamster. I promise."

"And you gave away Atma, too. That wasn't very nice." She squirmed away from Kristin's embrace.

Kristin's eyes watered, and she wrinkled her nose. "It was for the best. I just couldn't...take care of him. He missed you. Maybe we can get another Atma."

"No, I don't want another dog. I want Atma. And Shooting Star." She held her legs out, comparing the lengths.

"Dr. Clyde, are you here to ask me questions? Mommy said you would."

Clyde felt as if orbiting something far away, his mind racing. He wanted to see her drawings. "Of course, I want to ask you some questions, plus I just wanted to see you and your mom. What were you busy drawing?"

Mia looked to Kristin for support. "I guess I could show you, Dr. Clyde. Are you a real doctor?"

Clyde laughed. "I went to medical school like doctors do. I'm a psychiatrist, a forensic psychiatrist. And I would love to see your pictures." He started for the hallway, but Mia hesitated.

"Do you think I'm a crazy person?" asked Mia.

"Mia, the only crazy person is your daddy," said Kristin.

Clyde laughed. "No, but you know a lot, don't you? Think of me as an investigator, like I solve puzzles that involve the mind."

"Okay, but Daddy's not crazy. He saved me. He brought me back."

"You know what I mean, honey. Aside from that, just a little crazy. His humor attracted me. He always made you laugh, right?" asked Kristin.

"Yeah, he's funny. I miss Daddy."

Clyde cleared his throat. He was realizing the tightness of the bonds between Reece and Kristin and Mia. "So, those pictures. Show me. Is that okay, Kristin? Want to join us?"

"I've been looking at them and don't understand, but I never understood the music that's inside Mia, either. Did you know she can hear an orange and make a song from it?"

Clyde's attention drifted. "The most perfect of the arts, according to our good friend Schopenhauer. I, too, have some experience with music, but it always seems to be the girls who really get it. Always the little girls..." He remembered something very important. "Has Charlotte shown up? The feisty little girl with the perfect face, I'm told."

"God, Charlotte. Reece hated her. But you know, there has been a little girl like Charlotte who always latches onto us, no matter where we live, always living with grandparents. But, no, I haven't seen Charlotte since Mia was murd...I mean, went missing."

"Charlotte or Charlottes are a key to the puzzle. Make sure you let me know if she or someone like her shows up again." He wanted to use the word dangerous but held off in the company of Mia.

"I will," said Kristin. "Should I let her in the house?"

Markush seemed lost in thought. "I don't know, really. Just play it by ear. I'm sure Reece would forbid it, but we should ask him."

"I know you want to see Mia's drawings, but you have yet to say anything about Reece, about how he's been doing since returning. I mean, I called you right away. With him and the others, I didn't know what to do. Frankly, I was petrified. I just wanted to take Mia and hide and have them all disappear."

"Yeah, right. In short, he's doing well. He seems to have sustained some bruised ribs but is otherwise fine, as are the others. Let me go with Mia, and then we can talk more." He had hoped she wouldn't ask about Reece and maintain her disgust for him.

"Let's go." Mia took Clyde by the hand and led him

to the hallway and up the mahogany stairs. "This is my room."

Clyde took it in, the single bed against the wall, framed drawings on the wall, a desk covered with books and paper, a pile of crayons on the beige carpet beside a drawing book, glow-in-the-dark stars on the ceiling, a window looking over the back yard.

Mia plopped onto the carpet and opened the sketchbook. Markush perched on a rainbow beanbag chair beside her. She opened the book and flipped through the pages. "I ran out of red. Red sounds like ice dripping, but in a pretty way." She stopped on a drawing and then flipped back a page.

Markush leaned over to see the image of what appeared to be a black angel. "And what is that?"

"Dr. Clyde, that is Dahlia. The Abba showed me in his book, an old book. He kept whispering *Dahlia, Dahlia.*"

Markush felt his heart race. *Dahlia.* He had visited a small village in Ethiopia many years ago, early in the investigation, and had met an Abba, the Abba Paulos, but he had not shown him a book, just the magnets to facilitate travel. "And to you, who is Dahlia?" He felt his neck veins engorging and leaned back, his eyes fixed on Mia.

"She's like an angel, all perfect and everything. She's a little girl like me, but she can do strange things. I don't like Dahlia. She was hiding me in different places so that Daddy couldn't find me. She couldn't hear my music, and it made her mad."

"How did she get mad?"

"She wanted to know who her mommy was. I didn't know, and she took me to this place with no air and lots of bad music, like the music was trapped in there. I was floating, and the light was really blue. And then I could hear the real music, but she couldn't, and I figured out who her mommy was."

Clyde Markush held his breath.

Reece tried the doors, all locked. It was damn cold, and he just wanted to feel some sunshine and be free. The others were dying to get out as well and becoming paranoid that they were just some bacterium growing on a Petri dish. Cameras lurked in every corner, and who was watching them? After finding himself face down in snowy grass, Reece had been in a state of shock, along with everyone else. After eliminating broken bones, they had all filed into 47 Asterion Lane and gathered at the dining room table, stunned, Kristin holding Mia in her lap, asking how? and how? and how? receiving information that made no sense. Feeling ungrounded and helpless, although elated at finding Mia, Kristin had called Dr. Markush, and what followed blurred. Now he was captive within Organon, along with Emma, Afewerki, and Arthur Schopenhauer. *Katzenjammer!*

The open dayroom held a cluster of hospital chairs and short couches, tight gray carpet, interior walls of red brick, a balustrade, and above it gray, weathered wood, no windows. A separate sitting area faced a TV mounted to the wall, the TV always on but muted. The TV delighted Arthur, watching a commercial for an allergy medication. "So realistic, as if my eyes are being tricked." A wide hall with four rooms facing four rooms, very comfortable with single beds and a private bathroom. Reece had shown Afewerki how to work the toilet and helped him with hot versus cold water.

"This is plain shit." Reece paced, arms folded against

the cold. The others sat scattered among the couches and chairs, staring, thinking. A door opened, then closed, and a lone woman with a tight braid entered, pushing an upright vacuum cleaner. She plugged in and began her work as if all was well. Reece walked toward her. "Hey!"

Her name was Lenora, and she had never vacuumed this part of the facility, but there had never been a need until now. Hard blue veins rolled on top of her hands. She cut the power and looked at Reece as if he were a mailman. "Can I help you, sir?"

Reece glanced back at the group, hoping they could see he was taking action. "Can you open that door again? Does it lead outside?"

Lenora grinned, a front tooth missing. "What in the world for? You can't go nowhere on account of me. I just do the cleaning around here, me and Jed, that is. You have to have the pass." She flashed a badge hanging around her neck.

"Hey, Reece, go easy on her," said Emma. "She'll get in trouble. Markush said he'd be back."

"Yeah, what she said." Lenora thumbed the power switch and went back to work with a grim smile.

"Jesus, at the mercy of a cleaning lady, after I've been to the center of it all and traveled infinite light-years." Reece gave it up, though, for the moment, and walked back to the group. But were they a group or individuals? Did they *have* to work together? He just wanted to be home with Mia and patch up things with Kristin, or did he? He sat across from Emma, and his mind instantly calmed. She had saved his life back in 1986, after being shot. No, not this Emma, but the one in Hueytown. He had to remember that. But she was the exact same, although younger. He wanted to scream.

"Has anyone had the fortune of their bowels moving?" asked Arthur. He was large for the chair and looked like an antiquarian pathologist with his unruly white hair and whiskers. "Whilst in Gadam, 3981, that is, all there was to eat was the peculiar liquid dish called buster. Young Reece here can tell you about it. The various flavors were quite delicious and refreshing, but it makes one's bowels immotile as if there was never a need to evacuate them. I suppose there are advantages, but I found it quite distressing."

No one spoke for a moment, and then Afewerki laughed, and being shy, spoke with a lowered voice. "I am having the same problem. I am not eating the spicy food of home here. There is only salt, and the pepper is not real pepper." He seemed sad.

"Better than diarrhea, I'd say." Emma brightened at the frank talk of bowels, as most nurses do.

Reece chimed in. "Definitely. Damn, we saw some nasty cases of diarrhea. Remember that baby whose anus had everted, and we poured cold water on it to help it withdraw back into place, and then taped the little thing's butt cheeks?"

Emma had the look of knowing the situation, but not the we part. "Don't forget that we never worked together. That's the other Emma, the one who saved your life, right?"

"My my, what a tremendous mess we are in," said Arthur. "Not knowing who is who." He stood. "Perhaps I shall perambulate about the premises to stimulate some active force."

"Yes, just sitting and sitting," said Afewerki. "I will watch the television." He stood stiffly and walked that way, letting Lenora pass in front of him.

"I need to get back to Richmond asap." Reece admired the bit of ankle showing above Emma's sneaker.

"Seems like you have a better shot at going home than I do," said Emma. "I mean, how in the world am I here, and how do I get back, or do I just suck it up and stay here? I'm so confused."

"Markush is not taking very good care of our real needs," said Reece. "He used me while I was seizing to get at this great mystery he's been after for God knows how long. But I found Mia. That's what matters. What if he straps me down and tries to make me seize again? What's stopping him?"

"Paranoid, I see." Emma took a good look at Reece. Nice shoulders, a foot taller, thin, in shape, his major setback being his receding hairline. "Just stay focused on the short term for now. Like, what are we having for dinner? But tell me more about Mia."

Reece forced himself to relax the strain in his eyes. Mia. Mia. His only child, just seven years old, his pride and joy. "She's just a normal little girl, except Dahlia is after her, for her understanding of music, I think. Mia makes songs of everything, without trying. Dahlia has been after her for years. I tried to protect her, but at some point, Dahlia mapped her like she mapped me when I was a toddler."

"What the hell is mapped?" asked Emma.

Reece pushed back the hair over his ear. "Can you see it? The mesh, there and not there. But it shows up as a shadow on X-rays and CT scans."

Emma stood and walked over. "Not really, maybe the light?"

"Well, it's there. Even though I was only about two, I remember Dahlia in my room. There was a bright flash of blue light, and something went over my head. I was screaming bloody murder. I think my mother came, but I can't remember. And Dahlia got Mia, too, mapped her brain to discover whatever secret she's after. Primarily, Dahlia wants little girls, but she occasionally maps boys if they are in the line of a girl with musical powers like Mia. I was so vigilant all those years, watching and waiting, but she got her, mapped her, and then when that didn't work, she replaced her and whisked her off to never-never land."

Emma tried hard to believe what she was hearing. "Jesus, that's a lot to handle."

"Mia always had night terrors. We would let her sleep with Kristin, and I would sleep in Mia's bed. That's when the switch took place. The next morning, Mia called me 'father.' I knew it wasn't her. The music was all wrong."

"Wow, and then you did it?" Emma leaned forward, her hand on his knee.

"Yeah. I closed my eyes and did it, and went stark raving mad, winding up here in Organon. My other body's in this place somewhere. How, I don't know. I think Markush has an obligation to let me see it."

"That would be very weird," said Emma. "I'm sorry."

"Don't be."

Lenora closed in and asked Reece to raise his feet.

Dr. Glenelle Lock had a problem. Reece Myers had escaped from Organon and was on the loose. There were dense woods surrounding the Organon complex, and military police had not found him an hour into his escape. Her small office belied the importance of her position concerning Organon. Located in the basement of a large H-shaped building in Bethesda, Maryland, she was officially associated with the National Institute of Mental Health, holding a joint position as a psychiatric researcher with an office at the Pentagon that studied soldier survival in relation to specific weapons. Her dull, green, metal desk held two phones, one with a direct line to Clyde Markush that rang a special cell phone Markush kept on his person at all times. She had just talked to him. He had received the news of Reece's escape while visiting Reece's wife in Richmond. Using the other phone, Glenelle contacted the Pentagon office to speak with Major General Tom Watkins.

"Watkins here."

"Hey, General. We have a major problem. One of the Returnees has made a run for it. Reece Myers."

"Goddamn."

"I need you to authorize an all-out manhunt at Fort Knox. The folks on base don't give much credence to Organon, thinking it's just a psych ward," said Glenelle.

"Yeah, I can do that. I'll contact the base commander and get it going. I have Myers' photos, DNA, and fingerprints. What was he wearing?"

"Organon scrubs, dull brown, and house shoes, I'm told."

"Got it. I'm on it."

"We have to find him. He can't be talking to anyone other than us. This is damn serious. I'll check in later to hear about the analysis of their clothing. How's that going?"

"It's underway, checking for gases, metals, debris, chemicals, body fluids, radiation, and whatever else we can come up with."

Glenelle finished and called Markush.

Reece had it figured out. Two staff members, Jewel and Linda, entered the unit, pushing a cart that contained their dinner trays—roast beef, scalloped potatoes, and lima beans with unsweetened tea and a slice of vanilla cake for dessert.

"Hey, I can help," said Reece.

They looked at him like he was crazy, because all the patients were, right?

As the others gathered at the table, Reece made his move and grabbed a badge from the neck of Linda.

"Hey!" Linda grabbed the lanyard and held tight. Jewel stood back in shock as Reece wrestled with her.

"Reece! What are you doing?" asked Emma.

Reece yanked and had the badge. "Stay back, and I mean it."

Using the badge, he exited through the door and encountered a second, going through it easily. From there, he made his way down a hall past a kitchen and encountered a third door. He entered the reception area, surprising Denise, who was sitting behind the reception desk.

"Who are you?" she said.

Reece saw daylight spilling through the double front doors and dashed that way. Outside, he ran for the trees, a mix of pine and hardwoods, his feet being bruised by rocks and pinecones through his flimsy house shoes. As he ran and hobbled along, he wondered what universe he was really in. Was this the right one? It seemed to be, but he could not be a prisoner. He only wanted to be with Mia. It was around six, and darkness had fallen, cold with patches of snow in the shade. He slowed at a road and ran across back into the woods. A light rain fell. Within a quarter mile, he crossed another road. Soon, he stopped to rest and gathered his breath. The sky above looked gray and dirty, and he shivered, wondering why he had brought no food. Panting and frozen, he sat and leaned against a chestnut oak, most of its leaves fallen.

He thought back to Gadam 3981, where he had met Arthur and enlisted him to help find Mia. He had found Gadam strange, the people all with golden skin and most seemingly without work. They gathered in the establishments where buster was served, which was the only food available. There were bars too, and everything was free, but he learned that information and sex were the two things you had to pay for. Everyone seemed to know everything about him, that he was searching for his daughter, referring to the data fur. Soon, Reece discovered he could access this data fur and find information on everything he wanted to know, except where Mia was.

Gadam was small and contained nondescript buildings on steep lanes without names or numbers. At the edge of town, toward the east, things just stopped, and scrub appeared. There had been an Orthodox church, much like the ones in Ethiopia, where he had worked. He'd had an epiphany, recognizing Gadam as an alternate version of Godo, where he had worked and been shot. There would have to be an Abba in Gadam as well, and he and Arthur had set out to find him. He had not been sure why he needed to find the Abba, other than maybe he would have information about Mia, who he was certain was hidden in Gadam.

Arms folded and freezing and soaked with rain, Reece mustered and walked another quarter mile or so, until he reached a paved road that led into a cloverleaf off to his right. He hesitated behind the tree line and scouted beyond the road, seeing a chain-link fence. He waited until traffic cleared and darted across, vaulting over the fence onto rough ground. There were a few trees, and then the vista opened to a vast flat area with an imposing building, surrounded by an impressive barrier less than a thousand feet away. He thought back to his days as a kid living at Fort Knox and realized that he'd stumbled onto the gold bullion depository. He stopped, not knowing what to do. Suddenly a siren...He bolted back the way he had come.

Markush had been holding his breath, listening to Mia, as she revealed to him the mother of Dahlia. It was just as Helmut Grayson, a patient at Organon, had told him after he brought Grayson a bottle of Scotch. Time. Dahlia's mother was time. What that meant escaped him for now, but he and the others up north were working on it. Implications for the origin of everything hung in the balance. He was sure of that.

"Mia, thank you, but I have to make a phone call." He had just received the news of Reece's escape on his cell phone.

"Yeah, okay. I'll show you some more drawings when you come back. You're coming back?" asked Mia.

"I will soon, but have to go now." He trotted down the stairs and met Kristin there.

"Glass of wine?" asked Kristin. The heat kicked on with a hum, dimming the lights briefly.

"No time. I have an urgent matter to attend to. Just promise that if Reece shows up here, you'll call me."

"What? How could he get here?"

"Just promise."

"Is something wrong? I mean, I promise. I trust you, Clyde."

He forgot his blazer and stepped into the cold, running for his Volvo.

They had eaten without Reece, distressed that he'd escaped. He was the leader of this adventure, and they felt vulnerable without him.

A movie channel played, and with nothing else to do, they parked in front of the TV to watch *Rosemary's Baby.*

"The actors in this drama are quite amazing, knowing their lines. The apartment seems grand, very stylish." Arthur sat with his hands resting on his belly. "I am feeling some movement in my bowels."

Emma and Afewerki laughed. An ad for dog food appeared.

"It's quite distressing to break the drama with these short stories," said Arthur.

"They're called commercials," said Emma. "They want you to buy the dog food. The commercials pay for showing the movie."

"A necessary evil, I suppose," said Arthur.

Afewerki looked sad. "In my village, no one feeds the wusha, the dog. They are fighting night and day. You must throw the stone in case they will bite you."

"He's right," said Emma. "At night, it sounds like murder."

"I wonder how my dear little Atma is doing without me. She is my pet, and she eats only what I dine upon, not these crumbs from a colorful sack.

"Maybe Reece was right to escape. I wonder if they caught him?" asked Emma.

"He is very resourceful," said Arthur, "but I do wish for his return. While in Gadam, we had many interesting talks over glasses of liqueur and this bourbon of which he was fond. You know, in our travels, we met both you and Afewerki in a village, a Godo, I believe."

"But I had never met you before. I was in the village of

Gwar when we first met, where the little girls with knives... and then poof, here." She and Afewerki looked at one another. It was true.

"Yet another time and place, it seems, another you and another Afewerki, but the setting was the same, a rustic village of huts, steep lanes pocked with stones. There were the Icelanders, right?"

"Yes, there were Icelanders in Gwar, but in Gadam?" asked Emma.

"No, the village called Godo. I believe it was 1986. Oh dear, the Gadam where young Reece and I met was 3981. Dahlia lured us there, deceiving us. The real Mia was not there, but rather in your Gwar. The Abba sent me to you and Reece through the Ark, just as the girls were attacking."

"So, you met two Emmas, one of which was me. Then there's the 'original' Emma, who saved Reece's life, who lives in Alabama. And Markush told me about another Emma, a patient here who looks like me. She was shot. So, that's four Emmas I know of, and all with the Ethiopia connection. There's something special about that place."

"Indeed, an unlikely place for this drama," said Arthur.

Afewerki shook his head. "There are many mysteries in my home. Yes, the Ark of the Covenant is kept there, near Axum. But it moves, and no one knows how and where except the holy priest. The Ark can kill a man, possessing great power." They had forgotten the movie, caught up in their conversation.

Reece ran, soaked to the bone, his hands and feet numb, especially his right hand, which had a displaced radial artery. The house shoes proved useless, and he left them behind. The dim light of white clouds filtering through the barren trees, he plunged through brambles and scrub, crossed a road, and then another. He retreated and ran farther south, finding the road that ran into the cloverleaf. Nearby, a train track traversed the wide road, and he took it up and over, slipping on the ties and bruising his knees. A cold and silent wind froze him further. He had to get warm.

Once across, he veered left into a clearing and ran for tree cover just ahead, more thick forest but with less wind. He stopped to rest but began to cramp. A helicopter chopped in the distance, a beam of light searching the ground.

Within five minutes, staggering now and gasping for breath, he broke into another clearing and spied a small building. Perhaps he was in a park. He dashed headlong for the plain building, and it was a restroom. The first door, the women's side, he pushed into, and there was heat! Without thinking, he stepped into a stall and latched the door. On the toilet, he hugged his chest to his thighs, praying for warmth and mercy.

Base Commander Major General Phillip Borden scratched his bald head, standing in his bedroom, a mere half mile from where Reece was holed up in Thorne Park. The Pentagon had interrupted his dinner of rib eyes and baked potatoes with a seemingly innocuous emergency, an escapee from the nuthouse at Organon, but orders were orders. Thirty-two MPs in jeeps and an Apache helicopter with infrared sensors took on the search. Borden's biggest worry, though, was an intruder onto the grounds of the bullion depository, hopefully the same guy, a Reece Myers dressed in brown scrubs.

Inside the cockpit of the Apache AH-64, Chief Warrant Officers Brandon Cutch and Darnell Gibbs focused on the area around the bullion depository and the Organon complex. They could see the heat signatures of soldiers posted within the bullion depository grounds and circled wider.

"There's the bastard that cancelled my damn dart night," said Gibbs.

"Roger that," said Cutch. "In the park, moving north." He then got on the radio to MP headquarters to report target possibly located as Gibbs hovered the craft.

"His signature cancelled. He's in a structure," said Gibbs. "Goddamn monkey crazy bitch slapper."

"Alpha 5, suspect has taken refuge within a structure at Thorne Park. Will stay put until ground takes control."

"Battlefield illumination on target, looks like a shithouse."

"Fucking lunatic. Cut off his head and shit down his

neck hole."

Laughter and static.

"Get a dog on that fucker, Alpha 5," said Cutch, who had been uprooted from a quiet evening of *Beavis and Butthead.*

Reece could feel the chopper above, reminding him of the chopper thumping back in Ethiopia that brought grain and supplies to the village of Godo, so many years ago. He felt his temple and could feel the indent, where the bullet had entered his head and then cleanly exited on the other side. He'd been inside Emma's little mud and pole house, staying the night because he'd given up his bed to a man with a rotten leg that would need amputation. Undeniably, he'd had a crush on Emma, building from their close contact working in the clinic together, although he was engaged to Kristin. Massaging her neck, he had been standing behind Emma, and his hands slipped down... then the shots. Emma had controlled the bleeding and pumped him with IV fluids. He'd nearly died during the rough jeep ride from Godo to Alem Ketema, where Terry had flown him to Addis Ababa. He owed Emma his life.

Bright light poured through the frosted windows of the restroom, but he couldn't hear the jeeps over the noise of the Apache. He decided he would run for it and then couldn't work the stall's door latch, his hands still numb. He stopped at the sink and cupped water to his mouth. The door burst open.

"Down! Down! Face down!"

Reece eyed the leveled M16s and laughed.

Inside Organon, on the medical unit, Jim, one of two nurses on duty, made his way down the hall to room six to see Emma Smith, the nurse shot in the head. She could now flutter her eyes and move her fingers.

Jim, a solid beefcake with a round, tan face, checked her blood pressure, 90 over 60, heart rate elevated from 90 to 110 since entering the room. The room presented as plain with a hospital bed, an over-bed table, a side table, and a reclining vinyl chair. Dirty needle box on the wall. The TV stayed on during the day, now tuned to CBS and an episode of *Survivor*. A small bathroom with a shower and a sink completed the room.

"Hey, Emma. Jim here. You're doing well, just gonna turn you."

He used the draw sheet to turn her toward him and slid a blue wedge inside a pillowcase behind her back. He checked her tailbone.

"A little redness there." He popped on a glove and lotioned her lower back. Finished, he adjusted her head on the pillow. "Looking good." He noticed her eyes roll up and checked the EEG monitor. The steady buzz of alpha waves had gone spiky with gamma waves. Emma's body tensed beneath the white sheet ever so gently. "Seizing. Emma. Hang in there." He patted her shoulder, washed his hands, wondered where she was traveling to, and left to check on another patient, Timera Scocpol.

Inside the adjoining long-term unit, the lone nurse, Shelby, sat in the hallway outside Reece's room, the curtain pulled back, reading a copy of *The Thin Man*. The unit resembled an ICU on steroids, fully equipped to care for the dying.

Reece, on his back, breathed slowly at ten respirations per minute. EEG cables sprouted from his shaved head like a kohlrabi. The monitor showed a steady flat line, but with an occasional blip every ten minutes or so, having increased since his transfer a week ago. He looked like a ghost lying there perfectly still, his fingers loosely curled around rolled washcloths. Shelby was just about to recline when the EEG alarm sounded, bright and clear, like a perfect warble.

"What the?"

Shelby stood, book in hand, and stared at the monitor. Jagged polyspikes. He watched Reece's body respond as if in a full-body yawn.

"Jesus."

Shelby eyed the heart monitor, and the rate had increased to 130. He grabbed his penlight and shone it into Reece's eyes, and he swore there was a light constriction of his blown pupils. He would need to call Markush, but stayed with Reece until the spikes stopped, and the flat line resumed.

In the guest facility, eight o'clock neared, everyone bored beyond bored with watching TV. They were playing UNO. Back in Godo, Emma had introduced the team, including Afewerki, to the game, and it had been a sensation, even though one of the green threes had been missing. Arthur learned quickly and found it slightly amusing, although not on par with his favorite card game, Tarok. He also enjoyed chess and, in an essay, had written, "In chess, the object of the game, namely, to checkmate one's opponent, is of arbitrary adoption; of the possible means of attaining it, there is a great number; and according as we make a prudent use of them, we arrive at our goal." UNO was a poor man's grab at chance, while chess required logic.

Emma drew a wildcard and threw it down on a red nine. "Uno!"

"Well done, my dear," said Arthur. "I still have many cards, as you see."

"Ah, I am having only two cards. So close," said Afewerki.

The sound of a helicopter vibrated the air.

"They're looking for Reece," said Emma. "It's got to be damn cold out there. I hope they find him and bring him back."

"Yes, I am fond of the lad," said Arthur. "We worked very well together to find Mia, although this Dahlia was planting impostors in our way. It was the Abba who sent me to the correct location, and then what a commotion. Of course, you were there."

"I'll never forget it," said Emma. "First, we found the little girl who turned out to be Mia, and then Reece staggers in and starts seizing, and then that horde of little girls comes waltzing in like zombies with their little daggers, and then you drop in out of nowhere. If I—" She turned at a door opening. It was Clyde Markush, having learned first of Reece escaping, and then of the other Reece showing signs of returning from the dead.

Markush walked up to the dining table, and all eyes were on him. He breathed heavily, his long gray hair tangled. "It's great to see you, at least three of you. Why did Reece bolt like that?"

"Have a seat," said Emma. Empty cups of fruit juice littered the table. "He got jumpy. Wanted to see Mia. Are you just gonna keep us locked up in here forever? Have you found him?"

"He will be cold outside," said Afewerki.

"Yes, the frightful weather will result in his acquiring a dreadful fever," said Arthur.

"I've just been at the MP headquarters, where I was listening in. The helicopter located him, and MPs apprehended him inside a park bathroom. Before I could do anything, they threw him into the brig, but he's being brought here after being processed. It took a phone call to Washington to straighten things out."

They all looked at one another with some relief. "We're glad he's okay," said Emma. "But what about us being locked up here? Are you going to move us to even tighter quarters? It's obviously easy to escape."

"We are missing our home," said Afewerki.

Markush leaned his elbows on the table and shivered. He'd left his jacket at Kristin's and had been too busy to go home. He looked at each of them. "To be honest, your situation is unprecedented. We had a basic plan in place in case this happened, but no clue of the consequences or what we would do other than monitor and gather information."

"I am curious to know how you knew that such a possibility as ours existed," said Arthur, fiddling with an UNO card.

"That's complicated and confidential for now," said Markush. "Let's just say that bizarre things have been happening on our planet, at least since human history began to be recorded. But it wasn't really until the 1960s that we noticed a pattern and formulated this notion of Dahlia, a term created by a little-known physicist, Harold Leyman. I latched onto the idea in grad school after reading his dissertation and found that very few wanted to listen and that folks were thinking I was crazy. Leyman committed suicide. But there were developments. The Pentagon, the military, are inquisitive types and operate within a framework of organized paranoia. That's about all I can say for now."

"You never answered the question of when we will be free. This is a nice place, but it's not my home, not even my planet or universe," said Emma.

That particular thought dazzled Markush as always. "I just can't say at the moment. There are others, enemies of the state, who may have an interest in you. You're safe here, or so I thought. We'll have to increase security. There's nothing I can do for you now, except to keep you comfortable, and hopefully you'll remain cooperative, unlike Reece."

"He is a bit of a hothead," said Emma.

Arthur laughed. "That is a descriptive term, if I understand its meaning. If I were back in Gadam, the data fur would provide me with a definition."

"Data fur?" asked Emma.

"Yes, data fur," said Markush. "Reece mentioned it when he was on the medical unit, traveling back and forth from Gadam, the 3981 version. Tell me more." He searched for his pocket recorder, but it was in his lost jacket.

"Yes," and Arthur licked his lips, slightly purple with age. "This Gadam was on a planet, it seems, that did not rotate, and the sun was tiny but exceedingly bright. Thus, there was a light side of the planet and a dark side, much like the moon. On the dark side, I learned, was this data fur, miles in height, which contained a plethora of knowledge that one only had to question in one's mind. The subsequent answers were immediate, quite amazing. We tried, but there was no information about the location of Mia, seemingly erased."

"So curious," said Markush. "Fascinating. The dark side would have had to include the United States. I wonder if that's what we're headed for, a land piled to the heavens with data."

"In my home," said Afewerki, "the Abba Paulos is knowing everything. The people pay him to learn what they need to know."

"Yes, the Abba, always a factor in these various universes. He is key, I think," said Markush.

"Would you like to lock him up as well?" asked Emma.

"Honestly, I would love to have him here, as he is actively engaged with this mystery. It might be harmful to remove him. I do plan to pay him another visit, though."

Markush's cell phone rang. "Markush. What? Well damnation."

Reece paced the gray cell with smooth cement walls. He hadn't received his medications since returning and was feeling out of control, breathless. Reece took deep inhales and alternately sat on his bunk, stood, paced, and sat again with his head in his hands. Clutching a thin wool blanket over his shoulders, he still felt cold. They had offered him hot coffee, but that had only made the airy feeling in his chest worse. He wobbled to the steel toilet and peed long and hard. Thoughts of Mia tangled with thoughts of death. The thoughts raced through his brain, and he screamed.

A lone guard, Sergeant Bullock, watched the camera. He yawned and slumped in his uncomfortable rolling chair. Orders had been to have eyes on Myers 24/7, due to be released soon back to Organon. He glanced at the bank of camera monitors, and all seemed well, other guards doing their ten o'clock rounds.

"What the fuck?" said Bullock. He hit the alarm for cell A17 and called for backup.

Reece was banging his head against the wall, pretty hard, it seemed, just standing and throwing his forehead against the cement. A red light flashed on and off above the steel door. Within fifteen seconds, a guard unlocked the door, baton at his side. Another guard appeared.

"Hey! Stop!" said the first guard. "Hands behind your head, on your knees!"

Reece couldn't hear them. Only a vision of Mia played in his head. Perhaps he could induce a seizure or some state of unconsciousness and travel to her. He slammed his head against the concrete, stood erect, and did it again. The guards moved in and wrestled him to the ground, his arms pinned, a knee on his neck. He did not fight and instead cried.

Markush arrived at the prison within eight minutes, having sped there. Once inside and being given clearance, he made his way to a padded cell. The guard leading Markush asked if he would be okay entering by himself, and Markush nodded.

Reece lay naked in a fetal position on the thickly matted floor, his face a blank grimace. Markush kneeled beside him.

"Reece? Reece? It's Dr. Markush, your buddy. I'm taking you back to Organon. You're okay. Can you hear me?" He rubbed Reece's back.

Reece stared straight ahead. "I need...Mia. I'm...losing my mind. My medications."

"Shit," said Markush. "We forgot to put you back on your meds. I'm sorry. Can you sit up? I'll help."

It took a minute, but Reece sat up, his legs straight out. He'd never been able to sit cross-legged. "My head is racing. Won't stop."

"They gave you Valium, an injection. Are you feeling sleepy?" Markush noticed the large, raised welt on his forehead, turning purple.

"I don't know. I'm a failure. Mia is in danger."

With Markush in the back beside Reece on a stretcher, the military ambulance took them to Organon. Markush kept Reece overnight in the secure medical facility, back in his old room seven. Loosely restrained and now medicated with antipsychotics, he slept like the dead and awoke to find his pal Debbie looming over him with her short blonde hair and large breasts.

"Hey, Reece, it's Debbie. You're back in your room at Organon. You okay?" She checked the heart monitor and prepared to take his blood pressure. "Got a nasty bruise on your forehead."

"Hey." Reece felt somewhat normal, except his eyes

hurt. He closed them and then could feel the tight, dull pain in his forehead. "Is Mia okay?"

"Mia? She's with your...with Kristin in Richmond. All is well. Don't you worry. Checking your blood pressure, so hold on."

Reece stared at the overhead light, which was off. The TV played without sound, some sort of morning show.

"Pressure's fine. Let's check your temp." She shook down a mercury thermometer and placed it under his tongue, glancing at her watch and waiting. "Okay, temp is normal. Looking good. Just gonna have a little blood draw, check your lithium level."

He watched her palpate a vein in the crook of his right arm and slide in the needle.

"Great, all done. Need anything? Breakfast will be here soon." She dropped the syringe into the dirty-needle box.

"Maybe some grape juice." Reece licked his dry lips. "And untie my arms, if you don't mind."

"Gosh, I don't know. I don't have an order to do that."

"I'll be good, I promise. Not going anywhere."

"Okay, but you can't leave the room. Got it?"

"Got it."

Released, he stretched his arms over his head. "I need to talk with Markush. It's urgent."

Kristin listened, as Markush detailed the story of the previous evening. He had just spoken with Reece, who was anxious about Dahlia reappearing as that perfect little girl named Charlotte. After ending the call, Kristin ran upstairs to check on Mia, but she was asleep in bed. It was Christmas break, and Markush planned to reintroduce Mia to a new elementary school. No one other than Kristin and the folks at Organon knew that Mia was back. Markush said there was a plan. After all, the murder of Mia by Reece had been in the media. There had been a funeral. What would the public think when Mia appeared, alive? Markush had suggested moving out of state, but Kristin chose otherwise. They would portray the entire ordeal as a hoax, but Kristin would look seriously unstable, and Reece, if released, would be eyed with suspicion. But there had been a successful reintroduction of another little girl in Utah, Alicia, the daughter of Freddie Mentone, and he had been a patient at Organon. While traveling to find Mia, Reece found Alicia, and the Abba Paulos sent her back. The reintroduction of Alicia created a sensation, with nearly $100,000 spent on propaganda to protect her and her family. The doorbell.

Kristin hurried to the front door, worried that it might be Reece. She peeked through the narrow curtained window. "Oh my God." She didn't know what to do. Reece would know what to do. The doorbell rang again, and she decided to see what Charlotte could possibly want. How did she know? She opened the door.

"Hey there, Ms. Myers! It's me, Charlotte. Can I play with Mia? It's cold out here."

"Oh, right, cold. Come in, Charlotte." Kristin examined this little girl, whom Reece hated and associated with Dahlia, which Kristin still did not understand.

Charlotte pushed inside and looked around. She was Mia's age, had golden tan skin, and a perfect face. Her blonde hair hung shoulder-length, touching the collar of a black corduroy coat.

"Charlotte, Mia is asleep. She can't play right now."

"Let me go to her room and see. I have a secret for Mia."

Kristin's eyes widened. "Why don't you come into the den and let's talk? Do your grandparents know you're here?" She walked that way, but Mia lingered at the bottom of the stairs. "Charlotte? What's in your hands? Are you coming?"

"Tricked ya!" Mia bolted up the stairs two at a time, laughing. "Mia! Hey!"

Kristin froze for a second, but then ran after her. Mia's door slammed, and the lock clicked. "Charlotte! No! Mia!" She pounded on the door.

Mia sat up, clutching her blanket, staring at Charlotte. "What are you doing? Mommy!"

"This won't hurt a bit," said Charlotte, and then she was upon her, a magnet in each hand.

Kristin heard Mia screaming, heart in throat. She reached above the doorframe and found the Bobby pin there. She pushed the pin into the doorknob hole. "Mia!"

Charlotte sat on Mia's back, pressing her hands to Mia's skull as she thrashed and cried out. Flashes of blue light filled the room, making Kristin halt and push against a wall to keep her balance, sliding to her knees. She stared in horror as Mia went limp and Charlotte seemed to be pulling a spider's web from Mia's skull.

"Ha ha, got you now!" said Charlotte. She whistled "Ring Around the Rosy" off-key.

"Get out!" said Kristin.

Charlotte cut her whistle and crawled off of Mia, putting the bloody mesh into her pocket. "Now we have her secrets, don't we, Ms. Myers?" She jumped off the bed and tried to skirt around Kristin, but Kristin leaped and caught her around the throat, then she let go, realizing that Mia needed her attention. Charlotte coughed, but smiled, and then headed into the hall and down the stairs.

"Mia…" Kristin sat on the bed and turned Mia to her back. The mesh thing seemed to have been in two parts and pulled from two tiny tears on either side of Mia's head. Blood leaked from the small, neat gashes onto the pillow. Mia's glazed eyes rolled back, her breathing very slow but steady.

Markush was on North Dixie Boulevard, headed to see Reece, when his phone rang. He had managed a few hours of fitful sleep. It was Kristin.

"Hey—"

"She came! She hurt Mia!"

"What? Who hurt Mia?"

"Dahlia! I mean that little girl, Charlotte. She pulled something out of Mia's head. Mia's bleeding. She's like in a coma and won't speak. You have to come! Should I call an ambulance?"

"Is she breathing? Lots of blood?" He pulled onto the

side of the road, a horn blaring. A light snow fell.

"No, I mean yes. She's breathing but not responding."

"Shit. She has to come to Organon. We have a bed for her. She needs to be there anyway. I warned you, right?"

"Don't blame me for God's sake. How was I to know? She's just a little girl. But she's evil. I'm sorry..."

"This is fucked. Look, I'm on base but headed your way right now. Do not call an ambulance unless she has trouble breathing or loses a pulse. Got it!"

"Yes, but don't be angry at me. I just watched my daughter being attacked. Don't you get it?"

"Okay, I'm sorry. Reece's escape still rattles me and now this." He sped back onto the road, driving the Volvo wagon with one hand.

"Hurry, please."

"Not a problem. See you soon."

Markush called and let Debbie know he would be late and to have Shelby prepare a bed for Mia. Debbie was not about to mention this to Reece. He would go ballistic.

Inside the residential wing, the gang moped about, wondering about Reece. Why hadn't he returned, and why hadn't Markush updated them? They sat in the lounge area, Arthur explaining the delights of buster to be had in Gadam.

"The buster bars are all very similar on the outside, marked by green stars. Inside, though, the décor varies by establishment. Inside one, for example, there was a camel, inside another a giant fishhook."

"And this was your only nutrition, this liquid?" asked Emma.

"Yes, indeed, very nourishing, and coming in a variety of delightful flavors, whatever you wished, and it was free, as was the liquor at the bars. But the problem of moving one's bowels…"

"Everything is free?" asked Afewerki. "This is seeming strange."

"Yes, extraordinary," said Arthur. "Lodging was free as well, although it presented a major dilemma. Blue stars marked apartments, very comfortable, with cold air coming into the room through pipes of some sort, much like here."

Emma sat in her brown scrubs, arms folded against the cold. She had complained, but to no avail. "What was the major dilemma?"

"It seems there was a housing shortage. To acquire a room, the occupants were eliminated most brutally. Very bloody and grotesque. And you have to carry the body from the room and deposit it onto the lane where some entity comes and removes it." Arthur shook his head in disbelief at his own words.

"What a hell," said Afewerki.

"Yes, well said," said Arthur. "And then there were the red stars, where liquors, liqueurs, wine, and beer were served. Anything you wished, such as Strothmann from my country, a delicious caramel liqueur. There were waitresses with their tops removed, showing their lovely breasts." He seemed to be reliving the good old days, despite the strange circumstances.

Markush arrived at Organon with Kristin, who sat in the back seat, with Mia lying on her lap. After procuring a stretcher, they entered a side door leading directly into long-term care. With Shelby's help, Mia slid from the stretcher to the bed in room twelve, as far from the comatose Reece's room as possible. Shelby was a nurse practitioner, and the job of suturing Mia's head wounds, an inch in length, fell to him. Wiped onto a gauze pad, he showed Markush what appeared to be minutely thin fragments of a mesh material. Markush sealed the pad in a sterile bag for analysis.

Kristin stood beside Mia's bed, stroking her hair. She begged Markush not to shave her head to do an EEG. He agreed, noting that Mia responded when he ground his knuckle into her breastbone. She didn't appear to be seizing, although Kristin suspected a seizure just after Charlotte attacked Mia. The heart monitor clipped along at a very regular 98 beats per minute.

Markush sat in a rolling chair, just outside the drawn curtain. "Hey, come and rest."

Kristin kissed Mia's cheek and took a chair beside Markush. Mia's room was very bright, and the rest of the unit dim, making room twelve the center stage.

"Where do we go from here, Clyde? What do we do about Charlotte?" asked Kristin.

Markush's left knee bobbed up and down, a nervous tic. "She could have killed Mia. Do not let that girl near your house ever again."

"It wasn't my fault. I had no idea...So don't blame me." She folded her arms across her suede jacket.

"I'm sorry, but just be damn careful. Mia is precious in so many ways."

"No need to curse. Maybe you should leave."

"Leave?"

"*I'm* not leaving."

"Look, let me check on Reece, and then I'll go. You know that's him in room three?"

"Yeah, I know. I just hate to look at him. He seems so dead. Then there's the other Reece you have locked up in here, who is so alive. It bends my brain. Mia is my focus in all this."

Markush stood. "I think you need to spend the night in the guest house and get some good sleep. Shelby is an excellent nurse. He'll take super care of Mia. You can come back in the morning, maybe have breakfast, and visit with the Returnees." He thought spending time with Reece, Emma, Afewerki, and Arthur would help ground her in the complex situation. Since their return, she'd been distant, and he was feeling, he hated to say it, "unloved." He'd not had a serious relationship since his wife had perished in an automobile accident six years prior.

"I'd rather stay here. I can sleep in the recliner, but need to dim the lights."

"You sure?"

"Yes, I'm positive. And I think having breakfast with the Fab Four is a bad idea. It's like watching a play about how uncertain and crazy this world is. I'm grateful that Reece brought back Mia, but I still can see him strangling what I thought was the real Mia. He was so brutal, so callous. I'll never forget that."

"You can't mention that Mia is here to anyone, not yet."

Mia's bed quivered.

After a dinner of pizza and chicken wings with plenty of unsweet tea, the group was feeling highly neglected. Markush had failed to return that day, and Reece too. Emma turned off some of the overhead lights to give some semblance of evening, as there were no windows. As Jewel delivered dinner, a guard from the medical unit, Gumbo, accompanied her, a new protocol implemented by Markush. Markush now saw just how delicate this world of Organon really was, admitting that he would need more staff and security. With Reece in the medical facility, eleven of twelve beds held patients, and there would be a need for more beds. Markush had discharged Freddie Mentone back to his home in Utah, where he could be with his wife and his returned daughter, Alicia. Markush had fought with Freddie over his decision, but the reintegration of Alicia warranted his return to make things plausible. Right away, though, Markush had deemed it a mistake, thinking that Freddie and Alicia needed further debriefing. He planned to visit them, but he was being stretched thin at Organon.

"Movie, game, sing songs?" Emma walked in a circle around the others, still seated at the dining table.

Afewerki perked up. "What is the game?"

"Yes, what sort of game does one play in this time and place other than UNO?" asked Arthur. Chicken wing sauce stained his beard and his scrub top. He had protested at the sweetness and spice.

"I don't know," said Emma. "How about charades, where you act out something and we have to guess what it is?"

"An old parlor game," said Arthur. "Perhaps our times are too different to fathom the topic?"

"Right," said Emma. She thought. "I've got it! Truth or Dare. You have to choose to tell a truth or take a dare. Could be hilarious."

Arthur said nothing.

"She is walking the circle many times," said Afewerki. "She will make a path into the floor."

Emma stopped walking and sat down. "Okay, I say we play Truth or Dare. Who wants to go first?"

"I think that, Emma, you should be the first in this adventure to show us how the game proceeds." Arthur smiled and wiped his beard with a paper napkin. "I am like the pig eating from a tough, no doubt." Afewerki and Emma laughed.

"Okay, so one of you asks me, 'Truth or dare?'"

Arthur and Afewerki glanced at one another. "Truth to me is of utmost importance," said Arthur.

"Then truth," said Emma. She tapped her fingers on the table. "Ask me a hard question, maybe something embarrassing, and I have to tell you the truth."

"I am seeing this game," said Afewerki. "Can you make the sound like the rooster?"

Emma laughed. "No, you can dare me to crow like a rooster, but ask something like 'Have you ever had sex in a car?' Something like that."

"Oh my," said Afewerki. "I cannot ask such a thing. It is perhaps a sin, no?"

"I do agree with my friend here, and what is this car you speak of?" asked Arthur.

Emma laughed again. "You guys are killing me. A car, like a buggy in your day, I suppose. You know, a carriage."

"Ah, yes, a most daring supposition, making love in a carriage."

"So, that's what you're asking me...and then I say, 'No.'" Emma couldn't stop laughing.

"And what is the point of that, learning nothing, only what you have not done, which I am pleased to hear by the way." Arthur became grumpy, his eyes narrowing, his lips pursing, licking them, dry from the cold forced air inside Organon.

Afewerki watched in wonder as Emma hit the table, laughing louder and louder. He smiled, and then could not help himself. Arthur looked puzzled, watching these two guffaw. After a minute, both settled down with broad grins.

"Oh...damn. You guys are a hoot. I feel like I'm laughing

and not supposed to be, like in church or at a funeral. Say, Arthur, I'll take the lead here. Have you ever laughed at a funeral?"

Arthur looked bemused. "Not forthright, but within. There is a story in the history books, I'm told, of an incident that plagued me. There was a Frau Marquette, who greatly annoyed me. At her boisterous behavior, I gave her a nudge, and she fell. The courts forced me to pay her damages until her death. Upon her death, yes, I laughed, and famously, I am told, said, 'The bitch is dead.' Needless to say, I attended not her funeral, but had I done so, I would have been greatly tempted to laugh, in the manner of a minor demon feasting on a soul bewitched."

"You pushed an old lady?" asked Emma.

"No, she was middle-aged and quite the actress. You will find this strange, but in my travels with young Reece, when we had somehow crossed into the realm of a primitive village, this Frau Marquette appeared. I was appalled, but Reece understood she had come to aid in the discovery of Mia. She turned out to be of some service."

"Where is she now?" asked Emma.

"I don't know, other than lost amid universes, but, alas, she made her own fate."

"Are we playing the game?" Afewerki was thinking of home and the abandoned clinic.

Emma looked at both with a smile. "I don't know. It seems too hard, like telling a joke in another culture. I'll give it one last try. Afewerki, I dare you to kiss Arthur on the lips."

Silence.

Glenelle Lock punched the clock in her office, which was a thin ruse to disguise her as an hourly employee with NIMH, the National Institute of Mental Health. Her official title was just Research Assistant, partially assigned to manage data for an observational study involving the late onset of schizophrenia. The study contained 6 arms around the country, following 236 subjects aged 30 or older. Prior to inclusion in the study, subjects had no history of mental illness, but all shared one common variable: an affiliation with Ethiopia. What she was learning about select subjects no longer shocked her. But her actual role was to facilitate the operation of Organon and manage the data produced through Markush. Like Markush, she was becoming overwhelmed with her various tasks and the Organon findings. It was becoming obvious that she would soon need help, and that Organon would need to expand, but there was plenty of room next to Tobacco Leaf Lake in Fort Knox. The sticky issue was money, channeling funds so that no public or extraneous government interest should be shown in Organon. Walter Reed Army Hospital housed the closest arm of the schizophrenia study, and she was due to visit the following day. Markush's direct line rang.

Markush sat at his desk inside Organon, papers and books scattered. "Glenelle, lots to tell you." Markush updated her on the captured Reece, his establishment on the medical unit, the general condition of the other Returnees, and ended with the account of Charlotte attacking

Mia.

"God Almighty," said Glenelle. "That's a first. What to do about this Charlotte? You're not pursuing any criminal charges, right?"

"Oh, hell no. That would sink the ship in no time. I would like to interrogate her, though. But that seems impossible without kidnapping her."

"Maybe that's in the cards?"

"I thought about that. I still can't work out her being with grandparents, as she claims. Neither Kristin nor Reece ever met them. The little girls always live with grandparents, though. We have to learn more, but it's all I can do to keep Organon going, plus the recent developments with the Returnees."

"Clyde, I'm working on more funding, extra help, more facilities, more data. We all need more resources. We have the FBI connection that could help us with the girls like Charlotte, but it may be a matter for the CIA. Funding can be more slippery that way, more secure. We're learning as we go."

"Right. But for now, it's day to day with events piling up as they are. What I need is approval for a new medical unit and more nurses, guards, and cooking/cleaning staff at Organon." Markush wanted to say he needed a personal assistant or maybe a co-investigator, but was reluctant to give away any of his personal connection to the project.

"Work up the details in a report. I'll run it by the Pentagon. Glenelle scanned data on her desktop computer, connected directly to dozens of NIH databases and the Pentagon. We have leads on forty-seven of these little girls in thirty-two states. Forty-seven *Charlottes.*"

"And there may be thousands, and we haven't even scratched the surface in other countries, although I have a promising lead in Croatia, through a colleague of mine, an English professor who has a friend with an all too familiar problem."

She ran a query, watching the numbers fly onto her thirty-inch screen. "That's great, but stay focused on your territory. We have all we can handle here at home. Here's an interesting fact. All the subjects in my schizophrenia study are or have been married with children, but only one child in all cases. Strange."

"Curious. I was an only child. Mia is an only child. Alicia is an only child. Something I've wondered about but have no answer to. Oh, we have a sample of fibers to analyze that I'm sending to Watkins. It appears to be part of the mesh implants we've discussed. After Charlotte extracted the mesh from Mia, just ripped it out, she said something about having Mia's secrets."

"That's super. We thought maybe it was a control device, but maybe it's a data collection device as well." Glenelle put an unlit cigarette in her mouth, out of sheer desire, although she could not light it. She wanted to get out of the NIMH building just for that reason, maybe hole up in a repurposed house somewhere in the suburbs.

Markush pushed his rolling chair into a corner. "Yeah, probably both, like a hard drive and processor all in one, a brain on top of a brain."

"Ha, that's what our FBI contact came up with, more or less. She's a novelist, hired for her creative abilities, pretty smart cookie."

"As long as she doesn't write about it. That would be

like spilling our guts. I like the idea of her insight, but creative types can be tricky. We can't yet travel to another galaxy, but a writer can create one out of thin air." Markush slid down in his chair, looking at his maroon dress shoes. It was nearing lunchtime. He was starved, but he needed to make an appearance with the Returnees. Kristin had relented and gone to the guest house, and she would call soon, he was sure. "Look, that's all for now. Gotta see to the flock." He held the phone for a moment, dazed and exhausted.

Reece sat in the recliner, unrestrained and fully medicated. Cuts and scratches littered his feet and ankles from his dash through the woods. His feet blue, Markush worried about frostbite. Convinced Mia was in danger, Reece contemplated his plea to Markush to be released and head home, where he could protect her. Reece watched as the guards passed each other in the hall, mumbling to each other as they passed—"Suck a big one." "Your daddy's dick." As he passed, Shark glanced at Reece. Reece nodded.

Debbie floated into the room, having checked on Scocpol in ten. She had watched Reece seize and travel to parts unknown for nearly two months during his previous stay. His story, all the stories, amazed her. There was no one outside of Organon that she could talk with, being sworn to secrecy, and she followed the rules, being in love with her hefty paycheck and stellar benefits. "How we doing, Reece?"

Reece admired her shapely figure. "Doing fine, fed and watered, although my feet still hurt."

"Want another pair of socks?" She leaned in to check his vitals, holding a thermometer. "Under your tongue, big boy."

Reece said yes to the socks and opened his mouth. Debbie pulled the cuff from the wall and checked his blood pressure. His ECG traced neatly on the monitor in bright green.

"Okay, good to go," said Debbie. "Anything else besides the socks?"

"Yeah, I need Markush. I have to get home. Have you had any news about Mia? She's in danger, I'm sure. I can protect her. I'm the only one. Otherwise, I'll crash this joint and make it there this time." He was serious.

"No escaping, please? For my sake. Markush will be by soon. He's in the building. Mia is doing just fine." She knew Mia was lying comatose in the adjacent unit.

"Markush in the building? Just like Elvis." Reece smirked. "Get me some scrubs instead of this flimsy gown thing. I hate them."

"You're less likely to escape in a gown, my friend."

"Maybe."

Emma lay face down on the rocks and dirt, her respirations jagged. The Abba Paulos heard the shot and hurried from his simple house, spilling a wooden glass of talla, which he brewed in a metal barrel cut in half sideways. He looked over the ledge and could see a foot. Down the ladder he went, stepping on Emma's arm. Knowing this was the work of the Vulture, he raised his arms to heaven. He could not save her and knew of only one thing to do.

He scooped Emma from the ground, blood soaking his golden robe. Up the ladder slowly. At the top, he shoved Emma onto the stiff, wiry grass. Above, a scorching sun glowered. The ferenj was dying, sounding like a dying donkey. He lifted her once more to his shoulders and, panting, made his way to the church in the rock that he had been digging for the past eight years.

Inside was dark and cool. He placed Emma on the floor, in front of a wooden bier, blood running from her head, forming a small pool. The Ark was not present, and he trotted back to his house for the vest of precious stones. He lifted the heavy garment over his head and, muttering a prayer, returned to Emma. Her breathing seemed to have slowed, but still that ragged whine.

The Abba took his place behind the table, lifted his hands, and began an ancient chant in Ge'ez. He paused, and all was still. Soon, though, a blinding blue light filled the chamber with a noise that drove him to his knees and rendered him unconscious. Perhaps ten minutes passed. The Abba opened his eyes and smelled the burn of the sacred Ark. Remembering his duty to save the ferenj, he struggled to stand, careful not to touch the intricate chest topped with two golden cherubim with flaring wings. Emma's gasps had diminished further.

Once more, he began his ancient chant. The figures atop the Ark gleamed white hot, and an electric vapor played between the wings. As the brightness of the cherubim intensified, the Abba's voice rose louder and louder. The Abba opened his eyes and saw between the wings a flurry of images from universes past and present. He took a step back and raised his voice louder, although he could not hear it. There was a bright flash of blue light, knocking the Abba back toward a pillar. He hit his head and faded into black. The Abba had performed his task well.

For nearly an hour, Emma's body lay just twenty feet from the main Organon entrance. Clyde Markush arrived, parked his Volvo, and, running, rather than walking, nearly missed her.

"The fuck?"

He bolted to Emma's side, thinking she was dead. He put his ear to her bloody mouth and could feel a faint whisper of breath. Her pulse was irregular and thready, very weak. Instantly, he knew, although he wasn't sure how he knew.

"Hold on, sister. I'll be back."

Emma, although no one knew her name, had arrived two weeks before they committed Reece to Organon, after he strangled Mia's impostor. Emma had stabilized, escaping death narrowly. Markush had grass remnants on her socks analyzed, confirming to him that she had been sent to Organon from a rural Ethiopia. He imagined that Abba Paulos had something to do with it, but could not prove it. An X-ray of her head showed the vague shadow of the mesh with which he had become familiar.

It was Reece who gave Emma her name. As he became stronger, he learned of this young woman in the room next to his and convinced Debbie to walk him in. She looked very much like the Emma he had worked with in Godo, the Emma who had saved his life after being shot by the Hyena.

By the time Reece had his final voyage to parts unknown and his depleted body lay flat and brain dead, Emma could blink her eyes and respond to questions by squeezing a hand. Now, she could move her head and lift her hands, speaking in a whisper. She had a vague memory of Reece standing over her, but had not recognized him.

"Hey, baby," said Markush, still in his office, just having spoken with Glenelle in Bethesda.

"Don't call me baby," said Kristin. "I'm walking over. Can you meet me? I need to be with Mia and didn't sleep a wink, but then I did. I meant to come earlier, just so exhausted."

Markush frowned. "Yeah, right. I'll meet you in the reception area."

He arrived, and to him Kristin looked beaten, wearing the same clothes: jeans, a holiday sweater, and a green wool jacket. "You look great!" he said.

"Hey, Ms. Myers," said the receptionist. She was young, virile, a natural blonde, and had little idea about what happened beyond the reception area.

"Hey, Denise. Clyde, take me to her. I'm afraid she's gone or...dead."

"No need to worry. We have a secure facility."

"Then how did Reece escape?" She paused behind Markush as he scanned and opened the door to the long-term unit.

"But we caught him."

"If someone can get out, that means Charlotte could get in or Dahlia herself."

Clyde Markush felt his grip on Kristin slipping away. Since Reece's return, she had been distant and quite cranky. They had not been on a date in over two weeks. He wondered if Kristin was having second thoughts about the divorce, perhaps thinking about getting back together with Reece, but with which one?—*the walking and talking Reece, no doubt.*

"Hey, Dr. Markush." Scoot sat outside of Mia's room, room twelve, per Markush's orders. Mia had taken precedence over the lifeless Reece for now. "Hi, Ms. Myers, my name is—" But Kristin hurried past him into the brightly lit room.

"Has she moved or said anything, opened her eyes?" She didn't wait for a reply. "Mia, it's me. Mommy. Please stay with us..." She leaned over the bed, arranging Mia's gown.

Scoot gave Markush the rundown, vital signs, no further seizures, which Markush had determined were petit mal. He couldn't tell without the EEG, but he doubted Mia was traveling. She was too young, and now she didn't have the mesh. But on an X-ray, Markush had detected a small remnant of the mesh that had torn and remained roughly in place, perhaps the size of a quarter. Did the mesh enable traveling? If so, why? Why would Dahlia want her "victims" to traverse universes? It seemed like a game of sorts that Dahlia was playing, but she was, after all, a little girl.

Kristin remained stooped over Mia, brushing her cheek and hair, looking at the two sutures. Mia would have scars like Reece from his gunshot wounds, the bullet having traversed and exited his skull from right to left.

"Mother, mother, mother!" Mia's eyes flew open.

Kristin fell back, reached for a wall, but there was only the open curtain, and she crashed into the overbed table Scoot used as a desk. Markush lifted her up and stared at Mia, sitting up, a silly grin on her face. "Good God," he said.

Kristin moved around Markush to Mia's side. "Oh, Mia—"

"Stuff it in a hole, bitch," said Mia in a growly voice that made her cough, and then from coughing to laughing. "I'm sorry...mother. I need to dial it down."

Kristin's face looked old and shadowed, a pain in her eyes. Had Dahlia replaced Mia again? Was this Mia? She suddenly understood how Reece could have strangled her.

Markush moved in, giving Kristin a frown. "Mia. It's me, Dr. Markush. You've been asleep, and you just woke up."

"Yack, yack, yack. Put a lid on it, clown." She giggled and looked around the room. "This is a nice fucking setup. Who pays for the gadgets?"

"Mia, you're talking funny," said Kristin. "Clyde, what's going on?"

Mia suddenly looked afraid. "Who dat? In da hall, yo! He want to murder me and cook me up in da soup!" She pulled the sheet up to her eyes and stared at Scoot.

"Should I…?" Scoot stood and moved toward Mia, but kept his distance. "Hi, Mia, I've been taking care of you. You're in a hospital, at Organon."

Mia laughed like a grown man, and a definite heat radiated from her body, forcing the three backward. "You stay away! Mommy, make him leave!"

"Scoot, just leave us for a bit." Markush took it all in. He needed to de-escalate the situation and protect Mia, but he was afraid for his life, much like being in the presence of Helmut Grayson on the medical unit, but Grayson was strapped down with a full-body restraint.

"Yes sir," and Scoot retreated to the safety of the nursing station, encased in bulletproof glass.

"Mia? Mia, are you afraid?" Kristin, by Mia's side, looked as if slapped. "It's okay, Honey. I'm here with you. You're afraid, being in a strange place. Once we get you home—"

"Home!" The word swallowed the room and seemed to echo. "So Charlotte can fuck me with a knife! Are you insane, bitch!" She dropped the sheet and lay back down, her eyes wallowing in her head as if possessed. Slight bits of foam edged her dry lips. She shuddered, or was it a seizure?

Charlotte skipped along for days and days. She could forget about Mia for now, but had to find Dahlia in the Pinch. In all directions was white nothingness, completely silent save for the songs that Charlotte sang off-key. In her pocket was the mesh from Mia's head, barely nothing, like the finest lace modeled thinner than a snowflake.

She had encountered the occasional group of stand-arounds, folks trapped with nowhere to go, unless called by the higher power of Dahlia, and you had to fall into the Cylinder and maybe the Pinch, which everyone feared. Charlotte slowed her pace, feeling airy, forgetting to breathe for hours on end, but it wasn't really necessary to breathe. Up ahead, she saw the vague specks that soon turned into dashes and then into people, about twenty or so. She was sure to know them.

One man, dressed in a gown, saw her coming and squinted his eyes. "Here comes Satan." He pointed, and the others turned. They had been wandering for an eternity, stuffed into nothing.

Mia walked right into the middle of the group, not planning to stop. She fairly floated along with perfect posture, confident in her time and place, her mission. She wore a lilac dress with pleats and a black belt with a shiny gold buckle, and her feet bare. Neither heat nor cold existed in Dogtown. "Passing through, chumps. Passing through. Make way for Dahlia!"

"Charlotte, what are you doing here? On your way to butcher a bunny?" asked the man.

Charlotte stopped and turned around. "You bugger. I had you good. You and your little monster, Cecile. What a name, Cecile. She won't give up the goods, and here you stay." She smirked.

The man collected his thoughts. He wanted to murder her, but knew that it was useless. "Okay, I'll be nice. Just let me see Cecile to know that she's okay. I'll stay here forever if that's what it takes to free her."

The others stood about, some yawning and breathing occasionally. The same game playing, and without result.

Charlotte put her hands on her hips and stood on her tiptoes. "Be nice all you want, you old ham hock. When Cecile talks, she'll be free, maybe. You, never. You're just an old pile of dog poop." She laughed and continued through the group, parting them like minnows.

"Charlotte, please." The man went to his knees, watching her drift away.

"Please, my ass," and Charlotte was soon a dash and then a speck.

By ten-thirty, the group gave up on seeing Markush. Emma pressed the intercom button one last time to ask if he was coming, and she only learned that he remained tied up. They played another game of UNO before going to bed and facing another infernal night at Organon. Even Afewerki wanted to escape, like Reece.

"Tomorrow, I will teach you chess," said Arthur, holding his cards and sipping an apple juice.

"I'm up for it," said Emma. She threw down a red five.

"In my village, we play checkers with the bottle caps," said Afewerki. "Perhaps we can make some as well."

"I'm not familiar with checkers," said Arthur.

Afewerki gave him a summary, and Arthur listened with interest.

The door flew open, and it was Clyde Markush, disheveled and wild-eyed. He'd had six cups of coffee during the day, wired as tight as a piano string. Arthur stood.

"The gang's all here!" said Markush. "I am so sorry about neglecting you guys, but here is my corpse for you to roast. Playing cards? Good for you."

"What's going on?" asked Emma. Her scrub top was too big and untucked. A film of oil shone on her forehead. "Where's Reece?"

Markush plopped into a chair and felt that he would fall asleep, but sat up straight. "My God, lots to say. But remember, what happens at Organon stays at Organon." No one laughed, giving him sad blank stares.

"Yes, young Reece—"

"Right. Reece. I'm assuming you mean the alive and kicking Reece and not the brain-dead Reece? Right? I'm not trying to be funny. I'm just ex-haust-ed. So, we caught Reece in a bathroom, in a park, close to here. He was in pretty awful shape, with hypothermia and banged-up feet. He's on the medical unit, but I think we can bring him back here with our new security protocols in place. Maybe in the morning."

"That's good news, I suppose," said Emma. "He was worried about Mia. What's up with Mia?"

"I'm not privy to share the details, but Mia is safe, although there have been some curious developments. And to round it out, the comatose Reece is showing hints of brain activity. There, that's all I can share for now."

"Dear doctor," said Arthur, "how long are we to be incarcerated in this facility? We are wasting away with boredom."

"Working on it. Your presence here is unprecedented. We had vague ideas of what we would do in your situation, but we're flying by the seat of our pants. I'm sorry that you've been caught up in this, but it's all within the grand plans of Dahlia, which I have no control over. I can protect you from further harm, I think—"

"You think?" asked Emma.

"That's the best I can do for now. But you need to be here. I still haven't interrogated, umm, interviewed each of you properly. God, I need help and bad." Markush let go a long breath as if finished with a long race. "It's just been pure hell since you guys returned."

Afewerki raised his hand. "I would like to study in the United States and then return to my home."

Markush looked thoughtful. "That can happen, but you have to be patient. The study part is pretty easy to work out, but getting you back to your village is a big question mark."

"It is a question mark?"

"I mean, we have to figure out how to do that, whether it be through the Ark or maybe even through Dahlia. I just don't know."

Afewerki nodded, a look of relief on his face.

"Tomorrow, I promise to do the interviews. We also want to do X-rays, primarily of your head. Sound good? Break up the monotony."

"Afewerki wants to stay and study, but I would like to be returned to the village, finish my work there, and head back to my real home," said Emma.

"Oh my," said Afewerki. "I am feeling bad. Perhaps I, too, should return with you to work in the clinic. Who will be your interpreter?"

"No, you should stay and study, get your degree in agriculture like you want. I promised I would help you come to the States and study, but I didn't know it would work out like this." She laughed.

"And I should like to return to my apartments in Germany," said Arthur. "I miss my little Atma, such a sweet creature."

"Okay, I get it," said Markush. "We'll work on that for sure. I'm thinking that Reece or the Reeces will play a big role in getting you folks home. But we have a pretty enormous elephant in the room, Dahlia. The implications of her existence and her activity are exponential. Just realize that Dahlia is my focus."

"So, Dahlia before us," said Emma. "I think I need a hot shower."

Markush's phone rang.

Formed in 1992, the Army Research Laboratory, with headquarters in Adelphi, Maryland, twelve miles from Washington D.C., addressed an array of military research issues, including weapons and materials research. Building 205 housed a three-thousand-square-foot lab dedicated to the activity at Organon, with new equipment getting its first use. On the surface, the lab was an extension of a soldier survivability research center at the Pentagon led by Major General Tom Watkins.

Colonel Ignatius Lawrence, a member of the Director's Staff, sat twiddling his thumbs, waiting for Clyde Markush to answer.

"Markush, Colonel Lawrence. Get on the secure horn. I have some news. Been trying to reach you all day."

"A moment, please. I'm with the gang, the Returnees." Markush stood and excused himself, scanned through the door, walked by the empty kitchen, and returned to his office, the lights still on, the secure phone ringing. "Here I am, feeling lost with all that's happened. Have to brief Glenelle tomorrow."

"So, tests are ongoing on the clothing the Returnees were wearing, along with the tissue and blood samples. It may be a bit late, but we want scrapings from under the fingernails and toenails as well. But that's not what I called to tell you. You know that sample of mesh fibers you sent us from the little girl, Mia?"

"Yes!" Markush yawned, excited, but his mind dragging in a deep ditch of sleeplessness.

"Thallium. Thallium cuprate, to be more specific. Used in high-temp superconductors. That's what makes the mesh, very malleable in this case. Under an electron microscope, latticing is the primary physical characteristic."

"Wow," said Markush. "I hate to say I don't know what that means."

"We don't either, and we like to spread the ignorance around like fertilizer, hoping that we get a flower or at least a weed."

"An extended metaphor, very nice."

"I think you're right. I'm more clever than I suspected." The colonel pinched his black mustache. His broad shoulders filled out his civilian jacket. He was technically off duty, but that meant very little these days. It's a very malleable metal that forms a microfine lattice. It's a material used in superconductors."

"But thallium is toxic...It would kill anyone who had the implant. Right?" asked Markush.

"That is of interest. Gas chromatography shows that the cuprate has been doped with lithium oxide, which reduces the toxicity of thallium. What we have is a sophisticated material that conducts electrons extremely well. How the implants may control the subjects or gather data is unknown. Be sure that we're working on it." The colonel drew on his desk calendar a lattice structure similar to the mesh. "What I want you to do is test Reece—"

"Both Reeces?"

Colonel Lawrence laughed. He was thinking that his hair was getting too silver. "Where was I? Oh, test the *Reeces* and the other Returnees for thallium, just to verify its presence. The theory is that these folks have the implant, those with X-ray shadows."

"Right. I'll add that to the regular labs we're collecting," said Markush.

"Good man. Any developments I should know about since our last communique? I spoke with Glenelle today."

"Well, Mia woke up with a bang, cursing like a sailor. I was afraid of her for a few minutes. Like she had been rewired. We're keeping a close eye on her. Her mother, Kristin, is with her. She won't go back to the guest house."

"Curious. Make sure that this civilian, the mother, is not privy to classified information. It's best to get her out of there. In fact, I'm giving you an order only to allow her brief visits once a day. Too much is at stake. The Cold War may be over, but the Reds are still out there looking for every advantage, and this could be a big one."

"Uh, yes, sir. It will be hard to arrange. She's very protective, but we'll work it out." Markush wondered just exactly how he would limit contact with Mia. Kristin might get brash and run to the media. "That's about it. You know that the comatose Reece has been giving us some blips on his EEG?"

"Yeah, Glenelle told me. Where that will lead is anybody's guess, but stay in touch. It's getting to where we'll need to have regular face-to-face meetings with you, me, Glenelle, and Watkins, so keep that in mind."

"I will...sir."

The colonel stood and gazed out his window at the black sky. "Great. Over and out." He dropped the green phone onto its cradle.

After breakfast, Reece sat in the dayroom, watching a documentary about syphilis. He could see Jim, the nurse with the Fu Manchu, inside the office, chatting with the monitor tech Claire, who had long, stringy, black hair. He was still thinking about how to break out. In his earlier days as a nurse, he'd worked on a psychiatric unit with doors that locked with strong magnets, similar to those used by Organon. One day, he'd witnessed a patient, who had covered himself with baby powder, run the full length of the hall and, with a flying leap, kick the door open. He and another nurse had run after him, but he'd stopped in the hall, pushing the elevator button. They brought him to the ground and dragged him back inside the unit. Maybe that was the ticket out? Mia was definitely in danger. He could feel it in his bones.

Markush, having made his rounds on the long-term unit to see comatose Reece, Mia, and Kristin, entered the medical unit's nursing station through the connecting door. Reece saw him and rushed to the window, motioning for Markush to come.

Markush grabbed a chart, a million things on his plate. He figured Reece would give him an earful. "Be right out! Any major news?" he said to Jim.

"Everything's cool, so far. We got two traveling, Peters and Scocpol. Keeping an eye on them."

"Now to see what Reece is up to." Markush walked out of the station to the dayroom.

Reece met him, arms folded, his flimsy gown billowing behind him. "I'm outta here, asap. It's only what, seven days to Christmas? I have to be home with Mia, regardless of what you or Kristin say. She's not safe without me, Mia, that is." He stood a good four inches taller than Markush.

"Hey. Let's have a seat. There's news. I know you're frustrated. The others are frustrated as well." They sat in interlocking chairs next to one another.

"News? What news? It better not be bad news."

"I'm hesitant to tell you this, but maybe it will help you being here. Mia is next door on the long-term unit—"

"What the hell! In there with my lifeless corpse. Is she okay? Tell me, Doc." He started to stand, but then sat back down.

"It's Charlotte—"

"Charlotte! That freak. Did she hurt Mia? I knew it. You have no right to keep me here and expose her like that. Tell me what happened." Reece clenched his jaw and ground his teeth.

"Kristin let Charlotte in. That was against orders, I mean advice. Charlotte attacked Mia and withdrew the mesh, leaving two slits on her temples. She was unresponsive for a day or so, but she's woken up and with flair, I might add." Markush thought about the others and how he needed to talk with them. How he needed to gather more information from Freddie Mentone and his daughter, Alicia, in Utah. How he needed to get the construction going on new rooms at Organon. People to hire and train.

"Damn and damn and damn," said Reece. "I knew it. I felt it. Is Mia okay? How in hell did the mesh come out and why?"

"Yes, okay for now, just wired up is the best I can put it.

She went from zero to sixty in the blink of an eye. Charlotte somehow just pulled the mesh free, but there's a small portion left that we discovered on X-ray. We're guessing the mesh contains information that Dahlia wants."

"You have to let me see her, and not tomorrow, but now."

"Can I take care of some business first?" Markush noted the pleats in his tan dress pants needed ironing. Almost all of his clothes at home sat in dirty-wash baskets.

"No," said Reece. "Now, or I'll find my way there by myself."

"But Kristin is there with her. She's safe."

"Why the hell can't I see my daughter?"

Markush winced. He was afraid. "What if it's not really—"

"That she's been abducted again? If that's the case, I'll..."

"You killed the last impostor. That can't happen again. I'm pretty sure that it's your Mia. Whatever powers were being tapped or mapped by the mesh are no longer accessible, at least by means of the mesh."

"This is your fault, Dr. Markush. You and Kristin. This should have never happened." Reece stood and bent over to touch his toes. He reached for the ceiling, and the bones in his spine cracked. "Okay, I'm ready."

"Ready for what?" Markush felt vulnerable beneath Reece's gaze. Reece had murdered a little girl, even if she was a manifestation of Dahlia.

"You're taking me there, now! And then you're going to send me and Mia and Kristin back home to Richmond, where we'll have a lovely holiday together!"

Markush looked startled, thinking. "Okay, let's go see

Mia. But you can't stay there. Just a quick visit. But a warn-ing. She's being verbally abusive. Very strange."

"I wonder."

"Follow me."

Charlotte alternated between skipping and walking, occasionally doing a somersault. Mia's mesh was a tiny wad in her pocket. Nothing but white with a blue tinge radiated in every direction, the floor beneath her invisible. Unlike the stranded groups of stand-arounds, she knew where she was going and could hear its distant hum. She had no cares other than to give up her prize to Dahlia.

Weeks, months, years perhaps, passed as she glided along. The light had a bluish tinge, and she could feel herself being tugged toward the entrance to the Cylinder, which led to the Pinch. Everything that Dahlia had collected for an eternity existed there. The Pinch was like Dahlia's own special playground, where she puzzled about her mother.

The rushing sound grew louder and louder, and a blue light brighter and brighter, but it didn't hurt her eyes. Charlotte was just one of an infinite number of perfect little girls sent to the far corners of time and space seeking information for Dahlia. Charlotte laughed and sat on her butt, letting the force pull her toward the edge of an infinite abyss. She now heard single notes, plucked from tunes and stranded in a vacuum. "Here we go!" her glee unbounded.

An indeterminate time passed and Charlotte slipped over the edge of the cylinder, as if encased in soap suds 10^{34} thick. She fell, but there was no resistance, and so she floated, like a toy in a bathtub, without a care in the world. She giggled as the notes around her coalesced into songs she knew by heart. "Jack and Jill went up the hill!" she sang, her music in disharmony and always off-key. As she neared the Pinch, the music diminished, and her heart grew lifeless. She thought of fruit juice and cracker snacks and how awful little boys behaved. She heard a loud screech, as from a needle sliding across a record.

"Hello, Charlotte," said Dahlia, appearing in an angel's gown fringed with golden silk. A sparkly tiara rested on her forehead. She had that perfect oval face, brown, with shiny golden hair. Her lips made the shape of Cupid's kiss, and her ears seemed to be the perfect complement to her just-right nose. She lacked one tooth in front, where a permanent tooth should go, but that would never happen as Dahlia was timeless, ageless, just seven years old forever and ever.

"Hi, Dahlia! Do you still want a puppy? Mia had a puppy, but her mean old mother gave it away after you made Mia go away."

"A puppy would be so much fun!" said Dahlia. "They're all here, Charlotte. Look over there!"

Charlotte drifted, and she looked into the bright blue light. A little puppy chased its tail, yapping. And then a bowl of antifreeze appeared, and the puppy drank it. Charlotte watched as the puppy vomited and then died.

Dahlia was crying. "It always happens. The poor little puppies die, and the kitties too."

Charlotte had killed her share of pets and did not shed a tear. "Well, they just come and go, don't they?"

Dahlia wept into her hands for perhaps a thousand years. "If my mommy were here, she would take care of me and keep the puppies alive. I don't know how. Anyways, you have what I need."

"Yep," said Charlotte. She fished in her pocket for the tiny ball of wadded mesh. "Into the Pinch!"

Mesh in her little brown hand, Dahlia excused Charlotte. Charlotte kicked her feet and, traveling at the speed of light, soon reached the edge of the Cylinder, then headed back into Dogtown.

Dahlia drifted down, not in a hurry, because she had been disappointed so many times before. There was utter silence as the infinite interior of the cylinder narrowed toward the Pinch. There was a horizon that she struggled through, and soon she was being sucked along, but seemingly without moving. The sounds and smells of the universes began to whorl like tornadoes, and Dahlia held on for dear life, being tossed and buffeted against the quanta of time. No longer was there space, light, or darkness, just pure time. Spinning and spinning, Dahlia opened her hand and let the tiny ball of mesh spin with her. The mesh unfurled into a delicate fabric and sparked, losing its information to the Pinch. A flood of images crashed one against the other. There was heat. Entropy rising. Doors closing. Gum popping. Grass blades poking from ant hills.

"Where is my mommy?" asked Dahlia. "I want my mommy!"

From the void of voids came the answer, and Dahlia screamed, "No! That's not true!"

Reece walked onto the long-term unit, eyes flashing, led by Markush. Markush stopped him at room three, where the curtains had been drawn. Markush turned and looked at him. "We're about to pass your twin. Do you want to look?"

"I almost forgot." He wanted to see this shell of himself, but Mia came first. "No, I want to see Mia. That me can wait."

He followed Markush as the hall turned right. Around the next bend of the unit, he saw a nurse, Shelby, sitting in a chair in the hall. He pushed past Markush and walked into twelve, where Kristin slept in a recliner.

"Mia," and Reece rushed to her side. He put his hand on her head and looked into her eyes, knowing it was her. "Thank God."

Kristin's eyes flew open. "What the..."

Mia took his hand from her head and looked afraid. "Is it you, Daddy, or just another monster?" Her eyes looked hollow. A plate of half-eaten chicken fingers sat on the bedside table.

"Yes, it's me, Daddy." He looked at the small sewn slits on her temples. "Charlotte did this to you."

Mia's eyes grew wide. "Yeah, that little bitch, something something cum dumpster. She tried to kill me. She made Dahlia take me away. I know it." Like a professional, she pushed the button on the bedrail and raised the head of the bed. She made the bed rise two feet until she was looking Reece in the eyes.

Kristin stood. "Mia, it's okay. It's just Daddy, but I wonder why he's here." She directed the comment at Clyde Markush. Markush put his finger to his lips.

"Mia, we're gonna go someplace safe. Just you and me... and Mommy. It's almost Christmas. Have you thought about what you want?"

"Good God," said Kristin. "Is Christmas all you can think about? Plus, remember that we're divorced? And I have sole custody."

"The hell you do." They faced each other across the bed.

Mia's voice came out guttural, like a dying old man. "You two better suck it up and piss on somebody else's parade. Got it!"

Reece and Kristin stood back.

"She's not herself, since Charlotte..."

"This would have never happened if I had been there," said Reece. "This is all Markush's fault. Am I right, doctor?"

Mia said, in a little girl's voice, "You two cunts can play the blame game all you want, but for your information, it's that cock tease Dahlia who has the dirty hands here." She hummed a wonky little tune.

Markush convinced the stupefied parents to leave Mia. They stopped briefly to view the still body of the comatose Reece. Reece stood at the foot of the bed, looking at himself, wondering at the implications. The Reece before him looked peaceful, eyes closed, but gaunt and withdrawn. He wished for that peace in his own life. Kristin remained outside the room, looking at her shoes. When

Reece touched Reece's protruding foot, Markush saw no reaction on the EEG.

With Kristin back at the guest house, Markush brought Reece back to the residential facility, thinking that would somewhat satisfy Reece's urgent need for change. Markush would interview the other three that day, God willing. Once Reece changed back into brown scrubs, the four Returnees settled into a reunion, with Reece detailing his escape and capture. The interviews were scheduled for after lunch, and they decided the order they would go in, Emma being last and Arthur first. He said, "Beauty before age," in deference to Emma, but she insisted that the senior agent of the group go first.

Next to Markush's office were three successive interrogation rooms, each equipped with video cameras. As a precaution, he had summoned a guard to escort the Returnees. The brief search for Reece had cost upward of $160,000. Organon, being a private contractor, would have to foot the bill. But the media was the primary concern of Markush and his superiors, although he thought that even the media would one day have its place.

The interview room was two-hundred-feet square, grounded by a long table of walnut veneer and comfortable chairs. Dull, flannel-gray paint covered the walls, with the light bright but soft. Amanda, the guard, a cute thing and nicely rotund, escorted Arthur inside.

Markush stood and put forward his hand to Arthur. "May I call you Doctor?"

Arthur bowed his head. "I appreciate your formality, but I have quite become used to Arthur. May I?" He pointed to a chair.

"Yes, yes, please have a seat." Markush had managed a few hours of sleep but still felt weary. He wore a pair of gray slacks with a maroon cashmere sweater. Arthur, in brown scrubs and with rough features, looked like a butcher to Markush. "And you should call me Clyde, my given name, although not very pretty. I suppose my parents thought I would become a barroom jester."

"Yes, very quaint, Clyde. So what is it you wish to know, my dear man?"

"Well, everything, if that's possible. This is just the first of what I hope to be many fruitful conversations." The video light blinked red every five seconds. This was history in the making. "To start, tell me how you wound up in Gadam, 3981, and met Reece."

"It's quite a mystery, you see. I was in my apartments in Frankfurt, having left Berlin and teaching behind. My best memory, if one can call it that, is that I was ruminating over the death of my mother, having visions of her. I had fathomed the phenomena of magic, but had found the objective material rather disappointing." He paused and frowned. "And suddenly, I was lying on my back in a narrow lane, the scorching sun beating me into the earth. There was no explanation. Perhaps you are familiar with the first words of my major work."

"Not specifically," said Markush.

"*Die Welt ist meine Vorstellung.* The world is my representation. I could only fathom that perhaps the world was the same as I had left it, perhaps in a noumenal sense, but that my senses had been uplifted and now represented to me something entirely different. It was young Reece to whom I attribute this idea of another universe. And indeed, perhaps it was. The sun was very small, the size of a small coin, but hotter than I have ever experienced. This planet also did not rotate as did my Earth, leaving it much like the moon with a dark side and a light side."

"I've heard some of this from Reece. How did you meet him?"

"After arriving in such a rude fashion, I began the endless scorching days wandering the lanes of this Gadam and meeting its very queer people. They speak in an insulting manner and seem to have not a care in the world, everything being free, well, most everything, including alcohol and the exquisite liquid called buster, which provides the only nourishment."

Markush had heard of the strange people insulting Reece for no apparent reason, other than it was customary. "Ah, interesting. And then you met Reece."

"Perhaps days or even weeks passed. It's hard to tell when the sun shines with persistence. I met him in one of the very confusing lanes, all of which seemed the same. He stood out right away, and I knew him as a fellow traveler, which I called myself. Those I met knew immediately that I was not of their place. Henceforth, young Reece informed me of his search for his daughter, Mia, and enlisted my help. I found him to be quite earnest, although the complexity of his search puzzled me. How could it be?"

"And so you and Reece began the search for Mia."

"My first order of business and etiquette was to have young Reece nourished in a buster bar, denoted by the green stars. Our second order of business was to find lodging, which led to strange consequences, murder, I'm afraid."

"Yes, he's told me about the murders. But why you? Why were you sent, if that's really the case, to help Reece find Mia?" Markush, growing increasingly excited, leaned forward in his chair.

"At first, he did not recognize me as Herr Schopenhauer. When he did so, he related he was indeed a professor of philosophy, and that he was especially interested in my works, very flattering, as those of my time discounted my ideas."

"So, you had common ground, philosophically. Perhaps it makes rational sense? Perhaps even he chose you? He needed someone who could believe in alternate realities, such as you."

"That's an interesting supposition, Clyde Markush. I haven't thought of it quite like that. Our knowledge of the world is always indirect, being processed through the senses, a notion of positivism. Perhaps you've read Kant, whose ideas are important to my works."

"I'm vaguely familiar with his idea of transcendental idealism, which you espouse, that space and time exist within us and not outside us. Is that correct?"

Arthur laughed. "Correct enough. Yes."

Markush had planned to keep the interviews to two hours at a pop, but went for three with Arthur, and that was only the beginning. They had gotten into Dahlia, discussing what Dahlia really wanted. It all seemed very childlike that Dahlia only wanted to know who her mother was when the very foundation of existence was at stake.

Reece admired Emma's half-smile, as she related a joke she had heard in Ethiopia. The punchline was "We have enough of these" as two Ethiopians throw a Russian soldier overboard. Compared to the Emma he had worked with, who had saved his life, he couldn't get over how exact this Emma was. He had been in her little house, she in a chair, he behind her, massaging her neck, his hands dropping lower when the bullets came through the wall. Even though he was engaged to Kristin at the time, he was sure that she had been as attracted to him as he was to her. But this Emma standing before him had never met him. The other Emma lived in Alabama. He had seen her once since returning home to Birmingham, a brief encounter at UAB Hospitals, after marrying Kristin. He had mentioned the encounter to Kristin, a big mistake.

"Your feet look banged up, for sure," said Emma.

"Yes, you have cut them." Afewerki also had an affinity for Emma, viewing himself as her protector back in Gwar 1987, where Reece had found the real Mia, but also her guard in this new world.

"They're healing just fine, although one of my toes is still numb. So, what were the main things you treated at the clinic?"

Emma smiled. "Definitely disease related to a lack of sanitation, such as infected wounds, but also diarrhea and intestinal parasites, roundworms and tapeworms. Dead flies stuck in ears."

"Yeah, the same for me when I was there, in Godo, 1986,

in my time. The Emma I worked with, and the Afewerki, were exactly the same as you guys. I remember you, the other Emma, helping me irrigate ear canals with peroxide and pulling out globs of wax, pus, and flies. Totally disgusting, but with immediate results."

"Bizarre," said Emma. "Their hearing always came back right away. That was always the complaint, loss of hearing rather than 'my ear is clotted with flies.'"

"Very satisfying to see such immediate results. Did you guys see a lot of trachoma?" referring to the eye disease spread by black flies.

"God, yes. The eyelids inverting, scratching the cornea into blindness. Really sad. I often saw little kids with what looked to be black coals over their eyes, just a mass of black flies. The flies wouldn't budge. I had to physically wipe them away, and they would just zoom off and then right back in."

"Yes, the flies are a big trouble. We burn the incense inside the house to keep them away," said Afewerki.

"You could just catch them mid-air, they were so thick."

Afewerki laughed. "To catch them and then shake the hand to confuse and throw to the ground and step on them." Reece and Emma laughed. Emma reached and punched Reece in the arm.

"I don't mean to change the subject, but tell me more about this Dahlia. The little girls who stormed our compound, right before you shouted, and we were whisked away."

It suddenly hit Reece. He should try that here. Shout those words. Maybe he would be transported to Asterion Lane, but maybe he would be taken to some place far away. He was afraid to try.

"Dahlia. An entity, perhaps the original consciousness in the universe, the universes. Kind of like a God in the form of a little girl, seven years old. She holds power over the universes, is always here and there at the same time."

"If she is a God," said Afewerki, "why is she not to be worshipped?" He could only associate Dahlia with the angels, who had come to earth and had relations with women, creating giants. "There is no Bible for Dahlia."

Reece thought. "She doesn't care for worship. She's selfish and only wants one thing: to find out who her mother is. It's strange but true. I think that through the ages, she has been sending versions of herself to Earth and other planets where there is life, to find the answer to her question. Perhaps it's just now that her efforts are becoming more invasive and aggressive. Her focus has honed in on connections to Ethiopia. There is something special about the various Ethiopias that exist."

Afewerki perked up. "Yes, we have many mysteries in my country. But God is the ruler and his son Jesus Christ." Afewerki was quite religious, having accepted the New Testament teachings as taught by the Baptists he was working for in his village. The Orthodox Church of Ethiopia relied primarily on the teachings of the Old Testament, being reliant on angels, saints, and prophets. "The Ark is resting in my country, to speak with God."

"Afewerki, you have an Abba Paulos in your village, Gadam?" asked Reece. "There was an Abba Paulos in all the villages I traveled to."

"Oh, yes, the Abba, who is building the church into the rock. He is famous and wise."

"He controls the Ark and can make it appear. It's through the Ark that Arthur and I traveled from one place to another." Reece spoke in a matter-of-fact tone.

"Now that's crazy," said Emma.

"Perhaps it is possible. The Abba is a holy man," said Afewerki.

"It is possible. It happened to me. I experienced it. A great swirling of blinding blue light. It was between the wings of the cherubim that Dahlia spoke to me, and I saw an image of Mia."

The doors to the unit opened, and in walked Jewel, accompanied by the guard, Amanda. Jewel carried a tray of juice cups and ice cream for the refrigerator. The group stopped speaking as if their words were secret. Jewel and Amanda left as they came, in silence, and with wary looks.

"Is the Abba working with Dahlia?" asked Emma.

"I think so," said Reece. "Maybe she is just using him as a vehicle to allow traveling between universes, all to gather information on the origin of her mother. Dahlia just can't get it. She doesn't have the right music, as if stunted."

"Hmm," said Emma. "So, who is Dahlia's mother? Do you know?"

Reece tensed. "I learned the answer while floating inside the Cylinder, near the Pinch. I fell into the Cylinder, after wandering around in Dogtown."

"Oh God," said Emma. "Really? I hate to ask."

Reece laughed. "I've been there. Dahlia sent me to Dogtown, this endless white space with people like me wandering around, maybe to punish me. There's this Cylinder that is pinched in the middle where Dahlia seems to live amid endless information. I saw a drawing of the pinched

Cylinder in an old book of the Abba's."

"And Dahlia's mother? You know how to drag it out," said Emma.

"She is having a mother? She is like, how do you say, the ghost?" Afewerki rubbed his eyes and twisted his Exxon ballcap.

"I see what you mean, but Dahlia's very real, like a demon disguised as a little girl."

"And her mother? Tell us," said Emma.

"While in the Cylinder, amid the music, the answer came to me. I even told Dahlia what I thought, and she just got mad, saying that it couldn't be true. Okay, okay, I'll tell you. And I'm still trying to figure this out. I think Arthur may have some insight."

Emma stood and turned Reece's head toward her, and while laughing said, "Give it up, dummy. Enough!"

"What a hell," said Afewerki.

"Time! Her mother is time. But Dahlia doesn't believe it. I somehow know that time is her mother. It came to me as a truth and made complete sense in the moment, but now I have to think it through. Dahlia has probably known the answer for quite a while, but rejects it, and thus her mad search continues. Maybe if she just accepted time as her mother, the world would be a better place, no more famines, for example, assuming that Dahlia is something like God."

"Jesus Christ. That makes no sense at all," said Emma. "How can time be a mother, and why would this Dahlia even need a mother?"

"I am missing my mother," said Afewerki. "She is cooking the enjera and spicy wots."

"Exactly," said Reece. "Dahlia has the same need to be loved, and time certainly seems like a poor choice for a mother. Time can't cook dinner or put you to bed."

"I am to be like Emma," said Afewerki. "Why time is her mother?"

"I need to discuss it with Arthur and Markush, too, maybe a physicist. Have you ever wondered what there was when there was nothing? That has been a bothersome question for me, since I gave up religion after being shot in the head. Chucking God and Jesus Christ and the church left a big hole in my life, and I filled it with trying to understand the universe without a God."

"The Big Bang?" said Emma. "Everything was crushed into a point, and then it exploded, creating the universe."

"Yeah, but there had to be something before that point developed, when there was absolutely nothing. No space, no mass, no vacuum. Nothing. But there could be one thing when there is nothing, although perhaps science doesn't support this." He paused as if searching for words. "It's really quite simple." He looked at Emma and Afewerki. They looked back with blank stares.

"Okay, what was there when there was nothing? This better be good," said Emma.

"I'm thirsty. Anyone want a juice?" Reece stood, knowing that he was killing them.

Emma grabbed his arm. "No, just tell us. Juice can wait. You know, while in Gadam, I doubted my faith and wondered what it would be like to just give up God and the whole shebang."

"What is shebang?" asked Afewerki.

"I love that word," said Reece.

Emma was shaking her head. "It just means everything else, like the complete picture of God and religion."

"You are not believing in God?" asked Afewerki. "Oh my. God has made us all. He has been sending his Son to die for us."

Reece wanted to say that was bullshit, but held back. "So, time. When there was nothing, there was time, plain and simple. I see time as a thing, not just as something that passes or spaces events."

"So, time is Dahlia's mother?" asked Emma.

"Yes," said Reece. "Time gave rise to Dahlia. I'm not sure how or why, but I think and believe that is what happened. In essence, Dahlia has no mother, really, which is why saying that time is her mother confounds her and makes her angry. She wants a proper mother."

"I get what you're saying," said Emma. "But it's a new one on me. So, there's nothing, and time is passing. Then what? How did we get here?"

"God has created us," said Afewerki. "I believe this."

"I used to believe that as well," said Reece, "until I saw the famine and then was shot. Why would God rule such a cruel universe and allow such bad things to happen? If there were a God, then that God is quite the asshole. Pardon my French. There has to be a better explanation for why we're here. It's very simple. Instead of God, we have Dahlia, who seems to make more sense, being devious and cruel herself."

"How did we get here? You're avoiding the question again," said Emma.

"Okay, but the juice. Who wants what?"

"Thank you," said Afewerki. "I will have the orange."

"I'll have cranberry."

"Great, and I'll have grape." Reece stepped away into the mini-kitchen and brought back two juices for each. He seated himself, pulled back the foil lid, and drank a cup in one gulp. "Have to stay hydrated, right?"

Emma pinched his leg under the table.

"Ow! Okay, okay, time accumulated and reached a critical mass. Time yielded space and matter. I'm not sure if it was perhaps a single atom of hydrogen forming or of an enormous blast that ultimately resulted in the universe or universes. Maybe there were infinite instances of time accumulating, but I don't know how to explain that."

"Huh, so the universe is made from time," said Emma. "I just don't know about that. I would need some proof."

"And God would have to show me that this is true," said Afewerki.

Reece drank a second juice. "If I'm not outta here in twenty-four hours..."

Monday, December 19, 1997—Three lab techs, all with PhDs, stood busy over their instruments. Comprehensive blood analysis of the four Returnees had yielded nothing of import, although Arthur Schopenhauer had elevated triglycerides, and all the subjects showed traces of thallium. One tech, Maurice Landis, a botanist, was examining pollen under a microscope, recovered from the Returnees' clothing. Another was analyzing materials obtained from beneath the fingernails. The third was performing mass spectrometry on clothing stains. Thus far, pollen from grasses had been isolated, including *Themeda quadriraleis,* indigenous to Ethiopia, and *Poa pratensis,* the famous Kentucky bluegrass. The Returnees had definitely been in Ethiopia, but could they have traveled by plane and then dumped themselves in the backyard of 47 Asterion Lane? Or were they transported magically from an Ethiopia in another universe, as the Returnees claimed? There were skeptics, and Colonel Ignatius Lawrence, the lab director, was one of them, although he was willing to be astounded if the science was there. He respected Clyde Markush, but Markush had not convinced him of this outlandish story of Dahlia, time travel, and the multiverse. Nothing surprised him, though, and if national security was at stake, he was willing to do his duty.

Lawrence drew back the curtain, seeing Dr. Lily Nashburn in front of the Perkin-Elmer TurboMass Mass Spectrometer, the latest technology. Lily's white lab coat hugged her large body, splitting the tails from behind. The

Colonel moved toward her in a semicircle, admiring the precise machine more than its operator.

"Any updates, Dr. Nashburn?"

Lily turned, surprised. "Mostly nondescript body fluids you would expect, protein markers for saliva and blood. But I just ran a sample from the shoe of subject Arthur Schopenhauer and found evidence of what appears to be feces, a bit gross. I'm working on a sample now from the collar of the same subject."

"Sounds like a plan. Just let me know if something unusual pops up, as I know you will." He smiled, exposing his teeth stained from cigars.

"Yes sir, I will. But are you willing to give me some clue as to what we may be looking for here? The clothes from the subject Schopenhauer, I noticed, seem antiquated, but the rest are fairly modern. The sample we sent to the textile expert, of the Schopenhauer pants, is hand-woven of Egyptian cotton with a heavy black dye from logwood, *Haematoxylum campechianum,* with an inorganic oxide to fast the color."

"Any significance?" The Colonel leaned against a white counter, his finger to his chin.

"Only that the garment was probably expensive to make, especially if it's as old as estimated, perhaps the 1850s."

"I see." He wanted to say that made sense, but had to keep speculation at bay. Only he knew the true purpose of the investigation. "That's great information. Keep it coming."

"I will, sir, but it would help ever so much if we knew what and why." She sounded like a little girl asking for candy and felt slightly embarrassed hearing herself.

"Maybe in due time, but at present, just treat your work as raw data we will funnel to a larger purpose. That's about all I can say. Just know that your work is valuable, very valuable."

"I—" and there was an exclamation from beyond the curtain.

Reece existed, his idea that is, as Plato would say, within the Pinch. He was conscious of worlds forming and desisting, imploding into singularities, expanding to infinite reaches. His entire existence played within, over and over, an endless loop. He knew the last thoughts of a dying soldier at Antietam, as well as the harmony within the monk Thich Quang Duc as he immolated himself in South Vietnam. He knew how to execute the mawashi-geri, a roundhouse kick practiced in karate. He composed poems in Arabic and hummed the Piano Sonata No. 11 by Mozart. For ages, he watched a crystal develop on an unnamed planet. He was immersed in everything, every event, whether it be a Paleolithic sneeze or the adaptation of bacteria to sulfuric acid. Time, he realized, was simultaneous, and that time had ceased to gather and stretch once there was space and mass. Time brought itself to extinction, much as there was no time variable in quantum gravity, just a hop or skip from one probabilistic event to another, plotting the location of an electron.

And within this swirl of omnipotent perfection existed Dahlia, poking her nose into every nook and cranny, sifting, searching for her mother. Having been at it for an eternity, she had focused her efforts on those places with an Ethiopia, perhaps the perfect hiding place. At first, she had made angels who had come to the ancient land of Punt and bred with the indigenous populations, producing godlike creatures that the people worshipped. This had proven useless in her quest over the eons, plus there were an infinite number of these places with an Ethiopia, but the search had narrowed.

She had realized her error with the advent of worship, realizing that these creatures, these infinite humans, had correctly fathomed that there was a larger power. The people and their prayers annoyed her to no end. Why would they think she could help them? Time had stopped and become the infinite universes. Only the illusion of time remained, and these simple beasts lived accordingly, seeking lives of pleasure. She had no patience for that. Really, the audacity of a mere thing to believe that Dahlia would spend her time catering to basic needs, preventing broken arms and diarrhea, silencing wars. But amid that feigned intellect existed something very secret, and her one quest, now that the universes unfurled and continued to erupt and predictably evolve into static plasmas, her one desire rested with these lowly insects. If you lose a coin, the first place to look is beneath the light, but then into the nasty shadows you must go.

Life was eternal in the Pinch, an infinite storm of quanta that only she could fathom, or rather, thought she could fathom. She reluctantly shared this omnipotence with all those poor souls who called the Pinch home, mingling their quanta with ice cream and lungfish. But it was she who held power in this, her stronghold, this heaven. In a miasma of Brownian motion, there were streets made of gold and gates made of giant pearls. But there was no joy to be had, just the music of the "dead," which Dahlia found revolting.

There was an infinite source of those yet to experience consciousness, to experience a world through the senses, like little fetal demons waiting to burst forth. But there were legions upon legions of those who had lived long lives, and she feared their wisdom and strength. After all, she was just a little girl, deadened at the age of seven, never to grow older. She often wondered what it was about "living" that made her so anxious. She supposed it came with the territory and held her head high in the face of experience and this thing called life, but not without tearful ages of sorrow and scorn.

At random, she called together the quanta of a particular being, begging that same question about her mother. Why could these mortals possess such a beautiful thing and not her? She turned her attention to Reece Myers for perhaps a thousand years, and his basic particles gathered from the soup. She liked to see them whole on occasion, thinking it fun. "Mr. Reece! Oh, Mr. Reece!"

From within the Pinch, vastly dispersed quanta gathered into the naked form of a Reece Myers, the one she desired. At first, he was unaware of his assemblage, but soon the utter darkness of the Pinch blinded him, and he swung his arms wildly. "What? Dahlia? Send me home for God's sake." At first, she was behind him and then beneath him and then all around him, until she formed a glowing object, like a finely sculptured angel but in a thick, coarse dress that gave her torso the look of a triangle, much as in the picture he had seen in the book of the Abba Paulos.

"Hi, Mr. Reece. I'm just so bored. Have you learned anything new about my mommy? I bet she's pretty like me."

Reece felt himself spinning and stopped it with a thought. He looked at his arms, glowing in the dim light from Dahlia. "You keep asking, and I've told you before.

The answer is all around you. Just listen to the damn music."

"Ha ha. I just hear some silly songs about Jesus and playgrounds. I know what you said my mommy is, but maybe you've learned something new. After all, I gave you all this to play with."

Reece opened and closed his eyes. Words and music and something like apple pie surrounded him. His head felt as if full of crabs, and he jerked his head from side to side. "If I tell you, will you send me back, back to my home? Mia needs me. She's a little girl, just like you."

"Yeah, but she has a mommy, and I don't. Why does she need a daddy?"

"Maybe I need her."

"I hadn't really thought of that. But she's got a pretty mommy. Mr. Reece...who's my mommy?"

Reece noticed he wasn't breathing and took a deep breath. "Okay, I'll tell you one more time. It's damn time. Time is your mother. You have to believe me and let me go."

"You're using bad words, Mr. Reece. That's not nice, especially since I'm a little girl." She giggled and then sang a little ditty off-key. "No, that can't be true. How could time be my mommy? Time can't make me a sandwich or brush my hair."

Reece could feel the call of home, his body lying on a bed back at Organon. "If time isn't your mom, then you have no mom."

A great heat emanated from Dahlia, pushing Reece into a far recess, but Dahlia inhaled and drew him back. "You're a liar! A bad old liar!"

In an instant, Reece dashed to pieces and dispersed into mere nothingness.

And then she had the best idea ever.

"Holy jumping Jesus," said Shelby. He had been a wrestler in high school and looked like it, short and stocky with cauliflower ears. His guy friends had teased him about becoming a nurse, but he was raking in major dough working at Organon. The only sound on the unit was the EEG alarm connected to Reece Myers, detecting a grand mal seizure. Shelby stood by Reece, watching as he arched and his teeth and fists clenched, the bed trembling. "Damn." He had to call Markush and quick. But then Reece went limp, and the EEG returned to a flat line as if nothing had happened. He ensured that Reece's airway was clear and performed a quick check of his vital signs. "Shit."

Afewerki walked into the sterile interview room, not knowing what to expect. Nothing was clear. "What a hell," he said to himself as he sat across the table from Clyde Markush.

"Thanks for this," said Markush.

"For what?"

"For meeting with me."

"Oh," and Afewerki inspired deeply in affirmation, a curious habit of his people.

"I see we have your name and birth date as 6 Makawit 1965."

"Yes, the world has changed to the Ethiopian calendar, to show respect in our time of need."

"Interesting. So, you would be twenty-two, correct?"

"That is correct." Afewerki fidgeted in his chair, turning

from side to side.

"You were translating for Emma in a clinic. She was doing volunteer work during a famine?"

Afewerki nodded. "We are seeing many patients each day, perhaps one hundred on the market days. She is a good girl, a woman I am meaning. We are also to be in charge of distributing the food, the wheat and the sorghum and the soybean oil. We have the team and daily laborers to help us."

"And this was through a Baptist Mission? When Reece was a volunteer in Ethiopia, he was working with a Baptist Mission as well."

"Yes, I am told. We are working with the Icelanders, one doctor and two nurses. They are Gudmunder, Eydis, and Svana. They are good people." Afewerki coughed, wondering where this would all lead. He took another deep, whooshy inhale.

"Hmm, Icelanders. Reece has mentioned that to me. In your Ethiopia, there was a famine as in our Ethiopia. Reece worked with an Emma and an Afewerki as well."

"That is very strange. The little girl had arrived just a few days before. We are very frightened by these things."

"Right. His daughter Mia."

"How is she to come there, and he is to find her? He is speaking of Dahlia and saying that she was holding him."

"Okay, so he arrived, and then what happened?" He was getting to the exciting part. Reece had only told him briefly what had happened.

"Coming to the gate of the compound was the Snake. He is to be the village administrator, a terrible man. Next, there are many small girls...with the knives, and they will come to kill us. Reece is finding the pistol of Gudmunder and shooting shooting. So many, so many."

"Wow, a little army of Dahlias with knives."

"I am not knowing this. They are just small girls with the brown skin and looking the same, singing some songs."

"What happened next?"

"The Icelanders are running to the back and are climbing the fence. We have entered the dining hut. And there is a new man, the old man, a shimogele, Arthur. He is coming suddenly. We are surrounded, and knives are stabbing the walls. Reece is to raise his voice, and I cannot say what he shouted."

"And then you were all in his backyard, as if by magic."

"Oh, do not say such a thing. Magic is from the devil. Yes, we are lying on the ground, which is very cold, and there is some ice."

"Fantastic. This is fantastic. I really appreciate your testimony, if you will." Markush leaned back in his chair, and his phone rang. It was Shelby from the long-term unit.

A day-shift guard, Renaldo, led Afewerki back to the residential facility. The others sat mute, staring at a silent TV, a *People's Court* rerun.

"How'd it go?" asked Reece.

"There has been some trouble. The doctor has had to run for an emergency." Afewerki faced them, blocking the TV.

Reece sat up straight. "It better not be about Mia? Did he say anything about Mia?"

"No, he is only saying that he will come quickly."

"God, I hate being trapped in here. If it's the last thing

I do..."

"Hey, don't worry," said Emma. "He'll let you know. He knows how you are with Mia." She had showered, and her hair was still damp. She gave him a killer half-smile.

"Yes, Reece. Do not worry," said Arthur. "After all, Mia has traveled the galaxies and has proven quite resilient. I do crave a drink of something nice, perhaps some sherry. We have to inquire, don't we?"

Despite his alarm, Reece had to laugh. "Yeah, some bourbon would do me good about now."

"Just a good cold beer would suit me," said Emma.

"The alcohol will cause trouble," said Afewerki. "The Icelanders were drinking and drinking, making the people wonder."

"I'm sorry I didn't get to chat with them longer, but then Dahlia's troops attacked," said Reece.

"God, that was the freakiest scene I've ever encountered," said Emma. "I still don't believe it."

"Young girls, ah, so innocent," said Arthur. "Very disarming. One would never suspect such cunning."

Markush fumbled his pass key and looked up at the camera, flustered but eager as Shelby buzzed him in. At room three, Markush gazed at Reece's body, his breathing very slow, only six respirations per minute. Tape shut his eyes. An EEG strip lay looped on the floor. The jagged lines peaked and troughed tightly. Preceding the event had been messy, chaotic wave patterns, then waves forming a pattern of Ws, which then went flatline with just an occasional blip. The strip had kept printing, unspooling the entire supply of printer paper. Why had Shelby just left it on the floor? Markush heard muffled shouting and rounded the bend in the unit toward Mia's room. The shouting grew louder.

"Clyde, she's having a stroke!" Kristin held Mia's hand, bent over at an awkward angle.

Markush glanced at the heart monitor, 134 beats per minute.

"She just started moaning," said Shelby, his face red but his battered ears a waxy white. "She seemed to be trying to seize, just after Reece's grand mal. I had to leave him."

Markush stood opposite Kristin beside Mia. "Markush stood opposite Kristin beside Mia," said Mia. Her eyes slowly opened, as if coming unglued. "Her eyes slowly opened, as if coming unglued." She spat at Markush. "She spat at Markush."

"Clyde, say something," said Kristin.

"Mia, you're okay, gonna check your eyes." He flashed his penlight and watched her blown pupils constrict evenly. "Mia, have you gone anywhere? Away from this room?"

Shelby moved back into the hall, shaking his head. Organon needed to hire more nurses to handle the increasing workload, plus it was damn lonely.

Mia yanked her hand away from Kristin. "Where am I? Why is that man in my room? He's a boogeyman."

"Mia, it's Dr. Markush. You're safe. You're in the hospital. You had a little accident with Dahlia...I mean Charlotte. Have you just been somewhere different from here?"

"Maybe, but that's a secret, Clyde Markush."

"What's going on?" Kristin looked haggard from a lack of sleep and too much worry. "Mia, do you recognize me?"

"Why, of course, mother dear. You squeezed me out of

your pussy hole, remember, about seven years ago. How do you like them crackers?"

"What on earth? Mia?" Kristin seemed about to collapse and sat in the vinyl recliner, her head in her hands.

Markush stared at Mia, and she stared back. "Get the portable X-ray, Shelby." He wanted to shave Mia's head and slap on the EEG as well.

Shelby powered up the machine and drove it into room twelve, its motor humming. "X-ray of?"

"Her head."

Kristin seemed to have given up and just watched.

"Step out of the room," said Markush, "to protect your ovaries." He took a lead apron from Shelby. "Mia, I'm going to take an X-ray of your head, a picture. I'm going to put this cold plate behind your head, okay?"

"My head is a treasure ship," said Mia. "By all means, proceed."

"Thank you, Mia." Markush positioned the plate, and Shelby, in the hall with the remote, initiated the beam. There was a hum and a click. Markush handed the heavy plate to Shelby to process in the small lab.

Mia lay still, as if murdered, the left side of her face sagging slightly. "Got you behind the eight ball, don't I, Clyde Markush? This game is getting hot. But who are you really? You know who you are, don't you, Clyde Markush? You're just sucking on Dahlia's tit, waiting to write that book. Am I right? Oh, it'll be juicy, more than you could ever imagine. Clyde. Markush. I need a banana sandwich! Can't anyone get me a goddamn banana sandwich! Is that too much to ask!"

Kristin's mouth slacked, aghast. "Mia, baby, please just

be yourself. You're scaring me."

"Just settle down, my pet." Mia yawned and then went very still as if thrown into a sound nap.

"Wow," said Markush.

"Why did you ask her if she had been somewhere else?" asked Kristin.

"I have my reasons..." He left to go chart in the station and wrote an order for the X-ray and a round of blood draws.

By the time he finished with Mia, Markush was bone tired. He had convinced Kristin to repair to the guest house and had followed her there for a glass of wine. She had let him kiss her upon leaving, but neither was in the mood for love. Afterward, he visited the Returnees and let Reece know he would be the next interview on the following day. Reece gave him an earful and followed him to the door. Markush had come without a guard, breaking his own rule. He managed to talk Reece down and exit, but had been afraid. Afterward, Reece went to his room with the express idea of using the phrase that had transported them out of Godo and back to Richmond. He muttered the words, but nothing happened, and then said them louder, but without result.

The next day, Markush arrived. He had spent several hours after returning home working up a proposal for more staff and facility construction. Utterly depleted, he exchanged pleasantries with Denise, commenting on the gray skies and chilling cold. She had decorated the reception area with a few holiday wreaths and a small Christmas tree. Markush was Jewish and almost mentioned Hanukkah, but let it pass.

Right on time, as promised, nine a.m., Markush led Reece to his office with Amanda in tow, just in case. Reece was ready and champing at the bit. He had thought about putting Markush in a choke hold, but let go of the idea.

"Have a seat," said Markush. "Anywhere you like."

Reece took a rolling chair, but then changed his mind and sat on an austere beige loveseat. "What's up your sleeve?"

"Well, I mean, *really*. You've beamed back from another universe, bringing three unsuspecting innocents with you. We need to figure this out, and you are the man to help us do that."

"If I talk, you get me out of this place and back home where I belong with Mia, and Kristin, if she can stand me."

"Recent developments just might enable that, or maybe not. That's the second part of our conversation."

"Can you crank up the heat or at least give me a coat? Why is this place so damn cold?"

"It doesn't operate room to room but by building. Want my jacket? It's genuine tweed from the Outer Hebrides." He pulled out an arm.

"No, no. Forget the coat, but have somebody bring more blankets, if you don't mind."

Markush saw this as a minor victory, being able to provide Reece with something he wanted and gave an order over the phone.

"Okay, to start. You hurtled in from where, to land in Godo? I think you mentioned the Pinch?"

"Yeah, I had been wandering around in Dogtown—"

"Explain Dogtown again, if you would. Oh, wait, this is being recorded. Do you give your consent?"

"Not really." He looked up at the black camera. "But whatever. Dogtown is just an infinite white space with scattered groups of people standing around, waiting, for what I'm not sure. I somehow found the edge of what is supposed to be a cylinder and fell into a blinding blue light. Dahlia was there."

"And then you're in the Pinch?"

"I'm not exactly sure. I think I was near the Pinch but not in it. If this makes sense, I was floating, but perhaps at the speed of light. It's just the way my senses recorded things."

"And you spoke with Dahlia?"

"I actually saw her in Dogtown, but in the cylinder I didn't see her, just could hear her, and this scratchy music-box noise."

"What did she say?"

"That same lame question about her mother. She's obsessed. I told her what I know, that time is her mother. She didn't believe me, and to escape, I said the chosen words. Then I was in Godo and found Mia. Then the little army of Dahlia's with knives appeared."

"So, you told her that her mother was time?" asked Markush.

"Yes, and she was distressed. She wants her mother to be like, like Carol on *The Brady Bunch,* loving and practical."

"Why in hell is that so important to her?" Markush bristled with excitement.

"I dunno. Maybe she sees us earthlings with mothers and wants the same thing. The daddy figure seems to be just a matter of fact."

"That begs a question. How did Dahlia come to be? In our terms, she couldn't have possibly had a mother or father."

"It's all about time. Time is her mother. Before nothing, there was time, the only thing that could exist when there was nothing. I don't understand, but when there was nothing, there was time. So much time accumulated that it became substance, and Dahlia was 'born.' Her mother is time, plain and simple, no father to speak of."

"How could there be something when there is nothing?" asked Markush. "Isn't time a function of space and matter?"

"No. And it's just a belief. Time was once pure, separated from space and matter. There was absolutely nothing at first. Just time. In quantum physics, there is a lack of a time variable, so according to quantum theory, there can be space and matter without time, but it doesn't consider the opposite. If there can be space and matter without time, then why not the obverse, to get it all going? My thought is that time was absolute until time became so great that a singularity occurred, a climax, if you will. The original matter, which had to occupy space, formed from pure time. Maybe just a single bit of quanta and then a hydrogen atom and then helium and so on, until universes formed."

"So, if time made all that we know, is there still an ongoing accumulation of time?"

"I think the answer is no, at least for the initial infinite universes. Once there was an accumulation of a critical quantity of time, time ceased to exist. All time is now simultaneous and does not increase." Reece spoke as if sure of an absolute truth.

"I'm overwhelmed," said Markush. "We need some experts on the subject of time."

"That and an understanding of the ideas of my friend Schopenhauer. His notions of existence play well into the hands of time. We experience reality through the senses. There is no sense that actually commutes time. We have to use clocks. Einstein posited time as a fourth dimension, but time is an illusion. A place and time exist without the assistance of time. Regardless of a calendar, for example, John Hinckley shot Ronald Reagan. It doesn't matter the day or the time. It happened. The universes no longer need time."

Markush wanted to say, "crazy shit," but refrained. "So, what is the relationship of Dahlia to time? Was she an original being?"

"I can only speculate, but Dahlia emerged as time transformed into space and matter. In all things, there is the perfect idea of that thing, much as Plato's Realm of Ideas. There is the idea of a table and then, in 'reality,' there are innumerable representations of that perfect table. The original idea of time was of a little girl, Dahlia. Perhaps that is the most noble idea of existence, to be a little girl." Reece found that his heart was racing. "Little girls are made of sugar and spice. Little boys are made of snips, snails, and puppy dog tails, as the rhyme goes."

"I...I can't distinguish between little girls and little boys. They both seem precious."

"Have you had a daughter? Are you the father of a daughter?" asked Reece.

Markush drew back. "No, I've never had a child."

"Then how would you know, my dear professor?"

Glenelle Lock and Clyde Markush chatted on the phone. Markush brought her up to speed on the happenings at Organon, including the spontaneous brain activity of the inert Reece Myers and the strange behavior of Mia. After the call, Markush had a plan involving Reece and Mia, who were freaking him out.

"The proposal is just about finished," said Markush. "I'll email it by the end of the day. It's framed as a letter of interest, not a full-blown proposal. I need more staff for that."

"Right. Funding is basically capped, but only for appearances. You have new expansion and facility leeway to the tune of eight million for five years, with a million for staff in the next five years. Don't worry," said Glenelle.

"That's generous."

"Yes, very generous, but that's through a CIA link that we're developing. Ultimately, we need global clearance. I can't tell you his name just yet, but he's involved with funding covert activity involving an Islamic terrorist group known as Al-Qaeda."

"Really? Never heard of Al-Qaeda."

"They're on the move, funded indirectly through the Saudis."

"Whatever makes the cornbread rise," said Markush.

"You're cornbread yourself, Markush." She laughed and devolved into a fit of smoker's cough.

"Things are heating up. Three fresh cases of parents killing their daughters that seem suspicious, and an uncle and a niece as well, all with the Ethiopia connection. We have the four Returnees in the residential facility, and that number could increase, depending on how the traveling goes with our medical patients. I think we need another co-investigator here. I'm at my wits' end trying to keep up."

"Well, hell, Markush, are you thinking about the long-term or the short-term? We may need to commission an entire city just for Organon, or maybe buy an island."

"Hey, I can barely think about tomorrow, so all the help I get the better."

Glenelle tugged at an unlit cigarette in her mouth. She was small and wiry, with long, bony fingers and dull blue veins on her hands that popped. "Yeah, you need help. I'm working on it."

"Got it, I appreciate it. Hold up, I'm getting a call from Lawrence. We'll talk soon."

Colonel Ignatius Lawrence sat at his modern aluminum desk. He liked the sound of the drawers opening and closing, a brisk but sure *whoosh*. "Markush, Lawrence here."

"Hello, Colonel. Just interviewed Myers and need some caffeine."

"Got some more results for you. You'll find them in the online folder, but wanted to update you. The clothes from Arthur date to his period, mid-1850s. Pollen findings show that the subjects have been both in Ethiopia, which Ethiopia I'm not sure, and Kentucky. One of our lab geniuses got excited, found pollen from an extinct plant...and then DNA profiles. Those of subjects Emma Smith and Afewerki Nigussie came back with twenty-five pairs, but the DNA profile of Schopenhauer came back inconclusive.

Seems he has twenty-eight pairs of chromosomes instead of twenty-four. Very strange."

"Yes, but he is from another universe, different rules, but similar results."

"If you say so, Markush. Frankly, I was unsure, maybe still am, about the authenticity of these characters. I just don't know what to think. You're diving into completely uncharted territory." Lawrence eyed a photo of General Patton on his desk. He was old-school but bright.

"I don't think it pays to think any longer," said Markush.

Markush, despite the hectic activity, took Kristin out for lunch. At first, she said no, but then relented, being given the promise that she could spend the afternoon with Mia. He picked her up in his beaten Volvo wagon and drove toward Muldraugh, where they had had their first lunch date.

At The Ritz, a run-down diner next to a motel of the same name, Markush parked in the gravel lot. He had to powder his nose first, then joined Kristin at the window table. The day's special was skillet steak with two sides.

"Need some music?" Markush dropped a dime into the tiny jukebox at the end of the table.

"No. Well, okay."

Soon, the voice of Tony Orlando was crooning "Knock Three Times."

Kristin was a bundle of nerves and oh so tired. "I guess I needed a break."

"Yeah, you do."

The waitress, with a wide bottom and a fuzzy mustache, asked them for their orders.

Markush made a motion toward Kristin.

"Maybe the tuna salad plate, with sweet tea."

"I'll have the special...with mashed potatoes and the green beans."

The waitress waddled away, pushing a pencil into her tightly braided hair. Markush pondered what he should say. Should he keep it all business or take the opportunity to woo her? But there were just too many issues that needed to be discussed.

"There's a moth in the window," said Kristin. A giant gray moth lay on its back, spinning in a circle.

"So, there is. Look, I'm worried."

"About what?"

Markush cleared his throat. "About, well, us. You've really pulled back since Reece and Mia returned."

"Pulled back? It's all I can do to brush my teeth. I'm overwhelmed. Now isn't the time for romance. Don't you think?"

"It's just that I think we have something, and I don't want to lose it."

"Look, I have to think about Mia. Why is she acting so strange? I'm really worried she has brain damage. She's become so cold and just plain vulgar, cursing, like that little girl in *The Exorcist*. You don't think she's possessed, do you?"

Markush thought. "Possessed by Dahlia, perhaps. Okay, so I have to tell you. The X-ray of Mia's head didn't show the remnant of the mesh that was there. It's gone."

"What does that mean?" She could hear two men arguing about football.

"I even hate to say it. It'll just worry you to no end."

"What, Clyde? Tell me and now." She brushed back her long curls and stared him in the eyes.

"I think I would need Reece to confirm it."

"For God's sake, confirm what?"

"That it's Mia. I think Dahlia has pulled a fast one and replaced Mia again."

"What? That can't be! She's just come back and now she's gone again. But it's her, dammit, just different is all, the trauma, right? She's just in shock."

The waitress put Clyde's skillet steak on the table and shuffled away to return with the tuna salad. Steam rose from the plate.

"I want Reece to confirm it. He'll know by the music she emanates."

"No! He'll kill her again if that's the case. No, do not let him near her."

"It's the only way, Kristin, to confirm. We're back at square one. Reece will want to go looking for her, and what that entails, I have no idea." He unwrapped his fork from the paper napkin and poked at the green beans.

With only five days until Christmas, Reece paced the tight carpet. Markush had mentioned developments with Mia, but had provided no details. Reece was worried sick and feeling out of sorts, despite taking his medications. Afewerki and Emma sat at the dining table, learning how to play chess with Arthur.

Markush breezed in with the rotund guard, Amanda. "Reece, I need you. It's about Mia." He walked over to say hi to the others, leaving Reece with a blank look on his face.

"What's happened?"

Markush excused himself from the others. "Let's sit by the TV."

"Doc, what?"

"I'm worried about Mia."

"Why? What happened? Dahlia?"

"The mesh she had, the remnant, is gone. She's acting like a lunatic."

"But it was her when I saw her last."

"Something's happened after the other Reece had a grand mal seizure. Something's going on, on the other side."

"Damn. I need to see Mia again." Reece looked pale.

"My idea exactly. But we're afraid of your reaction. If it's not Mia, the right Mia, you can't freak out."

"Goddamn, Dahlia. I can't believe it. I thought we had won the day, that things were going back to normal. If I had been with her, this would not have happened."

Markush sighed. "Do you really think so? You were with her the first time Dahlia replaced her. If Dahlia is who she appears to be, this godlike being, what power do any of us have?"

"We have the music. We can hear it and parse through the information to find the truth. Dahlia can't. She's seven years old, stuck there. She should be innocent and wise, but she's twisted and cruel, just like the world we live in. The apple doesn't fall far from the tree, does it?" Reece glanced back at the other three, who were all looking their way. "Take me to her. I'm ready."

Markush had been unable to carry out Lawrence's orders and keep Kristin in the guest house. Night and day, she was terrified and insisted on being with Mia. Planted heavily in the recliner with a blanket over her, she saw Clyde. She saw Reece, with his hands cuffed behind his back, shouldered on either side by guards borrowed from the medical unit, Shark and Gumbo. They looked as if some sort of witchcraft was in the making.

"Hey, Father!" said Mia. "Why the long face?" She looked angelic sitting up in bed, a coloring book on her lap.

"Mia," and Reece slumped. The guards let him go to his knees.

"What?" said Markush. He kneeled to check Reece's pulse.

"Father, oh, Father, what is wrong?" asked Mia with a slight smile. "Does he have a tummy ache?"

"Damn!" said Markush, as Reece arched and seized. "Uncuff him. We'll put him in the next room."

Shark and Gumbo struggled with Reece's writhing body, first getting him onto a bed and then removing the cuffs. Reece's hands turned inward, and his eyes rolled into the back of his head, his teeth clenched, mouth foaming. Not knowing what else to do, Markush unwrapped an oxygen mask, plugged it into the wall, and fit the mask over Reece's face.

"Here we go again."

Glenelle hurried in from the cold, having killed three cigarettes in record time. She took the elevator down and, in her office, closed the door, which locked, and then got on the horn to Clyde Markush to make an introduction.

"Clyde?"

"Yep. Was waiting. A fresh development, but that can wait."

Glenelle coughed, a roiling of mucus in her lungs that lived in perpetual darkness. "Oh boy. It just keeps coming. Okay, I'm about to tie in CIA Technology Officer Jacob Jacobi. Organon has been tucked away in a division called Special Activities, which is perfectly generic, just what we need. He's contacted Adelphi and the Pentagon, and now he wants to get the goods from the horse's mouth, his words. He still likes to be called Agent, Agent Jacobi. And Jacobi is like Jack-uh-bi, three syllables, very important."

"Right, whatever you say, Glenelle." He could hear her labored breathing. "You need to cut back on the tobacco, for your own—"

"Hello, Agent Jacobi. Glenelle Lock here with Dr. Clyde Markush on the line from Organon. How are you?"

"Doing well. Let's just say funding is confirmed. Nothing more to be said. What I'm primarily interested in, Dr. Markush, is the long-term. When Ms. Lock and General Watkins briefed me about six months ago, my jaw hit the floor. I can't say you're my top priority, but who knows where this will lead us?"

Markush leaned back in his desk chair. He had removed the photo of his first wife, who had been killed in an auto accident. "So, you don't need a PowerPoint to justify the expenses?"

"Are you joking? This is no joke." Jacobi was swarthy with black streaks in his gray hair, smooth-shaven, and a sharp dresser.

"Sorry, sorry, sir. Just trying to be conversational," said Markush.

Glenelle was biting her nails, breathing heavily.

"Have you even thought of the long-term?" asked Jacobi.

"Yes, I've requested that our building here at Fort Knox be expanded and staff—"

"Look, Markush, that's not long-term. That's peanuts. We've run the numbers, and you could potentially be dealing with thousands, tens of thousands of subjects, and that's just in North America. I've done my homework."

"Maybe you're right, sir." Markush felt small.

"I know I'm right. My team here has been looking at the possibility of acquiring a decommissioned military base. I mean, you can't just lock people up in psych wards. They'll revolt. They need space, stores to shop in, bowling alleys, and gyms, at least the ones who aren't bat shit crazy or 'traveling' as I'm told."

"Wow, I appreciate the forward thinking. I'm just so caught up in the day-to-day. There are developments by the hour. We've just had an abduction, by Dahlia, right from under our noses. No one is safe, no matter how thick the walls are."

Glenelle broke in. "Really? After this call, I need the details."

Jacobi spoke. "And those details will follow to my office, uploaded to the Organon server only. Highly secure."

"Yes, sir," said Glenelle.

"Markush, I want you to buy into our vision for Organon. We're here to facilitate a grand undertaking that must appear simply as business as usual. No funny business with the media. Luckily, this all sounds so damned insane that no respectable news desk would believe it if they heard it." He laughed at his own words. "Think big, Markush. After all, and this may sound grand, but we're dealing with something akin to God. This could change the way we see life and death in very fundamental ways. And when that happens, all hell could break loose unless it's handled with care and long-term planning."

"I get it, sir. Forgive me for burying my head in the sand. I appreciate all the help I can get. I have one request. We're dealing with a complex view of time regarding Dahlia—"

"Ha, and you want the expertise of perhaps a physicist or maybe a logician, or maybe someone who specializes in the philosophy of mathematics?" Jacobi by now had his feet on his spacious mahogany desk, thinking himself grand.

"Wow, yes, exactly," said Markush.

"Got you covered, Markush. We're already on it."

With the addition of the formerly alive-and-well Reece, there were now three patients on the long-term unit. Kristin was going bonkers, dealing with Reece, who was seizing, and Mia, who was not really Mia. The brain-dead Reece seemed a million miles away and perhaps no longer mattered. But it all made sense to her now, Mia being replaced. Markush had pulled her aside and wondered out loud if Reece could locate Mia on the other side. Euthanasia and autopsy of the impostor were running through his head, but he couldn't say it.

"Hey, Mother," said Mia. "Remember that time you got drunk and fell? Father had to drag you up the stairs to bed. You vomited in the bed! Those were good times, right, Mother?"

"Mia, stop." Kristin couldn't bring herself to fully acknowledge this wasn't Mia. Surely there was some small part of Mia left inside that she could care for.

"Ha, you and Father used to have some bang-up yelling matches. You know what I think? I think he was in love with that nurse he met in Ethiopia. She saved his life. I think he just married you out of pity, and then you had me! Good times, sister."

Scoot, the evening/night nurse, came from the station to do rounds. He stood about five-five with a chiseled face. The work of three patients overwhelmed him. "You doing okay, Kristin?" She seemed to be more of a patient than Mia.

"Well—"

"Haha, look who dropped in, another boogeyman! Your tidy whities don't fool me. You like little girls, don't you? You'd like to crawl under this sheet and have a taste, wouldn't you, boogeyman?"

"Pulse, ninety. Mia, I'm going to check your blood pressure." Scoot wanted to strangle her, as Reece had strangled the original impostor.

"Oh yeah, baby. Put that cuff on my little virgin arm. You like that, don't you?"

Scoot pumped the cuff and listened to the *thump thump* through the stethoscope. "One hundred over seventy." He was trying to remain as objective as possible. "Anybody need anything, juice, water, late-night snack?"

"I'm fine. Maybe some coffee if you have any." Kristin stood and stretched, showing her belly. She was tired of battling Mia.

"Wait, boogeyman, I need to take a royal piss at the back of the plane. That should get your gears greased."

Scoot gave Kristin a pleading look. This was all beyond what he had ever expected, and he was not free to talk about it, not even with his partner, Will.

"I'll help," said Kristin. She scooted the bedside toilet away from the wall.

"Thanks," and Scoot moved to the next room to see about Reece.

"Little girl on the shitter!"

Reece had seized for nearly twenty minutes and then paused. Scoot had shaved his head and attached him to the EEG. Since the seizure, there had been only gamma waves, which, from experience, meant that Reece was in travel mode, zooming across the universes. Scoot pulled him up in bed a few inches and performed a neuro assessment. Reece just seemed to be sleeping. Markush had ordered a feeding tube and a feeding/water schedule to keep him nourished and hydrated. Feeling some simpatico, Markush had avoided placing an indwelling catheter, and Scoot had fitted a condom catheter, but it leaked as usual, thus the blue pads beneath him. He noticed a short run of polyspikes and held his breath, but the gamma waves resumed. "You're doing great, bud. Hang in there." He washed his hands and headed to the other Reece in room three.

"Holy cow," said Scoot. A solid line of gamma waves traced the EEG screen. He hit record for a sample one-minute tracing. "Back from the dead." He did routine vitals and headed back to the station. He looked at the clock, nearly midnight, and called Markush.

The three Returnees spent nearly two hours talking of home. Afewerki missed home the most, it seemed, and Emma the least. For her, this world was normal. The food was the same. The technology was mostly the same. She understood the cultural references from the TV. Arthur also missed home, and he had been away the longest, whether it was years or months, he could not tell.

"God, this is depressing," said Emma.

"They did bring the delightful tree adorned with baubles and lights," said Arthur. "In my home, we too brought trees indoors to celebrate the holiday, but living trees and not this material you call plastic."

"Four days till Christmas," said Emma. "And we're locked up in a secret hideaway that's in plain sight from what I gather."

"We must be re-leas-ed," said Afewerki. "We are prison-ers, and we have done nothing wrong."

"Where in the heck is Reece? Do you think he escaped, and Markush won't tell us?"

Neither Afewerki nor Arthur had an answer.

"Tell me more of the Icelanders," said Arthur. "Reece and I met them, along with you and Afewerki. It was a version of Godo that young Reece worked in when he was younger."

Emma yawned. "Again, I never met you before you just dropped in from nowhere, but there was an Icelandic team where we worked."

Afewerki brightened. "They are very hard workers. They have been weighing the children, Eydis and Svana, and Gudmunder is giving the vaccines."

"I really liked them," said Emma. "I wonder what happened after they went over the fence. Did the little girls catch them and chop them to pieces? God, what a nightmare. Reece, the other Reece, the one I worked with, went with them as well." They were sitting in the lounge area, the coffee table covered with empty juice cups.

"I am fearing to think of it," said Afewerki. "So many girls and so many knives. But the Snake, I am sure, has died. His bullets were not affecting."

"He was a nasty character, but I somehow felt sorry for him, even though he stole from us and arrested you. The Snake was just basically jealous of how the people liked us and didn't like him, I think."

"He is bully," said Afewerki.

"I believe you are referring to the fellow I know by the

title of the Donkey, a frightful man but harmless when drinking the local alcohol, very rough on the palate, I might add."

"Yes, the Icelanders are drinking with him, and he is falling down," said Afewerki.

"That was actually funny and painful to watch at the same time." Emma gave a half-smile.

The door behind them opened, and Markush entered, wearing a down coat. "Hey, just wanted to pop in." He took a quick seat beside Arthur on the couch. "I know it's late, but you're still up. Just so you know, and I'm being transparent, maybe to ease your mind or maybe not, Reece is seizing and is being held on the long-term unit for now. There's another development with the original Reece, but I'm not sure what it means. I'm on my way there now."

"This is getting complicated, more so by the day." Arthur stomped his foot as it was falling asleep.

"Ah, they are in danger," said Afewerki. "Maybe the Abba Paulos has called them."

"I hadn't thought of that," said Markush. "My mind always goes to Dahlia."

"Can they work together?" asked Emma.

"I don't know. I'll have to think about that. So, just wanted to check in. I have to go. Is there anything else you need right away?"

Arthur coughed. "Yes, my bowels are in need of a purgative."

Emma laughed. Markush laughed. Afewerki sighed and said, "What a hell."

Dahlia thought about her great idea as Reece materialized from the ether of information. He floated, his body bent double as waves of quanta flowed around him. All was black and neither hot nor cold, with just the faint outline of Dahlia in her triangle dress.

"Hey there, Mr. Reece. Sorry to bother you so soon, but I have this super plan."

Reece shuddered to life, his head empty. "Mia," is what he could say.

"Oh, you'll wake up in a minute."

"Mia?"

"You have to be my friend. I know you don't like me, but you have to. Maybe if you meet the other Mr. Reece, the two of you can talk and figure out who my mommy is. How does that sound?"

"The other Reece, Reeces. You...you've hidden Mia again. You have to stop."

Dahlia giggled. "Yeah, I'm good at hiding things, and I can play hide and seek too. Mia could never find me, and I ate her cookies."

"Charlotte."

"Yep, that was me. But you know too much, Mr. Reece. That's why I can't let you go back ever again. But you're safe here, nice and cozy with the unicorns and the teeny-weeny rolypoly bugs."

Reece's mind seemed as wide as a galaxy. "To you, I'm of no use. I told you who your mother is, and I have to find Mia."

"Well, guess what, abracadabra..."

Reece vaporized, and he noticed how slowly the light was traveling, just passing photons. There was something akin to the flipping of a pancake, and he stared into a gorgeous pink sky. He looked at his feet clad in green tennis shoes, Converse, like he used to wear as a kid at Fort Knox. He fingered his acrylic sweater, noticing the crazy zigzag pattern. Pants. He was wearing black cotton pants.

"Hey!" came a voice.

"What the hell?" He was standing over himself, it seemed, another Reece.

"It's me. It's you," said Reece. This Reece wore a single-piece jumpsuit that zipped up the front, just like his grandfather used to wear while gardening. Old black dress shoes, too.

Reece came to an elbow, looking around a meadow filled with wildflowers and an occasional tree. "I was at Organon. Mia had been replaced again. I passed out. I have to find her. Who are you? Me?"

"I'm Reece. I'm the original. You're like a copy. I came from the Pinch, Dahlia. But you know her."

Reece thought and sat up, feeling the soft green grass beneath his hands. "You came from the Pinch?"

"Yes, the Pinch, full of perfect ideas, except for Dahlia, I think. She's the question mark in all of this."

"You're the perfect idea of me? How can it really be?"

"You have a displaced radial artery that runs from beneath your thumb." Reece helped Reece to stand.

"How did you know that?"

"I just do. You're slightly flawed. There are an infinite number of you, many in the same boat as you."

Reece looked at himself, this perfect idea of a Reece. His hair was thicker and the hairline farther forward, but the thin body, sharp nose, and brown eyes were all the same. He tried to process what this other Reece was saying. "An infinite number. It occurred to me that was the case. And infinite Mias, but for me only one."

"That's right, infinite Mias, and impostors as well."

They were walking, side by side, toward a small hillock upon which stood an immense fig tree, the air cool, as if it had rained.

"Do we call each other Reece?" asked Reece.

Reece laughed. "I am ideal Reece, and you are real Reece. Maybe I can call you Real and you call me Ideal."

"That would be queer. Too didactic."

"Maybe."

"But maybe we just need to take on new names. Are there infinite ideas of you?"

"Ha, just one, but infinite expressions like you and your Mia."

"Right. Where are we going? Where do we start?"

"I think to a small town just ahead. It's like a part of me. I just know it's there. We're in Ethiopia. The town is called Solon. The idea of me includes this experience of walking with you to Solon. I'm going to help you find Mia. She's a part of my ideal experience, as she is your reality."

"Oh." Reece stopped and gazed at Reece, amazed at the detail of himself. Dahlia was certainly evil, it seemed, but what she looked after, all of everything, existing all at once, was quite remarkable.

Christmas Eve day. Ten patients to look after on the medical unit, and Markush was overwhelmed, now with patients in all three wings of Organon, plus Kristin. Glenelle Lock recruited a co-investigator to assist Markush, a general medicine practitioner from Star City, Arkansas, named Letitia Mumford. Exactly why Glenelle chose her was not clear to Markush, but he would soon find out. All he knew was that Arkansas had revoked her medical license, and then she had been accredited in Kentucky. Someone was pulling strings.

Helmut Grayson was Markush's favorite patient, although very aggressive and straight-up crazy. Grayson had drowned his stepdaughter, Lila, in a bathtub and seized once a week or so as he traveled to find the real Lila, assisted in his search by none other than Gandhi.

"Hi, Mr.—"

"The fuck, the fuck! Got a goddamn knife, you motherfucker! Help!" Grayson thrashed against his full-body restraint. He suddenly went quiet. "I know a little secret."

Markush checked the cardiac monitor: 88 beats per minute, regular sinus rhythm. The catheter bag hanging from the bed frame held 300 ccs of bright yellow urine. A mass of wires emanated from his scalp, connected to the EEG.

"What's the secret?"

"Don't *you* want to know? Yeah, it'll cost you big time. It's damn juicy."

"You've already told me who Dahlia's mother is. Is that

the secret?" Markush felt like doing some jumping jacks, full of nervous energy, plus looking at the catheter bag made him want to pee.

"I told you that? Damn."

"Remember, I gave you some Scotch for that secret, which I appreciate by the way. We've had confirming statements from others like yourself."

"Yeah, that damn Scotch! But I have another secret."

"Tell me, Mr. Grayson." Markush knew what was coming.

"Got any more of the Scotch, the Laphroaig. A big gulp ought to do it."

"Hold on."

Markush left room three and entered the nursing station. In the break room was a cabinet where he kept a variety of alcohol, including the Scotch. Grayson liked it straight up.

"Okay, I'm back with the almighty Laphroaig. Spill the beans, pardner." He poured two fingers into a plastic cup and dropped in a straw.

"Getting fresh, I see. I've been to Dogtown, snooping around, you see, and I hear things. Dahlia's not as smart as she thinks. Anyhoo, I was standing around staring into space when this fellow came walking up. Looked like hell, said he'd been in the Cylinder, had a little chat with Dahlia, and she let it slip."

Markush loved these stories. "Let what slip?"

"Gimme a sip first, Doc."

Markush leaned over Grayson, not willing to get within reach of his restrained hands. Grayson took a big slurp and coughed it down.

"Whooeee! Mighty fine. Mighty fine." He puckered his lips and glanced into the hall. "Who's that?"

"That's the guard, Renaldo. To keep us safe."

"He don't look right." Grayson's eyes narrowed.

"He's just fine. So, the secret..."

"Yeah, I'm getting to it. Gonna cost you another hit of that Scotsmack."

"I promise."

"Dahlia...Dahlia's got a goddamn..."

Markush was straining to hear. "A what?"

"A sister. Dahlia's got a sister!"

That floored Markush. "A sister? What else did she say? Anything else?" He scribbled on a chart at the end of the bed.

"A twin sister, by the way."

"Holy Toledo," said Markush.

Emma, Afewerki, and Arthur pushed back their plates, pancakes with margarine and syrup. They were all contemplating the situation of Reece, enlightened by Arthur as to his experience with Reece seizing and falling unconscious for hours during their travels together.

Arthur belched and rubbed his belly. "If my bowels do not move, I will certainly eat some powdered glass, an old remedy."

Afewerki shook his head. Emma laughed.

"I'll pray for your bowels to move," said Emma.

"I'm sure that the Father above will share your sympathy."

Afewerki looked flummoxed. "God is not hearing such things. He will be angered."

All three nodded as if it were the truth.

Just then, the door opened, and Claire, the monitor tech on the medical unit, entered with Amanda, the guard. She held a small green bottle and walked their way.

"Mr. Schopenhauer? I have your medicine. Dr. Markush ordered it."

Arthur took the green bottle, magnesium citrate, and examined it. "Am I to drink it? How does one access the contents?"

Emma reached for the bottle. "Here." She unscrewed the cap. "Right on time. This is a laxative, works like a charm. You may regret asking for it." She grinned.

Claire looked like a deer in headlights. She knew as much as the nurses, and these three Returnees stymied her. Amanda, more business than fun, grabbed her sleeve, and they left.

Arthur took a swig and made a face. "My, tastes like lemon and full of carbonization." He took slow sips and then upended the bottle.

"My prayer will be answered by dinner time, I predict," said Emma.

Afewerki laughed, even though it was an abomination.

Colonel Ignatius Lawrence sat at his sleek desk, his windows blacked out, poring over the latest information from the lab. Subject Schopenhauer had twenty-eight chromosomes, instead of twenty-four. That was a new wrinkle. Elevated but not toxic levels of thallium in all four. The mesh, no doubt. And the mesh itself, quite a bit of engineering. He did not understand how such a thing could be implanted within the scalp without surgery. He had been told of similarities among those at Organon, all with stories of being attacked when very young by a little girl with great flashes of blue light accompanying the scene. Markush seemed to think Dahlia used magnetic energy to place the mesh.

He turned his attention to another folder detailing radioactive findings from the clothing of the Returnees. They discovered nothing of import, except while analyzing the subject Schopenhauer's clothing—traces of gold-198, a radioactive isotope, and high levels of mercury-198. Gold-198 had a half-life of 2.697 days, forming stable isotopes of mercury-198. Lawrence definitely wanted to run that by Markush. Why had Schopenhauer been exposed to gold-198? The literature showed that gold-198 was used to fight cancer tumors, being implanted as radioactive seeds, specifically within the prostate. But this Schopenhauer was supposedly from a time before such technology was in use.

Nine o'clock was the time, and Lawrence headed home for the night. It was Christmas Eve, and his wife had been on his case to be home to celebrate with the kids. But this was more fun, and he dreaded putting the trampoline together in the dark after the kids went to bed. He needed a martini. Before leaving, he emptied his personal trash can into one in the hall. Cleaning staff were not allowed to enter the secure lab space. After locking the metal door, he took the elevator down and exited the building, only to see a flash followed by a voice.

Markush had asked the receptionist, Denise, to buy gifts for Mia, Arthur, Afewerki, and Emma. He loved the idea of playing a Jewish Santa Claus. Without family, holidays were lonely, especially since the passing of his wife.

He awoke at eight a.m. sharp, shocked that no one had called during the night, but then he saw the missed phone message on his cell phone. He decided it could wait. After washing his face with cold water and taking his vitamin D, he made coffee and had time to relax on his enclosed back porch, gazing through the frosted glass at his plain backyard, a cement bird bath that didn't hold water, and a barren elm tree. Having finished his coffee, he was putting the neatly wrapped gifts in a clothing basket when the doorbell chimed. Not understanding who it could be, he peeked through the glass and saw a man in a heavy black coat. In his driveway was a blue Toyota minivan. The innocuous minivan tipped him into opening the door.

"Can I help you?" he said through the glass storm door.

"Dr. Markush? I just need a minute of your time. I'm Jeremy Sims, *New York Times.*"

"What? *New York Times?*" Alarm bells in his head.

"May I come in or speak with you outside?"

A slight bile was rising in Markush along with a cold, sick feeling. "It's Christmas. I'm afraid I can't speak to you at the moment. What's this about?"

Sims was having difficulty hearing Markush through the glass door. "I'm sorry if this is a bad time, but it's an urgent matter related to your work on base. If it's not me, it will be someone else. I'm nicer than the others." He tried his best to smile.

"No comment. I'm closing the door." He closed the door and stepped back, waiting. He heard a door close and then, within two minutes, the sound of the minivan cranking. "Shit," and he followed up on the missed call.

"Dr. Markush, glad you called," said Jacob Jacobi. "The media are on to us. We had some snoops snap Lawrence's photo last night at Adelphi, yelling questions. Under no circumstances are you to speak with anyone, but you know that."

Markush then detailed his encounter with the reporter and gave him the guy's name, Jeremy Sims.

"Damn. It's started. I've contacted Glenelle and General Watkins. We'll have a plan of attack by tomorrow, Friday. Just stay low and say nothing. Reporters may tag you, but if they don't have base clearance, they can't follow you to Organon."

"Hell, I knew this was coming. There's been a leak; someone's talking. Could be an Organon employee," said Markush.

"Can you stay on base for now? To limit contact?"

"I can stay at the guest house."

"Great, do that. Carry on, but watch your tail."

"Will do." Markush put his phone in his pocket and grabbed his tweed jacket and an overcoat. It was above freezing but would dip to zero the next day. A business card pushed into the storm-door glass fell to the brick stoop.

Markush, carrying a laundry basket filled with gifts,

passed himself through security and waited for someone to buzz him onto the medical unit, which Claire did. He could hear Clark Peters yelling from room five, "Dah-lia!" and Markush nodded to the guard named Shark.

"Oh, presents!" said Claire. Jim and Debbie were in patient rooms.

"I'm sorry, nothing for the staff but for the Returnees, especially Mia."

"That's okay, Dr. Markush. Just glad to be here, making double time."

"Just happy you and the others made it. It's a lot to ask, working on a holiday." He wondered if Claire was the source of the leak. "Anything happened I should know about?"

"Not really. Emma is doing much better, sitting up in bed. She was just out cold for so long."

"Yeah, a gunshot behind the ear will do that to you. She's damn lucky to be here."

"Did she really just show up on the lawn outside?" Claire spoke, while scanning a bank of EEG and cardiac monitors, occasionally glancing at room cameras.

"So, you know about that?"

"Well, I was here when they carted her in. Just never got the full story."

"Right. Let's just keep the level of detail where it stands for now. Gotta head back to the other unit. Merry Christmas, by the way."

"And Merry Hanukkah!" said Claire.

That made Markush smile.

On the long-term wing, Markush walked down the U-shaped hallway to room twelve, carrying the gifts for

Mia and the others.

"Hey! Happy holidays!" Markush held the laundry basket as if it were a precious chest.

Kristin was asleep in the chair, wrapped in two blankets. Mia sat at a forty-degree angle in bed like a little princess.

"Hello, Clyde," said Mia. She smiled a big one. "Are those all for me?"

Kristin was coming out of a fitful sleep, her curls wonky, but Markush found her alluring in her discomfiture.

"What?" asked Kristin.

"I come bearing gifts. Not all of them are for you, Mia."

Mia frowned. "Damnation. Is there another little girl in your life?"

"Mia, be...polite." Kristin had been dreaming, just under the surface of sleep.

Markush placed the plastic hamper on the bed. He wasn't sure what was what and had to look at the tags beneath the bows. "Here you go, Mia." He handed her two brightly wrapped packages.

"Oh, wrapped to a tee!" She tore open the first and then opened a box. She peeled back a layer of tissue paper. "What the fuck?" She held up a red wool beanie with a pattern of white snowflakes. "Hey, I wanted a bikini to strut my stuff and show my junk."

"Mia," said Kristin. "Just say thank you and try it on." She knew that the Mia before her was fundamentally very different from her Mia, but she couldn't shake the illusion that she was still there.

Shelby appeared, holding a can of Ensure to push down Reece's feeding tube along with a bolus of water. "Everything okay? Presents, I see."

Mia looked disgusted. "You can just go away, boogey-man."

Shelby gave Markush a look and went on his way to the next room.

"Looks great on you," said Markush.

"What if it was the only thing I was wearing?"

"Then I would get you some clothes," said Markush.

"So persnickety, aren't we?" said Mia.

Markush ignored her, realizing that he was letting this Mia get to him. He had long forgiven Reece for strangling Mia's first impostor. Mia opened the second present, a book, *Harry Potter and the Philosopher's Stone.* She thumbed through the pages.

"I've already read this," she said. "It's bunk. Some kid with glasses catches a break and waves around a magic wand. Big fucking deal."

Kristin finally had the energy to stand, but pressed her hand to the wall, dizzy. "Mia, you've never read that book. I would know. It's new."

Mia looked a bit confused, as if she had spoken out of turn. "Well, thank you so much, Clyde. I've never read this before. Looks fascinating. Harry Potter, what a name!"

"You're welcome, Mia. Look, Kristin, I'm still looking for a present for you. Sorry."

She took his hand. "Don't be silly. So much going on. Can we talk?"

She led him into the hall and into the dayroom, which really had no function. The room was bare save one maroon couch and a ping-pong table. Markush had chalked it up to military contractors padding the bill. It was quite a nice ping-pong table with a steel and aluminum frame. They sat, knees touching.

"I can't take it anymore."

"Mia?"

"Yes, Mia. She's not my Mia. I totally get it now. It's like babysitting a tyrant. She's abusive, and I think I hate her. I'm afraid I'll do something foolish. Reece was right, after all."

"What if you step away, stay in the guest house for a while? I would much rather visit you there. I totally get it, I mean." He wanted to kiss her.

"I'm up to just go back home. I can't stand seeing the bodies of two Reeces, not knowing what the hell is going on inside their heads, the other places."

"That may not be a good idea. A reporter showed up on my doorstep this morning, asking me about my work. I don't know how he found me, what the motive is." He put his face into his hands as if he might cry.

"Oh no. What did you say?"

"I said nothing, closed the door basically, and he went away. There was another attempt at contact in Maryland. A testing lab. I'm afraid they'll mob you if you go back to Richmond, plus it's nice to have you here."

Markush led Kristin outside so that she could return to the guest house. "Anyone approaches you, say nothing and call me." He then entered the residential facility, bearing gifts, but no one was up except for Arthur.

"Guttenmorgen, my dear doctor." Arthur looked well rested and satisfied. "The medicine you prescribed has worked a wonder."

Markush had to think. "Yes, great. Nothing worse than being constipated."

"Perhaps being trampled by a horse." Arthur laughed. "I see you have what appear to be gifts. Is the holiday upon us? I am afraid I have nothing to give in return."

"Yes, gifts for everyone. No need to reciprocate. Your presence alone is sufficient." Markush placed the basket of gifts on a couch. It struck him now how small this residential facility was, with only eight beds. He had not really been thinking of the long term. "Arthur, until the others make an appearance, we can talk. I'm interested in your work, why you might have been chosen to assist Reece."

"That is of utmost importance, I think. My published thoughts stem from the transcendental idealism of Immanuel Kant. The world that one creates depends on an independent will, that is. The will is separate from what is known but assists in creating reality, in simple terms. To know the known, one must know the knower."

"That's what I've been thinking, having done some research on your works. Why might that be important to Reece and his journey to find Mia?"

"Perhaps he needed a grounded system of metaphysics to assist him. I'm really not sure what role I am playing, other than it helped lead him to Mia. This Dahlia would like us to see one thing rather than another. One must take for truth the validity of the senses, an idea of positivism, although perhaps my ideas have a bit of a mystical tone, which the positivist would deny." Arthur crossed his legs and coughed, as if discussing the sighting of a ship or a balloon.

"Arthur, how interested are you in the notion of time?

Time is of utmost importance here. I've learned through Reece and other patients that Dahlia's mother is time itself, plus there is all of this time travel that is occurring."

"Young Reece has mentioned this idea of time and Dahlia. I'm not sure what to make of it other than the Newtonian concept. I think that time progresses in a forward motion, as measured by clocks, but that time can flow regardless of its subjects. We are getting at an idea of Dahlia as being the product of time, which I cannot explain. That which is unknowable is unknowable unless we will it so."

Markush nodded. "Right, through your travels and those of Reece and others, the will is subjected to accept new knowledge of the world in a mysterious way. Maybe that's too simple. I really need to speak with Reece more about this, but he's off again to the neverlands."

"I do wish that I could be of service to him. I feel rather helpless moping about while he once again searches for his Mia in these neverlands, as you say."

"Right. I've been thinking of what to do with you, versus wasting your days here. There have been some developments that are prompting me to reconsider the secrecy of our mission here, but I require approval from higher authorities. What if you were to go on a lecture tour?"

"Oh, lectures. Mine in the past did not meet with much success, leading me away from academe. This world is very different, and ideas, I'm certain, have changed."

"But the fact that you have discrete knowledge of the past and that you are here to elucidate that past...There are legions who would love to hear your ideas and perhaps how they may have been altered by your recent experiences. It's just a thought."

"Ha, you would perhaps put me inside this television box to broadcast my thoughts?"

"That's an idea. We have what are called talk shows, where you could respond to questions. But you would have to speak in layman's terms to connect with a wide audience."

"Yes, I see, although sometimes it's most difficult to place down a stone versus a mountain."

"What are you guys up to?" Emma stretched and yawned. "Not time for breakfast?" She walked over to inspect the basket of gifts.

"Good morning," Arthur and Markush said.

"Yeah, good morning and Merry Christmas. Presents?"

"And here comes Afewerki," said Markush. "Right on time." He stood and placed the basket on the coffee table.

"My goodness," said Afewerki. "It is the day of Christmas." He wore his Exxon ballcap backwards.

For thirty minutes, Markush handed out the gifts one at a time, two for each. He had no clue what Denise had bought, and her choices surprised him: aftershave and socks for Arthur, a pair of earrings and a *Chicken Soup for the Soul* book for Emma, and a University of Kentucky ballcap and more aftershave for Afewerki. They all showed appreciation for their gifts, much to Markush's delight.

Markush's phone rang, and he excused himself.

Glenelle was back from a smoke break and had called Markush. She wore her typical tightly tailored dress with fake lapels. She had spoken with Colonel Lawrence at Adelphi, Jacobi at the CIA, and Watkins at the Pentagon about the media activity.

"Hey there, Markush. Sorry to bug you on a holiday," said Glenelle.

"There are no holidays at Organon, just like a hospital."

"Right."

She then told Markush that a plan was hatching to counter the media. So far, no stories had broken. The brief was on the server. Basically, all parties were to remain mum and act as if this media attention was just routine. General Watkins had approved the hiring of a publicity expert to map the future. "It's now or never," he said.

"Sounds good, Glenelle. I appreciate the hand-holding here, as I'm not one to deal with the media."

Glenelle laughed. She liked the idea of holding hands with Clyde Markush. "We've vetted the publicity agent, and we'll give her three days to come up with a plan. I may ask that you contact her, but we should follow her lead, even if it sounds preposterous."

"Preposterous is a strong word. Let's just hope that our funding remains a secret. I think the world would definitely be surprised at what is going on, maybe even shocked, but who knows? People do like a good story."

"Yes, they do. And like to see things crumple and fall, too. It's this whole idea of Dahlia that has me the most concerned, more than the time travel."

"Meaning that people's idea of a great God will be tarnished?"

"That's it precisely, too close to being an all-knowing creature, if you ask me. To be honest, I still need to be absolutely convinced. If the opportunity arises, I would love to see or speak with this Dahlia."

"You and me both," said Markush.

They wrapped things up and went about their business, Glenelle heading to her son's house for the great opening of presents. Markush strode onto the medical unit, taking off his tweed jacket and hanging it in the nurses' station.

"Hey, Claire."

"Hi, Dr. Markush."

Markush scanned the video monitors and saw Debbie and Jim in rooms. He scanned the EEG monitors. "Looks like Peters is back," he said.

"About twenty minutes," said Claire.

Markush walked to room five, Clark Peters. He had been traveling via seizure when Markush had last been on the unit. Peters suffered from schizophrenia and hallucinated around the clock. He had not only shot his daughter Beatrice but also his wife, and was traveling universes looking for Beatrice.

Peters lay flat on his back, his wrists and ankles restrained. "Argh, argh," he said.

"Hi, Mr. Peters," said Markush as he washed his hands. "Tell me about where you've been."

"Ark a doodle," said Peters. "Into the cave, deep deep deep."

"Have you been to the Cylinder?" He pulled a rolling

chair next to the bed. Peters, as far as Markush could tell, was being helped by a mysterious figure. He wanted to know who that was, but Peters was shy on details.

"Got me by the throat. Argh and grrr," said Peters. He looked down at his restrained wrists. "Scissors, mate! Need some damn scissors, arghhhhhh..."

Markush saw it was fruitless, as usual, but maybe he would talk to the nurses. Jim walked into the room. He stood a few inches above Markush and had prematurely silver hair, but without the receding hairline. His piercing blue eyes added authority to his muscled body.

"Peters say anything of interest to you?" asked Markush.

"He came out of his seizure screaming about a black bull. That's about it."

"Okay, I'm outta here. How about Emma? How is she faring?"

"Still improving. Tolerates sitting up in bed, moving her arms. Still has that glassy look, though."

"That's good news. Carry on, sir," and Markush left, headed to the guest house and Kristin. Was it too early for a glass of wine?

Two days later, Markush answered Glenelle Lock's phone call, just before noon. She had news about the publicity campaign. Sherri Loveless had been acquired from a firm on Wall Street to run the campaigns. Loveless was mid-thirties and somewhat skeletal, addicted to cross-training. She held the endowed Hermann Professor of Marketing at Stanford University. She no longer taught classes, paid primarily to hang around and impress others. As a partner with Graham Brothers of New York and Los Angeles, she had worked on publicity campaigns that had saved the skins of politicians and stars after unfortunate disclosures of either hanky-panky or outright crime. Her involvement with the CIA concerned propaganda to support the Gulf War, which went very well.

"Hey, Dr. Markush." Glenelle scooted back in her chair to ease the tension in her tight dress. She wasn't necessarily a looker, but liked to appear tightly packaged. "I've just finished meeting with Sherri Loveless. She's quite the pistol. In less than forty-eight hours, she has this master plan, but still wants to speak with you about the practical aspects."

"Sounds interesting. Did she have trouble buying into Dahlia?"

"She took it like a champ, as if she had always known such a thing existed."

Glenelle then laid out the basic plan to Markush. Instead of holing up and avoiding the press, the offensive was to be taken with press conferences and freely given interviews to those who mattered. Loveless was already on a tear, setting up interviews not only for Markush but for the Returnees.

"Is that really a good idea?" asked Markush. "I mean, what will people think? They'll think we're trying to destroy religion, philosophy, logic, and physics."

"That's just what Loveless wants. Chaos. Put the heat on everyone else to make or break claims we all hold dear. We are the wave, and we need surfers. Her words."

Markush couldn't believe it. "Will we give tours of Organon?"

"Yes, but not the medical or long-term unit, to protect patient privacy, but their stories, including the murders, Dahlia, and time travel, are all fair game. According to Jacobi, there's been a major leak from within Organon or possibly at a higher level. Instead of us being the prey, we become the predator, a kind of crazy predator that garners shock and awe. Once the truth is revealed, many people will just walk away. The rest will be fascinated and simply want more. Loveless wants you to write a tell-all book about Dahlia. She has a ghost writer in mind if you don't have the time."

Markush tried to take it in. This would change everything. "What about funding?"

"Clear and in the open, currently tied to arms sales to the Afghans and liberation groups in Africa. That's a funding stream, arms sales that is, that will never dry up. Nobody's social security check will be in danger. No one will protest that their taxes are undermining all that's scared. I mean sacred."

"Holy cow," said Markush. Ideas ran through his mind

like bottle rockets. This would change the lives of the Returnees and of anyone associated with Organon. Kristin. Himself. Arthur. Emma. Afewerki. And even the Reeces. "So, what do I do?"

"You wait to hear from me. I'll let you know about interviews and specific publicity campaigns that will involve you. One thing, though, General Watkins has agreed with Loveless that Organon needs a major security overhaul, including an electrified barbed-wire fence. There will be nut jobs who are drawn to you. You want to have control over who gets in and out."

"Right. What about Jacobi's ideas of expansion? Should we proceed with examining the long-term implications? Adding beds and a few staff won't cut it. I was being naïve."

"That's going to require an in-person meeting with the key players: you, me, Jacobi, Watkins, and Lawrence. It's gonna be big, probably add a Senator to the mix. I can guarantee that. Look, that's about all you need for now. Let me get outside in this damn cold and choke down a few coffin nails."

Markush laughed. "Right. I get it. Time to digest." He hung up his phone, and Denise buzzed him from reception. She said there was a man from the *New York Times* there to see him. He had base clearance and a letter from Loveless.

On the medical unit, Mia continued to sit in bed like a princess, as if the world served her. She was perfectly content to spend hours alone, watching TV and coloring. She took the nurses, Shelby and Scoot, with a grain of salt and kept them in line with her acid tongue. They had joked about making the little bitch pay somehow, perhaps an overdose of laxative or a good shock from a prime dose of insulin.

That afternoon, Reece's gamma waves continued in room eleven. He had not come up for air after his sustained seizure of over three days. The nurses were pumping him with Ensure and water to satiate his body's need for calories, which was enormous. No longer brain dead with the occasional EEG blip, the other Reece had also converted to gamma waves. The question on everyone's mind was where were they and what were they doing?

The Reeces walked among grassy hillocks with expansive views at their tops. The sky looked a perfect shade of light peach with no sun visible. Scrub trees and bush caught on their clothes.

"That's a jasmine bush," said Reece1. "And that's poinsettia, although not in bloom."

"You know things," said Reece2. "How much farther?"

"Within half a kilometer, it seems. There's a desert rose. And evergreens too."

"If you know so much, being a perfect idea, then where is Mia?" asked Reece2.

Reece1 seemed to glide along as if he were skating on ice. "The perfect idea of *me* doesn't know that. There are others who may know."

"Dahlia has set this up, for certain. She *would* pair me with one of us that wasn't privy."

"Does that make you angry?" asked Reece1.

"Maybe. What really makes me angry is your hairline. I have an egg head compared to you." He managed a laugh, feeling the thin atmosphere. "How high up are we?"

"About three thousand meters in the Highlands. There, just ahead." Reece1 pointed.

"Smoke, which reminds me I'm hungry. I'm absolutely starved."

"There will be food, eventually. They will be suspicious at first. Just follow my lead."

They walked into a gully of gray dirt packed with small rocks and fossils. They seemed to be in a tunnel.

Upon climbing some thirty meters, they came to an area of plowed land with foot-high sorghum. In the distance, on another plot of ground, a thin figure plowed with two oxen. He wore ragged pants that came to his knees, a rough shirt of thick cotton, and a makeshift hat. He had stopped to watch them.

Ahead sat house-sized boulders, and off to the left a collection of compounds, perhaps thirty, all with tall fences of sticks and living desert plants. Three women and half a dozen children stood by a well, watching them approach with hands over their mouths. As they came near, the Reeces passed by four depleted wells covered with poles and rocks.

"What do we do?" asked Reece2.

"We just introduce ourselves and see what happens."

A loud crack split the air, and a bullet ricocheted off a stone near Reece2's foot. "The fuck," he said and stopped in his tracks.

From between two boulders, a figure appeared, dressed in military garb, a Makarov pistol in hand. Behind him lingered two teenagers in jeans and dirty t-shirts, wearing sandals.

"The Hyena," said Reece2.

"The Hyena, the Snake, the Vulture, the Donkey," said Reece1. "Here, he is Wusha, the Dog." He walked toward the Dog with hands raised.

Reece1 spoke Amharic and engaged the Dog, telling him of their purpose, to find Reece2's daughter. Although she was absorbed into the quanta of the Pinch, Reece1 also had a daughter named Mia. Reece1 walked the twenty meters.

"Tenesteling," said Reece2. He knew a little Amharic from his time in Ethiopia as a nurse.

"You are twins," said the Dog. "This is a bad omen. You will bring bad luck and must leave." He spat, his lower lip packed with the narcotic leaf called qat.

Reece2 looked at the peachy sky, wondering where the sun was. There was no breeze, and the air felt sterile.

After a few minutes, Reece1 explained the situation. The Dog had demanded they leave, but not before a drink to wash away the bad luck.

As the group of five walked past the well, the women went silent, pulling their scarves across their faces. The children ceased to smile and clung to their mothers' ragged dresses. As they wound among the enclosed huts, curious eyes followed them with an occasional "Ferenj!" Reece2 swatted at the curious flies, which seemed translucent. He then saw something very odd. They approached a hut without walls, rather like a cabana, filled with shelves of books. A white man who seemed familiar lounged on a rough wooden chair. The man looked him in the eye as they passed and nodded. Reece2 drifted closer and caught the title of a fat hardback, *Three Trapped Tigers*.

They arrived at a hut with a piece of yellow plastic over the door. Inside was very dim and filled with smoke from tree resin burning in a dish. A small radio played Amharic music. A young woman of sixteen years, wearing a patched green dress and with a tattoo of an Orthodox cross on her forehead, stood with a definite frown on her face. Around the base of the hut's wall were large stones to sit on.

The girl gave them all red plastic cups and then poured a clear liquor. She mumbled, asking who would pay, and the Dog spoke. The girl turned away, disgusted, but what could she do? She took up her place on a low stool near the door and picked at her fingernails as the Dog spoke loudly to Reece1. Reece2 listened but without understanding. A man entered, lulling the conversation, but he withdrew right away.

"What is he saying?" asked Reece2.

"He says we cannot stay the night, but that we should speak with the bookseller before we leave. He may have information about Mia, and he's also telling me the story of Icelanders who worked here many years ago, and what fun they were, but they did not respect him. Their graves are near here."

"Good God, he killed them?"

"It seems that way, yes."

"Why is there a white guy selling books in this place? They seemed to be in English."

"He came here before the Icelanders and has an Amhara wife. The Dog says that he dropped from the sky as an angel or perhaps a devil. He has not sold a single book since arriving."

The young girl had refilled the Dog's cup twice with the fiery liquor, katikala, the vodka of the Highlands, and he drank in gulps, sighing loudly after each. His minions watched with eager, yet bored, eyes.

"Where did the books come from? Did they drop from the sky, too?"

"No one is knowing. It is said that they came from a cave."

"Have you asked this guy, the Dog, if he's seen Mia here?" asked Reece2.

"Yes, and he says that many years ago a little white girl appeared, but that she has gone."

"Maybe we arrived too late?"

"It's not clear, the timelines. Maybe we're too early."

"What?"

"Time has no direction," said Reeceɪ. "It's possible to travel to a point A but arrive at a further point B first, if you travel fast enough. Then going from B to A will take you back in time, making all time simultaneous." Reeceɪ looked thoughtful. Nothing seemed to disturb him.

"You'll have to run that by me when I'm not drinking. We should go and see the bookseller. I can't take much more of this katikala. I remember it well. Too smoky. I'm here for one thing, to find Mia. I've done it before, and I can do it again."

"Yes, we shall see." Reeceɪ turned and resumed his conversation with the Dog.

Emma missed Reece. She felt a connection with him, even though he was a little nuts. He had confided that he was bipolar and being treated, that at one point in his life, at his lowest point, a doctor diagnosed him with schizoaffective disorder. She knew he had a thing for her just by the way he acted, as if he was holding back, almost shy in a way. Markush wouldn't give her any details about his condition, other than he was engaged in prolonged seizure activity, which seemed awful to her.

She sat alone in her room on the single bed, staring at the ceiling. Afewerki knocked and walked in.

"The doctor is here with some news," he said. He wore his new ballcap.

Emma struggled to sit up and soon joined the gang in the lounge area with Markush. He looked tired.

"We are eager for news," said Arthur. "I hope it is good news."

Markush nodded. "There's been a development with how we will handle you guys. Thus far, we've been protecting you from outside forces, but that's all going to change. We're finding you homes nearby, and you'll no longer be cooped up like chickens." He laughed.

"Well, cock a doodle do," said Emma. "When?"

"As soon as we find you housing, perhaps in a few days. Afewerki, we have a special plan for you. There's more, too, that might be uncomfortable for everyone."

"What does it mean?" asked Afewerki.

Markush told Afewerki that he would enroll at Eastern

Kentucky University in their ESL program, that he would live on campus, free to study and work toward a bachelor's degree of his choice. That brought a huge smile from Afewerki and congratulations from Arthur and Emma. The kicker, for them all, was that they would be exposed to the media for what they were, time travelers from another universe. There would be staged interviews with the print and TV media. There would be ridicule, but they were to talk honestly about their experiences and could speculate on the meaning as they wished. No secrets, no holds barred. The media would seek them out, no doubt, and they were free to interact as they wished. Emma would be employed at the base hospital as a nurse, and Arthur would travel as a speaker to various universities and on talk shows. At first, the experience would be sensational but would soon settle into normalcy.

"Would there be people who want to hurt us?" asked Emma.

"I'm afraid so. It's only natural. We expect resistance from say physicists and philosophers on intellectual grounds, but what we fear most are the reactions from religious authorities and their followers. We're challenging the basic idea of God, putting in His place a seven-year-old girl named Dahlia, no less."

"Oh, but there is only one God," said Afewerki.

"That's precisely what I mean," said Markush. "But you need to follow your own beliefs. Not that you think Dahlia is God, but the implications for her existence push the limits of what people can believe."

"Reason alone discredits the existence of God," said Arthur. "But my recent experiences have highly discounted my reality of logical thinking and proof. I find I am in a constant battle with myself. What does it mean for a mere child to hold such power in her hands?"

"Yes!" said Markush. "You have to explore that with the public. Make it seem real and logical."

"A life's work, I'm sure. I do have need of pen and paper to write upon the ideas that are forming."

"I've thought about that," said Markush. "You'll have all the pen and paper you need."

"Excellent."

"When do I start work?" asked Emma.

"Give yourself some time to settle into your new home, perhaps a month. You have experience in cardiac intensive care, right? The ball is rolling with our office in the Pentagon, securing you a position at Ireland Army Community Hospital."

"I suppose the human heart works the same here as in my world."

"Don't worry. You'll go through an extensive orientation. Your license to practice in Kentucky is being secured as we speak, along with other documents such as a birth certificate and a social security number."

"That's all great," said Emma. "But I'm worried about the media."

"No worries. We'll have control over most of the coverage. We have a publicity expert coming in to meet with you tomorrow. She's the brains behind this effort, Sherri Loveless. I'm going to be a primary target, so I need to speak with her as well. To get us going, the first publicity *breach* will be the base newspaper, *The Gold Standard*. We've briefed a reporter, and he will be here on Monday to interview you."

"This is very exciting," said Arthur. "To have an audience for my view of the world, which I still hold, as represented to me by my senses, although I am questioning the reliability of my senses with current events. I should much like to return to my country and city if possible."

"I hear you, Arthur," said Markush. "I'm certain we can work toward that. This is an international issue as well."

"Do you mean inter-universal?" said Arthur.

Letitia Mumford saw a soldier dressed in green, holding a sign with her name on it. She had left her home in Star City, Arkansas, that morning, headed to Little Rock, where she caught a flight to Louisville, Kentucky. She was an Amazon with tightly braided cornrows that fell beyond her shoulders, with distinct cheekbones, somewhat like the model Iman.

After registering at the Fort Knox visitors' center, where she picked up a military ID, Mumford continued to Organon. Markush met her in the front lobby, wondering what sort of force he was being dealt to help him reckon with Dahlia and other worlds. He would wait to ask her why she had lost her license to practice medicine in Arkansas. Surely, Glenelle and General Watkins had Organon's best interest in mind.

After a tour of the medical facility, where she saw the fire of Helmut Grayson, the psychosis of Clark Peters, and the quiet suffering of Emma Smith, Markush led her onto the long-term unit to room three, where lay Reece.

"This is Reece Myers, the original Reece who murdered an impostor. He was successful in navigating time and place and found his daughter, Mia, and managed to get her back, along with three others. I just call them Returnees. We'll meet them."

Letitia Hubbard looked uncomfortable, rolling her shoulders, assaulted with this incredible information. She had been informed of the generalities of Organon, but had not expected it to be really true, although a similar incident with a patient of hers had occurred.

"Reece Myers," said Hubbard. "And there is another one in room eleven?"

"Yes," said Markush with a smile. He viewed his job as the best in the world, overjoyed to have someone he could closely talk with about the insanity of it all.

"How can there be two?" asked Hubbard.

Markush pondered the best way to put it. "Reece, at some point, was disabled in another universe, perhaps drawn into what is called the Cylinder or maybe even the Pinch, a unique region, maybe one of infinite unique regions. His body went silent, brain-dead basically. But then a double appeared. He had somehow escaped Dahlia and found Mia. I think it was a matter of psychology, or perhaps philosophy, that freed him. The Reece before us, though, has come back to life, so to speak. You can see the EEG activity."

Hubbard stepped into the room beyond the half-pulled curtain. "Gamma waves? Just like my patient back in Star City. I transferred him to Little Rock. He went in and out of seizure states, telling the most bizarre stories of Dahlia. I let him seize, did not treat him, and he lapsed into a coma. I lost my license after the family sued."

"Wow, I was going to ask," said Markush. "Sorry to hear it. I wonder how many more of us there are out there, those who are baffled, but know that something significant is at stake."

"You and me both," said Hubbard. "What I don't understand is how the other Reece returned if the Reece before us is also here. Was another Reece created? It seems that way."

"I've pondered that and spoke with the other Reece about that before he resumed his seizures and traveling, after his daughter Mia was replaced—again." He insinuated that the perfect idea of Reece existed in the Pinch. That perhaps his idea came to live among the rest of us, who are merely a representation of their perfect ideas. "I'm not sure which is which, though. The ideas somehow live in the Pinch, which I have yet to fully comprehend. Who was looking for Mia in those other worlds, and who has returned to us is just a representation of Reece. The bona fide original, for us, I suppose, lies before us, although just a shell. Or it may have something to do with how he returned, a duplication anomaly."

"I'm taking it in, Clyde. Can I call you Clyde?"

"Of course, and Letitia is fine?"

"That will do. Can I take a peek at the other Reece?"

"Right this way."

They walked and turned right twice, meeting Shelby. Clyde introduced them.

"Here we are, the Reece who returned from a version of a village that he had worked in when he was in his early twenties, a village called Godo. He found Mia there after outwitting Dahlia. Little girls with knives nearly annihilated the group. Reece saved them with an utterance that he won't reveal to me."

"So—"

"Doctor Clyde? Is that you?" said Mia from the next room. "I hear your tinny little voice and that of a stranger. Won't you pop in?"

Clyde gave Letitia a look. "You're about to meet *Mia*. Let's see what you make of her."

"Reece's daughter—"

"An impostor..."

Markush drew back the curtain, and Mia was sitting in the recliner holding a mirror and brushing her ginger hair. She produced a languid smile, as if she was eating mangoes along the banks of some ancient river.

"Well, who is this?" asked Mia. "She's certainly taller than you are and far better looking." She giggled.

"Mia, this is Dr. Hubbard. She's moving here to work with us."

"Hi, Mia—"

"Do you put on your underwear like Dr. Clyde? Yellow in the front and brown in the back?" She let out a hilarious laugh, ending in a controlled cough.

"Hmm, that's an old one," said Letitia. Her look at Markush said that she needed to leave, that she had seen enough for her first day.

"Mia, you should be nicer. You'll be seeing a lot of Dr. Mumford."

"Yeah, whatever, bitches. You can leave unless you brought more presents."

"I see," said Clyde. "We'll be seeing you, Mia. We have some questions for you, but we'll wait for a better time."

"Oh, did you mention time?" asked Mia. "You know I lied to that character, Dahlia. I told her that her mommy was made of time. I did lie, didn't I, Dr. Markush?"

The Reeces left the Dog and his buddies as they finished their katikala, backtracking to find the bookseller, who wasn't hard to find with BOOKS! painted in bright red on a sheet of wood. The book seller sat just under the hut's overhang, smoking a cigar that he had rolled himself. Reece1 looked at Reece2, insinuating that he should start the conversation. An old man leading a battered donkey along the dusty, rocky path passed them, his eyes bright. A group of children, all dressed in rags, had gathered some ten meters away, watching and murmuring.

"Hello?" asked Reece2. He imagined he sounded like a robot.

"Hey y'all." The book seller stood and stepped beyond the hut's sloping roof, made of corrugated steel, the only such material in the village. He held a fat hardback copy of *Ulysses*. "What can I do you for?"

"You live here?" asked Reece2.

"Do I live here?" asked the book seller. "Why Dwayne Turnipseed has lived here for an even score. Got me a pretty wife, a young thang, and two young 'uns. Of course, I live here. You got a problem with that?"

Reece1 intervened. "No, sir. We're just passing through and have to leave, according to the Dog—"

"Oh, the Dog! Damn the Dog. Why, you're here looking for your daughter, aint'cha?" He looked back and forth between the Reeces.

"Mia, my daughter...you know where she is?" asked Reece2.

"Yes, Mia, our daughter," said Reece1.

"I see now. A couple of buttfucks. Well, that don't shine particularly well 'round these parts. We are God-fearing people."

"Mr. Turnipseed," said Reece1, "you can think what you wish, but the fact is that Dahlia has hidden Mia, and we need to find her, he more than myself. My Mia, the idea of Mia, if you will, is safe. I'm just helping out."

"Okay, what goes around comes around, I s'pose. Look, I just sell books. It's my calling. Of all the places in the universe that needed a good bookstore, this here is the place. Not that anyone buys my books, but it's just the fact that they *might* buy a book. Get it? Course, my mama always said that mights come from chickens."

Reece2 swallowed some spit, thinking. This Turnipseed was as redneck as they come. "I have to ask. It always seems to come to this. Is there an Abba Paulos in these here parts?" He was letting the country flair get to him. His grandfather had been the first generation off the farm.

"Ho, ho, ho, the old Abba Paulos. That mother knows some tricks. You might hit him up for some in-for-ma-tion. He's a slick one, he is."

Reece1 nodded, as if he had known this all along. "He's nearby, building a church."

"Well, ain't you smart," said Turnipseed. "He'll talk, but you'll have to grease him up with some silver or some gold."

A couple of hooded vultures floated high overhead in the light peach sky.

"Where is this church?" asked Reece2. "We need to find him."

"I know where to find him," said Reece1. "Thank you, sir, for your time."

Reece2 stuck out his hand for a shake, but Turnipseed had settled back into his chair. "Let's get going. It may get dark soon. Not sure what time it is."

"There is no day or night here," said Reece1. They walked side by side along a steep path toward the edge of the village, a small troupe of children following at a safe distance.

"Where does the light come from?" asked Reece2.

"From high above, sulfide-oxidizing bacteria that produce light. This planet is riddled with volcanoes that spew sulfur. There's one." Reece1 pointed to a faraway wisp that seemed to envelop itself as it rose, like folds of time.

"Damn," said Reece2. "And there's no wind, just dead still."

"Part of the overall effect, a very stable atmosphere," said Reece1.

They continued up the hill and then down a steep, rutted path lined with brush and briars.

"Here's a clove tree," said Reece1. He pointed at a small shrub-like tree with bunches of what looked to be red berries clustered at the ends. He paused and picked a few of the red buds, something like pomegranate seeds. "Taste."

Reece2 bit into a stem with the red bud. "Wow, clove for sure, but bitter. How much farther?"

"I'm enjoying the walk, experiencing all the wonder that is unique to me. Just relax. Maybe half an hour and we'll be there."

Reece2 stopped. "I appreciate the nature lessons, but I'm not here for fun. This is serious."

"No worries," said Reece1. "Relax." He seemed to be in a reverie, soaking in every little detail.

Reece2 went to his knees and slumped forward.

The next day, the reporter from *The Gold Standard,* the base newspaper, arrived and was escorted onto the residential unit to interview the Returnees, minus Reece. Usually, he wrote cut-and-dry stories—a high-ranking promotion, the testing of a new tank—but this one had Darryl Hicks' head spinning. He was a civilian, dressed in slacks and a blue shirt without a tie, and lived off base near Radcliff.

The group gathered around the dining table, Emma drumming her fingers, bored out of her mind. She couldn't wait to get out of there and into her new job, although the prospect was frightening. Darryl introduced himself before sitting and had with him a notepad and pen, along with a 35-mm camera with a flash. Everyone glanced at one another, waiting.

"I received a press release," said Darryl, "which reports that you are from, uh, another place." He said "place" as if it were Mars.

"That is correct," said Arthur. "My year is 1856, Frankfurt, Germany, from whence I was whisked to a strange city called Gadam, its year being 3981. From there, my journeys carried me to various villages and thence to your country and time." He made a seated bow to affirm his declaration. Emma and Afewerki then told Darryl of their travels to the present.

"I see," said Darryl, but he did not. "Why are you here, locked up in what I thought was a psychiatric hospital?"

"That's a great question," said Emma. "I'd like to know the proper answer. We were just caught up in Reece's travels. He said the magic words and *poof,* here we are."

"Reece has saved us from the little girls with knives. I am still not believing it," said Afewerki.

Arthur focused on the question of why. "I think, sir, we are here at the whim of this being called Dahlia. Do your reports entertain her existence?"

Darryl scanned the press release. There was something about Dahlia, a young girl who was on a quest. "Yes, Dahlia. Now, who is she?" He scribbled on his notepad and scratched his head.

The three gazed at one another, and Arthur spoke. "She is a young girl who controls access to multiple universes. We are merely pawns in her tiny hands. What she seeks is mysterious, to learn the origin of her mother."

"I see," said Darryl, wondering at the ridicule the story would engender, but orders were orders. "Is Dahlia among us? She exists?"

Emma laughed, then spoke. "Reece told me that Dahlia exists everywhere. There are incarnations of her here and elsewhere, it seems. All the Dahlias, the impostors, are out to solve the riddle of Dahlia's mother, like Arthur said."

"So, there are many Dahlias?" asked Darryl.

"Yeah, copies, scattered around the country, maybe the globe, at least *your* country and globe," said Emma. "I'm not sure about my own, although there were little girls with knives who Reece said were Dahlia. But there's one Dahlia controlling them all."

Darryl stopped writing. "I guess I'm still stuck on why you're here."

"Because of Dahlia," said Afewerki. "She is the evil one."

"And you are from Ethiopia, I gather?" asked Darryl.

"Yes, but another. In this place, there is my village, I am told, but I am already there. I would like to see it."

"I hope you know this sounds crazy. Just not sure what to make of it," said Darryl.

"Indeed," said Arthur. "Dahlia is very stubborn. Reece has told her who her mother is, but she does not believe it."

Darryl searched his press release again. "And Reece is here, somewhere? The guy who killed his daughter some four months ago, but it wasn't really his daughter?"

"That is correct," said Arthur. "I met young Reece in Gadam, as he was searching for his daughter Mia. Dahlia had replaced his daughter with a veritable replica. That is from whom he took the life, as grisly as it seems."

"Reece is comatose?" asked Darryl. "In this building?"

"He escaped but was caught," said Emma. "I think he started seizing again. We're not sure why or what the details are. I've asked to visit him, but Dr. Markush has refused so far."

"Yes, the seizures," said Darryl. "He visits other worlds when he seizes?"

"He, and others," said Arthur. "All searching for their abducted daughters, the poor unfortunate souls."

"But he found his daughte and brought her back, along with you three? It says in the report that Mia is here as well."

"That's what we've heard," said Emma, "although we thought she was back home with her mom, Reece's, um, ex-wife."

"Uh huh, the ex-wife, Kristin, I believe. I need to speak

with her as well." Darryl put down his pen. "I just don't think we can contain this to a single story. It may need to be a series, but I need to get the general story down first. I have little idea of how to check facts, these other worlds, unless I actually go there, which is impossible." Darryl seriously worried that he would lose his job over this.

Markush had left Kristin in the guest house, having spent the night with her. He felt things were getting back on track with their relationship. He seriously worried she would gravitate back to Reece after realizing that he had been right about Mia being an impostor. Markush was on the long-term unit to talk with Reece, who had emerged from his days-long seizure, looking very thin despite all the excess calories being pumped into him. The other Reece's EEG had continued with sustained gamma waves, his body motionless, being turned every two hours by the nurse. Letitia Mumford was checking out housing on base and had the day off.

Reece spoke with difficulty. "We're in Solon, me and the other me. There was a bookseller, this redneck guy named Dwayne Turnipseed. The details are much clearer this time around. We were on our way to find the Abba, to help find Mia. We were talking, and then it's a blank. I don't need to be here. I need to be there. The impostor..."

Markush was recording on his mini device. "Yes, Mia is in the next room. She's quite a character, so unlike your Mia. It's like she can't be more obviously not like Mia, like she can't help it."

"Dr. Clyde," said Mia from the next room. "I can hear you!"

Reece sat up and then fell back. "It's her." He clenched his fists and sat up again, grabbing the bed rail, trying to get out of bed.

"Reece! No," said Markush. "You can't do it. I don't think she has to die. Just trust me. You're on a journey to find Mia. There's nothing she can do about it."

"Don't be so sure!" sang Mia. "Because I'm Mia and my father loves me!"

"Damn, that bitch," said Reece. He flopped onto his back. "I can't be on the same unit as her. You have to move me or her."

"That's becoming apparent," said Markush. "I'll work something out." He didn't want to say that the plan was to enroll the replacement Mia in school, to treat her as a normal little girl.

"You have to," said Reece.

"Hey, bumfuck!" Mia catcalled Shelby as he walked to room eleven with a can of Ensure.

"Hey, Reece," said Shelby. "Dr. Markush, do you want him to drink this or push it down the tube?"

"God, I can taste that shit in my stomach even now. I can't drink it. Can I have some solid food?"

Markush thought. "I would hate for you to seize while you ate, but this could be a protracted affair, so yes."

Reece ordered two ham-and-cheese sandwiches with two bags of chips and two Cokes. Shelby nodded.

"You need the calories," said Markush. "Seizing takes a lot of energy. I'm worried about the toll it takes on your body. I keep thinking that the other Reece just wore himself out."

"How are Emma and Afe..." His eyelids trembled.

Two days later, the story about the Returnees had broken in *The Gold Standard*. Simultaneously, the story flashed across the AP wire. Calls flooded the Fort Knox information service with reporters shaking their heads across the country, many viewing the story as a giant hoax. The press release had emanated from Sherri Loveless, citing the Pentagon and Major General Tom Watkins as the source.

"Pentagon embraces time travelers" *New York Daily News*

"Dahlia, the little girl who runs the universe" *The New York Times*

"Are aliens abducting our little girls?" *The Washington Post*

"Is Arthur Schopenhauer alive and well?" *The Christian Science Monitor*

"This seven-year-old will ruin your life" *The National Enquirer*

"Fort Knox: Lunatics or space heroes?" *Louisville Courier Journal*

New York Times reporter Jeremy Sims, who had contacted Clyde Markush just two weeks prior, was back in Kentucky, lodged at The Ritz, the only hotel with a room in the area. He had an afternoon appointment with *The Gold Standard* reporter Darryl Hicks, but was desperate to meet with Dr. Clyde Markush. He had acquired a phone number for Organon, but the calls went to voicemail, a message recorded by the lovely Denise: "Thank you for your interest in Organon. Because of the high volume of calls, we are unable to answer. Please leave a message after the tone." But the message box was full. Sims dropped the phone onto its cradle, cursing, and called his desk boss, Lucinda LeClerc, back in New York.

"Lucinda, no luck with Organon just yet. I need a direct line to Clyde Markush. Any success yet?" He sat on his hard motel mattress, burping a greasy breakfast from the diner next door.

"We're working on it. Just be patient."

"I have to have that number. He's not leaving the base. I sat outside his house for a solid eighteen hours, but I will try again. Just had to get some sleep." He ran his fingers through his oily black hair.

"Okay, settle down, Jeremy. We're in this boat together. We're working on the Pentagon angle and following up leads with the CIA. A press conference at the Pentagon is scheduled for eleven this morning."

"Wish I could be there. I just don't want the story to get away from me. Who's managing the Pentagon press event?"

"Can't you guess?" asked Lucinda.

"Not Banks?"

"Yes, Banks. The one and only."

"Goddamn, he'll run the story into the ground. You know he makes stuff up, just writes and lets it fly."

"No worries, Jeremy. This is your story, and you're at ground zero, it seems. We've got our fact checkers lined up. Just do your job there. Got it?"

"Right. Okay, I think I have to shit my brains out. Damn breakfast has me bent over double."

"Too much information, but I'll let you do your business. Bye, Jeremy."

Jeremy hung up and tried calling Organon one more time.

Major General Tom Watkins walked into the press briefing room, dressed to the nines in his military regalia. He stood six-four, lanky, with hollow cheekbones, looking like he needed a good meal. He stepped up onto the small stage and walked to the mahogany podium, and looked out over the room, reporters packed into stackable steel chairs. Behind him was the Pentagon logo, to his right, Old Glory. He laid his press brief on the podium and cleared his throat. The red digital clock at the back of the room read 11:00. He started.

"Good morning, everyone. Thank you for being here. I'll give a brief presentation regarding the work of Organon, a medical facility at Fort Knox, followed by your questions." He gazed beneath the bright light and could see stymied faces. He almost wanted to laugh at what he was about to say, but with each passing day, the story was becoming more real. Betting on Organon to push him to three stars, he hoped the wild ride would not lead to disgrace. But nothing ventured, nothing gained.

"Organon is a secure medical facility holding unique patients. These patients have seemingly committed atrocious acts, such as murder. Our position has been one of harboring and observing the 'criminally insane' versus dealing with status quo criminals. These patients, not convicts who have been tried for crimes, are unique and hold vast importance for the world, for the universe. I'm sure you are very interested in the specific story of one such patient, Reece Myers.

"On August 4, 1997, Reece Myers supposedly strangled to death his daughter, Mia. Following the incident, he was admitted to the Organon facility, where spectacular revelations have come to light. For a week, he remained in a protracted seizure state. Myers believed his daughter had been abducted and replaced; thus, the strangled girl was not his daughter. During his seizure activity, it has been determined that Myers somehow traveled through time and space to other worlds, seeking his daughter, who had been hidden from him. We believe Myers when he says this." Watkins turned a page.

"In the course of his inter-universal travels, Myers located his daughter in a remote village in an Ethiopia similar to the Ethiopia we know. Through what we can only call sheer will, he caused himself, his daughter Mia, and three others to be transported back to our time and place, Richmond, Kentucky, to be exact. These Returnees, as we are calling them, are safely housed within Organon, and they are undergoing extensive evaluation. What we are learning is groundbreaking and defies the imagination.

"At the heart of this matter is an entity called Dahlia, who appears as a girl of seven years. It is Dahlia, according to Myers and other patients at Organon, who is responsible for the abductions and replacement of young girls, which often leads to murder of the replacement. As of now, no charges are being filed against any patient at Organon, considering the ongoing investigations. I'm sure that you are as astounded as I am. I will now take questions."

The room erupted in a flurry of activity, with several reporters speaking at once.

Watkins held up his hands as a gesture for order. "Yes," and he pointed to a woman in the front row, dressed in a red jacket. He had been briefed on names and faces but could not recall them.

"Are the, well, murderers locked up at Organon insane, as you suggest? I admit that this whole story sounds insane."

"The insanity defense, which we are presupposing here, basically states that the person didn't understand what they were doing, failed to know right from wrong, and acted on an uncontrollable impulse. Considering the events that occurred and the mental status of the patients, we do label these patients as insane, but not to indict them, rather to grant us access to their stories in a controlled environment. Without our protection, these patients would face harsh penalties and possible retribution, in or out of prison. Note that the Returnees describe a new class of patients at Organon, except for Reece Myers, who have not been accused of any crimes." He pointed to a man dressed in a black suit with a blue tie.

"Who is Dahlia? How can you verify her existence? Are we supposing a supernatural being that rivals God?" He bit his pen.

"Yes, Dahlia. Dahlia, from what we gather, is an omniscient being who spans universes." Here, General Watkins had to hesitate, fearing that his words would create laughter.

"What—"

"I'm still answering the question. Dahlia takes the form of a little girl. We have verified her existence through almost all the patients at Organon, with evidence of Dahlia going back to the 1960s, within the work of a physicist, Harold Leyman. There is a supposition that we can find oblique references, some Biblical, to Dahlia. I would not characterize Dahlia as supernatural, but rather as a trans-universal force that we, and the patients of Organon, interpret as a little girl of seven years of age."

"So, is Dahlia a juvenile God?"

"What we understand to be God carries with it many meanings. We are very interested in allowing the public to reach their own conclusions." He pointed again, this time toward the back at a raised hand, the reporter on the edge of leaping forward.

"Why would this Dahlia figure want to kidnap girls and replace them with what I suppose to be lookalikes?"

"Yes, lookalikes, but immediately recognizable as a fraud to those who have the power to discern such things, such as a parent. From what we have learned, from interviews with patients, is that Dahlia is on a quest...to find her mother." A brief ruckus arose. "Bear with me. This is as hard for you to believe as it was for me, but the evidence is mounting. Dahlia has, in effect, *mapped* certain individuals with a mesh device, we think, to gather information. Her sole purpose appears to be gathering information to establish her mother's identity. That drives her to kidnap and replace little girls and to *map* individuals, sometimes little boys." He pointed to a petite woman from *CNN* that he recognized. "Yes, Hillary."

"To be honest, I'm floored. I've read the press brief and am stunned. Do you really expect the public to accept this story of time travel and a little girl as God?" She almost stood.

"We are as fascinated as you are. It remains to be seen how well the public can digest the events described here today. We have questions and are seeking answers. If what we suppose is true, this will impact every citizen of our planet. We are choosing to be proactive and curious, versus ignoring patterns that cannot be attributed to chance."

General Watkins took several more questions, affirming White House acknowledgement of the situation. Throughout, he was stoic, keeping as straight a face as possible, but felt that he was withering beneath the camera lights.

At The Ritz motel, Jeremy Sims watched the press conference disband, staring at the TV in disbelief but with a burning desire to sort out this unfolding mystery. He had determined that Dr. Clyde Markush was his number one target, along with Reece Myers. There had been hints that there was more of his story to be told. He also knew that Reece's wife was holed up on base, perhaps being restrained. He wasn't sure, but her story would be invaluable as well. His phone rang.

"Yeah, it's me. Okay, great." Jeremy scribbled a number onto a yellow legal pad. "Thanks a million."

Markush watched the press briefing on national news with Emma, Arthur, and Afewerki. The General had done a pretty good job of getting his facts straight with an honest, open tone. However, follow-up coverage, which they were tuned to on *CNN*, left him cringing. Like watching a train wreck, he couldn't tear away, but his phone rang. Markush excused himself and wandered into the small kitchen with its microwave oven and coffee maker.

"Dr. Markush. I'm Jeremy Sims, *New York Times.* About a week ago, I showed up on your doorstep. I apologize for the suddenness of my appearance, but this is just beyond belief, and I really need to speak with you."

"Are you in town?" Markush didn't ask how he got his number. He supposed he would find a reporter under every rock for the time being.

"Yes, at the fabulous Ritz. I can do anytime, anywhere. You name it, although I would love to see inside Organon, the patients, the Returnees—where should I begin—although I promise I'm more organized than I sound."

"You saw the press conference?"

"Yes, and it just raised more questions. If this shakes out as portrayed, no one will ever be the same. I just can't believe how candid the Pentagon is being about this, as if they are inviting ridicule. But when the Pentagon speaks, it speaks, and usually for good reason."

"Take my word, this is real *and* more insane—I hesitate to use that word—than you can ever imagine. I'm really tied up today, but could meet you tomorrow, here at Organon. I'll have a pass waiting for you at the visitors' center. Jeremiah Sims, *New York Times?*"

"Jeremy."

"Right, Jeremy. So, be here at nine. Just come into the reception area, and Denise will find me. I'm only doing this because the higher-ups have given their blessing. It's been somewhat of a cover-up until now. You were on the early train, though, and I suspect we had a leak. How did you know to show up on my doorstep last week, before the press releases and stories?"

"I took orders and basic details, but do not know the source. Anyway, that seems moot now. Anything goes, right?"

Markush had to think about that. "Maybe not anything, but they have cleared me to share the Organon story with the world at large."

"Okay, see you at nine tomorrow."

Markush took his feet off his desk, feeling jubilant but cautious. He did not know the consequences of this open-door policy dreamed up by a publicity guru. She would arrive in just an hour, and Markush went into high gear to prepare, skipping lunch once again.

At two p.m. sharp, Sherri Loveless arrived at Organon, shouldering a laptop bag. She had risen at four a.m. and run eight miles before catching a C-21, the military version of a Learjet 35A, directly from D.C. to Godman Army Airfield at Fort Knox. Her legs and arms looked like muscle sticks protruding from a lithe torso sheltered beneath a classic stewardess hairdo. Denise buzzed Markush, and he came to the front desk.

"Have you had lunch?" asked Markush. "We make a mean sandwich." He had to gaze up at this woman's perfect chin. He'd looked up her vitals—Vassar, Yale, Stanford, Wall Street.

"I don't eat lunch. Just one meal a day, dinner, but well-rounded and portioned, vegan to be exact."

Markush first gave her a walkthrough of the medical unit, commenting on patients and their histories. They made the full round of the U-shaped hallway and stopped beside Timera Scocpol's room, number ten. She was awake, sitting up in bed with a blank look on her face, the TV on mute.

"Timera? May we pop in?" asked Markush. He scanned the EEG, alpha waves. Timera still traveled frequently, looking for her daughter Lacie, being helped by the Ras Tefari, better known as Haile Selassie.

"Yeah, step in, Dr. Markush. You got a lady friend with you?" Timera was a large woman. Her shaved head gave her the look of a man.

"Timera, this is...Sherri. We're on a first-name basis, Sherri."

Sherri didn't miss a beat. "Well, hello. Nice to meet you, Timera. Just on a tour with Clyde here."

"My, you're a skinny thing. Need some meat on those bones," said Timera.

Sherri laughed. "I'll take that as a...What the fuck? Clyde?"

Timera went slack, then arched, and then straightened, her feet and hands trembling, her large eyes quivering. The EEG showed a mass of polyspikes easing into gamma waves. Debbie, the nurse, arrived.

"Doing good, Timera," said Debbie. "Just another seizure. We got you." She took a napkin and wiped at the foam in the corners of Timera's mouth.

"She's seizing, which is code for traveling," said Markush. "She visits another version of Ethiopia, somewhere far away." He spoke with reverence.

"Holy effing Jesus. Scared the s-h-i-t out of me. This place is real," said Sherri.

"Indeed, it is. And when she stops seizing, Debbie or I will debrief her on what happened on the other side. She's on a mission to find her daughter, as are all the patients here. You got her, Debbie?

"Yes sir." Debbie was prepping a warm washcloth for Timera's face.

"Shall we?" and Markush led the way out of the medical unit and down a hall to meet with the Returnees.

Once everyone had peed and brushed their teeth, Markush and a guard led the group out of the residential unit and to a conference room that accommodated eight persons around an oblong wooden table, veneered to resemble oak. He felt it was a slight gesture of goodwill for the Returnees to be off the unit and that it portended future freedom. Letitia Mumford hurried toward them and slipped into the room.

Sherri closed the door. "You guys cold? I'm cold." She hugged a thin sweater to her bony body.

"Nothing but cold, twenty-four-seven," said Emma. "Have to wrap up in a damn blanket."

Markush threw up his hands in defeat. He had no idea how to control the heat. "Have a seat, if you will. So, Sherri, this is Arthur, Emma, Afewerki, and Dr. Mumford, my new associate. Sherri is going to school us on how to deal with the media. I...well, it's just best if Sherri takes over. Yes, Arthur?"

"Explain this media to me. I understand it as the plural of the Latin medium." His voluminous sideburns, almost mutton chops, were especially bushy today and brilliant with silver.

"Yes, Arthur, excellent question. The media, meaning outlets for news and entertainment, such as newspapers and television shows."

"I see. It would be quite disturbing to see myself on this television. I'm still pondering just how it works. Perhaps molecules in the ether drawn by magnets are the best I can conjure." Everyone murmured, approving of Arthur's analogy.

"So, guys and gals," said Sherri, "let me start at square one. The media tell stories. Right now, you are the story. They want you badly. One element that makes a great story is conflict. If we had kept the course and taken the path of secrecy, we would have produced immense conflict, which the media would gobble up like a turkey dinner. We are dismissing open conflict by being completely transparent. They ask and we tell. It takes a fundamental zing out of the story they want to create through conflict and makes it far more likely that your amazing adventures will just become a part and parcel of the status quo."

Markush took it all in. "That's somewhat brilliant. In my field of forensic psychiatry, I'm interested in attachment theory, which posits that patterns of attachment, say with a child and his father, carry from childhood to adulthood. In essence, amid this media blitz, we are the child and the media is the parent. The expected relationship is one of poor attachment where the media, the parent, bullies the child, being us. But we're bypassing that attachment pathology and coming clean, turning the tables on the media. Yes, Sherri, I love it, and I apologize for interrupting, but go on."

"That's great insight, Clyde. New to me, but I like it. We're on this train together, and guess who the engineer is?"

Afewerki's lips were moving, then he spoke. "We are to be on a train?"

Letitia laughed, and Afewerki frowned.

"Yes, great question. No, that was just a figure of speech, figurative language. Um, I was just saying that we're all in the same boat. Well, perhaps we can put it this way: we are united. There."

"Oh, you are speaking in riddles," said Afewerki with a sly look on his face. "In my country, we have säm ena wärq, which is to mean the gold covered by the wax. One must hide the true meaning."

"Well, maybe that's the opposite of what we're doing," said Emma. "But I get what Afewerki is saying about understanding what he sees as a riddle, if that makes sense."

Sherri decided to just shoot straight from the hip. "We are a unit working together. You have incredible stories, and we want you to tell those stories openly and honestly." She felt a simile coming on and pushed it away. "Okay, so we take conflict out of the equation...we avoid conflict by telling the truth. Now, let's get down to the nitty-gritty." Sherri realized her mistake once again, seeing the puzzled look on both Afewerki's and Arthur's faces. "Let's talk about the basics of doing an interview beyond being honest."

"Now we're on track, dribbling the ball," said Markush.

Letitia sighed. "Clyde, that's a mixed metaphor, for-God's sake." She looked regal in a bright blue glove dress that hit above her knees.

"Okay, basic rules," said Sherri. "Rule number one: you will never be interviewed together. The focus has to be on you and your story. If your stories don't match up, that's not our concern. Just tell what you know. Let them stay busy trying to figure out discrepancies. Within two weeks, according to Clyde, you will live separate lives. You are individuals.

"Rule number two: demand respect. If you think you are not being respected, let the person or person(s) know. You have to be taken seriously and not portrayed as a clown, I mean, as someone you are not. Be firm. Remember that by giving an interview you are giving a gift, and that gift should be repaid in kindness." Sherri could tell that everyone was following.

"Rule number three: no drugs or alcohol before an interview. You need to have a clear head and an open mind. You will be asked hard questions, and you need to answer without hesitation and preferably with appropriate emotion. You are telling your story. Remember that. Any questions?"

Markush raised his hand. "When do we say no?"

"Rule number three and a half, you can always say no to an interview, but we do have a list of preferred media outlets that we encourage you to cooperate with. Play it by ear. I mean, take it day by day. I would suggest limiting interviews to only one per week. You have lives to live, right?"

No one spoke, all seeming to have had enough of the lecture, wondering how this honesty would play out.

Reece1 pulled Reece2 into the shade of a jacaranda tree. All was peaceful and somewhat fuzzy from the peach-tinted light. Reece2 stirred and kicked his left leg as if in a nightmare.

"You're fine. I'm here," said Reece1. He brushed red dirt from his green tennis shoes.

"What the hell? I'm back. Mia. The Abba." Reece2 pushed up on an elbow, saliva running down his cheek.

"Yes, back. We have just a few minutes' walk. Rest for a while longer."

"No, let's do it. I can walk." He stood and had to catch the trunk of the tree. "Damn dizzy."

"We need water. The Abba can help us."

They left the shade of the jacaranda tree and continued along a narrow rocky path, strolling. There was a sonic boom, and a jet screamed overhead.

"A war in the north," said Reece1.

The path leveled with large, flat-topped mountains in the distance. The dry altitude was such that neither perspired, although both struggled to breathe.

"That smell of sulfur, getting stronger," said Reece2.

They encountered a steep incline scattered with small bushes, a few cacti, and brimming with jagged rocks.

"It's only up or down around here," said Reece2.

"Just ahead, up the hill, five minutes."

Reece2 looked up the steep incline and could see what appeared to be a ledge and then a cliff face. They continued, panting, hands on knees, pushing forward, and reached the ledge, which was straight up, another three meters or so.

"We have to climb," said Reece1, and he went first, placing his hands and feet into small crevices, making it look easy. He stood at the top, watching Reece2 struggle and fall back to the ground.

"Try again," said Reece1.

After two more failed attempts and his fingers cramping, Reece2 scrambled over the lip, helped by his lookalike, who grabbed the back of his jumpsuit and pulled.

"This way," said Reece1, and passing through brambles and a cluster of small fruit trees, *Syzygium guineense,* came to an open green door in the cliff face. From within came the sound of metal on stone, a steady ring of iron on basalt, a remnant of ancient volcanic activity.

"Hallo!" said Reece1, peering into the gloom. He was very familiar with the Abba Paulos and his life's work of carving a church into the rock.

The pick ceased striking, and the Abba appeared gaunt and wiry with a thin, scruffy beard. His eyes twinkled in the darkness. He wiped his right hand on his robe and stepped into the curious peach glare. He said nothing and examined them from head to foot, as if creating encyclopedia entries for them both.

"Abba Paulos," said Reece2. He extended his hand, and the Abba reacted in kind.

"You are looking for your daughter, Mia." The Abba spoke in Amharic. "I have helped you before, yet here you are again. Have you not learned the ways of Dahlia?"

"He knows," said Reece1.

"How do you know?"

"Trust me."

"Abba," said Reece1, "can you take us to Mia, his daughter, set-lidj?"

"Ow, set lidj," said the Abba. He displayed his hands, empty.

"I knew it," said Reece2. "He wants money, and we have none, I think." He rummaged in his two pockets. "What's this?" It was a cheap pocket watch. He held it out to the Abba. The Abba examined it and then handed it back.

"I have no need of this small machine. It is only important to know how many strikes I have made with the pick. I count and then I rest."

"What's he saying?" asked Reece2.

"We have to find some real silver or gold, some coins perhaps, something he can trade with."

"Well, damn. The last time this happened, Arthur's friend Caroline, the lady he pushed down the stairs in Berlin, gave the Abba a piece of jewelry. Can we go back to Solon and earn some cash, or maybe trade for something?"

"There is a larger village to the south of here. We should go there. The Baptist Mission runs a clinic. There is famine in the land, and they are providing food relief and medical care."

The Abba looked at them blankly, waiting.

"Okay, we'll go there, but I'm afraid of what we'll find," said Reece2.

"Me too," said Reece1.

Markush finished a conference call with General Watkins, Glenelle Lock, Colonel Lawrence, and Jacob Jacobi. The response to Watkins' Pentagon briefing sparked a media firestorm across the nation and internationally. People were calling into their local police, reporting strange happenings, asking for help. The Pentagon had urged the President to follow up with a press conference of his own, but he had refused. Local and national authorities were reviewing cases of prisoners imprisoned for the murder of young girls. Religious leaders had reacted with clerical disdain for the notion of Dahlia as a competing God. Foremost in this effort was the Reverend Clarity Stillwell, leader of a fundamentalist church in Colorado Springs, with a national following via the Christian Instinct Network. There seemed to be nothing left to do but to ride this roller coaster that had taken the first plunge.

Markush downed a cup of warm coffee on the long-term unit. Reece was traveling again, along with the original Reece, who had not yet awoken from his journeys.

"That damn Mia is driving me nuts," said Shelby. He stood with hands on hips, his scrub bottoms riding low. With his bald head and black mustache, he looked something like a slouchy magician.

"God, I'm sorry. She is just literally the bitch from hell. She has no grace and no self-awareness. Enrolling her in school should be a hoot," said Markush.

"No doubt."

Markush ran his fingers through his gray hair. "Okay,

have to head out, appointment in just a few minutes. Keep me updated." Markush left the unit and returned to his office. Denise buzzed him. "Hey."

"Jeremy Sims here to see you, sir," said Denise.

"I'll come get him."

Sims took one of the two leather chairs facing Markush's desk, cluttered with papers and a copy of the *DSM-IV*. Markush was following Glenelle Lock's study on late-onset schizophrenia and had been focusing on schizoaffective disorder, which he found to be an intriguing diagnosis for some of the patients at Organon.

"You ask the questions, and I will answer," said Markush.

"Right. The recorder okay?" Sims dressed casually in a brown sweater and blue stretch pants. He was mid-forties, wore glasses that seemed tinted, with a swoosh of silver hair deckled with black.

"I suppose so. No holds barred per the big brass."

"Why are you here, at Organon? Just who are you?" asked Sims. He scribbled notes.

"Basically, I'm a forensic psychiatrist who specializes in the criminally insane. Initially, Organon was formed to house a select group of people who had committed atrocious crimes, who would have faced the death penalty in many states. Organon basically saves them. I'm in charge of their care. I always knew that the picture was much bigger, but the last few months, since the arrival of Reece Myers, have been earth-shattering."

"Why Reece Myers?"

"Reece strangled what appeared to be his own daughter. As soon as I heard about the case, and it was nearby in

Richmond, I stepped in, gained custody, and brought him here. He was stark raving mad for the first days and then, predictably, he entered a state of prolonged seizures, traveling to distant times and places in a search for his daughter, who had been replaced. What makes Reece special is that he is very lucid upon his return and can detail where he has been and what he has been doing with regularity. We have other patients who travel via seizure, but they prove to be unreliable because of underlying mental illness."

"And how can you prove he travels to other places and times? It sounds ludicrous to the average Joe, right?" Sims shuffled in his chair and pulled at the neck of his sweater.

"Yes. I admit that. There is an element of what fiction writers call the suspension of disbelief, a term attributed to the poet Coleridge. I've been doing work here at Organon for just three years, but I developed an interest in girl slayings, a gross term I know, and a connection with what seemed to be particular delusions held by the slayers. A psychiatrist in the mid-1960s, Harold Leyman, first noticed the pattern of delusions and wrote about them, but was dismissed as having lost his rocker. But back to the question. How do you explain the reappearance of Reece Myers in his backyard? His body at Organon, after a violent seizure, was brain-dead. But he returned, and now there are two Reece Myers at Organon."

"I don't explain, I just report the facts," said Sims. "How do we know that the first Reece didn't have a twin who suddenly showed up?"

"Write this down. We've performed DNA analysis on both Reeces, and the profiles are an exact match. It's the same person." Markush had crept to the edge of his seat, becoming excited at his own speech.

"Can I have the official results?"

"I can arrange that. In fact, I'm working on a dossier of evidence to be released to the media, along with our publicity expert, Sherri Loveless. You may or may not know that we have a dedicated lab in Adelphi, Maryland, run by Colonel Ignatius Lawrence. It would do you good to speak with him."

"I will." Sims wrote like a madman.

"Hold on." Markush answered his phone. It was Shelby. Mia had taken her clothes off, running up and down the halls, yelling that she was being raped. "Damn," said Markush. "Look, just make sure she doesn't hurt herself. Give her a dose of liquid Benadryl, fifty milligrams, and see if that will settle her down. Right. Okay, call back if things escalate."

"A recent development?" asked Sims.

Markush explained.

"And she has replaced the real Mia, and for the second time? It sounds like a possession. Before I go today, let me meet her."

"Maybe. If she settles down."

"I've heard the answer to this, but exactly why are these little girls being abducted and replaced? Is that the right language?"

"Yes, exactly. First, this is Dahlia's doing. She identifies young children and *acquires* them by placing a mesh-like implant within their scalp."

"Hold up. That's a new one."

"I'm just telling you what I know. These implants, to

use the language of Reece, map the person's brain. We can identify the mesh via X-ray, a shadow, exceedingly thin, and made of thallium cuprate, which is also used in superconductors. Dahlia follows these children, primarily girls but some boys, looking for clues to answer her one burning question.

Sims laughed. "I know what you're about to say: 'Who is my mommy?'"

"Laugh, but that's the central concern of what appears to be an omniscient being. And if the mapping doesn't reveal the answer, Dahlia takes it a step further and hides them, leaving a flawed replica. Just girls, though, as far as we know."

"Why hide them?"

"My guess is that she's hoping to break them. Plus, it's the perfect capricious act an evil little girl would do to abduct and hide something precious. I'm getting the idea that Dahlia is very jealous of these gifted girls and is striking back childishly, creating mayhem in the process." Markush had his hands on his desk as if to push up.

"My God. It just gets deeper. I was initially interested in you because of a tip that came through the desk that you were protecting child murderers. This is absolutely insane, though. I can't believe I'm writing about this, and I'm so grateful for your information. This is ground zero, it seems."

"Maybe, but ground zero for Dahlia are towns like Richmond, Kentucky, or Cedar City, Utah, wherever there may be little girls that Dahlia seeks. No one is safe. No family is safe. Already, since the Pentagon briefing, there have been thousands of calls and emails from around the globe, citing similar cases of supposed abductions and murders."

Markush's phone rang. It was Denise. Organon had hired four new nurses, and they were awaiting further instruction. Would there be an orientation? Markush said he was on it and scribbled a note on his desktop calendar.

"So, Dr. Markush, I have a million questions, but I have more than enough for my full story, which will break tomorrow morning. A summary is due at two p.m., and I need to get on it. One last question. Why does Dahlia want to know who her mommy is? If she is God, would she even have a mommy?" He laughed at his own words.

"That opens a can of worms," said Markush. "Reece has told Dahlia, and Mia has told Dahlia the answer to that question, but she doesn't believe it. Supposedly, time is Dahlia's mother. There are deep issues embedded within that supposition that physicists and mathematicians and philosophers have been dealing with for ages, the problem of time. My CIA contact, Jacob Jacobi, is procuring an expert to examine the question of time being a mother. I have one patient here at Organon, Helmut Grayson, who put it this way, after sipping on some promised Scotch. 'What was there when there was nothing?'"

Sims shook his head and thought. "I don't know. Hit me."

"Freaking time, man. Time. That's what there was when there was nothing. There had to be a *time* when there was nothing, pushing aside the existence of God. It seems that time precedes Dahlia and is somehow her *mother*. That's the simple version. Issues of existence follow with astounding complications."

"Wow." Sims scribbled a last line in his notebook. "Any

last words?"

"I dipped a man into the river of time and pulled him out on fire." Markush smiled.

The next day, with everything under control at Organon, with Letitia Hubbard in charge during his absence, Clyde Markush flew to Washington, D.C., for a meeting with the heavy hitters. The meeting was being held at a safe house in Georgetown. Of the group, Jacob Jacobi, the CIA lead, was the least approving of this openness campaign. He was old school and liked to stay in the shadows. As soon as Markush left the base in his trusty Volvo, a la *Winter Light,* three news vans with satellite dishes tailed him. He lost them in the parking deck at the Louisville airport because the vans were too tall to enter.

The safe house was a Victorian affair with a turret, gables, ornate woodwork, and a wrap-around porch. Markush hopped out of the taxi. At the front door, an agent dressed in a blue suit met him. Markush followed him to a downstairs library, where the rest of the group had gathered and were chatting.

Markush removed his plaid scarf and down jacket. The library was well-appointed with a collection of leather-bound books, including a set of the complete works of Voltaire, a French edition published in 1901. He saw the familiar face of the project manager, Glenelle Lock, who was sitting beside Major General Tom Watkins from the Pentagon. Standing were CIA Deputy Director Jacob Jacobi in a sheened black suit, and Colonel Ignatius Lawrence of the Adelphi Laboratory Center, dressed in civilian clothes.

"Dr. Markush! Glad you're here." Glenelle wore a tailored, stiff, green dress with a red collar straight out of

Norman Rockwell.

"Hey, Glenelle." Markush greeted the others in turn.

Glenelle took her place behind an elegant writing table. "Gentlemen! Let's get started." There were two matching chenille love seats and two leather chairs, and everyone found a seat.

"Much has happened in the past week. I thought we would go around the room and have an update from everyone. I hope you're ready for a long day, so let's get started. How about you, General?" Watkins wore his uniform with his two-star status displayed.

"Ha, you saw the press conference. Straight up and raw is the best way to put it. I have more requests for interviews than I can shake a stick at. In fact, I'll be giving a speech on C-SPAN tomorrow night. As you know, the general public is in an uproar. You've seen the headlines. Luckily, no damage control is needed, as no damage has been done. I was skeptical of the open-door approach, but I like the way it feels. No secrets."

Jacobi spoke. "I'm still hesitant about this dripping-with-honesty plan. Who's stopping private interests from capitalizing on our findings and creating a revolution that no one wants?"

"A revolution?" asked Colonel Lawrence.

"Riots, internecine warfare, terrorists," said Jacobi. "A group is marching in Atlanta. The consequences may be serious."

Watkins nodded. "I get you, Jacobi, but I can't see a revolution coming from this. The initial shock will wear down and dissipate. My guess is that folks out there are more concerned with Bowl Games right now than some crazy story about an alien being."

"Okay, the floor belongs to General Watkins. Save your questions." Glenelle picked up a small gavel and rapped three times with a serious face.

"Since the press conference, we've added a team of nine research assistants to follow up with abduction/murder leads, as well as stories involving time travel and mentions of Dahlia. Thus far, we have close to nine hundred U.S. inquiries. We're developing a standard questionnaire that needs approval from Dr. Markush. We want to be certain of what we're asking and what we're looking for." He continued, expressing concern over the sheer number of cases and that advice on how to proceed was welcome.

Glenelle then turned to Colonel Lawrence, a hulking figure, wearing long cycling pants with a plain brown acrylic sweater. He seemed the most relaxed of the group and spoke.

"The Adelphi lab has been working hard on evaluating materials from the Returnees. Work has slowed, but with the leads mentioned by General Watkins, I anticipate our workload will increase, necessitating the need for more specialists. We can handle what we have for now, but perhaps we were not cognizant of the prevalence of possible related cases. It's hard to say if we should prepare for analysis involving hundreds, thousands, or more." He cited budget numbers that now seemed too small. To investigate all leads would require an act of Congress, a group of labs, versus the one at Adelphi.

"Right," said Glenelle. "We initially just planned upwards of two dozen patients. Keeping things under wraps for the first three years prevented us from seeing the bigger picture. We have work to do, and fast." Jacobi raised his hand. He looked severe in his black suit.

"I'm raising the alarm bells," said Jacobi. "This is far greater than the Organon facility and our lab can handle. I'm looking at decommissioned military bases to fulfill a more long-term need. My best guess is that we'll need to serve and observe at least a thousand individuals. We need infrastructure, and lots of it, not to mention funding. I'm hoping we can keep this out of Congress to avoid delays, but it may be best to have our identity and purpose stamped with congressional approval, but then we get involved with constituents, many of whom will oppose us. It's early yet, but pockets of resistance are building around the country, especially from the far right. Many of you are familiar with Reverend Clarity Stillwell and his Christian Instinct Network. He's revving up his followers to denounce our work and has launched a fundraising campaign to battle us with. He's pretty slick, and there are more like him out there. We need facilities, but we also need to be prepared for war."

The group tried to discount Lawrence's views of all-out war and brought the focus back to decommissioned military bases that would require massive staffing efforts, akin to maintaining a small city. The idea was a good one, but perhaps it would be best to ride out the current storm first and get a better handle on the numbers.

Markush spoke next, perhaps the most practical of them all, providing an update and discussing the planned expansion of Organon at Fort Knox. Would it be wise to expand there first before acquiring a military base? There was plenty of room to build, plus he liked the land near the lake, his second home. To be honest, he could not imagine expansion on the scale that Jacobi envisioned.

"The storm is coming," said Jacobi. "We have funding to expand at Fort Knox, but to have the ultimate facilities, we'll need to be working on superfunding and a site or even sites." He was eager for everyone to believe in his urgency for the matter.

The group continued until having a catered lunch served at noon—roast beef, asparagus, salad, bread, and cherry pie. After lunch, a special speaker would appear, and the group would not be ready for what he had to say.

The Reeces climbed down the embankment and, instead of continuing straight down, followed a vague path that ran along the cliff line. Thorns and brambles caught their legs as they made their way to a village called Gobez. After twenty minutes, they climbed up and over a ridge and found two low buildings built of poles with tin roofs. A smell of wood smoke and urine filled the air. A group of five women sat, leaning against the shelter and weaving baskets. Others who stood with children stopped in their tracks, gazing at the two Reeces. "Ferenj!" said one little boy with a look of fear.

"These are shelters," said Reece2, "like there were in Godo. The women here are homeless, without husbands. Tenesteling," he said, greeting everyone.

The seated women stood, and others emerged from the dark shelters, shading their eyes and covering their mouths. The Reeces came closer, setting off an alarm of laughter from the children.

"What should we do?" asked Reece2. "I feel like I should do something."

"There's nothing to do here," said Reece1. "We have to find Emma."

"Oh, wow, Emma. She saved my life so long ago. But this one won't know me."

"Correct."

The barren hillside held the shelters, an outhouse, and a cooking hut leaking smoke. From their position, they could see the village below.

"What the hell?" asked Reece2.

A giant of a man, some three meters in height with long blond hair, walked up the path, carrying a staff, looking down at the many rocks. He wore a thick robe made of heavy cotton. A quintal of sorghum rested on his shoulder like a pillow. He looked up and stopped.

"Hello," said Reece1.

The giant continued forward, glancing at the women gathered in a group like starlings. His reddened beard reached his chest. He walked slowly and with purpose. "Hello," he said with a voice from a deep well. "You have come. Your brother awaits you."

"What's going on?" asked Reece2. He felt tiny in the presence of this enormous man.

"Yes, we have come," said Reece1. "Take us to Emma."

The giant walked with his load and dropped the bag in front of the cooking hut. "Follow me."

The Reeces fell in behind the giant, who was called Beo.

"The church," said Reece2 as they passed. He could smell incense from within.

They walked down a lane of thick, black mud hardened with drying puddles and many rocks. Adjoining compounds, surrounded by pole fences containing huts, sat off to either side. A frail woman with a single tooth, or was it a man, stopped and spoke to the giant. He replied with a laugh and continued.

They wound their way to a very steep path, leading downward with an open vista of hills ahead. A single cloud, a darker peach than the sky, seemed within reach yet far away. An old man struggled up the hill in silence, walking behind a donkey laden with straw. He stopped and removed his cap, waiting for them to pass.

Reece2 could tell they were approaching the clinic compound he had known so well. The path widened, and soon they were at a door in the fence made of corrugated tin. There was a line of patients squatting beside the fence. "You may enter," said Beo, and he knocked, looking over the fence at his leisure.

The guard, shouldering his ancient bolt-action rifle, creaked the door open and looked alarmed. He hurried away to the small clinic and shouted inside through the open door. Next to the clinic was a large warehouse used to store grain and oil. A woman poked her head out from the clinic, and it was Emma, followed by another head. Reece2's pulse quickened, and he floated toward the clinic made of poles.

"Emma," said Reece2. He stared at her and then at himself standing behind her.

"You've come," said Emma. "Beo told us you would come." She stepped down from the clinic and looked back at Reece3.

"Emma, you know me?" asked Reece2. "I'm looking for my daughter Mia. We have to pay the Abba for his services."

"I know *this* Reece," and she turned to Reece3. Her dirty blonde hair was cut short and parted in the middle. An aqua scrub top hung loosely on her thin frame.

"I'm not exactly sure why you're here," said Reece3. "But I'm amazed. Triplets, it seems, although I'm younger."

"Yes, triplets," said Reece1. He enjoyed seeing this version of himself doing good work.

"I have to finish with the day's patients. You should wait

for us in the other compound. We can talk then," said Emma. "Another twenty patients or so."

"Wow," said Reece2. "Yeah, I understand. Are you from Alabama?" he said, addressing them both.

Emma laughed. "Close, but we're from Georgia. I'm from Atlanta."

Reece2 gazed at Emma. He thought about the other Emmas back at Organon. His destiny seemed intertwined with this woman. He and Reece1 stepped back through the gate, where Beo had been waiting for them as if this were routine. He then led them back up the steep path to living quarters, a compound with a small house, a cookhouse, and a building with four rooms made of poles daubed with mud and painted white. A shintabet sat in a far corner beyond the dining hut. From one room stepped a fellow dressed neatly in Western clothes. Barra flashed a smile, and was very dark compared to most of the people who had golden skin.

"They have come," said Beo. He stroked his long beard.

"Yes, yes, it is true," said Barra.

They gathered in the dining hut, except for Beo, who could not fit. The two Reeces spoke with Barra about Mia, but he had seen no young white girls. Another worker arrived, Isaac, who wore glasses and a jumpsuit much like Reece2's. He joined them, and the conversation died down.

"Why are we here?" asked Reece2. "Mia's not here."

"But the Abba will help you," said Barra.

"Yes, the Abba," said Reece1.

There was nothing left to say, and Barra and Isaac excused themselves.

"We just need money," said Reece2. "Emma will have money." He felt it coming and placed his head on the table.

Everyone was eager to hear what Dr. Desmond Ory had to say. He was a physicist housed at the Institute for Advanced Study in Princeton, New Jersey. His specialty was quantum gravity, and he would have been a great friend of Albert Einstein and Kurt Gödel had they still been alive. He was especially interested in Gödel's idea of a universe where time travel was possible. Like Einstein, Ory had a plump belly. His dated clothes reminded one of mothballs.

Ory opened up by telling a joke, which brought mild laughter. Markush was especially interested in what Ory would say and had a thousand questions. Ory began by saying that the physics of Newton had made it possible to separate time from events, that time passes regardless of knowing the events that take place while time passes. But in his studies, he had refined that idea. Basically, time no longer existed. He explained that, in the sense of watching a clock, time passes, but that it is only an illusion. At the quantum level, which is where we should focus, he said that time is not a factor. He noted that Maimonides hypothesized that time was composed of short-duration molecules, much like atoms. He compared time to a photon, which only exists if it is traveling at the speed of light.

Markush raised his hand. "I gather that a physical system renders time mute. Are you familiar with Dahlia? How does she factor into this?"

"Yes, Dahlia. I've been briefed. I know she seeks the identity of her mother, and that the supposed answer is that her mother is time. This plays somewhat into my theory of time. If we mean by time everything that happens, then everything is time. But, back to Maimonides, think about time as a physical entity that pre-existed all physical systems." He paused long enough for Markush to interject.

"So, that's the answer, right? What was there when there was nothing? Time. Time preceded Dahlia, created Dahlia, created all physical systems as we do and do not know them. Dahlia's mother is time."

"This notion of time as a mother is perhaps too figurative. I am greatly interested in learning more about Dahlia, but to be honest, I find it hard to believe in her existence. I like the idea of God as a little girl, but, of course, that sounds preposterous. Am I right?"

"Yes, it sounds preposterous," said Markush, "but we have proof: the abductions and even eyewitness testimony. Patients at Organon have spoken with her. She is everywhere and all-knowing at all times."

"I'm open to the possibility of an *existant* that could be called Dahlia and that her origin is time. The origin of all things is time. We live now in a block universe where there is no distinction between past, present, and future. There are just interconnected events. If there is no past, present, or future, then there is no time."

General Watkins raised his hand, feeling like a child. "We've all been told that the Big Bang is the origin of our universe. What do we do with that in regard to this idea of time, or no time?"

"Ah, yes, the Big Bang, a rather dated theory considering recent developments. Where did that single point of matter that detonated into worlds come from? What preceded the Big Bang, if there was one? That matter had to come from somewhere, right? One has to ask that question in the absence of a God, or perhaps even in the presence of a God, considering Dahlia."

Markush was renting the edge of the love seat. "Yes, precisely. There was nothing, but there was time. Time accumulated in such vast proportions that time became matter and space, beginning as quanta and building first to hydrogen and then to the various other elements."

"You are following me somewhat," said Ory. "An infinity of time, an infinity of infinities of time, became like those photons that only exist when moving. It's simplest to think of time as the fundamental building block of matter, which then requires space."

Watkins wasn't satisfied. "So, there was no Big Bang?"

Ory smiled. "Time has always existed. One can't say that time began. Time has always been. But time reached a critical mass, and the entropy of the worlds, which approached zero, increased with the creation of quanta, atomic particles, atoms, elements, compounds, stars, planets, galaxies, universes. If our known universe is 13.8 billion years old, based on factors of expansion, then yes, there must have been some ungodly unleashing of power that formed this universe. However, the universe must be dated in terms of infinity and, given that universes have had infinity to develop, then there is no need for a Big Bang."

Jacob Jacobi was listening with a frown. "Well, what the hell happened? How did our universe get to be so large and complicated?"

"It could be as simple as a quantum of time. That single quantum formed an infinite universe. Another quantum formed, another universe. Those universes collided, and the quanta perhaps formed a neutron. The collisions continued, and soon a proton found an electron, and a hydrogen atom formed. Once that first quantum existed, we then had space, an infinite space, and time ceased to exist. The function of time was then simply to create more and more quanta, which led to hydrogen, which led to helium, which led to lithium, and so on until we have the universe as we know it, our state of entropy increasing to its present level. I call this simply the Tiny Bangs Theory. Imagine an eternity with just a single proton." Ory's eyes twinkled. "Of course, I'm giving you the simple version."

"Wow," said Markush. He gave Glenelle a side hug and raised his hand. "How do *you* explain Dahlia within this theory?"

"Spinoza said that God can play the role of a person, and I think that's important. We create God, and some claim to experience God through their senses. In that critical time surrounding the formation of the first atomic particle, inducing entropy, the tendency to disorder, there must have been a great void that became populated with the ideas of all things possible, a nod to Plato and his Realm of Ideas. Yes, there had to be a point when all things became possible, perhaps even before the first particle formed. To embody all things possible, there must simultaneously arise an entity that makes all things possible through being. That is Dahlia, the being that made all things possible, although we render such Gods in Spinoza's terms as 'the role of a person.'"

Markush had finally relaxed back into a chenille cushion, his heart racing. "How is it we still experience time if it no longer exists?"

"Well, we do not experience time. Time is no longer. Only clocks and calendars render time into crude increments. You are getting into the realm of positivism, which holds that we perceive reality through the senses only. Yet Ernst Mach pointed out that we cannot experience an atom. It does not yield to the senses, yet it exists. In this way, time exists, but only outside our senses, and it is now bound into the universe, being present all at once. Kant said that 'Time is nothing but the form of inner sense.' That is all that we can do with time and keep sane, at least for the average person."

"Jesus fucking Christ, this is brilliant," said Markush. "Dr. Ory, you have made obvious something that I have been pondering for years, since my time as a PhD student."

Glenelle coughed. "I can't say the same," she said. "It's terribly interesting but sounds wild."

"This seems to play well into the mystery of Dahlia, although I'm not quite getting this notion of time as nonexistent," said Watkins.

Jacobi spoke. "Are you a physicist or a philosopher, professor?"

Dr. Ory laughed. "When the physicist runs out of ideas, he turns to philosophy and vice versa, I think. One can inform the other."

Colonel Lawrence was lost but felt that he had to say something. "Are your ideas about time in line with Newtonian physics?"

Ory laughed again. "Einstein developed his theories

of relativity within a Newtonian framework, but he had to push beyond the limits of motion into what we know as quantum physics. But even he had to cheat a bit. To counter the forces of gravity, he introduced the idea of a cosmological constant to make his equations work in a more fluid manner. However, it is on his great work that I am pursuing my research in quantum gravity, which seeks to unite the mechanical Newtonian macroverse with the quantum microverse. There is much more to say, but without the aid of complex equations, I feel the need to stop there, although I would gladly answer more questions."

"Did Newton allow for God or a Dahlia?" asked Glenelle.

"In fact, he did, saying that God is 'eternal and omnipotent...his duration reaches from infinity to infinity,' but without direct proof."

There were plenty more questions, but when the questions veered into speculation about the motives and intents of Dahlia, Ory declined to speak, saying that he preferred to deal with more certain subjects. He left them with final words from Plato: "Time is a moving image of eternity."

Markush arrived at Organon the next day, getting updates from Dr. Mumford, who wanted to run a battery of personality tests on Mia and some of the patients. Markush had thought of that but had not had time for the involved testing. He briefed her on his time in D.C. and went into great detail about Dr. Ory's Tiny Bangs Theory and the origin of Dahlia. It seemed to lead to the conclusion that Dahlia's "mother" was indeed time, but why was Dahlia just seven years old? What element of perfection was there in that? She and Markush sat in rolling chairs in the medical unit's break room, very plain, with a small table and three chairs.

"Back to what's been happening here," said Mumford. "I'm feeling overwhelmed. How did you do it by yourself? The new nurses are working out fine, but that still leaves oversight for fifteen patients plus the Returnees."

"It's a lot, and I needed you a long time ago. Together, we can divide and conquer. Tell me what you learned while I was gone." Markush sipped his warm coffee.

"The most interesting patient I find is Timera Scocpol, the most involved with traveling and actively seeking her daughter, the most lucid too. The others, like Peters and Grayson, just babble and scream."

"So, what's new with Scocpol?"

"She's in the Lake Tana region of Ethiopia, traveling from island to island, visiting with priests and monks. Haile Selassie is with her, helping her out. He opens doors for sure. She was at a monastery called Debre Maryam, I think. The priest was friendly, and she'd had coffee and fresh figs with him. I can't get over how detailed she is."

"Any progress with finding her daughter?"

"Selassie thinks she is on one of the islands, in one of the many monasteries. She spoke of possibly finding the Ark, that it could be hidden there. That was yesterday, and she hasn't traveled since."

"Maybe she's getting close. She's been traveling for over a year now, crisscrossing universes, but Ethiopia is the one place where the missing daughters show up. That's what happened with Reece Myers, different versions of Ethiopian villages, different universes."

Mumford looked thoughtful. "Is there a way we can influence the finding of the missing girls? Something we can do? It's fascinating to hear the stories, but I feel somewhat helpless just observing without being able to influence the outcome."

"My main idea for helping comes from Reece Myers and a former patient, Freddie Mentone, whose daughter returned home thanks to Reece. They were traveling to the same universe and had this idea of helping one another. If we could somehow coordinate the travels, share information between the travelers, or somehow have them meet up in their travels, that could prove useful. That would involve them speaking with one another and scheming. A few of the patients here, though, live on the edge of psychosis, like Peters and Grayson, which makes that difficult."

A new nurse poked her head in the break room. She was short with tight braids and from the Philippines. "Dr. Markush, I haven't had a chance to talk with you. I'm

Carletta."

"Sorry that we had to throw you into the fire," said Markush. "Nice to meet you officially, although you come highly recommended. Found a place to stay yet?"

"I'm in guest house, but am looking, probably Muldraugh area. Seem like a quiet neighborhood. But I need run something by you, regarding Helmut Grayson. I know he angry and shouts, but I'm wondering if we un-restrain him? I have, what do you say, an *inkling* that he will settle down if he not tied down. It's just not best for his long-term health."

Markush sighed and felt guilty. "He can be violent when he hallucinates. Maybe now that we have three nurses per shift, we can consider that. I have to shape my thinking away from these patients as criminally insane to perhaps something less problematic."

"He's got such big hands, and he spits," said Mumford. "But I was thinking about the same issue. We need to be in the mode of rehab versus just straight maintenance."

Markush felt even more guilty. He had become blind to his patients' needs, getting from them what he wanted. "Let's do it. Get him up in a chair with the guards on standby." Before Organon, he had worked at a facility for the criminally insane in Philadelphia, supporting his habit of seeing these patients as inmates, although he exonerated them from their atrocious crimes. In the case of Grayson, he had suffered from late-onset schizophrenia but had done well until the drowning of his stepdaughter, Lila, in a bathtub.

"If you write the order for him to be up to the chair, I do it," said Carletta.

"I will," said Markush.

"Back to Scocpol," said Mumford. "Like you said, we could have the patients help one another, perhaps in a group session. The dayroom would be perfect for that."

"But they are subject to seize and travel without warning. We have to be careful. Don't want any seizures in the dayroom."

"We can work around that," said Mumford. She was taller than Markush while sitting and radiated a strong will.

"Okay, I'll let you organize the first session. And we'll see what happens with Grayson. I just hope it goes well. He's a big man."

After further talk with Mumford, Markush felt down, thinking that he had not had the patients' best interests at heart. But he somehow felt that he was a hero to them, having saved them from the penal system. He walked to the long-term unit to check on the two Reeces and Mia. She was going to be integrated into a school following the holiday break, which had him nervous but hopeful.

He stepped into the nursing station and met another new nurse, Sheila. She wore cat-eye glasses and moved slowly but efficiently, having thirty years of psych experience. She told him about Mia masturbating, but she had said nothing to her, just let her carry on. Markush entered the hall, hoping for the best.

"Well, well, Dr. Clyde," said Mia. She stood in the corner of her room, dressed in a loose gown. "Have a seat, big man."

"Thank you, Mia." Markush did as requested but

moved the chair closer to the open glass door. He always needed an escape path, which he had learned the hard way. He had an idea.

"Mia, tell me about Dahlia."

"Who?"

"Dahlia. She sent you here, right?"

"No. I'm Mia. I live with my mother and my father."

"How long have you lived with them?"

Mia had to think. "You're trying to trick me, Dr. Clyde. I don't like that. If you want to fuck me, then just say it and quit beating around my bush."

Markush winced. "Look, you know who Dahlia is. She created you and put you here to replace the real Mia. Reece and Kristin are not your parents." He felt kind of mean but wanted to see how she reacted when pressed.

Mia's upper lip trembled. "You, shut up! I'm Mia, and my mother and father love me."

Markush knew that Reece and Kristin had lived in Birmingham before moving to Kentucky. "Where did you live before moving here? Do you remember? What was your old house like?"

"You're tricking me, old man." She backed farther into the corner, a look of panic.

"You're an impostor, Mia, and you know it, don't you? You know where the real Mia is, don't you?" He felt anger toward this precocious little girl.

"Shut the hell up!" She deftly unhooked a suction canister on the wall. "I'll crush your skull."

A tinge of fear washed through Markush, and he stood, one foot in the hall. "Mia, put that down. It's okay. I'm sorry I upset you."

"My mother and father are real and don't you say otherwise. They love me." Tears welled in her eyes and slipped down her cheeks. She threw the canister against the wall and then fell onto the bed face-first, sobbing.

"Mia?" Markush was at a loss. He noticed Shelby emerge from Reece's room next door and shook his head. "Mia?" Markush watched Mia heaving on the bed.

"Need any help?" asked Shelby.

"I pushed her too far." Markush stepped next to the bed and put his hand on Mia's shoulder.

Mia turned and screamed. "Get the fuck away from me!"

Having settled down Mia, Markush stepped into Reece's room. Shelby had let him know Reece was back. Markush raised the head of Reece's bed to 60 degrees and sat in the vinyl recliner. Reece looked whipped and strange, with a feeding tube hanging from his nose, his head shaved and sprouting EEG wires.

"So fucking weak," said Reece. "A Coke. I need a Coke."

"I'll get one," said Shelby.

"Can you talk?" asked Markush. He held his small recorder.

"Yeah, saw the Abba, then went to a village called Gobez, just like the old Godo, and Emma was there with the team, but they didn't recognize me."

"The Abba is going to help you?"

"Yes, but he needs money. This one only takes the hard stuff, no paper."

"What else?" asked Markush.

"There was this giant named Beo, maybe eight or nine feet tall, a huge guy. Not sure why he was there, but the people seemed to respect him. In the Old Testament, in Genesis, giants visited the Earth and had children with the people."

Shelby handed the Coke off, and Reece gulped it down, belching. "Damn, that's good. I need another one." Shelby got the nod from Markush and left again.

"How is the other Reece helping you? Is he useful?" asked Markush.

"He seems to know a lot about where we are, as if he's

been there before. He says something like it's part of his ideal. I'm a copy of his ideal, if that makes sense, but I have imperfections, like the displaced radial artery on my right hand."

Markush hadn't noticed that before. Reece guided Markush's fingertips. "Well, I'll be damned. Strange."

"Yeah, he's just so calm about everything, as if he's having a really great time. I'm not quite getting it," said Reece.

"The other Reece, here, in room three, has been traveling nonstop, basically back from the dead. Can you tell if the Reece you are with is that Reece?"

"I don't know. I'll have to ask him. He seems to be straight from the Pinch, being the perfect idea and all."

"Has Dahlia appeared?" Markush turned and saw Mia standing in the hallway.

"Father," said Mia. "Don't listen to this *doctor's* talk of Dahlia. He wouldn't know Dahlia if she bit him in the ass." She giggled, looking somewhat like a ghost in her loose gown.

Reece gripped the bedrails. "You're not Mia. You're Dahlia. Where's Mia?"

Markush sat back, as if he were watching tennis. Shelby wiggled into the room with the extra Coke and left, not wanting to get caught up in the drama.

"I'm Mia, dear Father, your little girl. I wish I were perfect so that you would love me more."

"You little bitch, get out of here before I—"

"Before you strangle me? That's not very nice, Father. Don't you like what you see? You used to like it a lot." Mia made a frowny face.

"Get her out of here," said Reece.

"Mia, back to your room, please?" said Markush.

"I think I'll go visit my other father. He's nicer than this one." She left and walked around the halls to room three.

"I have to see what she's up to," said Markush,

"You're gonna have to get rid of her," said Reece. "The urge is too strong. She's the devil, but she looks just like Mia, except for that smirk, and her music is all wrong."

Markush rushed out. He sidled up to room three and stopped in disbelief. "Mia, what the hell! Get off!"

"Get back! This is my real father!" Mia was straddling Reece's body, no underwear on, and grinding her hips, Reece's face gripped in her fists.

Markush hit the room intercom. "Shelby! Room three!" Markush watched, fascinated yet nauseated. His gaze slipped to the EEG monitor, and there were irregular spikes among the gamma waves.

"Whoa," said Shelby, his bald head shining.

Mia had not broken her rhythmic hip movements. Markush went to one side and Shelby to the other.

"No!"

They each grabbed an arm and pulled her back. Reece's welted face bled. Together, they lifted her off the bed and into the chair. She put her face into her hands and bawled like a burning baby.

"God have mercy," said Shelby.

"Mia, let's go back to your room," said Markush. "You can't come back to this room."

"He's my real father!" she screamed.

"Uh oh," said Shelby. He pointed at Reece.

Markush stood dazed, looking at Reece, Reece's eyes open wide. His lips moved, but no sound. "Take her back," said Markush. "I'll take care of this."

Shelby approached matter-of-factly, not wanting to show fear, but he was afraid. "Here we go, Mia. Back to your room," and Mia did not resist, her eyes cast to the floor.

"Reece, you're back," said Markush. "You've been gone for over a month."

Reece turned his head from side to side. "Mi-a," he said.

"Yes, you've been searching for Mia. Are you with another Reece? Oh God, do you want some water?"

"Water," said Reece, his voice hoarse.

Markush fumbled a plastic cup beneath the faucet. He raised the head of the bed and put the cup to Reece's lips, and Reece sipped and drooled. Sheila, with her cat-eye-glasses, poked her head into the room.

"He's back?" Sheila looked all business.

"Yeah, back. Something to do with Mia."

Reece rolled his eyes from one to the other. "Mia, she... called me. But the music..."

Markush thought. "Mia is here, but not the real Mia. She's an...impostor. But she called you? I suppose that's the best way to put it."

"But I can't...be here...Needs me."

"Right, I get it. But you're here. We have to talk. Don't leave just yet. I need you." Markush looked desperate.

Having spoken with Reece for half an hour and sedating Mia once again with Benadryl, Markush trolled through a dozen voicemails, all wanting interviews. The nurses, even the new ones, had been approached for interviews. He had learned that Denise was going to be interviewed off base at a local TV station, but she knew relatively little, or did she? He wondered at the number of stories that would emerge, the conflicts of opinion, and possibly dirty laundry that he hadn't thought about. Markush had yet to see the front-page *New York Times* story titled "Doctor to the gods?" At the guest house, he'd had a quick dinner with Kristin and just wanted to sit on the couch with her and drink a glass of wine. He had some news for the Returnees and walked across the parking lot to Organon, letting himself in. The three were just finishing up a dinner of roast chicken with a vegetable medley and fried potatoes, followed by chocolate pie for dessert.

"Hey, I'm back," said Markush to the open room. The door locked behind him.

"Come on over," said Emma.

"Yes, please join us," said Arthur. "We have just enjoyed a plain but satisfying meal."

Afewerki struggled to swallow some peas and carrots. "We must have spice."

Markush pulled up a chair and took off his down jacket, which had a few flakes of melting snow on the shoulder. "New Year's Eve tomorrow night. You folks ready to celebrate? If I can remember, I'll bring some champagne."

"Delightful," said Arthur.

"If I weren't here, I might feel like celebrating," said Emma. "What's the update on cutting us loose? I'm eager to get my hands dirty." She glanced at Afewerki. "To get back to work, ha."

"Okay, I have news for all of you," said Markush. "Afewerki, you start school on January 19, just over two weeks from now."

Afewerki beamed. "Oh my, this is excellent news. I am very grateful for this. I will live there?"

"Yes, in a dorm room, but with a roommate, is my understanding, another international student. You'll have the first semester to prepare for your ESL exam, and once you pass that, you can start on your degree. Sound good?"

"Yes, wonderful. But what will I study? I am eager to study agriculture to help my village."

"That could be a problem," said Markush. "The school has a great criminal justice program. You could also get a degree in biology, which somewhat informs agriculture. You'll have a semester to decide, and there will be advisors who help you."

"I am happy. I will remember this day."

Markush felt pleased that Afewerki was pleased. "Emma, you next. We have you set up for a base apartment, two bedrooms, furnished."

"Cool," and she grinned.

"But wait, there's more! We'll provide a car, brand new, of course, for you to use. You can move out as early as next week, if you're ready. Your call. You'll have a week or so to settle in, then you start your orientation at the hospital. Everything is set."

"Holy cow, that is so good news. I can't wait to be alone in my own space. Sorry, guys." She ate the last bit of her pie.

"And what have you planned for me, dear doctor?" asked Arthur. "I am eager to hear."

"This is exciting. Sherri Loveless is working on this for you, scheduling a speaking tour for you at universities and on talk shows. I hope you don't mind traveling and seeing new places."

"Hmm, that is quite a curious task you have bestowed upon me. Am I that interesting? I certainly have plenty to speak of, but must know in advance who my audience shall be."

Markush laughed. "Absolutely, my dear man. Sherri, or one of her associates, will be with you on all of your travels, serving as a kind of personal valet. We don't want any harm coming to you or major discomfort."

"Harm?" asked Arthur. "What does it mean?"

"Just ignore me. No harm is coming your way, although you may face angry audience members who disagree with your ideas, your stories."

"That will be nothing new," said Arthur. "I rather like a bit of a challenge."

"All three of you are already famous, but Arthur is going to be a star." Markush rubbed his hands together.

"Yeah, we've been watching the news," said Emma. "It's too strange, seeing our faces plastered on TV and hearing the stories."

"The television makes me look rather frumpy," said Arthur. "Primarily, they show portraits of which I never approved, except for the sitting by my dear friend Jules. I wonder if I should have my hair coiffed in a more modern style?"

Markush nodded no. "You should be authentic. We've even discussed having clothes made for you from your time and place. What do you think?"

"Anything rather than these, what do you call them, scrubs? But I rather like the new styles for men, although of the more formal persuasion."

"The ladies will go wild," said Emma.

"Yes, the ladies will like," said Afewerki, cracking a smile.

"It will work itself out. And if the ladies love you, more power to you." Markush felt on top of the world, as if everything was coming together.

Arthur frowned. "At my age of sixty-eight years, I am quite beyond the tarts and salon debutantes. But who am I to deny love?"

Markush beamed. "That's the spirit, Herr Schopenhauer. Look, I need to escape this place before another emergency pops up. Dr. Hubbard is on call tonight, thank God. But I just wanted to be the bearer of good news." He stood to leave just as the dietary aide was coming onto the unit with a trolley for the trays and silverware. She looked tired and wary, the guard Renaldo right behind her.

The camera crew stood ready, but Reverend Clarity Stillwell was late, having been held up by a phone call from a major donor. Stillwell walked into the studio wearing a brown suit with a yellow tie. He was five-eight and soft but stocky with thick, blond hair parted on the side with ample, black-framed glasses. He muttered as he walked up to the set of the Christian Instinct Network.

"Hi, Honey," said Clarity to his wife, who had been sitting in position for the last hour.

"Need to brush you up," said Angie, the makeup artist. She took Clarity by the hand and sat him in a plain black chair. She combed his hair and patted his face with powder, adding some balm to his lips.

"Done?" asked Clarity. "Jesus didn't use makeup."

Angie laughed. "Jesus didn't have a cable network."

The crew of eight watched in amusement, checking their watches. Without being told what to do, Clarity stepped up on stage and sat behind his authorial desk that hid his legs. To his left was an American flag. Behind him was the Christian Instinct Network logo, the red letters CIN hanging from a cross. To his right sat his wife, Patricia, in a lavender chair with a Bible on her lap. She wore a pink cashmere top and a long pink skirt, accompanied by white designer shoes. Her makeup was flawless, and her red hair was swirled into a chignon.

The director, Todd, with a pretty big belly and dressed in jeans and a CIN sweatshirt, took charge. "You ready, Reverend?"

"Ready," said Stillwell, and he put on a solemn face. "And go!"

The dim lights brightened with the focus on the entire stage, Patricia smiling and nodding. Music swelled, a kind of staccato big band tune that made you think of apple orchards. The cameras switched, now focusing on Clarity. He got right into it.

"My dear congregation and fellow Americans, we are in a hot seat of tumultuous tomfoolery."

Patricia appeared on screen in a box that occupied the lower right portion of the screen. Her job was to nod the affirmative or the negative and comment on cue.

"This circus of lies and pandering to the ridiculous has brought me to my very knees in obfuscation. I have sought our Savior's will in this matter and only have been told by the Heavenly Father that we must fight this powder keg of lies." He paused for effect and glanced at Patricia. "The headlines are telling the story across the nation. Murderers being treated like kings in this hellhole called Organon, on the very soil of our sacred nation. A new god called Dahlia, a mere seven-year-old girl who is, as told by the liars, kidnapping our children and shipping them off to the far reaches of our blessed universe. And I said universe, for there is only one, just as there is one God."

Across the top of the screen began running text, informing viewers of how to call and donate to fight the nemesis and its lies.

"Patricia, my dear wife, what does the Bible have to say about this?"

Patricia's video box enlarged to the entire screen. She had the Bible turned to the Book of John. "Yes, dear Clarity. 'Jesus said to him, I am the way, and the truth, and the life. No one comes to the Father except through me.'"

"Amen," said Clarity, the main screen back to him. "There is but one God, and we are commanded to have no other gods before us. When Moses descended the mountain and saw his people worshipping the golden calf, he punished them mightily, and punish we must do. There has been no greater crisis within our faith than the sins of this so-called Organon. We've seen that our own government is supporting this outlandish chicanery, funding this outrage. We must take a stand and fall on the sword if we must, just as Christ gave his life for us. Get on the phone to your congressman this very instant and demand a retraction of this blasphemy against all that is sacred." His lips trembled, and he wiped a tear from behind his glasses with a tissue.

The filming continued for a solid hour, with all the details of Organon and Dahlia laid bare for the discerning eye. In an adjoining room, thirty-five souls sat taking calls and running credit cards. The entire building complex covered some thirty acres with a grand cathedral of wonder, the Pilgrim Sanctorum, at its center.

The lights dimmed, and the cameras ceased flashing. Spent, Clarity put his head on the desk.

In the dining hut, Emma stared at the two Reeces, both with heads down and not moving. "We have to lay them down." Reece3 looked over her shoulder. Behind him were the other team members, shaking their heads and whispering.

It took some effort, but with Beo's help, they carried the two Reeces to beds, just a slight twitching of their fingertips. Ready for dinner, the team gathered back in the dining hut, minus Beo, who ate alone inside Emma's house, which had the taller ceiling.

"What in dickens is going on?" asked Emma. A steaming platter of enjera and a goat stew smoked in the middle of the table.

"Well," said Reece3, "Beo said they were coming, and we didn't believe him."

"But why? Why three Reeces for God's sake?"

"He is to look for his daughter, the Reece, the Reeces?" said Afewerki.

"But why here?" asked Emma. "We've got enough to deal with as it is. This is too much."

"Because she is to be here?" said Barra, his white teeth flashing in the candlelight.

"Has anyone seen a little white girl?" asked Emma. "I haven't. I think I would notice."

"They said something about the Abba helping them. Beo says the Abba wants money," said Reece3.

"Well, good for the Abba if he can help," said Emma.

"Yes, he is wise, and he is also tinqway, having magic,"

said Afewerki. "But it is forbidden to speak of this. Many years ago, there was a white girl. She was lost. The Abba sent her away. He is powerful in this way."

"That makes little or no sense to me," said Emma.

"It is true," said Isaac. He pushed his wire-frame glasses onto his nose, speckled with tiny moles.

"Is Ketow keeping an eye on them?" asked Emma. Ketow was the guard.

"Yes, he is watching," said Afewerki. "He is frightened." He gave a nervous laugh.

Ketow raised the flap, babbling.

"Oh, it is the Dog," said Afewerki. "He is coming to bother us."

"Damn," said Emma. She knew the Dog very well. He often visited Gobez, which was without a village administrator, seeking to extend his influence, plus he liked to see Emma, who wore tight clothes, unlike the local women.

Emma, Reece, and Afewerki went to investigate the problem. The Dog leaned against the fence, high as a kite. His two minions with AK-47s stood near him.

"Where are...the intruders?" asked the Dog. "They must leave! They bring bad luck!" He stood straight and stepped sideways, looking at the ground. He hadn't made the connection that the other Reeces looked like the Reece before him. He put his hand on his pistol.

Emma looked to Reece3 for support and spoke. "They are ill. They are resting on the beds. We'll take care of them." Afewerki interpreted.

"Sick? They will make us all sick with the evil eye. I will shoot them!" He turned toward the bank of four rooms behind him and chose a door, motioning for one of his guards to open it. He peered in the gloom and, unsteady, walked into Reece2's room. This time he would avoid eye contact as that transmitted *buda*, the evil eye.

"Wake!" said the Dog. He peered at the lifeless Reece. "You must answer me!" He kicked the bedframe, being careful of his prized boots. There was no reaction. "Outside!" he said.

His compadres obeyed and grabbed Reece2, carrying him outside and laying him on the browned grass. They looked embarrassed and unsure.

"He's having a seizure!" said Emma.

"Afewerki, tell him," said Reece3.

Beo emerged from Emma's little house, belching and rubbing his beard. The Dog saw him and slouched a bit. "What is the problem?" asked Beo. He came to them, towering like a massive fig tree.

Reece2 lay nearly still, just small vibrations in his hands and feet, his eyes half open and darting.

Emma explained the situation to Beo. Without hesitating, Beo picked up Reece2, carrying him back to bed, when Reece2 jerked and then Beo was holding him upside down. Reece made a croaking noise and said, "Fuck."

Beo readjusted and held Reece2 like a baby before standing him up. Reece2 put his hands to his knees and took a few deep breaths. "I'm here," he said. He locked his knees and saw the group around him.

"You were seizing," said Emma.

"Yeah," said Reece2. "I was back at Organon, saw Markush. What's happening?" He sat on the ground. He craved food and water.

The Dog had been watching with interest, thinking that

Reece2 was faking illness. "You and your twin must leave."

"We have business here, the Abba Paulos," said Reece2. He looked for a four-leaf clover in the patch of grass between his legs.

"The Abba," said the Dog. "Yes, he will rob you, ha! He has no power over me." He staggered, and his guard caught him.

Beo spoke in a booming voice. "It's time for you to go, Shimellis." Beo knew the Dog's real name. He rubbed his massive hands together.

Ketow mumbled that there was noise from the other Reece's room. Emma went there and found him awake, staring at the ceiling. "You okay?" she said. "We're having a little dilemma outside."

"Yes, okay," said Reece1. "Where is Reece?"

"He's outside. He's back, too. You were both seizing."

"Thank you for caring for my body."

"You're welcome. I have to go back out. Just stay in bed."

"The other twin is no longer pretending," said the Dog. Like a flash, he bent over and projectile vomited, gagging afterward. He went to his knees, and his two pals rushed forward, unsure of what to do. Barra and Isaac emerged from the dining hut, looking on in wonder.

There was a knock at the gate and a loud "Hello in there!"

Ketow looked at Afewerki, who motioned for him to go and look. Ketow fumbled with his hat and braced an old rifle to his side. His wife had warned him that working with the ferenji would be dangerous. He opened the gate, astonished. Three little girls.

The girls, all with brown skin, golden hair, and perfect

faces, walked into the compound. "Hello, friends!" said one. "Is this a party?"

"What the holy fuck?" asked the Dog. Triplets, and he was sore afraid.

"Dahlia," said Reece2. "Why are you here? Shouldn't you be abducting little girls?"

"What a hell," said Afewerki.

"Who are you?" asked Emma.

"Our name is Betty," said one. "We just wanted to see Mr. Reece." The three girls, dressed in short pants and blue t-shirts, stood as if at attention.

"Which one?" asked Reece2. "There are three, if you haven't noticed."

"Well, you, of course," said another. "We don't like you. You're mean."

"Mean?" asked Emma.

Just then, Abebaw arrived. He'd had business in the village, trading oil cans for meat. He circled to stand with Isaac and Barra, putting on sunglasses, although he didn't need them.

Reece1 spoke. "We know who you are. What do you want? Do you know where Mia is?"

"You would like to know, wouldn't you? It's a secret. But we have a question. What was there before there was time?"

No one answered, but Beo was nodding his head. "How can you ask such a question, being a little girl?"

The three giggled among themselves. "We're smart," said one. "We like to ask questions," said another.

"Dahlia put you up to this. She wants to know who her mother is, and she can't accept the truth. Right?" said

Reece2.

"Who is Dahlia?" they said in unison.

"You know where Mia is," said Reece2.

"Oh, will that old Abba help you?" asked one. "He's just an old fuddy-duddy. He's a bad guesser."

The group coalesced into a semicircle, with Beo towering over everyone.

"These girls are wise," said the Dog. "The Abba is a fool."

"I will find Mia," said Reece2, "and damn you." He pointed at the Dog.

Today would be the first group therapy session, as suggested by Dr. Mumford. Both the Reeces had resumed traveling, giving Markush a break, but he was eager to hear about what they were doing.

On duty in the medical unit were Carletta, Debbie, and Richard. Carletta would assist with group therapy once they had a few patients gathered in the dayroom. All eyes were on Helmut Grayson, the wild card, and he would come last. Timera Scocpol was able to wheel herself in. Next came Clark Peters, loosely restrained in a wheelchair, his mouth gaping, his eyes wandering the room. Both Sebastian Necker, room one, and Dolores Thrift, room two, hobbled into the dayroom with assistance. That seemed a good number, and all three nurses and Clyde Markush gathered outside Helmut Grayson's room, ready for a battle.

"What are y'all donkey dicks up to?" asked Helmut. "Gonna rape me?" He laughed and tried to sit up.

"Mr. Grayson, we're going to try something new, get you up in a wheelchair and visit the dayroom. Can you help us with that?" asked Markush.

"Well, that sounds fine and dandy," said Helmut. "That'll be just like a slice of good old cherry pie."

Carletta took the lead, then Richard, one on each side of the bed. Debbie maneuvered the wheelchair.

"You going to be real nice, Mr. Grayson," said Carletta. "We untie you and help you sit on the side of the bed. You may be dizzy, laying in that bed so long."

A huge grin played on Grayson's face. "Wait till Gandhi hears about this." He watched as Carletta unfastened the buckles to his blanket restraint.

"Doing great," said Markush. "Just let the nurses help you."

Richard peeled off the restraint, revealing Grayson's massive body beneath a flimsy gown. Helmut flexed his huge hands as if preparing for battle.

"Damn, gettin' to air my balls. They need it," said Grayson.

Markush laughed.

"I put some powder on your balls," said Carletta. "When I give you a bath." She looked dead serious.

"Oh, she's a cheeky one!"

Carletta raised the head of the bed as high as it would go. So far, so good. She reached under and pulled his legs to the side of the bed, with Richard keeping him from falling backward.

"Doing excellent!" said Carletta. "Sit for a minute."

Grayson slumped forward, weak from lying in bed. In the past, he had started swinging when unrestrained. "I bet your pussy is dripping wet," he said and laughed.

"No, no, Mr. Grayson," said Carletta. Nothing could shock her.

Richard came around, and the two of them stood Helmut and pivoted him into the wheelchair. He let out a groan.

"Damn weak," said Grayson. "Now what are we doing? Gonna cut me up and feed me to the hogs?" He grabbed Carletta's scrub bottom and pulled her onto his lap.

Carletta just let him grip her and laughed. "Come on,

big boy. Let me go. You very bad."

Markush looked alarmed. He moved forward but stopped, staring at the spectacle.

It took a minute, but Helmut released her with a look of foolishness on his face. "Got me hard as a rock."

Carletta jumped out of his lap. "You naughty boy."

"Damn straight," said Helmut. "Now let's get this party started."

In the dayroom, the five patients sat in a circle, staring at one another. Markush assessed the situation, thinking that all was as it should be.

"So, if anyone feels ill and needs to go back to their room, let me know."

"What's this all about?" asked Sebastian Necker. He was mid-forties with an oily face and dark eyes that looked through you. He had throttled his *daughter* Felicia.

"This is a chance to leave your rooms, get a little exercise, but mostly for us to talk and share stories about your missions to find your daughters. Maybe you can help each other," said Markush. His argyle socks showed. "Who wants to start?"

"I'll start," said Dolores Thrift. She looked haggard, her long blonde hair stringy. Her thirty years on Earth had not treated her kindly, with two abusive husbands and two divorces. She had smothered her replacement daughter with a pillow. "I'm stuck in this weird place called G-land. It's the third world I've been to so far. Elvis is helping me out, which is interesting, but he's not so useful, always being hungry. I'm looking for my daughter Nettie. Anybody else got an Elvis?"

Clark Peters stared glassy-eyed at the ceiling. "Ain't

nothin' but a groundhog." He brushed away an imaginary spider web. "Peaches and scream?"

Dolores looked disgusted. "Anybody else? My Nettie is seven and has the cutest dimples."

"I wish I could help," said Timera, her large breasts sitting in her lap. "My daughter's Lucinda. She's on an island, I think. Haile Selassie is helping me out. Any of you folk been to the big lake in Ethiopia, Lake Tana?"

Helmut Grayson sat as mild as a kitten, looking on with interest. He raised his hand, flexing his fingers. "You got to get Dahlia in the Cylinder and pin her to the wall. She'll fool you, that little slut."

Markush perked up. "Why in the Cylinder?"

"She gets loosey goosey in the Cylinder. Gets real chatty, liable to spill the beans. God, I got to hock and bad."

"Oh, oh," said Carletta. "I take you to your room and you go bathroom." In a flash, she had Helmut out of the dayroom.

"Has anyone else been to the Cylinder?" asked Markush.

"I been there," said Timera. "Just floating in a blue light. Dahlia told me where my Lucinda was, but it was just a lie. Wants to know who her mommy be."

"Exactly," said Sebastian. "If we could tell her who her mommy is, she might reveal where she hid our daughters."

Markush explained the theory that Dahlia's mother was time.

"Yeah, that's what I told her," said Dolores. "She thinks I'm lying, and nothing gets settled."

"Maybe if everyone tells Dahlia the same thing, then she might believe," said Markush. "That's what's valuable about us talking, having a plan in place. Dahlia seems to be an omniscient being, but she's only seven, like your daughters. Think about reasoning with her as a seven-year-old."

Peters groaned, batting at the spider web. "Dahlia. Dahli-a. A ghost. The mesh, the mesh. She needs the mesh. To get her."

"You mean she needs a mesh herself?" asked Markush.

"Yessssss..."

"She implanted the damn mesh in my head," said Dolores, "when I was little. Does she have a mesh too?"

"Wow," said Markush. "I hadn't thought of that. What if Dahlia did have the mesh? What good would it do us?"

"We could read it," said Sebastien. "Understand her more."

"If we could read it," said Markush. "But that's an issue for our lab. I'll look into it. But how to get the mesh?"

"Rip it!" said Peters.

"Is he really being helpful?" asked Dolores.

"Anything that helps, helps," said Timera.

Letitia Mumford had been on the long-term unit and stepped in quietly, taking a chair near the group. Both Reeces were traveling.

"Timera's right," said Markush. "We have to coordinate our attack. It would seem useful for more than one person to travel to the same place. That way, you could help each other. Power in numbers. For example, Timera is currently in the Lake Tana region of a particular universe. If we can somehow send one or more of you there—"

"I think I can get there," said Sebastian. "That's a great idea, but how would that help me with my daughter?"

"One hand helps the other," said Markush. "It may

be that your side travel yields unexpected results. Sometimes Dahlia hides daughters in the same place. Recently, we had two patients, Freddie Mentone and Reece Myers. They were both in the same Ethiopia but in different cities. Reece found Freddie's daughter, Alicia, in a place that Freddie wasn't looking. And then he found his own daughter with the help of the Abba, whom some of you have met. Mr. Peters, you haven't mentioned the Abba to me, though."

"Argh, the Abba. A slippery clown with chicken feet," said Peters with glassy eyes.

"You've met him?" asked Markush.

"The Abba!" said Peters. "He knows. He knows."

Markush gave up on getting more out of Peters. "So, let's go around the circle and say where everyone is and what's happening. You're not traveling at the moment, but we know that can change, and quickly."

Dolores started, and then, one by one, they related their stories, with Helmut Grayson rejoining them. He mentioned once again that Dahlia had a sister, and Markush wondered at the significance of that.

New Year's Eve came and went. The Returnees enjoyed the loaded punch brought by Markush, all hoping for good things to come. They watched an NBC special report about Organon earlier in the evening, astounded at national reaction. After the report, the show's host held a Q&A with Jacob Jacobi, Senator Tom Janks from Nebraska, and the Reverend Clarity Stillwell, who put on quite a show, portraying the government as a bastion of blasphemy.

January held true to the cold of winter and promised fresh developments at Organon. A barbed wire fence was to be built within the week. The two empty beds on Organon's medical unit were to be filled that day with two new patients, one from Tennessee and one from Texas, both having murdered a daughter. On Monday, January 12, when school resumed, Mia would start school on base, and Markush held his breath, hoping all would go well. There were sundry other details to take care of, including acquiring clothes for the Returnees, as they prepared to leave the Organon nest.

At ten a.m., the first new patient arrived by ambulance, Loydell McNamara, from Cleveland, Tennessee. He had traveled to Ethiopia a few years back, visiting coffee farms, with the idea of importing the world's most delicious coffee beans. But he'd had bad luck, and nothing came of his venture. On December 27, he murdered what appeared to be a replacement of his daughter, known as Speck, and had been taken to a prison medical facility, raving mad.

The second patient arrived two hours later, interrupting Markush's lunch of tuna-salad sandwiches and tomato soup with Kristin at the guest house. Markush lived there for now to avoid media attention. He ran outside without his coat to meet the ambulance and the new patient, Demeter Preston, a grandmother living in Belton, Texas, who had killed her granddaughter Kisha with a knife. Strapped loosely to the stretcher, Preston mumbled, her eyes cracked like ice. Markush followed the paramedics inside and ushered them onto the unit where Debbie waited.

Markush had some charting to catch up with, but after an hour, he checked on Preston, the oldest Organon patient at sixty-nine. He walked into room twelve as Debbie checked Preston's blood pressure. She had given Preston an intramuscular dose of Haldol, an antipsychotic. Preston had straightened gray hair with bangs and deep brown eyes, a slight build, but with a noticeable belly.

"Ms. Preston? I'm Dr. Markush. You've had a rough—"

"Dammit to hell! Where am I!" She tried to touch her face, but her wrists were restrained.

"It's okay," said Markush. "You're safe here. We're at Organon, a hospital."

"This is a prison! You got me tied up!"

Debbie stood back, waiting on Markush, and decided to wash her hands and exit.

"Not a prison, a special hospital for people in your situation." He just got down to it. "You stabbed your granddaughter—"

"No! Not my granddaughter, a sneaky bitch. Somebody stole my precious Kisha. This one was all wrong. Called me MeeMaw. My name's Granny D! Her music was all wrong, like a sick dog."

"I believe you," said Markush. "There are others here just like you, who have lost their daughters."

"I got to find my Kisha, dammit to hell."

Markush noted from her chart that she had seized twice since being arrested and then hospitalized. "Have you been to a strange place where you might be looking for Kisha? Maybe it seemed like a dream?"

"I don't know my up from my down right now, mister. Why am I tied to this bed?"

"Would you stay in bed if we untied you?" asked Markush. "It could be dangerous for you to be walking right now. You've had two seizures in the past forty-eight hours."

"I suppose, if this really is a hospital and not a prison. I just need to find my Kisha. Somebody got to help me and quick." She watched Markush untie her wrists. "Thank you, mister."

"You're welcome. Was there a strange little girl who liked to visit Kisha?" asked Markush.

"Oh hell. That damn white girl, Loretta. Started coming around about a month ago. Wouldn't leave Kisha alone, always making her cry. I told her to git, and she just came back. How do you know that?"

Markush sat in the recliner. "It's just a hunch. The other people here have similar stories. Uh oh..."

Demeter Preston went rigid. Her neck cords drew tight, and her face grimaced. Markush made sure her airway was intact, ragged breaths swishing between her teeth, and then the trembling of the bed ceased.

Markush hit the call button. "Need to get the EEG on room twelve." Claire said she would let Debbie know. Granny D's head would need to be shaved, a protocol that Markush thought necessary for the best recordings. While in the room, he performed a physical assessment, going from head to toe. He would need to perform a skull X-ray to check for the mesh, but he was certain it would be there.

Markush made quick rounds, lingering to talk with the other new patient, Loydell McNamara, who had not yet begun to seize. McNamara seemed obtunded, having received IV Ativan during the ambulance ride.

"D...Dah..." said McNamara.

"Go on," said Markush.

There was nothing. Not no thing but nothing. This idea of nothing. Total nothingness. But to muse on nothing makes it into something. Here comes nothing but how can it come if it is nothing? There is no light or sound, no touch, no taste, not even an empty void to hold the lack of sensation or sense. Nothing is more than a lack of something. It is a lack of everything. Nothing, ironically, includes many things, or rather, the lack of many things. There is no space. Nothing cannot surround nothing. There are no objects. There are no tables or chairs or giraffes or worms. There is nothing to see. There is no air or particles, not even a vacuum, no electrons or tachyons, not even quanta that comprise particles. There is no radiation. No heat or cold. There are no magnetic fields. There is no God or anyone to recognize God. There is nothing for a God to work with. But there is a possibility of one thing in the blank face of nothing. Time.

Time, as we know it, seems to pass in seconds, minutes, hours, days, years. Time, though, needs no one or no thing to exist and accumulate. Time is eternal and infinite. There was no beginning of time, and there will be no end. Infinite infinities of time. Time accumulated, creating a singularity. Time created such a weight that it formed matter, thus being the key ingredient of bulldozers and eggs, the infinite universes. The burden of unfathomable time assembled itself into a single quantum. With the appearance of this single quantum came a universe of space, extending outward into infinity. And with this universe came the ideas of everything possible, and over time, everything possible came into being: grass, ice, and mountains.

This minute quantum existed alone, except that the infinity of time knew not the universe created and spat out another quantum, creating yet another universe, and so on, and this continues, for time does not pass but accumulates in a state of nothingness. Time accumulates. All time is simultaneous, but with the weight of time and the creation of quanta, infinite time reduces by an infinitely small increment. As time passes and worlds are born, less time from the infinite is available, and on no day will infinite time become less to such a degree that the magnitude of further infinities subsides.

Within the universes emanating from a single quantum, these universes collide. These colliding quantal universes, after an infinity of time, coalesce into particles such as protons and electrons, free within an infinite space. Universes of a single quanta collide. And soon we have hydrogen, then helium. The entropy of a universe becomes higher, and there is the slightest heat. Time churns and elements form bodies, hot clouds that become suns. These suns implode, explode, ejecting all elements as we know them, forming solid objects such as planets. This all came from nothing, from time.

After the first quantum formed, all ideas sprang into existence without a higher power to imagine them, but the call for such a power was immediate and immeasurable. Thus, Dahlia appeared, a reservoir of being to lead consciousness. Dahlia, God, did not know herself as Dahlia. She only knew that chairs and baboons were possible.

Her being swelled to infinite proportions as infinite universes spread before her. There was a finite point of understanding when Dahlia ceased imagining the possibilities and wondered at her own existence. From whence did she come, and she anchored there in raw wonder at her predicament, forever unable to move beyond her age of understanding.

Though quanta and helium were interesting, Dahlia had to wait for understanding, arrested in her development as a child of seven. She knew other beings would arrive after an eternal wait. There were bacteria and viruses, which shed no light on her burning question. Fish and ferns provided no clues. And then there were animals that Dahlia pondered, but they only sought to eat and reproduce. Dahlia waited and waited for those beings she could commune with who would recognize her higher power.

The three little girls skipped away with frowny faces, singing "Humpty Dumpty" in a screeching timbre. Reece1 and Reece2 had departed the village, carrying two large silver coins from Emma, known as thalers. They walked through the village and back toward the shelter, with Reece2 in the lead. The giant Beo followed them, curious and always up to visit the Abba.

Within half an hour, they reached the short rock face, and the Reeces climbed with difficulty, Beo taking it with ease. There was no sound of pick on rock.

"He will be in his home." Beo's thick hair and beard gave him the look of a lion.

The house of poles and mud was just a short distance down the ledge, smoke leaking through the open front door. A hen with three little chicks scuttled away.

The Abba sat on his bed, mending a sandal made from old tires, a small fire burning, heating a pot that bubbled with a spicy wot. He saw the Reeces and, as if expecting them, motioned for them to come inside. "Nah," he said.

The Reeces stooped and entered the dim hut. On a small table lay the Book of Dahlia, written in the ancient language Ge'ez on leather parchment, filled with crude but colorful ocher drawings.

Reece2 pulled the two silver thalers from his pocket and held them out for the Abba, who secreted them into the folds of his yellow robe. "My daughter, Mia."

The Abba stood and walked to the table, turning the stiff pages of the book. He skipped to a page that the Reeces had seen before, a drawing of a Cylinder that gathered in the middle, called the Pinch. The Abba pointed at the Pinch and then at the drawing of a black angel hovering above the Cylinder. "Dah-lia," he said and gazed at the Reeces.

"Yes, Dahlia," said Reece2. "I need you to send me to Mia. Mia."

"Ow," said the Abba, meaning yes. He turned to a page filled with stars and what seemed to be planets. He waved his hand over the page and then swirled his hands in the air.

"Perhaps he means she could be anywhere," said Reece2.

"I think he will know," said Reece1.

The Abba turned to a page of text and read aloud, his voice rising and falling. Beo kneeled at the open door to get a better look.

"What is he saying?" asked Reece2.

Beo spoke. "Dahlia has a sister. She is the one who can help you."

The Abba nodded as if he understood and then stooped over a small wooden chest. From the chest, he lifted the tailored vest studded with twelve precious stones and lifted the vest over his head. "Nah," he said and stepped into the everlasting peach light.

At the entrance to the church in the rock, the Abba spoke.

"He says that I must go with you," said Beo.

"Really?" asked Reece2.

"Perhaps Beo can help us," said Reece1.

"Will there be sufficient, how to say it, power for all

three of us?"

"The Abba is wise," said Beo. "You must listen."

The three followed the Abba into the dark, cool cave, a pile of rock chips at the back wall next to an iron wheelbarrow. Before them was the empty wooden bier with the Abba standing behind it. He motioned for them to kneel and raised his arms, mumbling in Ge'ez.

A globe of light appeared over the table, and the Abba's voice grew louder. The light grew brighter, blinding them with flashes of blue. The three who kneeled felt a mighty power, a roaring vacuum. All three hunched over with eyes closed, and then there was a loud crack, and the Ark of the Covenant stood upon the table with flashes of static bursting between the golden cherubims' wings. The Abba went to his knees, breathing hard.

"Dah-lia," said the Abba, forcing himself to stay conscious.

A fuzz of electric charges played between the cherubim's wings, blue lightning. Particles of radioactive gold-198 spun from the static.

"Hello?" came a little girl's voice.

Reece2 dared to look up and saw her face in the electric glow.

The Abba pushed against his knees and stood. He spoke.

"Oh, hello, Abba," said Dahlia. "You're so nice to help these poor people, but they don't really like me, except maybe Beo. Have to go! Lots to do!" and her image faded into a mist of electrons.

"What next?" asked Reece2.

"Silence!" said the Abba. He again lifted his voice, and the chamber boomed. The bright blue light multiplied, and they were gone. The Abba collapsed onto the floor.

Afewerki had been taken to Eastern Kentucky University, along with new clothes and things he would need, including shampoo and a nice backpack. Emma was in her new apartment, feeling lonely. Organon had purchased her a Toyota Corolla, and she spent her days exploring Fort Knox, but was not yet allowed to drive off base. Arthur was living in the guest house, enjoying his extra freedom, imbibing the selection of wines that Markush had provided. He liked to leave his small apartment and walk around the lake.

Monday was Mia's first day at school, and what might happen petrified Markush. Kristin had taken her to the PX and bought her clothes and a heavy blue coat. Mia looked the part of a bright-eyed second grader and was excited to see Van Voorhis Elementary School. The small school sat on a slope, with a paved play area in front and playgrounds off to the right.

Markush pulled his old Volvo wagon into the parking lot with Kristin and Mia in the back. Most of the kids walked to school from the surrounding apartment complexes. Kristin had definitely given up on loving this Mia but felt it was her duty to show some semblance of care for her, even though she was effectively an alien creature and a naughty one at that.

Mia wore her pink backpack proudly. "Well, here we are! This place seems just dandy!"

"We hope you like it," said Markush. "You have to behave, though, and not draw attention to yourself."

"Yes, Mia, just do as you're told," said Kristin. "Be respectful."

"Let's go!" Mia ran ahead of them up a sidewalk, skirting dark green bushes.

"This is gonna be a disaster," said Kristin. "I mean, she should be under a microscope somewhere."

"It's been suggested," said Markush. "I was fine with DNA sampling, but draw the line at biopsies."

They walked into the school and followed directions to a second-grade classroom. The woman who met them in the visitor's office had seemed very nervous. She knew all about the Returnees from the news and that Mia was one of them.

The square classroom held five rows of metal desks. Already, fifteen students sat at their desks, babbling with one another in excited tones. Colorful hand-cut paper decorations outlined the chalkboard. Around the room were small posters with phrases such as "Be Nice!" and "Always Say Please!"

"Hi!" said the teacher, Ms. Diane Butterworth. She looked teacherly in her sage cowl-neck dress, which reached just below her knees. She was thin with swaying hips.

Kristin took over with Markush standing in the doorway. "This is Mia. She's a new student."

Diane's lavender eyes widened. "Yes, Mia. Welcome, Mia." Diane leaned over and held out her hand for a shake.

"This classroom is primitive," said Mia. "And I can see the top of your boobs." She giggled.

"Mia!" said Kristin.

"Oh," said Diane. "I'm sorry, well, maybe surprised.

We're glad to have you, Mia. Just take a seat where you would like."

"Bye, Markush and Kristin. You can go fuck now."

No one said anything, and Mia walked right up to a girl sitting in the front row in the center. "I need to sit here, please and thank you."

The girl named Cecily looked terrified, and her face contorted into a cry.

"Mia, that's Cecily's seat. You can have the one behind her."

"I need to sit in the front to maximize my potential," said Mia. "So, move it, sister."

Tears burst from Cecily, and Diane looked frightened. "Mia, you have to be nice. She was there first. It's okay to ask if you can change seats, but you can't be mean."

Mia smirked and gazed at the faces, looking at Diane as if she were a monster. "You're not very familiar with the human condition, are you? Hate, pain, misery. We're simply wallowing in it." Mia laughed.

"Mia, you *will* sit behind Cecily. Maybe later, someone in the front will want to change seats. Please do as I say." Diane's eyes strained.

"Well, dog shit," said Mia. "If you say so, Diane."

"What? How did you know my name was Diane, and do not use curse words." She took Mia by the arm and led her to the desk behind Cecily.

"You touched me, bitch," said Mia. "If you want to lick my cunt, just say so." She sat in her chair.

Diane looked flummoxed, having trouble forming words. The bell rang, and Mia put her hands over her ears.

"Class, I will be back in just a moment, and we'll get

started." Diane hurried out of the room to the principal's office.

Mia gazed around at the humanity. She locked eyes with a boy wearing a plaid shirt named Billy. "Hey, Billy. You look like your momma died. Is she dead or just the walking dead?"

Billy turned red. "You shut up."

"Oh yeah," said Mia. "Shut me up, you little turd." She stood from her desk, knocking her backpack onto the floor. "Look what you made me do!" She navigated her way to stand beside Billy, who leaned sideways to avoid her.

"Go away. I'll tell the teacher," said Billy. He had red hair and freckles on his cheeks.

"Tell what you will, Billy, and I'll eat you for breakfast." She raised her fist, and Billy cowered just as Diane entered the room, followed by Principal Humphries, who had quite the belly roll and oily black hair.

"Mia! What are you doing?" asked Diane. She wanted Mia to perform so that Humphries could see.

"Who me? I was just telling Billy how cute he is, and he's such a sharp dresser. I'll return to my seat. I'm sorry that I left my desk in your absence. Is everything okay?"

Humphries and Diane looked confused. "Mia, will you come into the hall for a minute?" asked Humphries. He was well aware of the stories of the Returnees, but none of it made much sense. Was the Army conducting yet another social experiment?

"Yes sir," said Mia, and she followed him into the hall.

Humphries said with some difficulty, "Hi, Mia—"

"You're Principal Humphries, and that mean old Diane

told you some lies." She crossed her arms. "Your wife's name is Miracle, which is unfortunate."

"What?" asked Humphries. He stood. "How did you know that?"

"I just do. Let's just call a truce. I promise to behave. I know that's what you were going to say, and I'll try and watch the language, but English is so rich."

"Yes, Mia, you have to behave, and you can't use curse words. Understand? Otherwise, we'll have to send you home. Does your mommy let you talk like that?"

"She more or less taught me, if that helps. She's not the brightest tool in the shed. But I have to make do."

"You are very adult." Humphries leaned against a bank of lockers, pondering Mia's fate.

"You look like you're pondering my fate," said Mia. "That's alarming."

"Wow," said Humphries. "Okay, Mia, I'm returning you to the classroom. You must do as the teacher says, and no cursing. Got it?" He smoothed back his oily hair.

"You want to smell your hand, don't you? I mean, yes sir. I'll be a model student from now on."

Back at her desk, Mia sat at attention, drilling holes into Diane with her eyes. At the door to the classroom was a reporter from *The Gold Standard,* wanting to take a picture of Mia on her first day at school.

General Tom Watkins had been working closely with Jacob Jacobi on funding streams for Organon. They'd had to drop the Al-Qaeda hush money because of public outcry and knew that the funding from arms sales would soon need to be dropped as well, in favor of direct funding through the Department of Defense and Congress. The White House was still leery of the whole Organon blow-up but had begun to listen as the story continued to grow. Another Pentagon press conference with Watkins had been arranged for two o'clock Eastern Standard Time.

All went quiet as the two-star general took the stage. He gazed at the reporters and cameras, coughed, then began reading from his notes.

"This is an update on Organon and its activities. As you know, Organon houses patients who have been accused of murdering young girls, and what we have come to know as the Returnees. These Returnees are in the process of being reintroduced to society, and we greatly appreciate any leniency regarding reporting that you can give them. Their position in history is sensitive. What we are discovering has been described as disturbing but is also groundbreaking in terms of global security.

"Our primary lab at Adelphi continues to examine materials from the investigation with surprising results that we have subsequently released, being transparent in all matters. Funding is being mainstreamed through House Bill 4103 and Senate Bill 450. We urge our Congressmen and Congresswomen to pass these important bills to support the massive efforts needed to study and manage an escalating situation effectively. More than thirteen hundred murders of young girls have been identified, going back to 1887, that are suspicious. Currently, there are some eighty persons being held in prisons whose circumstances need further investigation in light of Organon's findings."

Watkins paused and continued reading. "We understand that the American and world public have been caught by surprise since we first announced the situation at Organon. This is understandable, but we ask that all seriousness be given to issues of time travel, the abductions and replacement of girls by the entity known as Dahlia, and the return of the abducted, of which we have documented two cases thus far. We ask that the religious community be open to new ideas, and we ask that they continue to ask meaningful questions.

"Looking ahead to the long term, we are following up on thousands of leads nationally and internationally. To accommodate an expected influx of patients and their families, the decommissioned Griffiss Air Force Base will be acquired and refitted to house them. The cost of renovations, adding housing, a medical facility, shopping, and schools is estimated to be in the amount of 350 million dollars, a small price to pay for such an urgent situation, with national security at stake. I will now take questions." He stood over the ornate podium and grabbed the sides to ease an ache in his lower back. Hands flew up. Watkins pointed at a middle-aged man wearing a sweater with a tie.

"General Watkins, we continue to be baffled by this entity you have named Dahlia. Has contact been made with this being, and is she a form of God?"

Watkins knew that was a tricky question. "Dahlia is apparently an omniscient being, as far as we can tell. It's hard to say just yet if she is omnipresent or has the capabilities to be such. We speculate she is omnipotent, able to do as she pleases. We have patients at Organon who have had direct contact with Dahlia, usually within a special realm known as the Cylinder and the Pinch. She has also been reported to visit Dogtown. I have released descriptions of these locations. We speculate that the Cylinder, the Pinch, and Dogtown are where Dahlia lives or exists. But the impostors that Dahlia sends to replace young girls, we theorize, are organic copies of Dahlia. Dahlia is among us, is the best way to put it."

Watkins pointed at a young woman in a red power suit.

"Can you give some clarity to the idea that Dahlia is seeking to find her mother? And that is why she is abducting and replacing young girls?"

Watkins was doing a great job of keeping a straight face, although the words coming from his mouth seemed ridiculous to him. But there was so much evidence, and Markush from Organon was so convincing.

"Yes, Dahlia seems to be on a quest to find her mother. That is her preoccupation and reason for her interest in humans of our Earth and others. We have experts working on the significance of this idea. The primary factor to be considered is what came before Dahlia, that is, what we could recognize as her *mother*. Dahlia is reckoned to be of a finite age that is eternal. So, what was there before Dahlia? In our deliberations on the topic with physicist Dr. Desmond Ory, who is a proponent of the Tiny Bangs

Theory of the origin of our universe, we have accepted the idea that indeed there was nothing, yet one thing could exist in that nothingness, and that thing is time. Patients at Organon have confirmed this. Time, we think, is the origin of Dahlia, and thus, time is her mother. The fact of a physical mother seems impossible. Regarding abducting and replacing young girls, which often results in the replacement's murder, it seems this is a method of Dahlia, gathering information in her quest to discover her mother. How long she has been doing this is not clear, but we believe similar events are happening in other universes." Watkins scanned the crowd of twenty-six reporters and pointed to a large man with glasses in the back row wearing a dark blue sweater.

"This issue of Dahlia and time has the religious community in an uproar. How could there have originally been nothing but time? It's been stated that time no longer exists, that all time is somehow simultaneous. How can it be that time no longer exists? I wear a watch as most of us in this room do." There was a light murmur within the crowd.

"That's a significant question. One that I am struggling with as well. I am told that the burden of infinite time led to the creation of matter. Note that this happens in an infinite number of instances where there is only time. Once matter exists, time ceases to accumulate and continues to create matter, one quantum, one universe at a time. There must be an infinite number of universes, each perhaps with its own Dahlia."

The same reporter raised his hand and spoke. "How is it we experience time? For example, the time is two-thirty p.m. I have been awake for eight or so hours. The sun will set in approximately four hours."

"Yes, I see your concern," said Watkins. "I, too, wear a watch and experience what seems to be time. The best way to put it is that we confuse events with time. One thing happens, and then the next. It's just a series of events. Time does not matter, except that we live with the illusion of time, which proves useful in conducting the world's affairs. I hope that makes sense."

The man in the back was taking notes and shaking his head.

"To add to that further, birds migrate at specific times of the year and can migrate thousands of miles, navigating by the night sky, the position of the sun, and magnetic fields. They can travel vast distances and reach the same tree that they nested in six months prior. It appears that birds rely heavily on the passage of time to determine their migration. What is actually happening is photoperiodism. The length of a day and its change triggers the instinct to migrate. It's just circumstantial that time is a factor. Birds simply distinguish one event from another, which leads to their choices, much as humans do, but humans have the aid of clocks for organizational purposes. Next question."

The questions kept coming for another twenty minutes. One reporter asked about the mesh found within the scalps of patients at Organon. Another wanted to know why Dahlia was supposedly hiding little girls in other universes. General Watkins took each question in stride, sharing his information until a question concerning quantum gravity stumped him, for which he had no prepared answer.

Reece rolled onto his side and sat up. There was bright red grass in his hair and mouth. He spat. Fog filled the air. High above, a giant orange sun frowned on the place. He was wearing the same clothes—green sneakers, black cotton pants, and an acrylic sweater with a crazy zigzag pattern.

"You are okay?" came a gruff voice.

Reece turned and saw Beo towering above him, wearing his long, thick cotton robe and sandals made from old tires. "What? Where's Reece, the other Reece?"

"Dahlia has sent him elsewhere. We are two." Beo reached down and, with his hand as large as a skillet, helped Reece to stand.

"Why are you here?"

"I entered the church in the rock and was taken. I am here to assist you." He pushed aside his red beard and scratched a tooth.

Reece scanned the area, clusters of small trees with bright yellow leaves, the bright red grass. The scene hurt his eyes, and the fog was hard to breathe. "Where the fuck are we?"

"I am not knowing. There is a path of stone just there."

With Beo leading the way, they walked on the smooth paved path, two meters wide. Reece felt the cold and shivered. Soon, from the top of a slight rise, a boy on a bicycle sped toward them. He braked and came to a skidding stop, then remounted and left the pavement, giving them a wide berth.

"What the hell?" asked Reece.

A motorized bike, similar to a moped, appeared, carrying a thin man wearing a red jacket and a matching red helmet. He buzzed up to them. "Seen a kid on a bike?" His cheeks were sunken, his eyes heavy. There was a crest and the word "Tangler" on the back of his jacket.

Reece looked at Beo. "Uh, yeah, went that way." He pointed.

"Thank you," and the man sped off.

"Maybe a thief?" asked Reece.

Beo nodded and took the lead. At the crown of a steep hill, a small city opened before them, surrounded by a four-meter-high fence with razor wire at the top. Just ahead, outside the fence, sprawled a complex that looked like a quarry paired with an industrial structure of silos, belts, and tubes. It was a cement plant. Large cement trucks idled in a line, waiting to be loaded. Clouds of white dust filled the air. The ground was parched, as if it had not rained for weeks, but the fog persisted.

"There is a gate," said Beo.

They soon stood at an arch with the words "Welcome to Gordian" at the top, beneath which was an iron figure of a mother and child.

A door stood beside the gate, and Reece knocked. A small window opened, and Reece saw a yellowed face.

"What's yer business?" asked the man.

"I'm looking for my daughter, Mia."

"Ha, another runaway. Where'd she run from, the big city?"

Reece didn't know what to say. "Yes, the big city. My friend here is helping me."

"He's a big fella. I'll have to open the damn gate."

The solid wood and metal gate swung outward.

"You'll need to register at the Tangler Office," said the man. His clothes were patched and stained.

"Right," said Reece. "Yeah, we'll do that."

Before them lay a long street that came to a roundabout with a statue of a mother and child in the center. Tidy but aging two- and three-story tenements with shops on street level ran along the avenue.

"Damn, where to start?"

"Perhaps we need housing? Good food?" asked Beo. He rubbed his red beard.

"Yeah, a base of operations. Let's look."

They wandered the streets, passersby gazing up at Beo in wonder. They turned onto a smaller street, and a gang of older children ran at their approach. One stopped and threw a rock, which hit Beo in the chest, but it was like hitting a brick wall with a pencil.

Reece stopped at a restaurant, but they had no money. A lanky woman with huge breasts sat at a table along a plank sidewalk, eating fish.

"Excuse me, ma'am?" asked Reece.

"Ma'am? What's that?" asked the lady. She wore a double apron over her shoulders with a ten-pound weight in the back. The front part supported her large breasts.

"Oh, it's just...Anyway, we're wondering how we might find housing in your lovely town."

"That's easy. Just look for the flats with a red sign in the window."

"Thank you."

Reece had seen several red signs in windows but hadn't

paid them much attention. They walked for a few minutes more, encountering another pack of children who flew away like a murmuration of starlings.

"There," said Beo.

Reece sidled up to the yellow wooden door. The colors in the town were dazzling but aged. He knocked with the brass rapper. A minute passed, and he rapped again. A woman with huge breasts opened the door, and she was wearing the same apron as the woman eating fish, with two ten-pound weights in the back. Her hair was a bright yellow, her smile upside down. Beneath the apron was a long brown skirt that reached her ankles.

"Well, hello there. You come to tangle for us? Look at that tall fellow. I'll bet he has an appetite."

"I'm not sure, the sign in your window," said Reece. Beo stood behind him a few feet.

"Yeah, to tangle. Come in and I'll show you the room. We do breakfast and dinner, but lunch is on you. Name's Cleeda."

Beo stooped to enter, and his head just brushed the tall ceiling plated with decorative tin. On a couch sat three children near a fireplace, who looked very much alike, all with the same bright yellow hair and unsmiling faces. The plaster walls showed cracks in places. This was the main living area, then a narrow entrance into a large dining room, and then a kitchen beyond. A strong smell of meat cooking filled the warm home.

"Your room's upstairs with the tough meat." She led the way up the wooden stairs.

There was a landing and a large bathroom with three toilets side by side. Down a hall, there were six rooms off to the right and left. There were no windows, and it was very dim, without lighting of any kind. The metal doors wore heavy locks.

"Your room is here at the end, although the bed's gonna be a kerfuffle for the big man." She cackled. "But a tangler's got to do what a tangler's got to do."

The bright blue room was square with two small beds. Beo groaned, but he was used to such discomforts. There was a dresser and a round table with two wooden chairs. The only light came from a window that looked into a narrow alley.

"Is there electricity?" asked Reece.

The woman laughed, her giant bosom heaving. "You must be from the big city. No such thing here except at the cement plant. Well, are you gonna do it? You have to take the tough meat to the bathroom twice a day. If you let one get away, then the skin's on you. The tender meat needs watching. Can't let 'em out of the house, under no circumstances. They get locked up at night, so you got to be on your toes. And you have to tangle two runaways. The last tanglers we had let 'em get away. Got it?"

Beo looked confused. "What is the tough meat and the tender meat?"

This time, the woman looked alarmed. "Why the big ones versus the little ones? You really are from the big city. I'm hiring you as tanglers to keep 'em in check and find the runaways. My husband, Bertram, works at the cement plant, but it don't buy us meat." She laughed as if all was well.

"So, we get the room and meals? Is there any pay otherwise?"

"What? Other pay? Man, maybe you should head back to the big city. You're joking, right?"

Just then, an orange crush of light flashed in Reece's head, and he slumped to the floor.

The blackness dominated, and Dahlia hummed a little tune. All around her were the perfect ideas of everything, including Reece. Perfect ideas caught up in the Abba's transport were automatically diverted back to the Pinch. At Dahlia's whim, Reece's quanta reassembled, and he felt squeezed and nauseous, his mind racing.

"Well, Mr. Reece, what did you learn, good buddy of mine?" Dahlia flitted to and fro in the infinitely small space.

Reece felt as if he was doing somersaults, and he concentrated on answering. "I successfully inhabited Reece Myers' body and met Dr. Markush. He thinks I'm the real Reece. You sent me to Gobez, and then I'm back here..."

"I know all of that, silly. What did you learn? That's why I sent you, to learn something. Did Reece say who my mommy is?" Dahlia licked her little finger.

"He's only concerned with looking for his daughter."

"What did he say! Who is my mommy!"

"I know what he knows, and time is your mother. When there was nothing, before you, there was only one thing, and that was time. You emanated from the particles of time, if that makes sense. I feel sick. Can you return me to the darkness? I'm tired of existing. It's much too hard."

"No, and hold your horses! I have a mommy who is sweet and cares for me. She wants to buy me princess shoes and make me cookies. My mommy loves me. And I have to meet her!"

"It's not possible to meet her. Time gave itself to become you, and then the rest. Time no longer exists. Your mommy is...dead." He regretted saying the word as soon as it left his lips.

"No! My mommy is alive! You cunt! You bastard! Back you go, you no good devil."

Reece swirled, reduced to his most basic parts, the quanta squeezed into nothing.

Dahlia was so upset that she took a long walk in Dogtown. Her sister lived there, that goody little two-shoes. Dogtown opened before her in all of its empty glory, bright white light with glows of blue suffusing the eternal space. Dahlia skipped along, singing badly a little tune she had learned in the Pinch. She saw a gathering coming into view and prepared herself,

"Here comes Dahlia," said a wispy woman with strong eyebrows and a frown.

The group of twenty souls turned and watched as Dahlia skipped into their midst. Dahlia pretended to be interested in her bare feet, waiting.

A large man spoke, dressed in the simple paper robes of everyone else, "Dahlia, please, have some mercy. I need to get the hell out of here and find my daughter."

Dahlia grinned her perfect grin. "Mr. Andy, you still here? You'll have to pray real hard, Mr. Andy. You're here for a reason, and you know that."

"Why then are we here?" asked the wispy woman.

"Oh, because you won't share. You know who my mommy is and won't tell me, plus I gave you a chance to look for your precious daughter. You should be saying thank you."

Andy got down on his knees. "I'm praying, okay, for

some small mercy. You're the only one who can help me."

"Who's my mommy then?"

"Your mother is Jennifer Aniston."

"Oh, really? Then why was she born in 1969 or 1980 or 2001? You're just pulling my leg, Mr. Andy. At least you didn't say that time was my mommy. That makes me hot-headed." She performed little practice bows.

"But your mother is time!" said two voices at once.

"Stop it! You'll never get out of here if I have anything to say about it." Dahlia stomped her foot and clenched her fists. There was a collective groan. "Well, I'll be going now. Got some work to do."

"Dahlia, please," said Andy.

"Bye bye," said Dahlia, and she skipped along her way, and soon the group was just tiny specks.

She headed away from the Cylinder, going toward the far reaches of Dogtown. After what could have been days or weeks, and passing one small group after the other, all with the same pleas to be sent home or released to find their daughters, Dahlia saw a lone figure in the distance walking toward her.

"Hey, Sis!" said Dahlia. "Up to no good?"

They looked like twins, except Dahlia wore a plaid skirt and a red sweater.

"You would come here and be so happy," said Julia. "Why are you here?"

"I've been sad about our mommy."

"We don't have a mommy. You know that."

"Yes, yes, we have a mommy and she loves us, or at least me. You're worthless. I'm glad I put you here with all the other dorks."

"You're so mean. Why don't you help people? I would help people and not hurt them like you do. You just make messes," said Julia.

"You have no clue how hard I try to make things work. All those people praying to me. You're lucky you don't have to deal with all that stuff. And we do have a mommy. How could we be little girls without a mommy?" Tears forced themselves, but Dahlia held them back.

"Why just a mommy? Why not a daddy too? That would be nice," said Julia. "You're such a crybaby."

"I don't need a daddy. Daddies are mean. They don't like little girls."

"Then why are all of those daddies trying to find their little girls?"

"I don't know, and I don't care, so there." Dahlia folded her arms across her chest.

"They love their little girls, and you're making them kill the replacements that you create."

"Don't be a know-it-all, Sis. I use stuff I find in the Pinch, plenty of stuff. The daddies and some mommies somehow know that something's wrong. I don't get it."

"You can't hear the music. You make trouble, Dahlia."

"But I got the upper hand on you, Sis. You're not very smart. I tricked you real good, and we don't have to hear about all of your talk about puppies being cute and how you wish everyone had ice cream. If it were you instead of me, everybody would be weak. I make them strong."

"I wish you could just see the good stuff and not look so hard at the bad stuff." Julia sat cross-legged on the invisible floor. "I could kill you, you know, right now, but that's just you talking and not me."

"Ha, you couldn't kill a flea. In your world, people would catch ants and put them back outside. And no more murders? Murders always give me the creeps, but there have to be murders."

"Why?"

"Just because."

"Because you're evil, that's why."

"Maybe so," said Dahlia. "I like it that way. No one's pulling the wool over my eyes. Well, you've been *so* helpful." Dahlia vanished back into the Pinch.

Arthur was scheduled to give his first public lecture at the on-base Officers Club in a conference room within the Saber and Quill. The event would be a trial run for a wider audience. He had become constipated once more, requiring another bottle of magnesium citrate, which worked wonders, although it made him cramp. The event started with a meet-and-greet with Arthur and Clyde Markush.

"This cocktail is very bland." Arthur wore period clothes from his hometown in Frankfurt, Germany: black linen pants with wide legs, a white shirt with ruffles, a collar resembling a priest's, a black wool double-breasted coat, and black clogs. He looked every part the German philosopher with a grumpy face and demeanor.

"Yes, a little bland," said Markush. "Can I get you another drink?"

"Perhaps schnapps would be delicious," said Arthur.

Just then, the base commander appeared, Major General Phillip Borden in full dress. His medals shone brightly, much as his shaved head.

"Professor Schopenhauer, so nice to meet you." Borden put forth his hand for a shake and introduced himself.

"My pleasure," said Arthur. Small talk followed an awkward silence.

Markush returned with a snifter of schnapps for Arthur, who was appreciative. The General was boring Arthur.

"This is quite the spectacle," said Borden.

"Why a spectacle?" asked Markush. He nursed another

cocktail, which was bland but with plenty of vodka.

"Indeed, why?" asked Arthur.

"I mean, you have come to us from...another universe, it seems. To be honest, I find it hard to believe, although you are standing before me."

"Yes, I am now a part of your world," said Arthur. "I was taken from my home and carried to a strange place called Gadam. No one recognized me, seeming to be a place far in the future of my own."

General Borden had had a few whiskies and talked freely. "So, why are you here? Why here and now?"

Arthur glanced at Markush, who was content to listen to this mild argument. "Reece, Reece Myers, brought me here. I somehow became enmeshed in his journey back home along with his daughter Mia, whom I helped to find."

"Right," said Borden. "Time travel, more than one universe. It just sounds crazy, don't you think?" He slapped Arthur on the back.

"My, we are being forward, aren't we?" said Arthur.

"I get what you're saying," said Markush. "It's very puzzling, and you have to see the larger picture. Arthur has been caught up in a drama perpetuated by Dahlia. She is using Arthur to gather information."

"I hate the idea of being used," said Arthur. "But it seems to be so."

"It's like being at Disney World and meeting Goofy." General Borden laughed and slapped Arthur again, then squeezed his arm.

"I'm not privy to Disney World or this Goofy. Should I take offense, Dr. Markush?"

"Oh no, Arthur. He's just using figurative language to make sense of your appearance." Markush needed another cocktail. He gave the General a dissatisfied look.

"Excuse me," said Borden. "Special guests have arrived." Without ado, he left them.

Arthur and Markush entertained two officers for twenty minutes, and then it was time for Arthur to speak in the adjacent conference room, which was dimly lit. Chairs for fifty souls held fifty, including Darryl Hicks from *The Gold Standard*, with two standing in the back.

General Borden, swaying slightly, introduced Arthur as "...a curious fellow from another universe, having traveled through time to be here. Perhaps you are familiar with his written works, such as *The World as Will and Representation*." There was light applause, and then all eyes were on Arthur, who walked slowly to the black podium. He spoke but was too far away from the microphone, and a tech explained the situation to him. Arthur seemed stymied when he heard his voice amplified.

"What wonderful gadgets you have in this world," said Arthur, gripping the black podium. To his right was an American flag. "Yes, I am Arthur Schopenhauer, dead to you in this world, but alive and well nonetheless." There was light laughter. "I am most honored to be here and share some of my ideas with you, which have been somewhat revised, considering my recent experiences. My primary thoughts have been based on the writings of the great philosopher Kant, and I use them to counter what you may know as German Idealism, the absolute realists, to be more precise. My ideas embrace transcendental idealism, influenced by readings of Hindu philosophy."

The crowd began to fidget, but Arthur continued for nearly an hour, with many in the audience checking their watches. When he finally finished to light applause, Markush stood from the front row and asked if there were questions for Arthur. No one was really interested in his philosophy.

"Sir, how do you explain this character known as Dahlia? Is she a God?" asked a woman, an officer's wife.

"Primarily, it is important to note that I am an atheist. I do not believe in God or Gods, but I now have to modify that. I have experienced Dahlia and learned much of her through my young friend Reece. Although I am troubled by her existence, I cannot deny her existence. She certainly has godlike qualities. It was Dahlia who effectively uprooted me from my home and placed me in Gadam with Reece. That is a power I do not understand but am forced to ponder. It is Dahlia who is creating havoc within families, taking young girls and replacing them with near duplicates. The gifted parent can discern right away the substitution based on the music emanating from the replacement. As I have written, music is the most sublime of the arts, and Dahlia lacks in this capacity, for what reason I am not sure. I do hope that answers your question." He spoke now from in front of the podium with his hands behind his back. A slight sweat glistened on his wrinkled forehead. He waited.

A hand rose. "Do any of us with young daughters need to be afraid of this Dahlia?"

Arthur nodded. "Yes, I would say so. Dahlia is seeking a truth about herself and will stop at nothing to reach her goal. If your daughters exhibit the gift of music, I would be especially concerned."

Darryl Hicks, sitting in the back row, stood. "It's nice to see you again, Professor Schopenhauer. I have a question for you. There is a character who keeps appearing in your story, as well as in the stories of the other Returnees and the patients at Organon. What role does the Abba Paulos play in all of this?" He sat with pen ready.

"Quite a lovely man, very industrious, building a church into the rock with only a pick and an iron wheelbarrow. He sends one to faraway places using what appears to be the Ark of the Covenant as his tool. He is quite clever, but rather like a priest in that he wants payment for his services. I suspect he is in league with Dahlia, but cannot be certain."

Three others had questions, none relating to his philosophy. The event ended with several coming forward to have their photo made with Arthur as he sipped from a glass of water. The event over, Markush drove Arthur back to the guest house.

"All they wanted to know was about my trials with Dahlia," said Arthur, his hands on his knees, the window down, cold air rushing into the Volvo.

"It's interesting," said Markush. "In the future, you'll have to speak of your experiences with Dahlia, with Reece. Maybe try to summarize your philosophy in simpler terms in relation to Dahlia. Your next appearance is on a morning talk show in New York City. Millions of people will see you via television."

"My, that will be exciting," said Arthur. "I'll need to prepare within the terms you mention.

Markush's phone beeped. "Hold on."

After seeing Arthur into his small guest-house apartment, Markush declined a glass of wine and headed for the long-term unit. There, he saw that Reece had lapsed back into a flat-line EEG, but the other Reece was awake and talking. He spoke with Scoot, the Reeces' nurse, and then headed to room eleven.

"Glad you're back. Give me the details," said Markush.

"So much has happened," said Reece. "The Abba sent me and Beo to another world, a place called Gordian. It's so strange having Beo tower over everything. Anyway, I'm expecting to find Mia there. The Abba Paulos is usually spot on. The other Reece didn't make it, and I'm not sure where he wound up."

"Yeah, his EEG is flat if it's the same Reece. What's Gordian like?" asked Markush.

"It's like a quaint village, poor but painted in really bright colors. There's a cement plant outside of a huge barbed-wire fence. We found lodging, but we have to work as tanglers. We have to find two children who are runaways. It's strange. There are young children in the house, but upstairs are locked rooms with what I suppose to be older children. Not sure why they're locked up. Just getting a bad feeling, but we can look for Mia while we're looking for the runaways."

"Interesting," said Markush. "I wonder if the runaways are replacements?"

"I don't know, but there seem to be a lot of runaways. I guess the barbed-wire fence is to keep them in. Not sure why, though."

"Sounds somewhat sinister," said Markush. "Is the giant helpful?"

"Seems sincere. Just kind of fell into my lap like Arthur."

Markush told him about Arthur's lecture, and Reece laughed. He knew how formal and dry Arthur could be.

"Hey, can I get a meal? I'm absolutely starving here, and there too."

"Sure, I'll have Scoot order you some dinner. Two Cokes?"

"Beer would be better, but the Cokes are fine."

Markush scribbled some notes. "Look, I have to check on Mia and Kristin, so just keep trucking." He stopped by the nurse's station with the order for Reece's dinner and left. Dr. Hubbard was on call that night so that he could get some sleep.

Kristin answered the door, looking frazzled in a cream bathrobe, her hair wet from a shower. "I'm at my wits' end," she said, closing the door.

"Where's Mia?" Markush took off his down coat.

"In the bedroom. I hate sleeping with her. She talks in her sleep." She sat on the tight floral couch.

Markush sighed and sat on the opposite end of the couch. "How was the first day of school?"

"Pretty frightening, for the teacher, from what I understand. Mia was picking on other students and using foul language." She had to laugh.

"I wonder if she's capable of learning anything new," said Markush. "We know little about these replacements as they age. Usually they're *taken out,* to be nice."

"Hey, big boy!" Mia waltzed into the small living room,

wearing only underwear. She hopped onto Markush's lap and fingered his long gray hair.

"Mia!" said Kristin. "For Pete's sake, be decent. Go put on your pajamas."

"That's a good idea," said Markush. He pushed Mia off his lap and onto the couch.

"Don't be so rough, honcho," said Mia. "I'm just glad to see you."

Kristin returned from Mia's room with silky pink pajamas. "Put these on right now, young lady."

"Christ!" said Mia, but she complied and then sat alone in a wing-back chair. "This is a circus."

Markush regained his bearings. "Mia, how was school, your first day?"

"Kind of like a big fat joke. Ms. Butterworth, or rather Diane, is a piece of work, a real control freak."

"What did you learn today?" asked Markush.

"I learned I can't sit in the front row."

"What about a lesson, spelling or math?" asked Markush.

"Uh, she talked about a lot of stuff. Can you believe Cecily took my seat?"

"Who is Cecily?" asked Markush.

"A little bitch. She deserves to be…but never mind."

"She has her schoolbooks, but there was no homework, or so Mia says," said Kristin. "Reading, math, social studies, and she gets to take a music class and a PE class."

"Like I need a music class," said Mia.

"Mia, can you read?" asked Markush.

"Of course I can read!"

"Can you show me?" asked Markush.

"No! I can read, dummy."

"Mia, it's ten o'clock, and you need to get in bed," said Kristin.

"Yeah, whatever. Markush is being a dick anyways."

Markush and Kristin exchanged glances.

"Who's gonna read me a bedtime story? Isn't that what you're supposed to do?"

"Mia, that's a great idea," said Markush. "Is there a book to read from?"

"I guess we need to buy some," said Kristin.

Markush instead volunteered to tell her a story and went with her to the bedroom, which held a queen-size bed with a yellow comforter and a nightstand. The room looked sterile, much as a guest bedroom should. He sat at the foot of the bed while Mia sprawled beneath the covers. He wasn't quite sure what story to tell, but had an idea.

"So, there was a little girl—"

"What's her name?"

"Her name is...Hildegard."

"That's a fucked-up name." Mia smiled.

"Right, so Hildegard is two years old, and she's all alone in her big crib. Her room is dark, and she has a big doll and a teddy bear."

"Oh, dark!"

"And then something happens." He glanced at Kristin standing in the doorway.

"What happens, Markush?"

"Well, there was a little girl, about your age, who was under the crib. She listened to make sure the parents were asleep."

"Is she gonna kill Hildegard?"

"No, but she sneaks up on Hildegard, and there's a flash of blue light. She's putting something into Hildegard's head. She has magnets. Hildegard screams."

Mia looked dumbfounded. "Don't be cute. I know what you're doing."

"The blue light is gone, and Hildegard's mother rushes into the room and finds her standing in the crib, crying and crying. It's very sad, isn't it?"

Mia pulled the comforter up to her chin, staring at the ceiling. "That all sounds dandy, but Hildegard had it coming. She thought she had the music, but she didn't. None of them do."

"Oh, none of them? Who are *them?*" Markush was getting short of breath.

"Don't be so clueless, Markush. You know who they are. You can't fool me."

"Are they little girls like you?"

"Maybe so, but what does it matter?"

"Was the girl under the crib Dahlia?"

"Dahlia? Who's Dahlia?" A smile crept onto her lips.

Emma was getting the hang of her new environment, although she'd never had a cell phone, and marveled at the technology. A week had passed, and she was lonely, especially missing Reece, but her orientation at the hospital started today. She wondered if she should wear scrubs, but opted for a pair of black knit pants and a dark green turtleneck instead. She'd gotten used to her new car, but a couple of things were off, such as the horn sounding funny, and the steering wheel wasn't in the middle like she was used to. Markush had offered to meet her at the hospital, but she had declined his kindness.

She drove into the Ireland Army Hospital parking lot, gazing at the nine-story tan building shaped somewhat like a T. The lady at the reception desk directed her to a conference room, and she walked the clean halls, arriving fifteen minutes early. There were pastries and a silver container of hot coffee. Tasting the coffee, she frowned. It was too hot and bitter.

There were six others attending the general orientation, which covered hospital policies and included filling out paperwork. Susan Randall led the orientation, a stark blonde who worked in human resources. The morning went by quickly, and in the afternoon, Emma had a chance to visit the coronary care unit where she would work. Everyone there knew fully that Emma was a Returnee, and all eyes were on her, trying to fathom just where she had really come from.

The unit she would be working on was rectangular

with a central desk station, the rooms going around the perimeter. Right away, some of the technology surprised her, such as the IV pumps and indwelling cardiac catheters. Many of the patients also had urinary catheters, which were frowned upon back at her old hospital. Emma kept her concerns to herself, but the head nurse, Octavia, seemed to be somewhat leery of her.

"Are the patients required to confess?" asked Emma.

"Confess?" asked Octavia. She was curvy and overweight, with very short hair.

"Yes, confess the destructive behaviors that led to their illness. That's standard, right?"

The two stood in a corner of the unit beneath glaring bright light. IV pumps were beeping and ventilators cycling.

"Is that what you're used to? You mean like with a preacher? Confess?"

Emma laughed. "Not with a preacher, but with a medical confessor, to own up to their unhealthy behavior and seek guidance on how to change. It's critical, right?"

Octavia frowned. "Maybe come to my office." She led the way out of the unit and across the hall. She closed the door. "I was told that you have experience as a coronary care nurse. That's true, right? Maybe we do things a bit differently from where you come from." She finally asked, "Where do you come from?"

Emma thought. She was supposed to be transparent. "Home for me is Atlanta, a small city in Georgia. I guess you know that I'm from another universe, or that's the best I can explain. Very similar here, though."

"I see. I'm not sure that *very similar* is good enough.

I'm worried that your world might be a bit too different in terms of patient care. You're just one of a few civilians working here, and the only one from, as you say, another universe. I have to be confident that you know what you're doing. Are you familiar with ventilators? Just for example."

"Yeah, of course, the breathing apparatus that cleanses the lungs with blessed air," said Emma.

"Blessed air?"

"Blessed air, blessed by the Priest of Breathing. The air has to be blessed, right?"

"No, it doesn't. The oxygen is precious, of course, but whether it's blessed is not an issue here." Octavia looked alarmed, her eyebrows rising.

"Oh," said Emma. "What about the Priest of Digestion or the Priest of Circulation? They have to be consulted. The doctors know what they're doing, but they need spiritual guidance. The body is a temple."

"Lord, Lord," said Octavia. "We might have a problem."

Kristin dropped Mia off near the elementary school, hoping for the best. "Goodbye, Mother," said Mia. Kristin watched to make sure she entered the front door. Mia walked the spotless halls and made her way to the classroom, thumbs inside her backpack straps.

"Good morning, Ms. Butterworth," said Mia.

"Hi, Mia. You seem more cheerful today," said Diane Butterworth. She already had a dusting of chalk on the back of her black-and-red dress.

"Well, times be a changin'," said Mia. She glared at Cecily and then whispered into her ear.

Cecily turned red and up shot her hand. "Ms. Butterworth, Mia said she would...cut my throat."

Diane went pale. "Mia, take your seat and never say such a thing again."

"Yes, ma'am," said Mia, taking the seat behind Cecily. She glanced around and saw the ginger, Billy, and locked eyes with him, trying to hear his music, but it was tinny and sad.

The bell rang, and all twenty students sat at their desks. Ms. Butterworth scanned the timid faces, noting that Mia was staring holes through her.

"Our first period is math," said Diane. "We're going to review adding and subtracting first and then move on to simple multiplication." She turned and wrote 2 + 2 on the chalkboard. "Who can tell me what two plus two is?" A hand rose. "Yes, Amanda."

"Four," said Amanda, grinning.

"That's—"

"Excuse me," said Mia. "Two plus Two is an equation. The sum of two plus two is four, so Amanda is wrong, and so are you. You said *is* and not sum."

Diane looked tired. "Mia, please raise your hand before you speak. What you said is technically correct. I should have been more careful with my words, but Amanda knew what I meant, and so she gave the correct answer."

Mia raised her hand. "So, it's just okay to butcher the language?"

"That's enough, Mia." Diane turned and wrote 5-3 on the board. "Class, what is this? I mean, what is the sum of five minus three?"

A hand went up, but this time Mia stood. "Look, Diane, sum does not apply to subtraction. The sum only applies to addition. With subtraction, we are looking for the difference. So, the answer is a difference of two." She sat down with a blank face.

"Mia, I need to speak with you in the hall," said Diane. Mia stormed out after her.

"I'm just trying to help, Diane. You obviously need it. Can't you just be open to a little help?"

"Mia, call me Ms. Butterworth, and not Diane. It's disrespectful."

"Will do, mighty Ms. Butterworth. Just trying to keep things on the down low. No need to get your panties in a wad."

"Listen to me, Mia. One more act of disrespect, and I will send you home. Do you want that?"

"To be honest, no. Where I live is a hellhole of absolute boredom. Kristin is clueless."

"Let's just pretend that we're starting over, okay? Now, back to your desk."

Lunch came quickly, with Mia mostly behaving. The class walked to the open dining hall and formed a line with Mia being first. She soon approached the entrance to the steam table and read the sign. "Pigs in a blanket! What the hell is that?" She grabbed a tray, then a carton of milk. She watched the tired lunch lady, wearing a hairnet, put the hot dogs wrapped in biscuit dough on her plate. Then came tater tots and a lemon pudding. "Good God, what a mess!"

Mia found a spot at a nearly full table and sat down. Diane tapped her on the shoulder. "Mia, you have to sit with your class. Over there."

"Where does it end?" said Mia.

Afewerki's dorm room thrilled him, sleeping on a top bunk with his roommate Maurice from Senegal on the bottom. The building was old red brick with a spacious covered porch out front, looking over the campus to a deep depression where there was an amphitheater. For the first semester, he would take ESL classes with the goal of passing the TOEFL exam, then enter a mainstream program. He was not so thrilled with the food in the cafeteria, missing the spicy wots and enjera of home.

After his appearance on campus, rumors spread that he was a alien being. His Senegalese roommate, being very superstitious, had become wary of him and went to the length of preparing a magic potion to protect himself from any evil.

It was Saturday, and Afewerki was out and about, exploring the campus. He was somewhat aware of the rumors, but no one had directly accosted him yet. There were baseball fields nearby, and he walked that way. A man with a microphone and a cameraman appeared out of nowhere and backed Afewerki against a massive pin oak tree.

"Hi, Afewerki? I'm John Collins, with a news crew out of Lexington. Can we talk?"

Afewerki's heart beat in his throat. "I do not know. To talk about what?"

"You are one of the Returnees. You come from another universe is what we've been told." He pointed the microphone at Afewerki.

"I am a student from Ethiopia, but yes, perhaps, a different place. I am here by accident. I did not ask to come here, but I am happy to be at this college." His voice trembled.

"Tell us about getting here."

"I am not sure. Reece has been shouting, and then I am here."

"What about the little girls with knives? You were being attacked?" The reporter wore slacks and a white long-sleeve shirt with a tie. His neat hair lifted in the wind.

"You are knowing many things. They were just girls, many girls, coming with knives, and then Arthur appears, and Reece is shouting. He is having a pistol, but there is no effect."

"He shot little girls?"

"Yes, but they are not wounded. It was to save our lives." A news van with a satellite dish pulled into a nearby parking lot.

"Do you think these girls are a part of Dahlia?"

"I am not knowing Dahlia. It is said to be true."

"But what exactly is Dahlia?"

"There is only one God," said Afewerki. "We must live by the Bible."

"So, Dahlia is not God?"

"She cannot be God. She has strange powers that must be from the devil."

"Interesting," said Collins. "But how could you travel across universes without the help of God?"

"I do not know. It is cold. I must be going now." He inched away from the tree and turned, but there was another camera and a woman in a dark blue dress, wearing a satin jacket.

"You guys done?" asked the woman.

"Not really," said Collins.

"I am to go now," said Afewerki.

"Mr. Nigussie, Afewerki, please, just a few questions."

Afewerki broke into a fast walk back toward the dorm beneath a gray sky, thinking about a new word he had learned, debacle.

Beo and Reece sat on their beds, Beo's knees rising above his chest. He would have a fit sleeping, the bed being three feet short. Reece handed the two grainy photographs of the runaways to Beo.

"Must be eighteen or nineteen, hardly runaways," said Reece.

"The lady says we must look in the city and beyond the east gate," said Beo.

Cleeda had offered them boiled meat, bread, and milk, and they both had eaten the meal with care.

"Well, shall we?" asked Reece. "Get on the job?"

"Yes, it appears we must work for our room and board."

They walked down the stairs, Beo ducking the ceiling. The three children with yellow hair were still sitting on the couch, hands on knees, with blank stares. Reece tried to engage them in conversation, but all he got was one "Yes sir."

At the street with no sidewalk, they randomly turned left, keeping the photos at the ready. Reece kept an eye out for any little girls, but he had yet to see one. There were men on bikes and a scooter here and there, but no cars or trucks. They wandered a few blocks past houses that looked the same, except painted different vibrant colors that were hard to look at. There were no trees or lawns. The fog had lifted, but low-lying clouds hovered over the city in front of the enormous orange sun.

They entered a stretch of businesses, most made of dull red bricks. There was a bicycle shop, a hardware store, and then a butcher with racks of ribs hanging in the front window. Reece took a close look and saw a few flies on the meat.

"There is a group of young adults just ahead," said Beo. "They have turned down the street, seeming afraid." He nodded to a woman passing by with several wrapped parcels.

"Let's check it out."

They reached the street, and Beo peered around the corner. "They are moving away as one."

Reece turned the corner and saw the group of twelve or so. One was walking backward and alerted the others. In a flash, they had run and turned another corner.

"Damn," said Reece. "This is harder than it looks."

"You go that way, and I will go this way, and they will perhaps be trapped."

Reece trotted forward for a block and stopped, careful not to expose himself, waiting for Beo to come from the other way. He made himself count to thirty and then stepped into the narrow street of compacted sand and gravel. The group had just broken into a run as Beo rounded the corner. There was shouting as Reece ran and caught up with Beo, who had caught one of the ruffians by the neck with one hand. The boy, about eighteen years of age, put up no struggle and was silent but panting.

"Are you a runaway?" asked Reece. The young man did not have bright yellow hair. Reece consulted the photos again. Beo held the captive by his arm.

"What's it to you?" asked the boy. He let out a long whistle.

"We're looking for two runaways," said Beo. "Show

him."

Reece held out the photos to the boy. "Do you know them?"

"Will you lemme go if I tells you?" The boy wore high-waisted pants and a rough gray sweater with a knit cap. His face looked youthful, but his eyes held secrets.

Reece looked at Beo. "Yeah, of course, but tell me why there are so many runaways first."

The boy sneered and laughed. "Ye must be from the big city. If ye don't know, then why are ye lookin'?"

"Well, that's a great question, and I'm asking you to help us understand. Are you a runaway?"

"Of course, I'm a runaway. Why wouldn't I be?" asked the boy, sneering.

"What are you running from?" asked Beo, loosening his grip.

The boy wrenched free and took off at a gallop, whistling loudly.

They started after him, but stopped when the boy flew into an alley.

"Damn, I didn't get to ask him about Mia," said Reece. "If anyone knows, they will know."

"But these runaways seem to be older," said Beo. "I do wonder what they are afraid of."

"The older ones at our house are locked up day and night, maybe that's why," said Reece.

"Perhaps, but something is not quite right," said Beo.

They walked another two blocks, glancing at derelict homes, none with open doors, even though it was warm.

"I would love a cup of coffee, but we have no money," said Reece.

"The coffee will not be as good as that of Gobez," said Beo.

"Right. Shall we go to the east gate? I wonder how far?"

They stopped in front of a small shop that advertised glassware and went inside. A large woman with tremendous breasts and the apron with its weights met them. She told them that the east gate was less than a mile away and pointed in the general direction.

They walked mostly forward, but had to navigate side passages as well. Beo's sandals clopped in the relative silence. Twice, they saw groups of teenagers, but they were quick to get away. There was a strip of bright red grass with a barbed-wire fence at the end. They looked left and right and went left. They had to walk through piles of junk, but soon arrived at a large gate in the fence, guarded by a small man wearing overalls and work boots.

"Hidee, fellas. What's yer business? You headed out to do some tangling?"

"Uh, yes, that's right, to tangle," said Reece.

"And you, sir, are an impressive specimen. Never seen the likes of it."

Beo tried to strike a pose of amusement. "I am a son of God, sent to your place."

"Well, ain't that mighty interesting. You just go on believ'n, and it might come true." He cackled while fishing out a large key. "Y'all catch us some dinner, you hear?"

With that, Beo and Reece walked through the gate, Beo ducking beneath the arched wood. There were rough patches of the red grass, a taller yellow grass, and scattered trees that neither recognized. The neatly paved path was relatively straight, but steep in places. They noticed two figures approaching, a man leading a boy by a harness. The boy's hands were cuffed behind him. Neither the man nor the boy said a word as they passed, just a raise of the hat. Reece turned and called to the man, "Have you seen a little girl, seven years old, with light red hair?" The man just kept walking, towing his captive.

Soon they came to a vast slope dotted with mounds of earth, some fresh but most overgrown with grass, each mound backed by a gravestone. They stopped to look.

"Huh," said Reece, "these are all young people."

"I am having a bad feeling," said Beo.

"Me too. Do you think they were runaways, maybe murdered?"

"It is not clear just yet, but I fear the worst."

"Damn, we have to produce the goods if we want to stay at the house with Cleeda. I'd hate to be contributing to something like murder. Why would they do such a thing?"

"It is not yet for me to say. We should continue looking, perhaps, off the path."

"Right."

For two hours, they scoured the lower half of the slope, which was pocketed by limestone grottos and what looked like cedar trees. They checked inside various nooks in the rocks.

"There must be caves here," said Reece. "The limestone and the cedar trees indicate caves."

"A good hiding place," said Beo.

"Yeah, we'll have to come back here, but we should go for now. We have to see to the kids."

Seven-thirty a.m., five minutes until show time, Arthur fidgeted in the backstage green room, waiting to be interviewed by Lauren Sculler of the *Today Show*. To suit his stolid frame, he had opted for modern clothing, including black suit pants and a colorful sweater. He'd had his white hair cropped closely and combed straight back. He looked like an aged Hulk Hogan, but without the muscles. Sherri Loveless, the Organon publicist, sat beside him, looking bony and drawn.

"The truth, that's all it takes," said Loveless. She wore an elegant green suit woven with gold fibers. "You good?"

Before Arthur could answer, a production staff member stood in the door. "Ready, Professor Schopenhauer?" He motioned with his head to get a move on. "Two minutes."

"Ah, the television," said Arthur. "I hope to do dear Dr. Markush justice. If you will excuse me."

The previous guest, speaking about the Monica Lewinksi scandal, had vacated the hot seat during the commercial break, and Arthur sat down, feeling the warmth of its previous occupant. He wanted to touch his face, feeling the makeup there, but resisted.

"Lauren Sculler," and Lauren sat in her chair in front of the plants and background squares of decorative glass. She leaned over and shook hands with Arthur. She glanced at the timer. "One minute and we're on."

"Well, my pleasure," said Arthur. He found this young woman quite attractive, with her high cheekbones and distinct chin. He wanted to say more, but Lauren seemed meditative as she glanced at a teleprompter. And then they were live.

"We're with one of the Organon Returnees, Professor Arthur Schopenhauer. Professor Schopenhauer, you are looking very comfortable, a change from the photos we've seen." She laughed.

"Thank you. I wished for a more contemporary flair."

"And you've got it," said Sculler. "We're all wondering, Professor Schopenhauer, as a philosopher, what the recent events concerning Organon mean."

"What does it mean? It means that existence has become fluid in my estimation. We are no longer contained within the past, present, or future. There are forces at work that strain the imagination."

"How did you help Reece Myers find his daughter in another universe?"

"He carried the impetus to succeed, and I was merely a helpmate, in my estimation. He used some choice words of mine to extricate us from a dangerous predicament, being confronted with hundreds of young girls with knives."

"Yes, tell us more about the young girls with knives," said Sculler.

"They were charming, in appearance, but with blank faces. They were singing some children's songs and marching forward, brandishing their knives. Had Reece not spoken, we would have been doomed."

"I see," said Sculler. "What was the intention of these little girls?"

"My understanding is that they were sent by Dahlia, the primary culprit in all of this drama, to prevent my young friend Reece from rescuing his daughter, Mia."

"It's amazing that he found her. I understand that his daughter was replaced. And this is where it gets dicey. Reece Myers actually murdered what everyone thought was his daughter, including his wife. That seems, no, it's just brutal. How could he have murdered his own daughter even though he thought she had been replaced?"

"That question is hard. He knew that his daughter had been replaced by the replacement's music. As long as she lived, he could not locate the real Mia."

"Describe this music more," said Sculler. She crossed her legs and scolded herself for doing so.

"There are those who have a connection with music in its perfection. Both Reece and his daughter possess such qualities. The universe or universes can be reduced to the various musics that are created. Music is the most perfect of the arts and is noble. Dahlia and her helpmates lack the gift of music and seek to gain that knowledge from those who are gifted."

"To wrap up, what do you hope to accomplish by speaking openly about your experiences?" asked Sculler.

"It is my wish that Reece and others like him be enabled to find their daughters and be absolved of any crime of murder. We must expose Dahlia for the trickster she is and somehow remove her from her seat of power. The work of Organon is critical in this matter."

"To summarize, what seemed initially impossible, time travel and talk of Dahlia as God, has become somewhat mainstream, and although questions remain, evidence is mounting that the strange events centering around Organon are truly real. Thank you, Professor Schopenhauer."

"And thank you."

A production assistant led Arthur backstage, where he met up with Loveless, who was beaming.

"That was super, Arthur," she said. "Straight from the hip and without a lot of mumbo jumbo. You're spending the night in a hotel near the airport. I'll get you there, but you'll have to navigate your way back home."

They stepped onto a busy Sixth Avenue from the NBC building in Rockefeller Plaza. Right away, a crowd enveloped them, many shouting, "Arthur, Arthur!"

"What is this?" A small throng jostled him, and many in the crowd wanted his autograph.

"You are instantly famous," said Loveless. "Just keep walking. I'll get us a cab."

But Arthur had stopped and accepted a pen and notebook from a small woman in a wheelchair. "What shall I do?"

"Your autograph, Arthur!" said the woman, her legs strapped to the chair.

Loveless was in a hurry. "Arthur, just sign your name!" she said over the small crowd's roar.

Arthur did as he was told and added "What a lovely day" to his autograph.

"Dahlia!" yelled a middle-aged man in a sweatsuit. "Draw a picture of Dahlia!"

"Last one," said Loveless.

"I'm not an artist," said Arthur. He did his best to draw a crude figure of Dahlia that resembled her likeness in the Abba's book, wearing a triangle dress. He was pushed and pulled, teetering back and forth amid the commotion. "I must be going!" he said to the wind and struggled to follow Loveless, who was creating a path. She was thin, but she was strong.

Loveless snagged a yellow cab and dove in, looking back. A reporter and cameraman had waylaid Arthur, none other than Stuttering John from the Howard Stern Show.

"Ya, ya, ya, you, get a lot of, a lot of ass?"

Arthur seemed transfixed. "I do not follow."

"Arthur! Into the cab," said Loveless.

Arthur sat in his seat with his legs still in the street.

"Ya, ya, ya, ev, ever, squeeze Dah, Dah, Dahlia's tits?"

"Such a question," said Arthur, and someone slammed his door.

"Dear God, what an uproar," said Arthur.

The cab lurched into traffic, stopping and starting.

"Yep, you're famous for sure, and people seem to like you."

"This television is magic. I do think I like it."

"That's swell," said Loveless. "Really swell."

The two new patients, Loydell McNamara and Demeter Preston, had been traveling off and on and were pretty lucid about their experiences, and Markush decided to include them in the group discussion. Also present were Clark Peters and Helmut Grayson, adding mirth and mystery to the proceedings. Dr. Letitia Mumford presided, along with Markush and the nurse Carletta, who had proven to be very helpful with difficult patients. Nothing fazed her. At the last moment, Timera Scocpol, in her wheelchair, joined them.

"Letitia, you want to get us started," said Markush.

"I think we need a summary from everyone, of where you are traveling and any progress that is being made. Demeter, you want to start?"

"Just call me Granny D," said Demeter.

"Granny D!" said Helmut. "In the house!" He roared.

"I'm in some awful place called Gland, looking for my daughter, Kisha. I know some of you got some interesting characters helping you out, but me, I'm stuck with Betty Crocker. Wears an apron and got rosy cheeks."

"Betty Crocker?" asked Loydell. "Well, burn my buns. I ain't got nobody helping me yet."

"Better crockware," said Peters. He swatted at something in the air.

"Okay, moving along, Loydell, how about you?" asked Mumford.

"Looking for my daughter, call her Speck," said Loydell. "I'm going to this place called Gacci. Looks like a coffee farm I once visited, but everything is shiny and made of metal. Not a cup of coffee to be found."

"Timera?" asked Mumford.

"Right. Still on Lake Tana, going from one island to the next, looking for Lacie. Got me the Haile Selassie to help out, speaks the language, otherwise I'd be lost." Timera leaned forward, a bit out of breath.

"Clark? How about you?"

"Bzz, bzz," said Clark. "Beatrice! Beatrice!" His eyes looked wild.

"Beatrice is your daughter," said Markush. "Are you getting close?"

"Gettin' close, yeah, not so close, but close. Dah-lia," said Clark. "I seen her." He pointed at Timera.

"Really? You saw Timera in your travels?"

"Yesssss."

"I ain't seen him," said Timera. "Maybe I don't need his help."

"Let's see what happens. You never know what might happen," said Markush.

"And Helmut, what's happening with you?" asked Mumford.

Helmut laughed, gripping his thighs. "Yeah, just in that same old dump, Gimmi. Garbage everywhere, plastic bottles choking the ditches, but I can smell her, can smell Lila. She's got to be there. I need to get back for sure. In fact, I'll just take a walk and get there."

"Helmut, no!" said Markush.

Helmut stood from his wheelchair, but his wrists were tied to the armrests, and the wheelchair hung from his backside.

"Don't mind me." Helmut staggered to the doorway

and headed left for the unit door.

The guard, Shark, at the end of the hallway, saw what was coming. He barked into his walkie-talkie for Gumbo to get his ass over there.

Carletta followed Helmut. "No, no! Mr. Grayson!"

Grayson kept walking toward the door, but Shark, who had a baton at his side, met him. "Sit down, brother," said Shark. "We don't need no trouble." He saw Gumbo running up the hall.

"What the hell?" asked Sebastian Necker from room one.

Grayson breathed heavily. "Out of my way, shit-face. I'm on a mission!" Grayson plowed into Shark, who stumbled against the locked door.

Gumbo got involved, and they wrestled Grayson into the wheelchair.

"Goddamn it!" bellowed Grayson. He fought like a wildcat, but Gumbo had him around the neck.

And then Grayson went rigid, his body quaking.

"Holy Christ," said Markush. He could see that Mumford was shaken. "Back in the bed, but wait for him to relax. He untied the restraints, and Carletta retrieved a pillow so that they could lay the massive Grayson on the floor as he twitched and trembled. Loydell and Timera had entered the hall to see the excitement, leaving Peters all alone in the dayroom. Peters pawed at the air, pushing away demons.

"No more therapy sessions for a while," said Markush, kneeling beside Grayson.

"Got that right," said Mumford.

Octavia, from the base hospital, had called Markush and expressed her concerns about Emma. She felt that Emma's past experience in a critical care unit, being in another universe no less, did not meet the standards of this time and place. She worried that a patient would die. Markush had listened, disheartened, but was not surprised. Reintegrating Returnees into society was a new thing. There were bound to be complications.

Emma returned from her orientation, confused and disappointed, understanding that they would not hire her. Octavia had suggested that she would need to earn her nursing degree again to be seriously considered. In her spare apartment with its matching gold couch and armchair, she ate a bologna sandwich, turned on the TV, and thought about Reece. The Reece she had worked with in Gwar had become a genuine friend, and she had begun to have feelings for him. The Reece she had returned with looked exactly the same, but older, and he was divorced, whereas the Reece in Gwar had not been engaged or married. She longed to see Reece in whatever form he may have taken. Reece could understand her life-changing experiences in Gwar. Reece was a Returnee like her. Tears rolled down her cheeks. Damned lonely and discouraged, she would never see her family again unless a miracle happened. She thought about her mom, who worked in a barbecue joint in Atlanta. From what she understood, the Atlanta of this land was much larger than the small city she knew. The phone rang, and she silenced the noon news. It was Markush.

"Hey, I'm so sorry about the job," said Markush. He leaned back in his office chair, doodling on his desktop calendar.

"Yeah, the lady thought I was a lunatic. She had no idea about the Priest of Breathing. Is that really not a thing?"

"I'm afraid not, although it sounds like an interesting idea. Is there a Priest of Thinking?"

"Well, duh, of course. Highly paid where I come from."

"Wow," said Markush.

"I also didn't understand the part about getting paid. Back home, doctors and nurses work for free, and healthcare is free for everyone. We just get housing and meals. I'm shocked that you would take money to help people."

"Wow, again," said Markush. "That certainly had never crossed my mind. Were there enough doctors and nurses to go around?"

"Actually, too many, I think. Because we had so many nurses, I was always taking days off."

"I get it. That was your life."

"But I was working in Ethiopia, and that's really where I need to be, to finish what I started. It hurts me to think there are people there who relied on me and now I'm gone."

"Having you return to either place is an unknown. Our only guess is to have you visit Ethiopia and commune with the Abba Paulos. He seems to be the key to time travel, other than the seizures. Although Dahlia, I think, would have the power to send you home. I suppose it would be a matter of having an audience with her. Not sure she's the type to listen to prayers."

"I'm open to any suggestions, no matter how strange. I'm just lonely. If Reece could be out and about, I feel we would really get along. What's his status?"

"I'm not supposed to breach patient confidentiality, but I can make an exception with you. Both Reeces are traveling, although the Reece in room eleven popped back in for a short while and then resumed seizure activity. The Reece in room three has gone dormant again, a flat EEG. It's as if he's disappeared on the other side. Hey, I have an idea."

"What?" asked Emma. "Give it to me." She thrummed her fingers on the armrest of the gold couch.

"If you really feel that working for free is the way to go, we could use you on the medical unit. You could serve as a nurse, but not in an official capacity. You could be near the two Reeces in the long-term unit and maybe have some insight into what they are experiencing."

"Huh, that sounds like a great idea. I'd like that. Could I just come back and live in the guest house to be closer?"

"For now, that will work, but you're sure you want to give up your apartment? You can keep the car, either way," said Markush.

"Yeah, back to the guest house. I'll be close. Won't have to drive. Just like my old job. Thanks, Dr. Markush. I was getting down in the dumps."

"No Priests of Urination, though."

"I get it, but you guys should really look into it. The priests add an extra level of care."

"Certainly, something to consider," said Markush.

Reece and Beo made their way back and passed through the east gate, having learned nothing of the runaways or Mia. Beo had a good sense of direction and navigated to the roundabout with the statue of the mother and child and then found the house from there. Reece tried the doorknob, but it was locked. He guessed it was approaching dinner time as the light outside was dimming. Beo knocked on the door with his giant knuckles, hunched over and ready to stoop.

A man answered, Cleeda's husband, Bertram. He was skinny as a rail, had a red nose, and a head full of black hair that stood straight on end. He wore dusty blue pants with a coarse cotton shirt.

"You the new tanglers, I take it," said Bertram.

"Yes sir." Reece noticed the three yellow-haired kids still on the couch, one reading a book.

"That's them!" said Cleeda, coming from the kitchen.

"Any luck?" asked Bertram. He spoke with a slight lisp.

"We went beyond the east gate, didn't see them," said Reece. "I'm looking for my daughter, too. Have you seen—"

"Hold up now," said Bertram. "Yer working for us. We ain't rooming and boarding ye to look for yer daughter, got it!"

"Okay, yes sir. We'll do that." The living room seemed small now with him, Beo, Cleeda, Bertram, and the three kids.

"Yes sir, indeed. You need to get upstairs and take the tough meat for a potty break. The keys stay in the kitchen.

Cleeda?" Bertram entered the dining room, where sat a cup of hot broth he had been drinking.

Cleeda took Reece and Beo into the kitchen. She showed them the ring of keys and said to take one boy at a time, making sure the log stayed attached to their leg. "They's the two of them on the left-hand side. Dick and Dingle. If you don't watch 'em, they'll make it to the street and then you gotta pay by golly."

Reece took the keys and led the way upstairs. Beo then blocked the entrance to the stairs. Reece tried the keys, found the right one, and opened the first door. The smell hit him, sweat and pee. Sitting on a plank bed was a young guy, perhaps sixteen, plump and soft, with black hair. The red wallpaper hung in peels. No curtain covered the barred window, and the floorboards bucked in places. There was no closet, but a wooden chair held wads of clothing.

"Uh, Dick? Dingle?" asked Reece.

The boy, Dick, stared at his bare feet, which had long, yellow nails.

"Time for the bathroom." Reece felt terrible being this poor boy's jailer, but what could he do otherwise?

"Done gone," said Dick.

"Really?"

Dick pointed, and there was a newspaper in the corner with the evidence.

"You should wait or knock on the door when you need to go. You need to pee?"

"Yeah," said Dick. There was a short, thick log shackled to his left ankle.

"I'll carry the log."

Dick laughed and stood, his thin shoulders slumped.

Reece carried the log and followed Dick into the bathroom. He thought about putting the log down, but just held it as Dick took a long pee. Beo stood in the hall, frowning.

"He shit in his room," said Reece.

"What shall we do?" asked Beo.

"I ain't cleaning it." Dick smiled, showing two blackened front teeth.

Reece checked with Cleeda about the protocol, and she laughed, telling him it was his job, that he could very well "flush the turd" and that it would be a daily occurrence, no doubt.

After cleaning up Dick's mess, it was time for Dingle. He was thinner and had yellow hair with his front teeth bucked. His bright orange room was just as soiled as Dick's, but had a spittoon that he obviously peed in. Reece went through the motions with Dingle, learning his name, and stood back as Dingle seated himself on one of the three toilets and just stared into space. Reece tried to discern if Dingle was moving his bowels, but there were no sounds. He let ten very long minutes pass. Dingle was spoiling for time out of his room, so Reece squatted in the hall behind Beo, who was sitting, blocking the stairs. Another five minutes passed. Reece could hear shouting from below.

"Okay, Dingle, time to wrap it up. I hate to rush you," said Reece

Dingle hocked a big one and let it drop between his legs. Reece turned away as Dingle stood and buttoned up.

"Sure yer a tangler?" asked Dingle. "Seem kinda soft to me."

Somehow, that made Reece feel better. "Yeah, me and Beo, two tanglers from hell." He gave a short laugh.

"Yeah, right." Dingle shuffled back to his room, carrying his log. He went back to his bed and sat. "What's fer dinner, Glenda or Norbert?"

"Oh God, I was afraid of that." Reece looked at Beo, who was peering into the room. "Look, you just relax and take it easy. I'm a good guy," he whispered.

"You're the toughest meat of all," said Dingle.

Reece locked the door and sighed. "Are you thinking what I'm thinking?"

"Yes, they talk of meat and runaways. I am worried." Beo could touch the ceiling sitting down.

"Hey, you!" came from Cleeda downstairs. "Dinner's ready!"

"Uh oh," said Reece.

They descended the stairs and headed to the dining room, where everyone but Cleeda was seated, including the three children who looked hollow.

"Did you make 'em wipe real good?" asked Cleeda. "They don't like to wipe."

"Um, maybe next time," said Reece. "Do they really need logs tied to their legs?"

Bertram coughed. "Course they do. They'll run off otherwise, like those other two. Now sit down and eat."

Beo took a chair and pushed it against the wall. He could lean forward and reach the table with ease. "Thank you for the food," he said in his deep voice. He scanned the items on the table: a bowl of brown broth with bones, mashed potatoes, and then a roast of some sort, bleeding juices on its plate.

"Those potatoes look mighty fine," said Reece.

Clarity Stillwell had decided to fight fire with fire, hiring his own physicist, Dr. Newton Frasier, to shine a light on the Dahlia situation. Frasier was in the studio, along with Stillwell's wife, Patricia, who sat in her lavender chair like a Kewpie doll with red hair. Clarity dressed casually for the event, to appear more earthy, and looked like an adult Linus with glasses from *Peanuts*. As the director and technicians scuttled about, Clarity sat at his desk. He was cued. "Action!"

The opening montage of Clarity preaching at his mega-church played with its uplifting music, then a clip of him sitting on a stump in Guatemala surrounded by kids dressed in rags, ending with Clarity shaking hands with the President of the United States.

The camera opened with a wide shot of the stage, showing Dr. Frasier sitting to the left of Clarity, with Patricia off to the right, holding her King James Bible and smiling. Another camera zoomed in on Clarity, capturing his glare against the backdrop of the Christian Instinct Network, CIN. There was a fade, and the words "Make God's Earth Great Again," then a fade back to Clarity.

"My friends, and even if you're not a friend, welcome to today's show. God is working miracles through our network. Our church, Pilgrim Sanctorium, has had to add a second drive-through Starbucks to meet demand on Sundays and Wednesdays." He paused. "We Christians like our coffee...but what we really love is the Lord Jesus Christ."

A third camera captured Patricia. "Amen!" She held up the Bible.

"And the Lord loves being the Lord and taking care of his flock. I am your pastor, but Christ is our shepherd. Amen?" Clarity's neatly parted blond hair shimmered with hairspray.

"Amen!" said Patricia.

"And in the news, and across the land, we have the abomination of Organon, eating away at the very fabric of our God-fearing society. We've seen the news, the talk shows, and jibber jabber on this new thing called the internet. The Devil has amassed his army and is flooding the land with lies and tomfoolery. We are drowning in propaganda and being sucked into downright evil."

"Amen!" said Patricia, her image now in the lower right corner of the screen.

"We've heard the ideas of the enemy's spokesperson, a physicist, this Desmond Ory, who claims to be a scientist but who sounds like a regular Pied Piper. They are bamboozling us with twisted facts, and we must respond with air strikes of our own. To that end, today we have Dr. Newton Frasier, a renowned creationist who can balance the facts with what's really going on. Welcome, Dr. Frasier." The camera zoomed out to include Frasier. His frowsy black hair was combed back, revealing a shining dome, but the hair around his ears bloomed. His maroon sweater over a button-up without a tie gave him a homey appearance.

"Thank you," said Frasier.

"You believe in God and you are a learned man," said Clarity.

"I think so."

"Hallelujah!" said Patricia.

"God created the heavens and earth six thousand years ago?" asked Clarity.

"That is correct," said Fraiser.

"Time travel is impossible, except for God. Am I correct?"

"Yes, you are."

"Is God a seven-year-old girl named Dahlia?"

"I really don't think so."

"Amen!" said Patricia.

"What do you make of this Desmond Ory, who is a tool of Organon? First, we had the Big Bang theory, and now we have what he calls his Tiny Bangs theory."

"Both scenarios doubt the truth that God created the Earth in six days. We have to work with that. As regards the Tiny Bangs theory, time cannot be the origin of anything, not even a mote of dust. There was never just nothing. There was God and not just time, as Ory claims. God is time, if that makes sense."

A text feed to donate and a phone number scrolled at the top of the screen.

"Yes, you have harpooned the whale and drowned the myth," said Clarity.

"I suppose I have," said Frasier. "Dr. Ory, if I may call him that, implies that there are infinite universes all created from time, beginning with just a single quantum, or can I just say tiny particle? Just one teeny weeny particle and a complete universe. These vacuous universes collide and become more complicated with each collision. It's actually quite an interesting...I mean, it's primarily preposterous."

"Praise Jesus!" Patricia radiated a warmth and fever, highlighted by her large red hairdo. The production staff stood stiffly, always waiting for the next thing to happen.

"Amen!" said Clarity, and the interview continued for another twenty minutes.

"So, to end this, we need to absolutely refute this idea of Dahlia. She, or it, cannot be allowed a foothold in the imagination of the uneducated masses. God is God, and that is that."

There was a cut to Patricia with her Bible: "To our God and Father be glory forever and ever. Philippians chapter four, verse twenty."

"Ab-so-lute-ly, Reverend Stillwell," said Frasier. "How could a seven-year-old girl create the universe in six days? Why she can't even make her own breakfast. She may not be able to tie her own shoes. How could this wonderful world we live in come from the mind of a little girl? It just doesn't make sense."

"That's the way a scientist who loves the Lord talks," said Clarity. "I mean, could a girl come up with the Declaration of Independence?"

"I highly doubt it," said Frasier.

Glenelle Lock dialed Clyde Markush from her office at the NIMH. She had spoken with the key players, including Jacob Jacobi and General Tom Watkins. She was beat with coordinating a national study of late-onset schizophrenia, a genuine interest of hers, and keeping up with Organon. If anyone had their finger on the pulse of Organon and its implications, she did. She wasn't a big drinker, but had lately been drinking herself to sleep with expensive red wine. Her head felt a little fuzzy, and her cigarette break was wearing off.

"Hello, Clyde, some updates for you." Glenelle fingered a turtle brooch on her plaid suit coat.

"Hey, Glenelle. I'm all ears."

"First, there's progress with the decommissioned Griffiss Air Force Base. It looks like there's a deal in the making to lease it to the CIA for a dollar per year for fifty years. Of course, this all hinges on the passing of the Senate and House bills that would provide operational funding."

"How's that going? I've been too busy to watch the news." Markush sat in his office, wearing his down jacket, wondering why it was so cold.

"There's opposition, of course, primarily in the Senate Subcommittee on Military Construction and Veterans Affairs, and Related Agencies, specifically Senator Dalby McCutcheon of Wyoming. He's a big supporter of the religious right and has come out publicly denouncing Dahlia and Organon as the devil's work."

"That's to be expected," said Markush. "What is our PR

genius, Sherri Loveless, doing about this?"

"She's still riding the transparency train. We spoke on Tuesday, and her new idea is to somehow humanize Dahlia, make her more real."

"Kind of like bringing Jesus Christ to earth to make God more real."

"I thought of that. If we can accept Dahlia as a real little girl, but one who is misguided and needs help, that's what we need to work on. People need to feel bad for her in some way," said Glenelle.

"Even serial killers have their adoring fans. Look at Ted Bundy. Women want to marry him."

"God, Markush, don't even make that comparison. Bury that. We need sympathy."

"I get it." Markush doodled on his desktop calendar, noting the requests for interviews.

"There's been another interesting development. One that may hurt us or help us. There are six groups that we know of, who have started churches intending to worship Dahlia. A group in California, Bakersfield, no less, has begun work on what would be a Bible dedicated to the teachings of Dahlia. The group is small but making waves."

"Holy cow," said Markush.

"Yeah. The leader is Simon Klinefelter, a former polygamist from Utah. He seems to be married to most of the women in his group of eighty or so. They have a meat processing plant in Bakersfield, but most of the group lives on a vast ranch near McKittrick, right along the San Andreas fault."

"What's their angle?"

"Pretty simple, that Dahlia is the true God. That the replacements are her angels on earth, and that we should worship them as prophets or something like that. If I were you, I would expect to be hearing from them. Fort Knox might become a weird Mecca of sorts."

"Huh, I received a strange letter from a group in California. I just glanced at it. I'm getting dozens of letters every day. So much to do."

"It surprised me that you got the okay to send Mia to school. How's that going?"

"Ha, Mia is a handful. She's so damn confrontational. We've had at least three phone calls from the principal. Mia's a real bully, but can be so sweet at times. Without testing her, she fits the mold for a mixed personality disorder, very antisocial. Kristin takes the brunt of her abuse, and I'm afraid she might break at some point."

"Monitor her, Markush. Mia's a valuable asset."

"I will. She's a smart cookie. I was afraid she wouldn't be able to learn, but she's a whiz with math and spelling. She hates her music class, though."

"This whole idea of music and Dahlia isn't clear to me," said Glenelle.

The line from the medical unit buzzed. "Hold on." He took the call and went back to Glenelle.

"Sorry, just some excitement on the unit. Clark Peters has returned from a two-day seizure. I'll need to check on him soon."

"The music?" asked Glenelle.

"The music. Yes, the music. There are those among us with unique musical abilities that Dahlia doesn't understand. I think the music attracts Dahlia to her victims. It's the change in their daughters' music that tips off parents that their child has been replaced. Arthur says that music is the most perfect of the arts, that music is an ideal quality that can exist without us."

"You never told me this, and I've been wondering. Are you one of them?"

"One of whom?" asked Markush

"Like one of the kids who were mapped by Dahlia."

"I'd like to think I'm that important, but no, I haven't been mapped. I don't have the mesh."

"This is your life, Markush, Organon, time travel, replacements, Returnees, Dahlia."

"It is. Ever since I discovered the writings of Harold Leyman in grad school, working on my PhD, I've been hooked. No one else was interested. Everyone thought he was a lunatic."

"I have a collection of his writings, only one that was published, but that was on schizophrenia among the elderly."

"Which is interesting. We have a couple of patients here who are definitely living with schizophrenia, especially Clark Peters. After the murders of the replacements, the murderers all exhibit signs of acute schizophrenia, even though they often have no history of mental illness."

"We'll have to talk about that more, Markush."

"Look, the medical unit is calling me again, so I need to hop off for now. Keep me updated."

"Will do...Clyde."

The next day, Reece awoke in his lumpy bed. Beo had put his mattress on the floor, his legs shooting off the end. Bertram had asked to see their tangling papers and had been quite upset that they had not registered with the tangler office, which could result in a fine.

"Rise and shine!" Cleeda knocked like a maniac on their door.

"Shit," said Reece.

Beo lifted his massive head from the flat pillow.

The door opened, and Cleeda appeared. "The tough meat's got to go potty, you slow pokes. I done fed 'em and let out the tender meat. You 'uns need to get on it."

"Uh, yes ma'am," said Reece. "Is there breakfast for us?"

"Yeah, but after you git them boys pottied. Now get a move."

"Shall we?" asked Beo.

They repeated the chore, first taking Dick and then Dingle to the bathroom. Dingle had defecated in his room on the bare wooden floor, and Reece cleaned it up with a filthy rag. There was no soap in the bathroom, and he washed his hands as best he could. Dingle had refused to leave the bathroom, and Beo had reached in with one hand and solved the problem.

Breakfast consisted of bread and a clear, brown broth, accompanied by a glass of milk.

"Why don't y'all drink your broth? Good fer yer body," said Cleeda. Bertram had left early for the cement plant.

"The bread is delicious," said Beo.

"Yes," said Reece.

"If you ain't gonna eat it, then I'm not gonna serve it."

"We have simple appetites," said Reece. "We're vegetarians."

"Vegewhatians? Why, that's just plain crazy after all the trouble we go to for good meat. I got more growing right in here." She pointed to her large belly that was obscured by her breasts.

"I suppose that is exciting," said Reece. He pushed the glass of milk aside. "Is there water? I really like water." He looked at Beo.

"Well, get it yerself from the kitchen, why don't you? Have mercy." Cleeda shuffled to the kitchen with the bowls of broth and poured them into a large pot on the coal stove.

After drinking their fill of water, Reece and Beo made their way to the tangler office to get their papers. They walked a half mile through winding streets, asking directions along the way. Twice, they saw groups of teenagers scatter at their approach. The two-story tangler office, made of cement walls painted a bright turquoise, spanned the entire block. Inside was spotless, with a counter and two hallways going left and right, each with a staircase.

"What can I do you for?" asked a man in overalls, wearing a red cotton jacket. His name was Juniper. There was a logo of a mother and child on the left breast with "Tangler" in white letters on the back.

Reece explained the situation, that they were from the "big city," and they were looking to work as tanglers. The man didn't ask for any ID and pulled out two forms, which they filled out. The pencil in Beo's hand looked like a toothpick. There were no fees, and he handed Reece a red jacket from a closet behind him. It was obvious they didn't have a jacket large enough for Beo, but the man just said for them to keep together.

There was a commotion outside, and a skinny man led in a girl of fourteen with a rope around her neck. Reece stared at the girl, who seethed foam between her lips.

"Got me a good one," said the tangler.

"Well, there she be, the Toodler girl." Juniper turned and took down a ring of keys from behind him.

"I hate you!" screamed the girl. She struggled, but the tangler yanked the rope. Her face went purple, and she fell to her knees.

"Get yerself up and don't be a crybaby," said the tangler.

Juniper reached under the counter and pulled out a steel box. He unlocked it and withdrew three bills and two coins, put them in a neat brown envelope with a button and string, and handed it to the tangler. Together, they walked the girl upstairs, where she was shoved into a cell with three other girls. Reece and Beo walked outside onto the dusty concrete street. The enormous sun loomed in the west.

"Damn, that's hard," said Reece. "I wonder how many they have up there. Maybe Mia is up there."

"Very sad," said Beo. "I hate to see it. But now we are a part of this system."

"It seems you get paid, and we do need money."

"What has to be done has to be done."

The tangler exited and walked away, whistling, the rope looped around his shoulder.

"While we're here, I need to look upstairs, just in case,"

said Reece.

He and Beo walked back inside.

"Forget something?" asked Juniper.

"Hey, I just want to check and see if you might have two boys here." Reece pulled out the photos with the boy's names written on the back.

"You ain't been tangling without a license, have you?" asked Juniper.

"No, no, just getting started is all," said Reece.

"I don't recognize 'em, but you can have a look." He hitched his thumb toward the stairs.

Reece and Beo ascended the clean cement stairs and found themselves at the end of a long hallway with forty cells, twenty to the left and twenty to the right. There were windows at the ends of the hallway, and the light was very dim. They approached a cell with a steel door and a barred window. The smell of urine and feces was quite strong. Beo stooped as usual.

Squinting, Reece peered into the first cell. He saw lifeless bodies sitting on mats, seven teenage girls sitting shoulder to shoulder as if for warmth. There were two buckets. "Y'all okay?" asked Reece. He wanted to do something, but what?

No one replied. Reece knew Mia was not there. "Anybody hear of a little girl named Mia?"

"Get the fuck away," said a small but firm voice.

"Right," said Reece.

They continued down the hallway, Reece peering into the cells but seeing only older girls and boys, all in the same filthy conditions. But then he spotted a young girl, and his heart raced. "Mia? Mia?"

A few faces turned toward the small window, but no response.

"You, the little girl, what's your name?" asked Reece. "Please? I can help."

"Help? How in hell can you help? You're a goddamn tangler," said one of the shadows.

"Just tell me the little girl's name. I want to help. Trust me."

The little girl didn't look up.

"Her name's Lila," said the same girl. "We woke up one morning and there she was."

"Lila?" asked Reece. "Lila, how did you get here?"

Lila seemed to come from a deep sleep. "I don't know. I want my daddy and mommy."

Reece turned to Beo. "She's one of us. She's been replaced. Lila. I have to ask Markush." He noted the number on the cell, twenty-one.

They completed the length of the hall and made their way downstairs.

"Did ye recognize 'em?" asked Juniper with bright eyes.

"No, but there's a little girl named Lila in cell twenty-one. We're looking for her too," said Reece.

"Yeah, that's a curious one. Just showed up out of nowhere," said Juniper.

"She's wanted, from the big city," said Reece. "We can split the profits? What do you say? I'll get her back home. She's some real good tender meat, for sure."

Juniper thought. The girl, Mia, had messed up his books, and he was eager to balance them. "Well, you got a deal." He fished out cash from the box and handed it to Reece, then made an entry in his ledger. "I'll get her for you. You got a rope?"

"Uh," said Reece.

"I have." Beo withdrew a length of rope from around his robe.

Markush suspended the group therapy sessions, but all the patients were being encouraged to get out of their beds and walk the hallways and spend time in the dayroom, much to Carletta's delight. Helmut Grayson was still the wildcard and had to be restrained when he was up in a chair. Markush had asked Emma to work on day shift, more or less as a nursing assistant, and this was her first day. There was the issue of the other Emma in room six, who had been shot in Ethiopia and who was recovering slowly.

The unit buzzed with activity. Four patients lounged in the dayroom, playing poker, and Clark Peters sat in a wheelchair in the hallway near the exit door, bumping into Shark's rolling chair, fumbling his words, and looking at the ceiling with wonder in his eyes. The guards were not excited about this more active approach toward the patients.

"So, Emma," said Markush, "we have a full house, as you can see. I'll let Debbie give you a rundown of who is here, but you know about the other Emma. I think you should meet her first." He pointed at the camera screen for room six.

"Jesus," said Emma. "Looks like me. How did she wind up here?"

"She just showed up on the lawn outside. She hasn't been able to speak just yet. We sampled her clothing for pollen, and the results indicate she had come from Ethiopia. Reece recognized her as the Emma he had known, but she has to be from another universe. The Emma he knew now lives in Hueytown, Alabama. So, there's three of you on this planet that we know of."

"Jesus," said Emma.

They exited the nursing station and arrived at room six. Emma lay in bed, her head raised to forty-five degrees. She did not have the shaved head or EEG leads, as she did not seize, or at least not yet.

"Emma?" asked Markush. He went to one side and Emma to the other.

Emma opened her eyes slowly and looked straight ahead, then toward Markush. Her lips moved, but no sound.

"Emma, you're doing well," said Markush. "We're taking good care of you. I have someone I want you to meet. Her name is Emma, too."

"Hi, Emma," said Emma. She seemed ready to cry. She took Emma's hand in her own. There was slight movement of the fingers. A TV game show played at low volume.

Emma shifted her gaze to Emma. There was a slight movement of her facial muscles into what could be a smile.

"I'm gonna be working with you," Emma said. "Take good care of you."

Emma's other arm lifted, and she placed her hand on Emma's hand.

"Very good," said Markush. "She's regaining motor control. Look, I have to go, but you two get to know one another." He left, winking at Emma.

"You were in Ethiopia?" asked Emma.

There was a slow nod from Emma.

"Yeah, me too. I was a nurse working in a clinic, where I ran a feeding program. Is that what you were doing?"

Emma nodded again.

"I can only guess who shot you. In the village I worked in, there was this evil administrator named the Snake."

Emma's eyes widened, and she tried to speak. Her mouth formed a word.

"I knew it," said Emma. "He probably had a different name, but it was him. Am I right?"

Emma nodded and squeezed Emma's hand. For half an hour, Emma lingered with Emma, telling her story, how she had been transported to this world. Debbie, Emma's nurse, entered the room.

"Good to have you with us," said Debbie. "You two getting along? You can help me turn her. Gonna get her up in the chair later."

"Yeah, just telling her my history. I'm sure the Snake shot her, or maybe he had another name. I'll bet the Abba Paulos sent her back. That's the only way that I can see."

"Dr. Markush had a similar thought," said Debbie. "Gonna turn you, honey." She took the draw sheet and pulled Emma toward her. Emma took the foam wedge inside a pillowcase and placed it against her back.

"Let's push a can of Ensure," said Debbie. She handed the can to Emma. "The syringe is on the table."

Emma drew up 60 ccs of tan liquid Ensure and slowly pushed it through Emma's feeding tube. Emma made swallowing motions, feeling the liquid enter her stomach.

"After the Ensure, push a hundred ccs of water," said Debbie. "She still gets most of her fluid through the IV. It would be great if you could give her a bath, and then I have some other stuff you can do. Just check in with me or Carletta or Jim."

"Sure thing," said Emma. "Like taking care of myself. Very strange."

"Everything is strange at Organon." Debbie laughed.

Spinoza said that God can play the role of a person. I have now observed three separate cases that baffle me. Three men who have murdered their daughters but who say that the daughter murdered was not the actual daughter. They claim that their daughters have been replaced, and they all mention Dahlia as the God behind this. One has communed with Dahlia in what he describes as a Cylinder, a vacuous space that seems infinite. He spoke with her, Dahlia inquiring, strangely, who her mother was. The subject did not know the answer prior to entering the Cylinder, but it came to him there. Dahlia's mother is time, a most unique solution into which I have been putting a lot of thought.

Dahlia is a little girl, perhaps the same age as the "replacements," being seven years old. According to the subjects, she is intelligent but wanton and refuses to believe that time is her mother. Kant thought that time "is nothing but the form of inner sense." Time does not exist without a person sensing it, but I now know this to be wrong. There was a time when there was nothing, nothing but time. Einstein made this more real. There are instances in nature that we cannot sense, such as atoms. They exist, yet we do not sense them. Yet Einstein does not intuit that time can stand alone but thinks that time hinges on a state of motion. Wittgenstein says that "space, time and colour are forms of objects." He is getting close, yet time is not an object. Time is the absence of objects in its purest form. He also said that *"The limits of my language* mean the limits of my world." My world is no longer limited.

With the burden of time came the single quantum, spilling out to form a universe. Suddenly, everything is possible, yet there must be a knower to know this. The power to know was upon us, and the knower came into being, Dahlia. But why a young girl with evil intentions? I've learned from my subjects that Dahlia has a sister, a goodly girl, different from her twin. Why there must be good versus evil, I am not sure. It is a kind of *faute de mieux,* a want for the lack of something better. Dahlia and this sister are like the microcosm that we cannot sense. Instead of a discrete knowing, we rely on probability. Dahlia and her sister are a probability, one that I must now accept as significant. *Dear heavenly Dahlia...*

Juniper tied the rope around Lila's neck, but as soon as they were out of sight, Reece undid the knot and set Lila free. She was big for her age, had oily black hair with bangs, and narrow brown eyes. She wore light-blue jeans and a striped, yellow polo shirt.

"Thank you, mister," said Lila. She needed a bath. "He's tall."

They were standing on the road in front of a café. Reece could smell hot coffee.

"You hungry, Lila?"

"Yeah, all I had was a piece of bread and a cup of water. I just want to go home and see my mommy and daddy."

"We'll talk about that," said Reece. "Beo, you up for some coffee?"

"Yes, and now we have money."

"We have three hundred firkins, according to the bills," said Reece. "Not sure what that'll buy."

The café was rather small, with just three tables made of barrels. Beo tried to make himself as small as possible, and Reece perused the menu. He found what appeared to be a soup with bread for Lila. There was a glass case filled with bric-à-brac and a thin, sad woman behind it. She had a small bosom and did not wear the apron with weights. Behind her were mugs and glasses, along with the town's emblem of a mother and child. To her left was a large percolator on a charcoal stove, and a tiny kitchen through a door.

"We'll have two coffees and then the soup with bread,"

said Reece.

"My, what tender meat," said the lady. She gave Lila a knowing smile. "He a tangler?" she said, pointing at Beo.

"That is true," said Beo. "The red jackets are too small."

"I see," said the lady. Her name was Irma. "That's two free coffees and the sandwich and soup. She gonna have a drink? How about a Dr. Feisty for the young one?"

"What's that?" asked Lila. "Is it sweet?"

"Yeah, a soda drink, real sweet." Irma batted her eyes, as if talking to a queen.

"Sounds good," said Reece.

Irma went into motion, drawing down two large mugs of coffee. She then made the Dr. Feisty with soda water and a thick black syrup. There seemed to be no ice in Gordian. The soup and bread appeared in a window near the door.

"Three fifty for the food and drink," said Irma. "Not many young 'uns get such a treat."

Reece handed her the bill, and she made change. "Free coffee for tanglers? Anything else free for tanglers?"

"No, just coffee," said Irma. "I wish I had one just like her. She's a real doll, real tender meat."

Reece and Lila sat at one of the small tables, but Beo had to sit on the floor, leaning against three burlap sacks filled with coffee beans.

"What's in this soup?" asked Lila. "Tastes like it has cinnamon in it." She continued to eat without getting an answer. She sipped her sparkly drink. "Tastes like vanilla. That lady keeps staring at me."

"She just likes you," said Reece. "Lila, how did you get here?"

"Dahlia's hiding me from my daddy. I lived in a cage in the circus. There were lots of little girls, and the people would come and stare at us. I didn't like it." She picked up the bowl and drank the soup. "This is good."

Reece had an idea. "What's your last name?"

"It's Grayson," said Lila. "Lila Grayson."

"I'll remember that," said Reece. "Coffee good?"

Beo took another sip. "I prefer the coffee of Ethiopia, but one can't be a chooser in our circumstances."

"Right," said Reece. "Lila, have you met Dahlia?"

"Yes. The Abba Paulos sent me to her. I couldn't see her, just heard her voice. Everything was swirly and bright. She wants to know who her mommy is."

"Do you know?" asked Reece. He held his coffee mug with two hands.

"I'm not sure. I think her mommy is time, but that doesn't seem right because Dahlia got mad at me and sent me here to that jail."

"If only she would believe," said Beo, "then this whole game of stealing little girls could be over."

"I just want to go home. I'm tired." She finished her soup and ate her bread, taking little sips of her Dr. Feisty.

"I think I can get you home," said Reece. "I'll try, anyway. Okay, hold on, I'm going to try something. This worked once before. Everybody ready?" He was about to say it. "No, not yet. We have to look for Mia first."

"And we must look for the two runaways," said Beo. He placed his empty mug on the table.

"I wonder if we can bring her back to the house?" asked Reece. "I'll let you sleep on my bed."

"I was sleeping on straw in the cage at the circus," said

Lila.

"That sucks," said Reece. He watched Lila finish the last of her drink. "For now, we have to keep looking for the runaways to keep our room."

"I may have an idea," said Beo. "Show her the photos."

Reece pulled the two photos from his back pocket. "What's the plan?"

Since it was near and Afewerki was there, Markush had Sherri Loveless set up a speaking engagement for Arthur at Eastern Kentucky University. The event would take place in Brock Auditorium, which held 750 seats. By the day, Arthur was growing more casual and had even begun to say "y'all" with flair. Markush had acquired an unmarked van from the base motor pool, as reporters were watching for his gray Volvo wagon. His Jaguar was locked up in the garage at his off-base house. In the van were Markush, Arthur, Emma, Kristin, and Mia, who had received a stern lecture on how she should behave.

Afewerki waited in the lobby, standing stock still, waiting for the gang to arrive. For a few days, reporters had accosted him, but his reluctance to talk had thinned the efforts to interview him. He saw one of his ESL teachers and waved a small wave. When he saw Markush and the others walk through the doors into the high-ceilinged lobby, he was all smiles and broke into a run, but there was a ring of cameras around the group with reporters shouting Arthur's name.

"You are here!" he said. "Oh, thanks to God." Afewerki muscled his way beyond the reporters as if he were taking the last seat on a crowded bus. "Emma!"

Before she could say anything, Afewerki was on his knees, tying her loose shoelace.

"Afewerki, no!" said Emma.

"It is okay," he said as he finished.

Arthur was backed into an alcove where he stood with

his hands folded in front of him. Markush just let happen what would happen. There was an hour or so until Arthur would speak.

"Arthur, you seem to be adjusting to life in this universe," said one reporter.

"Yes, quite well. I find the people friendly and curious."

"Arthur!"

"Arthur!"

The group of twelve reporters tussled to be up front as cameras flashed and recorded. A small woman in a black dress suit and heels stuck out her hand, and Arthur shook it. "Arthur, what will you be speaking about tonight?"

Arthur wore new black Levis and a colorful sweater with a red down vest. His shaved face and trimmed hair withdrew twenty years from his chiseled facial features.

"I am here tonight to speak of the strange and mysterious Dahlia and her adventures. That is what everyone wants to hear about. I will need a bit of room to breathe, though." He smiled, but his face registered mild distress at the pressing crowd. At the behest of Markush, two security guards intervened and extricated him from the crush.

"Arthur, this way." Markush pulled Arthur along to a book signing station. There was a table set up with a white cloth and fifty English translations of Arthur's magnum opus: *The World as Will and Representation,* in two volumes. A young woman named Dawn, with a bookish gaze, stood there wringing her hands. She worked with the campus bookstore.

"You're handling the signing?" Markush felt Arthur being pulled away from him. "The people have to make a line."

"Yes, is he ready?" Dawn looked small, standing beside the stacks of books.

The vast lobby, the floor polished, was filling quickly. Quite enjoying the attention, Arthur had resumed giving interviews.

"Arthur! Arthur, how is it you speak English?"

Arthur entertained the question and smiled. "I do not know the answer to that, other than my new language comes through the agency of Dahlia."

"Arthur!"

Kristin, Emma, Afewerki, and Mia formed a tight group and held their ground. "What the hell is happening!" said Mia. Two reporters were whispering and looking her way.

Markush intervened and took Arthur by the hand. "Arthur, we have books you need to sign."

"Oh yes, the books. I'm eager to see them!" He spoke loudly over the din of the bustling crowd filled with suits and a growing contingent of students. Cameras flashed as Arthur momentarily struck a thoughtful pose.

Arthur arrived at the table and examined the blue books, Volume One, and the red books, Volume Two. He glanced at the name of the translator, a fellow named Payne.

"Mr. Schopenhauer," said Dawn. "If you'll take a seat, I'll take payment for the books and then pass them to you to sign." She blushed.

"Yes, little creature, you are very kind to assist." Arthur sat in the stackable chair behind the table. "I do look like such a stodgy old man," he said, gazing at the book covers.

The two police officers were shouting for people to form a line, and something like a line formed. The reporters set up a perimeter off to Arthur's right, cameras flashing. "Arthur! A big smile!"

Outside, the crowd was backing up as it pressed toward the six columns of the building that held the auditorium. There had been no ticket sales, just a few announcements in the local media that had gone viral.

Arthur took the first books from Dawn. There were five pens on the white tablecloth. He looked up at the man, who was wearing a blue suit and a red tie. "I thank you," said Arthur, and he wrote his name with a flourish. Markush stood behind him, thinking that the crowd would smother them.

"Can you make that out to 'Emily, my dear wife'?" asked the man.

Arthur wrote "to Emily, my dear wife" and felt that he had made an error. The man was trying to shake his hand, and Arthur obliged with a concerned smile. It was all Dawn could do to keep up. She took cash and credit cards, placing the receipts inside the books, pushing them toward Arthur.

A semicircle of reporters now faced the other Returnees and Kristin.

"This is a shit show!" said Mia.

"Mia!"

"Mia Myers!"

"Oh no," said Kristin. She clutched Mia by the shoulders. "Don't say anything."

"Let me go," said Mia. She stuck out her tongue at a camera as it flashed.

"Mia, are you an alien!" shouted a stout blonde with a microphone.

"Stop!" said Kristin.

"Did your father kill you?"

"I'll kill you!" said Mia.

"What a hell," said Afewerki, wearing a new EKU cap.

"We gotta get out of here." Wearing tennis shoes, Emma was ready to run.

They stood pressed to the wall beneath a portrait of a former university president. One of the campus police officers saw their dilemma and intervened. "You guys need to back off and give them some room!" he shouted at the reporters. He had already called for backup. "Come with me!" he said, and the group fell in behind him, not sure of where they were going.

Arthur's books sold out within forty minutes. The entire group was backstage in a small lounge with mirrors and spare lights. Arthur paced, working off the frenzy of excitement.

"I keep learning," said Markush. "The whole world is here, a packed house. I'm sorry I let the crowd get to you," he said to a rattled Kristin. She looked lovely in a dark-blue pinafore dress over a white sweater.

"Like a carnival," said Kristin. "They wanted Mia badly. She just can't be out like this, unprotected."

"Oh, Mother," said Mia. "Maybe now I can get my front-row seat at school. I'm more famous than that damn Cecily."

"Don't call me mother," said Kristin. "I'm sorry." She seemed on the verge of weeping.

Afewerki and Emma sat in a corner, talking about the clinic back in Godo, and the work that remained to be done.

"Arthur, are you ready?" Markush wore one of his two suits with a bow tie. "Should be less than five minutes. The university president will introduce you."

"My mind is racing with possibilities. My lectures were never anything of this magnitude and were poorly attended. I do think the tables have turned." Arthur laughed.

"Do you have notes?" asked Markush.

"I simply have the tip of my tongue, and that will suffice. I do think that I am learning what the people would like to hear."

"Dahlia and more Dahlia," said Markush.

"Precisely," said Arthur. "Perhaps with a subtle flair of my philosophy, but not too much. I had the feeling that those who bought my books had little interest in the contents and merely wanted my signature. One fellow had me dedicate the book to his cat. Amazing."

"Old Arthur's getting a hard on," said Mia. Kristin had picked up a brush, combing her reddish blonde hair over and over. "Don't skin me, Mother."

A woman from the publicity office, known as Kluge, arrived out of breath. "Professor Schopenhauer?" She had neat bangs and small teeth like ivory corn. "Come with me. The rest of you can sit behind the curtain, but please, don't let anyone see you."

The group filed out, led by Kluge. They arrived behind a dark maroon curtain, where there were chairs. The university president, Doug Lindesfarne, had taken the stage and stood behind the podium. To his right was an organ with its pipes. There was a great ruckus in the packed house. His initial words went unheard.

"Ladies and gentlemen!" he said for the third time. The crowd settled down. "Tonight, as part of our Humanities Lecture Series, we have the world-renowned Professor Arthur Schopenhauer. We all know that he is one of the Returnees, perhaps hailing from another universe, but alive and in the flesh nonetheless." He thanked donors and gave a brief history of the theatre auditorium. He looked back and got a thumbs up from Kluge. "Ladies and gentlemen, Arthur Schopenhauer."

There was tremendous applause and even whistles. "You're on," said Kluge. "Speak into the microphone, okay?"

Arthur understood and walked through the curtain onto the stage that bowed out slightly in front. The overall light dimmed, and a spotlight settled on his stately but casual figure as he made the podium his own. He looked out over the audience on the lower level, split into three sections of fixed theater chairs that curved away from the stage like sound waves. The lights blinded him, but he relished in the fresh applause. Shading his eyes, he raised his arms and gazed into the packed balcony. For a solid minute, there was clapping and an occasional hoot, and he just let the din die of its own accord until there was silence.

Beo suggested sending Lila with the photos and a small supply of cash. The roving gangs of teenagers would not fear her and might betray one of their own with a bribe. Beyond that, they would just see what happened.

They walked the streets, passing the tightly spaced homes and businesses, all painted with bright colors, except for the occasional cement or brick building. Most people were walking, with a few on bicycles. A giant sun glowed orange in the sky, seeming to give little heat, but the weather was warm and the air placid. They crossed a street and came to a park with a concrete statue of a mother and child. There was a central area with benches and shrubs.

On a wooden bench sat a portly woman. Her apron was unfastened in front, with her massive breast exposed and resting on her lap. Attached to the saucer-sized nipple was an infant swallowing milk, his mouth foamy. She paid them no mind. The benches were arranged in a circle, and the three passed to the other side, somewhat hidden by the tall shrubbery.

"Lila, you'll need to go up and down the street and look for groups of kids," said Reece. "Show them the pictures and offer them five firkins, that's like five dollars, I think, if they can identify the boys in these photos."

Lila took the photos. "Are they bad boys?"

"No, they have just run away from home," said Beo.

"Yeah, their parents want them back," said Reece. "We'll stay here in the park and wait for you. So that you don't get lost, just walk down the street as far as you can and then walk back."

"Why did they run away from home?" Lila looked small in her jeans and polo shirt.

"We don't really know," said Reece.

"When will you take me back to my mommy and daddy?"

"We have to find a way first. We're working on it. But for now, we need to find these boys," said Reece.

With the pictures and money, Lila turned left onto the street. Every adult she passed gave her a strange look, and one man asked what she was doing. She explained her mission, and that seemed to satisfy him. Passing rows of tenements, she walked several blocks when she saw a group of kids duck into a side street. She picked up her pace. The corner was blind, and as soon as she turned, a gang surrounded her.

"Who are ye?" asked a lanky teen, looking like Oliver Twist with a homemade cap of felt. "Ye look different. Ain't seen ye before."

Lila's eyes widened. "I'm Lila. I'm looking for my friends." She showed the pictures to the teen. The group of ten pressed in closer. Lila could feel their heat.

"Ha, that's old Laramore and his brother Mickey," said Oliver Twist, who was the ringleader.

"Why are ye looking fer them?" asked another. "They be outside the east gate, in the caves."

"Hush yer mouth!" said Oliver.

"Oh, I have some money," said Lila. She pulled out the bill.

Oliver plucked the money from her hand in a flash.

"That's mighty fine. Thank you kindly."

"Hey!" said Lila. "I have to find them. They're my friends."

"They don't want to be finded," said Oliver. "You leave be what needs to leave be. Yer one of us now. Got any more firkins?"

"No," said Lila. "I have to go now."

Reece and Beo decided Lila had been gone for too long and went to look for her.

"Damn, we can't lose her. Dahlia replaced her, like Mia. Maybe this was a dumb idea." Reece struggled to keep up with Beo's long strides.

"We will find her," said Beo.

They passed a butcher shop and a row of single-story buildings selling strange fruits and vegetables. They glanced down each side street but saw nothing, but when they passed a three-story home painted pink, there they were. Beo leaped forward and grabbed one by the collar. The others galloped off with Oliver in the lead, leaving behind Lila, who was crying.

The boy thrashed, and Beo grabbed him around the waist and held him above the ground.

"Traitor!" yelled the boy named Karl, and he reeked of dust and sweat. His black, beady eyes sat close together. He went limp like a lamb in Beo's grasp.

"Lila, you okay?" Reece knelt in the lane and hugged her. "It's okay. We won't do that again. I'm sorry."

"They were mean and took my money," said Lila. She let Reece wipe away her tears.

"It's okay," said Reece.

"I'll tell ye where they be," said Karl. "If ye let me go. Ye have to be kind sirs, to such a lowly lad as me."

Beo lowered Karl to the ground, gripping his arm.

"You saw the pictures?" asked Reece. "She showed you?"

"Yes, and criminy. They be Laramore and Mickey, hiding in the caves beyond the east gate," said Karl.

"That's great," said Reece. "Beo, tie your rope around his waist and let him lead the way."

On a Tuesday, the big players met at Organon to discuss an upcoming Senate hearing, where they would testify on behalf of Organon funding. The hearing was being led by Senator Dalby McCutcheon of Wyoming, Chair of the Senate Subcommittee on Military Construction and Veterans Affairs, and Related Agencies.

By noon, Agent Jacob Jacobi, General Tom Watkins, Dr. Glenelle Lock, Colonel Ignatius Lawrence, and Dr. Desmond Ory arrived at Fort Knox. Aside from Lock, this was the first time the others had visited Organon. After a brief tour of the long-term unit, where the two Reeces lay in their respective states, the group gathered in a stately conference room, which had never been used before. The room was oblong with walnut panels from floor to ceiling. A narrow, oval table with comfortable rolling chairs took the center of the room. Markush was present, as well as Dr. Mumford. After a few minutes of socializing, Glenelle Lock got the ball rolling.

"Listen up," she said. "The future of Organon is at stake, and we have to be on our toes for the hearing. Senator Mc-Cutcheon, as you know, is our primary barrier to the passing of Senate Bill 450, which, with House Bill 4103, will provide above-board funding for Organon. Currently, we have eight million for five years, with a million for staff in the next five years. That all happened before acquiring Griffiss Air Force Base. If the bills pass, we'll get the base for fifty years with four-hundred million for renovations."

"When would we acquire the base?" Jacobi looked

sharp in his dark blue suit with a black tie.

"Initial renovations are blocked out for fourteen months, but won't begin for six months pending the passing of the bills. We could occupy the base as early as August 1999." Glenelle sipped her bottled water.

"In the meantime, what will we be able to do about all of the cases we're stumbling across?" asked Markush.

"Good question," said Watkins. "There are over a thousand suspicious murders going back to the late nineteenth century."

"And eighty-two persons we have identified," said Glenelle, "who are currently incarcerated for murdering their daughters under suspicious circumstances. I suggest that Colonel Lawrence take charge of the investigations into those cases. The work for his lab is slow at present, and we need to keep those talented personnel of his busy."

"Glenelle, work is slow," said Lawrence, "but what if we have an influx of Returnees or new patients here at Organon? I don't want to get mired down in research." His silver hair glowed in the fluorescent light.

"Don't worry, we'll back you up. For the hearing, you need to be prepared to state that you are on the job. For now, the international cases will be on hold, but once the base is up and running, we can expand our horizons."

"It seems, Glenelle," said Jacobi, "that you're neglecting my expertise here. I think the CIA should be in charge of the murder investigations."

"What about a joint effort?" asked Watkins. "I agree with Jacobi. At the very least, he should be involved." Watkins was as thin as ever and looking famished.

Glenelle ran her hand through her short red hair. She

needed a cigarette.

"Okay, agreed," said Glenelle. "Let's put Jacobi in charge of case research with the personnel at Adelphi labs under Lawrence at his disposal. How does that sound?" Everyone murmured their approval except Dr. Ory, who seemed to be in his own world. "So, back to the actual hearing. We're going to be grilled. Senator McCutcheon is a hard-ass, dead set against the work of Organon. Each of you must present the facts and," she smiled, "with a straight face."

"What are his major concerns?"

Dr. Mumford's phone beeped, and she excused herself to check on a patient.

"Primarily, Dahlia," said Glenelle. "McCutcheon and many others see Dahlia as a rival to the idea of a Christian God. Uncharacteristically, he's extended his sympathy to the Islamic community, where there is also opposition."

"How do we counter that?" asked Watkins. "So far, I've just run press briefings with somewhat cooperative journalists. They love what I have to say. They love the transparency."

"Yes, we have to have a plan for adversity. The Christian right has acquired their own physicist, Dr. Newton Fraiser, to support their objections to Dahlia and time travel. Perhaps we should hear from Dr. Ory?"

Dr. Ory twiddled his thumbs, deep in thought. He wore an old camel-hair jacket that was too big for his shoulders but too small for his belly.

"Dahlia," said Dr. Ory. All eyes were on him. "For the purposes of this room, Dahlia is the closest we will ever get to God. She is merely a young girl, but she holds the keys to the unknown. Since the writings of Harold Leyman, I have been curious about a greater power that works among us, tying that in with a unified field theory of how the universes work. I am finding solutions within Dahlia to the Little Bangs theory, as it is known."

"That's great, but we can't really say that at the hearing, can we?" asked Jacobi.

"Are we not to be transparent here and speak the truth?" asked Ory. "If God created the heavens and the earth, then Dahlia is not God. You can say that with certainty. Dahlia only emerged after the first quanta were formed, and there arose a need for the possibility of everything to be contemplated. Dahlia did not form our solar system. That took an eternity of universal collisions, universes that through collision after collision accumulated the basic particles to form life. We can say truthfully that Dahlia is not God, but that she co-exists with God, if that is what they want to hear."

"Wow," said Markush. "But will that be enough?"

"Is Dahlia a kind of helpmate for God? Can we say that?" asked Glenelle.

"Perhaps, but I don't believe in God," said Ory. "God exists in the mind. Dahlia exists, out there, here, is alive and well, and willing to show herself."

"So," said Watkins, "It's best to deny that Dahlia is God, but that Dahlia exists and that she is actively engaged with the people of our planet. She's an alien of sorts."

Dr. Ory's face pained. "If that must be the official line to preserve our work, then it must be so." He closed his eyes and whispered, "Dahlia..."

With a rope around his thin waist, Karl led Reece, Beo, and Lila beyond the east gate back to the area of cedar trees and limestone outcroppings. They followed a cliff line of jagged rock that led downward through brush and briars.

"Yer going to let me go, right, sirs?" asked Karl, showing his moist buck teeth.

"If we find the boys, yes." Reece's tennis shoes were having a hard go at the rocky ground.

"I'm so tired," said Lila. "Can we rest?"

"Karl, how much farther?" asked Reece.

"About half a mile, sir."

"I should go ahead with Karl, and you can remain here with Lila," said Beo.

"Okay," said Reece.

Beo took the rope and fell in behind Karl. Along the way were declivities in the rock face to their left, one the size of a house. Beo peered inside and found a ring of rocks with charred wood, but no kids. Within ten minutes, Karl came to a stop and pointed at a sinkhole, which had a set of natural stone steps leading downward. An opening at the bottom was a meter across and about a meter in height.

"In there, sir," said Karl. He wiped sweat from his brow with his ratty hat.

"Will they come out?" asked Beo. His gigantic feet, clad with sandals, ached.

"Got to go in and catch 'em," said Karl. "They might've seen us coming. They's a dozen lives in the caves."

Beo saw the dilemma. He could not fit through the entrance. "You will go inside and flush them out." There was a large boulder he could hide behind.

"Right away, sir!" He watched with beady eyes as Beo untied the rope from his waist.

Karl stepped down to the cave entrance, which exhaled a cloud of cool air. He entered and disappeared. He stooped to navigate a tunnel of wet rocks. Where the tunnel led into the first chamber, he whistled three times. Against the far wall of the oval room, the sides piled with broken rocks, a match was struck and a candle lit.

"Who ye be?" came a young voice.

"It be me, Karl." He walked toward the light, careful of the mud and smooth, slick rock. Water dripped from the ceiling into a cold, clear pool.

"Aye, Karl," said the voice that belonged to a youth named Burlie. "What's the news?" Underneath the candle sat a crate of apple-like fruit. Old, soggy newspapers and broken glass lay about. The candlelight showed Burlie's round face with deep-set eyes.

"I give 'em the slip, I did," said Karl. "He's a big one, a giant, with another tangler and a young lass." He grabbed a fruit and bit into the soft flesh.

"Yeah, good job. You're a randy sort. Let's go back to the others."

Karl fell in behind Burlie, seeing mostly shadows as they navigated a rocky passageway. Gradually, there was more light, and soon Burlie was in a chamber of ten meters by twelve, with a stalactite in the middle. In the room, seated on wooden chairs with rotten bottoms, were six teens, four boys and two girls. One boy was Laramore, whom Reece and Beo were looking for. Karl retold his story, telling of giving the giant the slip.

"Them's the crackers," said a scraggly boy wearing a heavy wool coat.

"He's outside the hole, waiting. The tanglers are looking for you, Laramore, and Mickey, too."

"Well damned," said Laramore. His yellow hair flashed in the light of a kerosene lantern. "You led 'em to us, you filthy bastard. Ought to cut yer throat."

"I had to, otherwise it was the butcher. He don't know about the back door," said Karl, his breath short.

"I say we stick him," said one of the girls called Lawless. She dressed like a boy and wore a loose bonnet.

"A lot of sticking would be needed. He's a giant, I say, new to these parts, from the big city no doubt." Karl sat on a small boulder, feeling the wet and cold through his cotton pants.

"Hell, Karl, the back door's a ways off if ye don't forget, plus there's the Abba Paulos to deal with," said Burlie. "Ye said there was another tangler."

"Yeah, a ways back, with a little girl, tender meat. She seems to like 'em. Strange, if you ask me," said Karl.

"We gots to have a plan, boys," said Laramore. "I ain't going to no butcher."

"There's us girls," said Lawless. "Maybe the tanglers like a sweet young thing?"

"You leave it to us boys. They'll take you just as well as me," said Burlie.

Worried and with Lila rested, Reece took off in search of Beo. They found him standing above the sinkhole with a frown. He explained the situation to Reece.

"We may have lost him," said Reece. "You let him get away, Beo."

"I could not enter," said Beo. "Perhaps you should try." Beo pointed to the hole.

"I don't know. They could have weapons, plus I don't have a light."

"Are you scared, Mr. Reece?" asked Lila. "I'll go."

"Hell no. I mean heck no. If anybody goes, it'll be me. It's just too risky, it seems. There could be another way out, too."

"We are done here?" asked Beo.

"We could try and wait them out, but who knows how long that will take?" He surveyed the giant sun. "Dark will be soon. At least we know where to look. We can come back with a weapon."

Just in case, though, they waited for another half hour, but there was no Karl. Feeling duped, they made their way up the steep incline, found the path, and walked for an hour back to town, passing through the gate.

"How are we gonna explain Lila to Cleeda and Bertram?" Reece looked for landmarks to lead them back to their home.

"My, what a sweet and dear little thing," said a woman with a sweet smile. "You better tie her legs together lest she run off." She continued on her way.

"Why are people so mean?" asked Lila.

"Maybe because Dahlia is mean," said Reece. "She sets the tone."

It took another half hour, but they arrived and knocked. One of the younger children answered the door with eyes cast down. There was tremendous bellowing coming from within.

"What the...?" said Reece.

With Emma helping on day shift, things went more smoothly. She enjoyed the patients but had taken a special interest in her double, Emma.

"Coming up," said Emma.

"Easy does it," said Carletta.

Emma dangled in a Hoyer lift, headed for the reclining chair. Emma's eyes showed fright as she swung in the air, and she reached and held the straps suspending her.

"Whoa, great job, Emma," said Emma.

They rolled Emma's reclined chair to the dayroom where the TV was on and a game of rummy was underway between Daisy Klinger, James Kirkpatrick, and Timera Scocpol. Daisy had drowned an impostor, and James had ended the life of his impostor with his bare hands. Timera's murder had been the most brutal of all, having bludgeoned her daughter Lucinda's replacement with a swingblade. Carletta rolled the chair up next to the three.

"You guys. You guys!" said Carletta. "This Emma. She looking so good."

The three turned and greeted Emma, who managed a brief smile.

"You need anything to drink?" asked Emma to Emma.

Emma mouthed "ice cream."

"Ice cream, sure. Vanilla or chocolate?" asked Emma.

Emma mouthed "vanilla."

"No worries. I'll order that for you. You'll be able to eat regular food soon, and we can get you off that Ensure and pull that feeding tube out of your nose."

The three patients resumed their card game.

"You don't think Markush is getting rich off us, do you?" Daisy wore her blonde hair in pigtails and had a slim figure, despite her wide hips.

"I wonder that myself," said James. He was short, thirty-three, and looked like Jesus Christ.

"Now, why do you think that?" Timera's cards looked good, a possible royal flush.

"Just watch the damn TV," said Daisy. "Every time I turn it on, there's something about Markush and Organon. He's getting mighty famous. I like Dr. Mumford better. I don't see her on TV."

"He's using us for his own gain," said James. "It's like he's in charge of Dahlia. Everybody wants to know about Dahlia, and he's got the keys."

"I don't care what he makes as long as I'm not in jail for doing the right thing," said Timera. "You ready to show 'em?" She laid out her final card and took a stack of checkers they were using as chips.

Markush appeared, chatting with Emma and getting the update on the other Emma. "She's really clicking now that you've put your healing hands on her."

"I just can't get enough of her. I want her to talk so badly and tell her story, how she was shot, how she got here. It makes my story seem lame," said Emma.

"Not lame. You are history. The first group of verified Returnees. Keep up the good work." He headed to speak with Helmut Grayson, with whom anything was possible.

"Hey, Mr. Grayson. It's me, Dr. Markush." He surveyed the neat room, the cardiac monitor showing a normal sinus rhythm, and the EEG showing awake and alert.

"I know who the hell you are," said Grayson in his deep voice. He rested in the recliner with his wrists and ankles restrained loosely. Since Carletta had gotten him out of bed routinely, he had mellowed but was still cantankerous. "You're the big man. You dot the i's and cross the t's. You're a bowl of butterscotch pudding."

"Thanks a lot, I guess. Listen, I want to know more about this sister of Dahlia's. What can you tell me?" He knew what was coming.

"That'll cost you, dear doctor. I'm thinking some twenty-year, straight up, and I drink it from a glass and not through a goddamn straw."

"Right, I'll be right back." Markush headed to the break room inside the nursing station, where he kept the bottle of Scotch. There were no glasses, and he poured a stiff three fingers into a coffee cup. "Here you go, my friend."

"Untie me, Doc."

Markush untied Grayson's right hand and handed him the triple shot. Grayson looked deep into the amber liquid and then down the hatch in one gulp. For a second, he seemed paralyzed.

"Hoo whee! Might fine, mighty...fine." Grayson coughed. Before he knew it, Markush had re-tied the restraint to the chair. "Hey, you sneaky bastard."

"Okay, I got you the Scotch. Tell me about Dahlia's sister."

"You think you got me over a barrel, don't ya?"

"No, just curious, is all. You're the only one who's mentioned a sister, other than Harold Leyman."

"Okay, Doc. I'll tell you what I know. Got your listening ears on, Doc?"

Reece followed the loud moans and saw Cleeda flat on her back, on top of the dining room table, the tablecloth wadded beneath her. The weights from her apron had been tossed aside, denting a dish cabinet and marking the wood floor.

"Help me!" Cleeda pulled up her dress, and a tiny head was bulging her vulva.

"Hell, you're having a baby!" Reece went into nurse mode. "Beo, get a pillow or something and find a towel."

Beo did as he was told, not eager to see Cleeda's hairy privates. The three children had resumed their seats in the living room with frightened looks.

"It's a comin'," said Cleeda. She bore down, and Reece watched the wet head push out farther. He pulled her dress up higher, ready to catch the baby,

"Deep breaths," said Reece. "Push when you feel the contractions." He gave his hand to her, and she squeezed it hard.

In an instant, the baby slid out, face up, too quick for Reece to catch. "Lord, a tiny thing. A boy." He picked up the baby and held him on his forearm, face down, and patted his back vigorously. The baby coughed, turning blue, and then began screaming, still attached to the umbilical cord. "Beo, scissors, or a knife!"

Beo dumped a pile of towels on a chair. He had grabbed a cushion from the living room and dropped it on the floor. "A knife!" He squeezed into the kitchen, where there were plenty, and returned with quite a large and sharp blade.

Reece retrieved a towel and was cutting the cord when Cleeda screamed. He glanced, and there was another slimy head. "Shit." Not knowing what to do, he rushed the wrapped boy into the living room. "Here, hold your new brother," he said to the girl with bright yellow hair. He rushed back to Cleeda, and the next one, another boy, was already on the table, his left foot still inside.

Reece slapped the back of the boy until piercing cries erupted. Reece looked at the boy's face, and it seemed so angry. He wiped mucus and blood from his eyes, cut the cord, and wrapped him up, but there was another head. He handed off the package to Beo's giant hands.

"Dahlia, help me!" said Cleeda.

"Dahlia?" asked Reece.

Reece focused on the next head, which was coming out face up. It should have been face down and then turned face up once out. The nose and lips emerged, the head jamming against the pelvic wall. Reece went in with his hand to lift the head and force it upward. Cleeda's screams kept him focused. He stood back and watched as Cleeda strained. The head pushed out and then went back in. In a mild panic, Reece took both hands and thrust them inside Cleeda and pulled. Like a spurt of blood, the baby girl shot onto the table, blue and turning purple. This one he held almost upside down and slapped quite hard on the back. The girl's mouth moved as if gasping for air. He held her right side up and placed her on his shoulder, thumping her back. Nothing. He turned her back over on his forearm and gave a mighty slap. A plug of mucus shot from the baby's mouth, and a weak cry ensued. Reece cut yet another cord and wrapped the baby, expecting another, but what followed was a great groan from Cleeda and a clot of tangled placentas burst forth onto the table with a liter of bloody amniotic fluid.

"What in tarnation!" said Bertram, just returned from the cement factory. He pushed past Reece and went to Cleeda. "Oh, you beautiful thing. The babies have come, the best meat of all."

"It just came on me," said Cleeda, her face still red and wet with tears. "This fella helped me. Couldn't have done without him. Can I see my babies?" She sat up on the table and swung her legs over, with Bertram supporting her.

"How many?" asked Bertram. He had a wild look in his eye.

"Three," said Reece. Fluids and blood covered his clothes. He still held the little girl. "Never seen the likes of it."

"It is a miracle," said Beo. He clutched the second boy to his chest, his head grazing the ceiling.

"Get me to my chair," said Cleeda. She slid off the table, and Bertram walked her into the living room and sat her in a plain soft chair with a cushion, where Mia had been sitting. "Get this damn apron off me." Bertram struggled with the straps and buckles, then lifted off the heavy apron, revealing Cleeda's massive bosom with areolas like dinner plates.

Reece handed her the little girl, and Beo handed down the little boy. They each rooted for milk and soon latched on, the third having to wait his turn. The three children on the couch stared at the baby they were holding with curiosity, but remained silent.

"I'm sure grateful to you fellas." Bertram was dusty and

dressed in a gray jumpsuit labeled CEMENT on the back, wearing a blue felt hat.

"No worries," said Reece.

"Who's the little girl?" asked Bertram, pointing at Mia, who was standing by the door with wide eyes.

"She is a runaway," said Beo. "We have caught her and are returning her to her parents."

"Got some business on the side, I see. Normally, I wouldn't allow it, but seeing you've saved my babies..." He walked over to the little girl who was holding the other little boy. "Gimme that baby, you brat." Shaking, she handed the baby to him. "Hoo wee! He's mighty fine. Look at them cheeks. Kinda small, though." He held the baby straight out in front of him like a doll. "Ye didn't forget to get the dinner going, did ye?"

"What, dinner? And me having these babies? You better stick yer head in a hole." The babies lay on her knees, sucking, searching.

"Table's a damn mess," said Bertram. "Couldn't ye get on the floor like a damn horse should?" He laid the third baby on top of Cleeda's breasts. "I'm damn hungry for some meat."

Reece stood with his arms folded, leaning against the doorway into the dining room. "We'll clean up the mess and get you some dinner."

"That's mighty kind of you," said Bertram. "And then we need to get them babies into the barn out back. We got a program to follow."

Markush assured Grayson that he had his listening ears on. He sat in a wheelchair that was to the side of Grayson's bedside recliner. "Give it to me, pal."

Grayson craned his neck and looked to make sure no one else was listening. "I've been to the Cylinder, my friend, on more than one occasion, and had some little tête-à-têtes with Dahlia. After bawling me out for not telling who her damn mother was, she got all teary and said she hated me as much as her sister. Yeah, my ears perked up on that one."

"Does her sister have a name?" asked Markush. He watched as Debbie passed by, and Grayson put a finger to his lips.

"Name's Julia, the best I remember. Well, I had to ask her about this sister. My thinking was that maybe this sister could help me find my Lila. Anyways, she spills the beans. She put Julia in Dogtown and won't let her out. Of course, I asked why, and she said that Julia was not a reasonable sort, that she was always harping on helping folks and doing good. Dahlia's a mean bitch, she is."

"Why is Dahlia more powerful than Julia? Are they twins?" Markush adjusted the sleeves of his blue button-up.

"I don't rightly know. They seem like twins, but altogether different. I looked for Julia when I was in Dogtown, but she must be really far off."

"What else did you learn about Julia?"

"Dahlia realized her mistake, telling about her sister

and shut down, calling me names and dumping me in that place. You know that village, Gimmi. Old Gandhi is a real helper, but he doesn't speak the language, and neither do I. But, anyway, Dahlia let it slip that if she found out who her momma was, she'd let Julia go."

"Wow, interesting. We just have to make Dahlia believe us. Maybe we're taking the wrong angle," said Markush.

Debbie poked her head in. "You guys okay in here?"

"Hey there, good lookin'!" said Grayson. "Wanna sit on my face?"

Debbie didn't reply and just kept going.

Markush wanted to laugh. "You've got to be a little more respectful, you know?"

"Hell, just having some fun is all." Grayson dwarfed his recliner.

Following his session with Grayson, Markush headed to the long-term unit to check on the Reeces. He walked into the original Reece's room, and nothing had changed. Reece looked peaceful, lying there with zero brain activity. He walked around to room eleven, where Reece the Returnee lay in bed. Everything looked neat, sheets clean. Reece lay on his side, a feeding tube looping from his nose. He had been traveling for several days, and Sheila, with the cat-eye glasses, had inserted a urinary catheter. Markush glanced at the EEG, and there was a regular pattern of gamma waves.

"Come back soon." Markush was worried and curious to know what Reece was doing. While standing there, he had a brilliant but elementary idea. Sheila popped in.

"Nothing much to report," said Sheila. "You making it?"

"Yeah, doing okay, just busy. Call me when he returns,"

said Markush. "I'm headed out to the guest house. Need anything?"

"Nope, got it covered."

Markush exited back onto the medical unit, where he had left his down jacket. He glanced at the bank of video monitors, patted Claire on the back, and left Organon, saying hey to Denise on the way out the front door. Kristin was watching TV when Markush knocked. It was one o'clock, and she picked up Mia from school at three.

"Hey, babydoll!" said Markush. "Looking good."

"Babydoll? What are you so happy about?"

"Sit down for this one." He sat on the floral loveseat and patted the cushion beside him. "Warm in here."

"Organon is an ice box," said Kristin. "So, what's up?"

"You know how Dahlia wants to know who her mother is?"

"Yeah, very strange."

"All she's been told is that time is her mother. Time is technically her precursor, but that's as close to a mother as we can get. What if we come out and tell Dahlia that her mother is alive and well on this Earth?"

"You're kidding?"

"No, I'm not. She's so desperate and has the mind of a seven-year-old. If we give Dahlia a name, reassure her that the woman in question is her mother, she just might bite. I haven't told you yet, but Dahlia has a sister named Julia trapped in Dogtown. Julia sounds like the polar opposite of Dahlia, a kind seven-year-old. I learned from Grayson today that Dahlia would release Julia if she found out who her mother was."

"That's a lot of information. A sister, really? And who

will Dahlia's mother be? Who would be crazy enough to take on that role?"

"You ready?" asked Markush.

"For what?"

"You, Kristin Myers, are Dahlia's mother." Markush beamed like a little boy.

Reece helped Bertram carry the three newborns out back to a wooden shed that sat some ten feet away from the house, with a cement yard between them. A brick wall on either side made a courtyard. A coal bin sat next to the fence with an opening into the alley. The shed had a tin roof but was well-built and fitted tightly, with two windows. Inside were four stalls, each with homemade beds with thin mattresses about belly high. The triplets screamed their lungs out, their lips pooching, looking for Cleeda's nipples.

Reece watched Bertram lay down a baby and cover it with a blanket. He did likewise with the other two.

"Hush now, you little brats," said Bertam. "Mommy will come see you and give you some milk."

"Just leave them out here?" asked Reece.

"Yeah, this is the baby barn. They like it. Yeah, they'll holler, but they'll pipe down. No use havin' 'em crowd up the house."

"I see." Reece watched as Bertram blocked the door with a heavy board and then attached a large lock.

"Don't want no one getting the best meat," he said.

Reece had to say it. "You eat babies?" The day was warm, with half the courtyard in bright yellow sun.

"I know you big city folks think different. Course we do, but just one. We'll raise up the other two to tender meat. I got to get busy and fertilize Cleeda. Just what I gotta do."

"Oh," said Reece. "I guess Cleeda stays pregnant?"

"Sure does. Gotta keep the meat coming in."

They entered the back porch, where there was a bucket with food scraps and a garbage can, along with a broken chair and some wooden boxes.

"'Bout time for a potty break," said Bertram, once they were in the small kitchen.

"Yeah, Dick and Dingle," said Reece. "We'll do that now."

In the living room, Cleeda sat in her chair with the three straw-haired kids sitting on the couch with their hands on their laps. Beo sat on the stairs with Lila on his knees.

"Are the babies okay?" Cleeda's face had gone from bright red back to her pasty usual. A thin film of whiskers covered her upper lip. Her breasts lay exposed on her lap.

"They're nice and tidy," said Bertram. "But ye got to do your job and feed 'em proper and don't be bitchin' about it. I know how ye get."

"Hey, Lila, why don't you come and sit in the dining room?" said Reece.

"I'm thirsty," said Lila.

"Cleeda," said Bertram. "Get off yer ass and get the girl a glass of milk."

"Damn," said Cleeda. "I just brought three new ones into the world. Need the milk for them. Got to change this bloody dress."

"Well, get her done, woman."

"Gimme my apron," said Cleeda.

As Bertram was helping Cleeda back into her apron, Reece told Beo that it was bathroom time for Dick and Dingle. They trudged up the stairs, and Reece knocked on Dingle's door, unlocking it with the key. He pushed open the door into the orange room and then closed the door just as quick.

"What is wrong?" asked Beo.

"Look." Reece opened the door again.

Hanging from his neck by a torn bedsheet was Dingle. He had tied the sheet to the bars over the window. Reece moved in to check for a pulse, but there was none. Dingle's face looked lavender with his tongue hanging out.

"This is terrible," said Beo. Feces littered the floor and urine filled the spittoon, a dry crust of bread on the stained mattress.

Reece went downstairs, Cleeda still in her chair. Lila sat at the table with a small glass of milk and a funny look on her face. Bertram shuffled around the kitchen, and Reece stood in the doorway.

"Um, Bertram, Mr. Bertram. Dingle has hanged himself. He's dead," said Reece.

"The hell! Oh no, we got to act quick." He pushed past Reece and ran up the stairs and squeezed past Beo into Dingle's room. Without a pause, he whipped out his knife and cut Dingle free, his body thudding to the floor. "Hey, big fella, get in here!"

Beo stooped and entered the room.

"We gotta get this here meat down to the butcher lickety split before it spoils. Goddamn it."

Reece had climbed the stairs. Beo gave him a look, and Reece just nodded.

"Hurry up, big fella!" said Bertram. "Follow me!"

Beo winced and gathered Dingle into his arms. A rush of yellow liquid spewed from his mouth, and Beo gagged. As if carrying a princess, he carted Dingle down the stairs and then onto the street, following Bertram. The butcher was only two blocks away, and Beo took long strides, passing a group of three men who were gawking.

"Lay him down, and I'll strip him," said Bertram. He made quick work of it and left the pile of stinking clothes on the road. "Take him inside. Go on now. It's a tangler's duty."

Beo gazed at the racks of ribs hanging in the window. Inside, all was spotless, but a faint odor of death lingered.

"What'cha got, Bertram? Some tough meat, I see," said the butcher named Adolph. "Just bring him in the back. Been dead long?"

Bertram had his hands in his pockets, feeling the holes. "No, no, just up and died a few minutes ago."

Beo walked past a display of sausages and organ meats. In the back were two steel tables and buckets. Hooks hung from the ceiling.

"Hold him upside down by the legs," said the butcher.

Beo did it with ease but gagged. He watched as the butcher took a sharp knife and made slits behind Dingle's Achilles tendons.

"Spread his legs a bit," said the butcher. He then slid a hook behind each tendon, poor Dingle hanging with his arms flopped to the floor. "You're a handy fella."

Beo shook his head and left as quickly as possible, headed back to the house.

Kristin's eyes went wide, and her jaw dropped. "Me? Dahlia's mother?"

"Yes, it's perfect. Dahlia knows what a great mom you are. She's jealous of Mia. She would love to be your daughter. You look like the perfect mom in that dress. Laura Ashley, right?"

"I look like a mom? Is that actually a good thing?"

"Well, yeah, you look great. I like the plaid."

"What does being Dahlia's mother entail? How do you be a mom to a supernatural being who thinks she's God?"

"Supernatural? Dahlia is real. And I suppose she is a form of God, but she wants a mother and badly," said Markush.

"It's hard enough being *this* Mia's mom, plus there's the real Mia out there somewhere that Reece is looking for. That's what's important here, the real Mia."

"If you were Dahlia's mom, you could tell her what to do. She would have to return the real Mia and hopefully take away the impostor," said Markush.

"I don't know, but if it would end this game of hiding Mia, I can't say no." She sat on the blue wing chair, and Markush took the loveseat, pushing aside a pile of books.

"Perfect. We just have to let our patients know the plan. They occasionally meet Dahlia, and she always asks the same question about her mother. Plus, you need to tell Mia that you're Dahlia's mother. Somehow, I just know that Dahlia stays in touch with replacements, gleaning information from them."

"Okay, sounds good, as long as I don't have to really do anything?"

Back on the medical unit, all was quiet, with four of the twelve patients in travel mode. Timera Scocpol seemed to be closing in on finding her daughter, being helped by Haile Selassie. Loydell McNamara, in room four, had just returned from a small town called Gacci, where he believed his daughter Speck was being hidden. He was still weak from his seizures, but was talking.

"Tell me more," said Carletta. She had changed her braids into a frizzy black ponytail.

"Everybody's rich and makes computer parts." Loydell looked beat and like an alien with the EEG wires sprouting from his skull. He had a broad face with a padded chin. "The people are stuffed with themselves, right down annoying, like pigs rolling in mud."

"Does anyone know where Speck is?" asked Carletta.

"Nobody seems to care except this elderly gentleman named Bor-hays. He seems lost just like me, says he's from Argentina, worked in a library, and he's blind, so I've taken to leading him around."

"Oh, the writer," said Carletta. "He is dead in this world."

"I suppose so, but don't rightly know. We're staying in a hotel for the unemployed, free of charge. The food's decent, but they serve damn wine with every meal, even breakfast. They don't even know what orange juice is."

"Strange," said Carletta.

"When can I get the hell out of here?"

"You cannot for now. You are important. And you would

be in jail without us, I'm afraid."

"Has my wife called? I know she hates me for what I did, but it had to be done."

"Nobody called," said Carletta. "We take care of you, and you find Speck."

"Yeah, the receptionist at the hotel said we should see some guy called the Abba who lives outside the town in a cave or something."

"Abba is good. Other patients go to see him. Make sure you find the Abba. He is the Abba Paulos. You need lotion on your back. Was red when I looked."

"That'd be dandy." Loydell rolled to his side, and Carletta rubbed him down with hospital lotion. "Damn, that feels good."

Carletta washed her hands. "Yes, you go to see the Abba. He will help."

"If you say so."

In room six, Emma was working with Emma, having lifted her into the recliner from the bed. After making the bed, she gave Emma a quick bath, as Emma watched her with increasingly bright eyes. Emma had begun to speak, making the faintest sounds.

"Reece," whispered Emma. She looked ghostly, sitting in the glare of the overhead light, wearing a loose gown.

Emma moved in closer to hear her.

"Reece," she whispered again.

"Reece?" asked Emma, sitting on the bed. "He's a nurse. Was he working with you in a clinic?"

"Yes."

"Wow. I worked with a Reece in a clinic too. There's a Reece here at Organon, well, two Reeces, kind of like there are two of us. I know this all sounds like a fantasy, but it's true. I wonder if you could chew on some ice chips. Want to try?"

Emma nodded and poked out her dry tongue.

Emma ran to the nursing station for a cup of ice and a plastic spoon.

"Got it. Just open your mouth a bit." She slid in an ice chip, and it slipped out. "Oops, let's try again." This time Emma closed her lips around the ice chip, moved it around her mouth, and swallowed. "That's great!" Over the next few minutes, she spooned in one ice chip at a time. "Maybe in a few days we can try some solid food."

Emma made a tiny smile and nodded her head. "Reece," she whispered.

With Beo gone, Reece took Dick to the bathroom. Somehow, Dick knew Dingle was dead, but showed no emotion, dragging the log that was attached to his ankle. Reece then set about making dinner to keep Bertram at bay and found flour and potatoes in the larder. He decided to make potato soup and biscuits. There was a cabinet in which hung portions of dried meat, but he decided against cooking it. Beo returned and stepped into the courtyard, and he could hear the babies crying from the shed.

"Want to help peel potatoes?" said Reece to Lila.

"Sure," said Lila. "Are you supposed to have your babies on a table? She was screaming, and I was scared."

Reece laughed. "No, but that's just what happened. I suppose she suddenly had to have them and crawled up there."

They peeled potatoes together, and then Reece made biscuits. Bertram showed him a small lard bucket, which made Reece queasy, and the can of baking powder. A large brick of butter sat on the counter, and he used that instead of the lard. A slight bed of red coals glowed in the iron stove, and Reece added fresh coal from a steel bucket. There was a ruckus in the living room, Bertram yelling, and soon Cleeda was in the kitchen, still in her bloody clothes. Lila hung back behind Reece.

"Got to feed my babies." Cleeda walked like a zombie into the courtyard and to the shed door. She unlocked the lock but was having trouble with the plank that blocked the door.

"I can help." With one hand, Beo plucked the plank from the iron hangers.

"Thank you kindly," said Cleeda. "Oh, my babies are a cryin'."

Curious, Beo watched from outside as Cleeda undid her apron and let down a breast into the first crib. She positioned her nipple near the baby's mouth, and he went silent as he sucked. The other two, sensing milk nearby, raised alarming cries.

It took nearly thirty minutes for Cleeda to feed all three, and she shuffled back inside, peeking into the soup pot and looking into the oven.

"No meat?" asked Cleeda. "That'll make Bertram right mad."

"It's a rough day for everyone," said Reece.

"She's a cute one, looks real tender," said Cleeda, looking at Lila, who was hiding behind Reece.

"Yeah, we gotta get her back to her parents," said Reece. "But we're still looking for your two boys. She'll just have to stay here until then. We'll take her with us to keep an eye on her."

"I appreciate ya," said Cleeda, and she went to take her chair in the living room.

Reece checked, and the biscuits in the iron skillet had risen, browned on top. He took a towel, removed the heavy pan, and placed it next to the enameled sink. Grease and bits of food spattered the wall. A wide cabinet with three doors hung from the ceiling. The light through the window was fading, and Reece worked in increasing shadows.

When all was ready, with biscuits and potato soup on the table, Reece gathered everyone, eight in all, filling the large table that had that afternoon served as a birthing platform, although Beo stood, holding his bowl.

Bertram eyed the food warily. "There ain't no meat in these taters."

"No meat, but lots of butter," said Reece.

"Butter's expensive," said Bertram. He held his spoon like an oar.

"Oh, I didn't know," said Reece. "Sorry about that."

"Damn, Bertram," said Cleeda, "just be glad you got some food to eat. I'll fix you some damn meat for breakfast. Least I got one meal off for having three babies."

Bertram grumbled. "Eat yer soup," he said to the three kids, who looked petrified.

"Yes sir," they said in unison.

"It's yer duty," said Bertram to Cleeda. "Never heard of a tangler making dinner."

"Shut your face and eat." Cleeda dipped her biscuit in the soup juice and chewed. "Mighty good if you ask me."

"I like it," said Lila.

"Who asked you?" asked Bertram. "Shut your trap and eat."

Lila's breath caught, and tears threatened.

"Lila, it's okay." Reece wanted to say they were leaving the next day, but didn't want to start a ruckus with Bertram. Suddenly, his eyes rolled back, and he slid down in his chair.

Scoot paged Markush that Reece was back, and Markush rushed from Kristin's to the long-term unit. He entered the unit and then the nursing station, glancing at the EEG monitors. The Reece in three still showed a flat line.

"How's it going?" asked Markush.

"Fine," said Sheila. "Scoot's in eleven with Reece."

Markush exited into the hall, room eleven right there. Reece was sitting up in bed, drinking a Coke through a straw, his eyes hollow.

"Say, you're back," said Markush. "I see Scoot's taking good care of you."

"Got him two sandwiches ordered," said Scoot.

Markush nodded.

"I'm famished," said Reece. "Everywhere I go, I'm hungry."

"Still in Gordian?" Markush had left his coat at Kristin's and felt chilly.

Reece emptied the can of Coke with a slurp. "Yeah, and lots to tell. They eat their young. Kids are like hostages, the teenagers locked up all day. There's butcher shops. The lady in the place we're staying gave birth to triplets and kept referring to them as meat."

"Jesus," said Markush.

"That's what I said."

Scoot left the room with a frown.

"So, you're living there?"

"Yeah, me and Beo are what they call tanglers. We have to find two runaways. The parents give us room and board.

We got close, but no cigar. Plus, I wouldn't catch them, knowing what will happen."

"Beo, the giant?" asked Markush.

"The same. Oh, this is the best part. We found a little girl named Lila—"

"Lila?" Markush knew Lila was Helmut Grayson's missing daughter.

"Yeah, Lila, same age as Mia. She's definitely been abducted and hidden in Gordian."

"Wow, you have to bring her back. She may be the daughter of one of the patients on the medical unit."

"Yeah, I'm wondering about that, but I need to look for Mia. There are caves outside the town where the runaways hide. She could be there. I can only hope."

Markush then told him about the idea to tell Dahlia that Kristin was her mother.

"That's insane, but that might do the trick. What does Kristin think? I'm out of the picture, so I can't be the dad unless Dahlia is into divorced parents." Reece laughed.

"But she only seems to want a mother," said Markush. "It's perfect. We have to send the message somehow to Dahlia. Have you seen her?"

"No, that only happens in the Cylinder and Dogtown. Although she appears when the Ark is present, with the Abba Paulos."

"You should pray to her, let her know Kristin is her mother. I'm going to let the other patients know as well, and Kristin is going to tell Mia that she is Dahlia's mother."

"I can try the prayer approach, but a face-to-face would be better."

Scoot came in with two hamburgers, pickles on the

side. "Here you go, special order."

Reece took the tray and laid it on his lap. "One second, doc." He ate a burger in four bites, nearly choking, and then followed it with ice water. "Shit, that's good." He belched.

"A face-to-face would be perfect, but the odds of that are unknown," said Markush.

"Probably impossible. Excuse me." Reece took a bite of hamburger. "Gonna make myself sick."

"Yeah, slow down," said Markush. "Although you could pop out at any minute back to the land of the cannibals. That is so unexpected that it's happening somewhere right now."

Reece finished his burger and ate the pickles. "The women are basically baby machines, to produce meat. I think we're out of there as soon as I get back. I can't be a part of that whole scheme."

"No blame. Just keep your eyes peeled for Mia, take care good of Lila, and have that meeting with Dahlia if you can."

At the elementary school, it was the final class of the day for Mia, PE, which she hated. Today, they had warmed up with jumping jacks and then played freeze tag in the gym. The gym was half the size of a basketball court and floored with honey-colored wood. Cecily and a boy named Hubert were the taggers. Cecily gave Mia a wide berth as she was running, trying to tag other students and make them freeze.

"This is stupid." Mia sauntered along, as if the game did not concern her.

Hubert ran up and tagged Mia. "Freeze!" he said.

Mia ignored him and kept walking. The PE teacher, Mr. Klim, was watching, and he yelled for Mia to freeze. Mia tapped herself on the head and yelled, "Unfreeze!"

Klim was leery of Mia, somewhat afraid of her, and just let it go. Mia burst into a run, feeling silly in her shorts and t-shirt, and she began tagging people and yelling, "Freeze!" That created confusion, and Mr. Klim had to intervene.

"Mia, you're not *it*. You can't freeze people," said Klim. He looked dumpy in his gray sweatpants with a University of Kentucky sweatshirt.

"You're a fool. I can do what I want. You know very well I'm not of this place. I could turn you into a pumpkin and then some." Mia spoke with her hands on her hips. The game all around them came to a slow stop.

"You can sit down and watch," said Klim. He looked frightened, his small eyes shining.

"I prefer to stand, if you don't mind. The floor is dirty."

"Fine." Klim blew his whistle and started the game anew with two new taggers.

Unfazed, Mia slipped out to the locker room and changed into her red dress and black loafers. She decided to leave school early and walk around until Kristin arrived. She walked into the empty hallway and began skipping to the front door, stopping at her classroom to get her coat. No one seemed to notice her escape, and Mia walked up onto the asphalt play area, holding out her arms and spinning in a slow circle. And then she felt it, a calling from beyond, from Dahlia. She sat next to a large oak tree on a pile of rotting leaves and closed her eyes. She could feel the mesh in her head hum as Dahlia uploaded her information. "Dah-li-a," she said, and felt cold and empty.

At first, Kristin couldn't find Mia in her usual spot out-side the school door, and then spotted her red dress. Mia seemed to be in a trance, something she had seen before.

"Mia, what are you doing?" Kristin had bundled up in her long, light purple parka with a hood. She was so thin and did not like the cold of January.

Mia said, "Hmm," and opened her eyes.

Kristin was about to burst with the news. "Guess what, Mia?" She helped Mia to stand and brushed leaves off her dress. "Put your coat on first, though."

Mia focused and slipped on her denim coat, which had a wool lining. "Hi, Mother." She held onto Kristin's hand as they walked to the parking lot.

"This is so exciting," said Kristin, her cheeks red with the cold and flushed with excitement.

"What is, Mother?" Mia sauntered, as if drugged.

"Well, this will come as a surprise, but I'm Dahlia's mother. It's been me all along!"

Mia stopped and looked straight ahead. "You?"

"Yes, me. I've just been keeping it a secret, so you can't tell anyone, not even Dahlia."

"Who's Dahlia?" asked Mia.

They arrived at the Civic. Kristin opened the door for Mia and helped her inside. "Where's your backpack?"

"In class."

"No homework?"

"No. Dahlia?"

"Yes, I'm Dahlia's mother. She's wanted to know for so

long, and now I'm ready to let her know." She cranked the car, and the heat blasted full force.

"Oh, that's nice. To have a sister, I mean." Mia yawned and let Kristin buckle her in.

"Yes, of course, a sister. You have a sister. Isn't that exciting! Now don't tell anyone."

"Okay," said Mia.

Markush dropped by Arthur's apartment, next to Kristin's, to check on him and give him news of his latest gig. Arthur enjoyed taking walks to Tobacco Leaf Lake, his gloved hands held behind his back. He had struck up a friendship with the Military Police who patrolled the area in their jeeps. They had all wanted his autograph, and he had obliged. Arthur ushered in Markush with a bow. The guest apartment was decorated in fall colors, the couch being dull red and the two wingback chairs a rusty yellow.

"What brings you here?" asked Arthur.

Markush took a chair. "Just wanted to let you know about a string of speaking engagements. You're in very high demand." Markush noticed a slight hint of body odor.

"Lovely! I am quite bored here, as you know. Tell me more."

"Sherri Loveless has ten events in the making, all across the country. Your next show, because it will be a show, is in Dallas, in Texas."

"Ah, Texas, with the cowboys and native Indians," said Arthur.

"Yeah, something like that. And I have some news about Dahlia's mother." Markush told him of the plan for Kristin to pose as Dahlia's mother.

Arthur laughed. "Do you think she will believe?"

"We're hoping. She wants a mother so badly."

"And what do you hope to gain from this ruse?"

"If Dahlia finds her mother, maybe she will return all the hidden little girls and stop abducting them in the first place. There is a new twist as well—Dahlia has a sister who seems to be quite the opposite of Dahlia. This sister, Julia, I'm told, has been alienated by Dahlia, perhaps held captive in some way. If Dahlia finds her mother, she has let it slip that she will release Julia." Markush was out of breath with excitement.

"I see. The plan sounds of great use. I wish to know more about this Julia."

"Yeah, me too," said Markush. "This could be ground-breaking for the future of the universes."

On the medical unit, Dr. Mumford made her rounds. Three patients were in travel mode, and one had just returned, the sassy Demeter Preston, aka Granny D, the oldest patient on the unit, who was searching for her granddaughter, Kisha. This was Granny D's second traveling experience since being admitted, and she lay limp in bed with her head raised and the rails down.

Mumford sat in the recliner, eye level with Granny D. "You look tired."

"Yes, ma'am, wore plumb out. Lord, give me strength. That's all I can hope for."

"Tell me about where you've been and what happened. Are you getting close to finding Kisha?"

"To tell the truth, I don't know. Of all people, I'm tangled up with Betty Crocker. I never knew she was real. Funny brown-haired white lady, real plain and simple. Well, at least she speaks English."

"You're in a village in Ethiopia called Gland?" asked Mumford.

"That's right. The people be so poor but happy as clams. That food they eat is so damn spicy, makes my head sweat. Old Betty's taken an interest in the cooking. They have potatoes, and she made me some fried. They were sure good, and I thanked her."

"I see. Have you found any little girls yet?"

"No, but we found a nurse named Emma working by herself in a clinic. She said there was a famine going on. Big warehouse full of sacks, wheat and such. The line to the clinic runs up the hill, a sad sight to see them poor folks squatting in the sun."

"Want me to turn off that overhead light?" asked Mumford.

"Yes, ma'am, and please. Hurts my eyes. Thank you."

"You're welcome. So, is Emma helpful?"

"I think so. She's working with these local guys, and they speak some English. One's real handsome, named Abrehem. Real polite folks. One told me and Betty about going to see a priest, or maybe it was a monk."

"I see. Did he mention the Abba Paulos?" asked Mumford.

"That's right! Sure did. How do you know that?"

"Other patients have visited him. He may be able to send you to Kisha or bring her to you. You definitely have to see him," said Mumford.

"I surely will. You know what's funny? There's two

moons in the sky at night. A strange sight."

"You're in another place, another solar system, perhaps another universe," said Mumford.

Carletta waltzed in with her hands on her hips. She was short, but looked powerful. "Everything okey dokey here? Dinner coming soon. You need something to drink?"

"Some apple juice would be nice," said Granny D.

"Thank you, Carletta," said Mumford.

Lenore, the cleaning lady, knocked on the glass panel. She grinned, showing her missing tooth. "Y'all mind iffen I sweep?"

"Oh no, darling," said Granny D. "They got you working."

"I'll step out," said Mumford, and she did.

"Didn't mean to run that doctor off." Lenore ran the push mop under the bed and in the corners.

"No, no, you got to work, baby."

Lenore made a little pile of dust and pushed it into the hall. She then turned to Granny D. "What they got you in here for?"

Granny D. looked thoughtful.

Markush drove Arthur to the airport in Louisville and saw him off. The innovation of flight still amazed Arthur, and he thoroughly enjoyed the experience, sipping white wine in first class, sitting next to a woman who was a vice president at a healthcare corporation. She had recognized him from news reports and kept up a lively conversation, but the man in a turtleneck across the aisle had accosted Arthur, calling him the devil. The stewardess had intervened, but Arthur was shocked at the verbal abuse.

Sherri Loveless met him at the airport in Dallas, and they took a hired shuttle to the downtown Sheraton, a vast hotel complex with conference facilities. After checking into his executive suite on the sixteenth floor, Arthur rewarded himself with a hot bath, as he found showers to be unpleasant.

A taxi dropped Arthur and Sherri at an Italian restaurant on Commerce Street, and Sherri hustled him inside, fearing he would be recognized. She wanted to do room service, but Arthur said he wanted to be out and about to enjoy the experience. A waiter seated them at a table for four in a back corner. The light was dim, the tablecloth shockingly white. A few heads turned, and eyes were on them.

Before the waiter asked them if they would like drinks, he said, "You're Arthur, from another world. Wow, so nice to meet you." He seemed star-struck and dropped a serviette without noticing.

"No interviews or questions, please." Sherri wore a red

bodycon dress that outlined her slim, athletic figure. "And the wine list, please."

Arthur coughed and frowned. "Despite my friend's reluctance, I am very pleased to meet you. What is your surname?"

"Oh, it's uh...David. Yeah. David." He placed a serviette on the table along with silverware from his apron. "So, you've met Dahlia?"

"I said no questions," said Sherri.

"Miss Loveless, please," said Arthur. "What do you know of Dahlia?"

"Uh, she's like a little God who runs the universe, a girl, but she sounds a little wicked," said David.

"Perhaps. She is perpetually young and lacks wisdom, seeming somewhat cruel. But our future hinges on understanding Dahlia. That is very important."

"Wow, I see, and yes, the wine menu coming right up. Thank you, Mr. Arthur."

"My pleasure."

"Don't encourage these people. They'll crawl into bed with you if you let them. It's great we're being transparent, but you have to keep the public at a distance. They'll suck you dry."

"Such language, being sucked dry. I'm an old man and can quite take care of myself. This is as fascinating for me as it is for my, what do you call them, fans?" Arthur smiled to himself.

"Fans and more. There's a group of nuts in California who have formed a church to worship Dahlia. They have named you as a primary disciple of Dahlia, a prophet of sorts. People are taking the bait and running with it."

"Yes, Dr. Markush has mentioned these cults of Dahlia, but I was not aware that I am a prophet. I rather like it, though." He struck a pose as David handed him the wine list.

Arthur spent the night in relative comfort, enjoying the view from the sixteenth floor. Overnight, news crews had learned of his whereabouts and camped on the street outside. His speaking engagement at the hotel would take place in the Texas Ballroom, on the second floor, at five p.m., with a poster signing afterward. The 11x17 posters had been an idea of Glenelle Lock's and had Arthur's new, more modern face with a genuine smile. He looked like a grandfather on his way to the park.

Before the event at five, hotel security escorted him, along with Sherri, to a small conference room on the twenty-seventh floor, where there was a buffet with wine. In attendance were special guests invited by Sherri, including the mayor of Dallas, Debbie Rodriguez, and a state senator, Jasper Wilson.

Wearing a soft brown cashmere sweater and knit slacks, Arthur entered the room of thirty or so people. Light jazz played. His eyes brightened, and he headed straight to the buffet, but Sherri caught him and steered him toward the mayor. "I'll get you a glass of wine, red or white?"

"Yes, white will do, thank you." Arthur examined the mayor, wearing a blue power suit with a Texas flag pin on her lapel.

"Professor Schopenhauer, so nice to meet you." Debbie then introduced her husband and an assistant.

Arthur took her hand and held it briefly, looking into

her eyes. "My pleasure."

There was small talk about Dallas, and Arthur had his second glass of wine in hand. He found himself in the senator's company for a full ten minutes, who spoke of the national interest in Organon. Arthur excused himself and made his way to a group of five older women, all with the city's arts and museum scene. They tittered at his approach like a bundle of sparrows.

"My ladies, how are you this fine evening?" He sipped his wine.

The ladies seemed rooted in place. One spoke. "Very well, Arthur. May I call you Arthur?" She wore a black evening gown with a draped neckline.

"Certainly, my dear. And you are?"

She smiled. "Gretchen Potts, if you please."

Arthur focused his attention on Gretchen, ten years his junior, but answered questions from the others. He found his element in the company of these admiring women.

"Tell us about that place you lived. It's called Gadam, right? Where the food and drinks were free?"

"Ah, yes, Gadam. The year was 3986, another universe altogether, or so I assume. I met young Reece Myers there, as he was looking for his daughter Mia. The sun in the sky was tiny but hot, and it never rained."

"What was the buster like? I can't believe I just asked you a question."

"Buster, a frothy liquid with body, coming in any flavor you can imagine. There was no other food available, although there were bars with the finest alcohols."

"Jesus Christ, Arthur in the flesh," said Gretchen. "Can I hug you?"

Arthur licked his lips. "Of course, my dear lady," and he embraced her, smelling her French perfume.

Time passed quickly, and Sherri removed him from the group of adoring ladies, and with hotel security, a tall man in a suit, they made their way to the vacuous ballroom with its thirty-foot ceiling. Four hundred chairs faced the stage, where a podium stood. On either side of the stage stood floor-to-ceiling screens that showed the center stage from a close angle. Several crews had set up their cameras behind the last row of chairs. Music played from Fleetwood Mac's *Rumours*, a choice made by Sherri Loveless. She wanted to pitch Arthur as an all-around nice guy who could connect with the curious masses, and it was working.

Sitting on stage, Arthur listened as the mayor of Dallas introduced him as "a kind German professor who has traveled the universe." The chairs were filled, and perhaps fifty stood. Tremendous applause greeted Arthur as he took the podium. He thanked the mayor, Dr. Markush, and Sherri Loveless, and then appealed for ears to hear and minds to believe.

Reece opened his eyes and saw the dirty white ceiling as if candles had burned for years in the room, which smelled of mold. His brain fuzzed, and he raised his head and saw Lila sitting on the mattress. Beo was gone.

"Hey." His mouth was dry, and his mind dry as well.

"Oh, Mr. Reece!" Lila jumped up. "You were sleeping for so long."

"I'm back. You okay?"

"Yeah, but I'm hungry. Mr. Beo told me not to eat the meat. I just had some carrots for lunch and a big glass of that weird milk."

Reece thought about the milk and Cleeda's giant breasts. "Maybe just drink water. Where is Beo?"

"He was mopping the floors downstairs to help the mommy."

"What time is it?" He sat up.

"I don't know, after lunch. Why won't those kids go outside? They just sit on the couch all day and go to the bathroom."

"I think the parents are afraid they'll run away," said Reece.

"There sure are a lot of kids running away."

"Yeah. Can you get Beo? I have to tell him something."

"Sure," and she was down the stairs in a flash.

Beo lumbered up the stairs and stooped to enter the room. "You are back. It is good."

"Thanks for taking care of me," said Reece. "Listen, we have to get out of here. We can't catch those two boys knowing what we know. We would just be accessories to... murder."

"Yes, we must leave. I have already taken a loaf of bread. It is there," and he pointed to a pillowcase.

"Great, plus we have money." Reece lowered his voice to a whisper. "We should take Dick, set him free; otherwise, he'll end up like Dingle."

"We must do it before the man comes home and while the woman is in the barn feeding the babies."

"I almost forgot about the babies. Wish we could take them too."

"I went out back and could hear them crying," said Lila.

"Yeah, kinda sad," said Reece. "So, let's do it."

"The boy, Dick, has the log attached to his ankle," said Beo.

"Yeah, the keys."

Reece retrieved the keys and ran back upstairs to Dick's room.

"Dick, we're going to take you out of here."

Dick looked stymied. "What fer?"

"To make you free." Reece fumbled through the keys to unlock the chain from his ankle. "Damn, none of these work. Do you know where the key is?"

Dick always took a while to respond. "Daddy keeps it."

Reece followed Dick to the bathroom and closed the door while Dick did his business. Cleeda was busy cooking dinner, making sausages from organ meats.

"How long since lunch?" asked Reece.

"Perhaps four hours," said Beo.

"Damn, Bertram will be home any time. Lila, you let us know when Cleeda goes out back. We'll leave together with Dick when she feeds the babies."

Within minutes, Lila climbed the stairs. "She went out the back door to go see those babies."

"Let's go," said Reece.

Beo opened the bathroom door, and Dick was sitting on the toilet with his hands folded. "Come, I will carry you."

"What?" asked Dick.

Just then, the front door opened, and it was Bertram. "Hello!"

Reece descended the stairs. "Hey! Cleeda's out back. She wanted to see you."

"Huh, you come back, I see. Ye weren't pretending to be sick, were ye? I expect ye to be tangling for my boys. And by God, there better be meat for dinner." He sat in Cleeda's chair.

Lila came down, and then Beo appeared with Dick slung over his shoulder, the log in Beo's hand.

"What the hell?" asked Bertram. "Get him back in his room! That's some tough meat, but it's meat by golly."

Reece looked back and forth between Beo and Bertram. "We have to go for a while, give Dick some fresh air. We'll be right back."

"That's plumb crazy. He don't need no fresh air. Now get him back up them stairs." He approached Beo and looked up at Dick's face.

"Let's go," said Reece. "Lila, stay with me."

"The hell!" Bertram grabbed Lila by the neck of her shirt.

"Hey!" said Lila.

Bertram put his arm around her neck. "Y'all are stealing my meat!"

Beo maneuvered close to Bertram and slapped him hard across the face. Bertram went tumbling, knocked out cold.

Without speaking, they exited through the front door, leaving the three straw-haired kids gaping on the couch. Reece led the way, holding Lila's hand with Beo in tow, shouldering Dick, who was limp as a rag. They trotted the streets, passing houses and shops. The people they met looked on with curiosity but didn't speak. Within half an hour, they reached the east gate. The man there, short and with a beard, wanted to know what they were up to.

"We're headed out to tangle," said Reece. "Gonna use that tough meat there as bait in the caves."

"That's a new one," said the man, a cigar drooping from his lips. He took his keys and opened the gate for them, and they were free.

"Damn, that was close," said Reece.

"Where are we going? I'm thirsty," said Lila.

"We can walk slowly now," said Reece.

"Shall we leave Dick at the cave?" asked Beo.

Dick came alive. "The caves? You lettin' me go?"

"That's a good idea," said Reece.

They made their way down the smooth path, passing fields of red grass dotted with fruit trees. The orange sun hung low in the sky, emanating a steady warmth. They arrived in the area with limestone outcroppings and cedar trees, and proceeded down the hill until they reached the sinkhole. Beo let Dick to the ground.

"Yeah, this here is the cave," said Dick. "Hot diggety dog." He stood lackluster and pale, with stooped shoulders. He looked dirty in the light, his fingernails long and caked with grime.

"Beo, can you get that log off his ankle?" asked Reece.

"I think so. Come with me." He walked to a smooth boulder about knee high and picked up a large stone. "Lift your leg here," and he pointed.

Dick did as he was told with a grin on his face. Beo palmed the stone and crashed it onto the chain near the log. The stone shattered in his hand, and he found another one. On the third try, the chain broke and Dick was free, except for the shackle attached to his ankle.

"The boys'll get that off me," said Dick. "If they can't do it, then that old man, the Abba, can do it. He's got powers."

"An abba?" asked Reece. "The Abba Paulos?"

"Yeah, that be him. He's a real sharp one, at the other end of the cave where it comes out. He's building something."

"How do we get there?" asked Reece.

"Down through that hole," said Dick. "Or go up over this here cliff and find the hole on the other side."

"I cannot enter the cave here," said Beo.

"Do you know if there are any young girls in the cave?" asked Reece. "I'm looking for a little girl."

"Don't rightly know. You just have to see fer yerself." With that, Dick leaped down into the hole, ducked, and disappeared.

Dahlia was at one with the circles and triangles, the perfect ideas of cats and dogs. She felt safe in the Pinch, being surrounded by an infinity crushed into a point. Prayers from infinite universes reached her there, and she processed the doggerel of sentient beings, often laughing at the absurdity of their requests. She made a point of letting be what will be and ignored the pleas for love and peace. Humans in their various renditions were problematic by nature and prone to self-interest, which she understood and propagated. She had received news, though, from Mia's replacement, and Dahlia wasn't sure what to make of it. A version of Kristin Myers, on the planet called Earth, was claiming to be her mother.

She was quite excited and curious about the news, but skeptical and called into being the perfect idea of Kristin and a visit with her in Dogtown to see in more detail what her mother could possibly be. Could it really be true? A thrill ran from her chest as if a long ribbon was being pulled from her heart.

A swirl of blue light pumped in all directions, and Dahlia stood silent in Dogtown. She would have to find Kristin Myers and began skipping along with a nervous smile. For days and weeks, she wandered, passing through schools of those she had damned to an eternal waiting, all wanting to find their little girls. She had an idea and turned to face a particular direction with nothing in the distance. For a while, she ran, and then began skipping again, singing a children's song about bumblebees. Perhaps an eternity passed, and then she could see two figures in the distance and slowed her walk. What would she be like?

The specks soon became small dashes and then became figures. Dahlia felt her heart in her throat and found that she was afraid of what she would find or would not find. She dreamed of fresh chocolate chip cookies and glasses of cold milk, cuddles, and kisses. By the time she could discern faces, she could barely contain herself. And then there they were, her sister Julia and Kristin Myers.

"Here she comes," said Julia. "You are her mother. You are my only hope, the hope of all that is to come."

Dahlia walked to within ten feet of the two. "Mother?" she said, arms hanging limply by her side.

Kristin Myers, dressed in a gingham sweater, checked white and soft blue, opened her arms. "Dahlia, come to me. I've been waiting for you, darling."

Dahlia stood rooted to the translucent floor of Dogtown, her mouth ajar. She wore a simple dress of white with red trim. Dahlia watched as Kristin approached her and then felt the warmth of arms around her. She pushed her face into Kristin's chest and felt a welling of emotion she did not understand.

"Mommy," said Dahlia, melting.

"Dahlia, it's been such a long time coming. We're finally together." Kristin kissed the top of Dahlia's head and then ran a hand through her golden hair. "I love you so much, baby."

Dahlia withdrew and looked up into Kristin's thin and shining face. She noticed the tears and could smell her sweet breath, like flowers. "Mommy."

"Yes, I'm your mommy. I've been there all along. You

just had to find me. I think you're so pretty."

"You're my mommy," said Dahlia, and suddenly she understood the pain she had caused, separating little girls from their mothers. She moved in for another hug, and Kristin gave her a squeeze. "Why are you with Julia?"

"I'm her mommy too," said Kristin. "You're sisters, and you have to love one another so that I can love you both equally. You are both so precious."

"She's our mommy," said Julia. "What you've always wanted."

Dahlia beamed with joy, making plans to visit the real Kristin Myers, who would love her forever and ever.

As Beo was too large to fit into the cave entrance, the trio walked farther down the cliff line and found a passage up and over that they could climb. The sky loomed dark. Beo went first, bridging a smooth embankment. Reece used him as a ladder, and then Beo passed Lila to him. The limestone was old, damp, and covered with moss and rock paper. The sinuous path up leaned steeply, about twenty meters in all. At the top, a dense thicket of thorny trees met Beo at eye level. Reece led the way, then Lila, and then Beo. For fifty minutes, they walked, soon reaching a grassy slope pocked with large boulders.

"The other entrance must be at the bottom of this slope," said Reece.

"I'm hungry." Scratches from the thorny trees covered Lila's arms.

"Hopefully we can find food," said Beo, "But I have the bread."

They continued downward until reaching a ledge and then a ten-foot drop. Beo looked over and saw a narrow path. He went to the ground and lowered himself over the edge. "Step down on my shoulders."

"Will I fall?" asked Lila. "It's raining."

"No, Beo will catch you. Hold my hand and go to your belly," said Reece.

Lila did so, and Beo grabbed her by the waist. Reece then swung his legs over the ledge and lowered his foot onto Beo's shoulder. Beo reached and grabbed him by the waist as the rain poured and the wind picked up. There was a great flash of light, followed by a loud boom a second later. A small stream tumbled along, paralleling the path.

"I'm scared." Lila's wet hair plastered her face.

"It's okay, sweetie," said Reece. "I think we should follow the stream."

The rocky dirt path hugged the low cliff. Large trees grew on the other side of the stream, which reminded Reece of beeches. One tree had fallen over but was still growing horizontally on the ground. For five minutes, they walked in silence, with occasional lightning and thunder. The air felt crisp and warm.

"Smoke!" said Reece. Ahead, thirty feet away, white smoke spiraled out of a jumble of large boulders.

They arrived at an opening in the cliff face, roughly the height and width of a man. The smoke smelled sweet and wet with the rain.

"Hallo!" said Reece. He came to the entrance and peered into the darkness.

"Abet!" came a reply.

"The Abba. I know it." Soon, Reece saw a dim shadow approaching, a person with a tiny kerosene lantern. The Abba Paulos motioned for him to enter, and Reece slid inside an open cave twenty feet square with a high ceiling. Lila followed, and Beo turned sideways to squeeze in. The roof of the cool cave was a foot shy of his height. Reece noticed a passage in the back of the room.

"Nah," said the Abba, meaning come.

The entry into the passage was smaller than the first, and Beo went to his knees to get through. The group entered a larger room that held a rickety bed, a crude desk, and three wooden chairs, the seats made of laced leather. A small fire burned, sending up a plume of white smoke that leaked out through fissures in the rock above. Off to the left was a wide passageway where water trickled and ran back into the cave.

Holding the candle, the Abba looked like an apparition, wearing a golden robe and a matching skull cap. He spoke in Amharic, and Beo translated.

"He says that we must rest, to sit," said Beo.

Reece and Lila took chairs, and Beo sat cross-legged on the cold floor. Over the fire was a steel tripod and an iron pot, the contents of a spicy wot bubbling. Against the wall sat three clay pots filled with water below shelves made of old boards.

"He says that the young girl is named Lila," said Beo.

"He knows," said Reece. "Lila, have you met the Abba?"

"Who's the Abba?" asked Lila.

"This man."

"I don't think so. I'm thirsty and hungry." She shivered.

"I will ask him for food and water," said Beo.

The Abba went to the shelves and brought down a loaf of hard bread. He took a knife and carved a hunk and handed it to Lila. Over the pot's spouts were purple cups, and he poured a cupful of water for Lila.

"Thank you, sir," said Lila.

The Abba spoke, standing and holding the lantern.

"He says that you are here to find your daughter," said Beo.

"Yes, Mia!" said Reece.

The Abba took a chair and placed the lantern on the ground, its flame spinning in the draft.

The day dawned bright and chilly, the sun seeming alive but cold. Kristin readied Mia for school.

"Mia, out of the bathtub! You've been there for twenty minutes. We'll be late."

"Hold your horses, you old nag." Mia arched her body out of the warm water, creating waves.

"Out, now!"

"Okay!"

Kristin looked in her purse for Mia's lunch money and only had a ten. The day before, Mia had slipped out of school and headed to the convenience store in the officer's quarters, using her leftover lunch money to buy snacks. The military police took an hour to find her, and Kristin had been in tears.

Out of the tub, Mia dressed herself in black corduroy pants and a fluffy brown sweater. She combed back her wet hair. She stopped, and her mouth dropped. "What?"

"It's me, silly," said Dahlia. "I'm here to see my mommy."

"What? Here? Your mommy?"

"Do you like your mommy? But she's not really your mommy. She's my mommy." Dahlia hopped onto the bed and pulled the floral comforter over her legs.

"Mia, are you dressed?" Kristin walked into the bedroom. "Good, you look nice. Thank you, Mia. What's wrong?"

Mia looked at the bed. Dahlia had pulled the comforter

over her head.

"Boo!" said Dahlia, sitting up straight as a board.

Kristin's throat closed, and her heart stopped for a second. "How? Who?" She looked at Mia.

"Hi, Mommy!" said Dahlia.

"That's Dahlia," said Mia.

"Oh, my God." Kristin had practiced meeting Dahlia, but this was so unexpected. "Dahlia. Yes, Dahlia. I'm your mommy." She stood frozen.

"Can you come and snuggle with me, Mommy?" asked Dahlia

"Hey, she's my mother!" said Mia, still combing back her hair.

"Bye bye, Mia," said Dahlia, and with just a tiny flash of blue light, Mia was gone. She patted the space beside her on the bed.

"Mia's gone."

"Yeah, I sent her back to the Pinch. You didn't like her anyways. Aren't you going to comfort me? I want you to make me some snickerdoodles."

"You're a little girl with golden hair. You're Dahlia." Kristin sensed her feet were moving, and then she was on the bed, sitting next to Dahlia. "You're my little girl." She touched Dahlia's very real hair.

"I love you, Mommy. You always have to take care of me. I'll be the best girl ever."

"I, I love you too. What should I do?"

"Oh, just hug and kiss me."

Kristin put her arm around Dahlia and drew her close. Somehow, she felt as if the real Mia had returned, and she kissed Dahlia's cheek. "I'm so glad you're here, baby."

"Me too."

For half an hour, Kristin held Mia, who had melted into her. Kristin desperately wanted to call Clyde Markush and tell him the story. Would Dahlia bring the real Mia back?

"Honey, I have to make a phone call. Is that okay?" Kristin wore jeans and a black wool turtleneck. "We'll get some things at the store to make cookies."

"Okay, Mommy. I'll come with you."

"Why don't you just stay warm under the covers?"

"No, Mommy. I want to be near you."

"Well, okay."

Kristin walked to the small kitchen and took the phone from its cradle on the wall. Mia looked in the refrigerator and took out a carton of orange juice.

"Hello, Clyde?"

"Hey! My favorite lady in the world. Why are you whispering?"

"It's just...You have to get over here asap. It's an emergency. Dahlia."

"Dahlia?"

"Yes, Dahlia. Hurry."

Clyde Markush grabbed his tape recorder, not knowing why, and hurried into the lobby. "Going to see Kristin," he said to Denise, the receptionist. He walked out into the brisk air and across the parking lot to the guest house. He knocked.

"Get in here," said Kristin. "It's Dahlia, out of nowhere, and she made Mia disappear."

"You're kidding." He seemed to be rooted to his spot, then stepped into the warm hallway. He followed Kristin past the kitchen and into the living room, where he saw a little brown girl with perfect features drinking from a red tumbler. "Hello?" he said.

Emma stayed busy with Emma the patient. She had been pushing Emma up and down the halls and then taken her into the dayroom. A group of five played rummy.

"We'll just sit here for a while," said Emma.

Emma nodded and whispered, "Thank you." With Emma serving as her private nurse, she was recovering her motor and speech skills with rapidity.

"You really liked Reece, didn't you?" asked Emma.

"My friend," said Emma with difficulty.

"Yeah, my friend too. I visited him this morning, one of the Reeces that is. I told you there were two. But then there's the one you knew where you came from. They're all skinny, but with pretty good legs."

Emma smiled. "Yeah."

"Maybe there's one for each of us." Emma laughed.

Emma nodded her head.

"Are you from Georgia?"

"Al...abama."

"Right. There's another Emma, just like us, who lives in Alabama. So, there's three of us. That's crazy, right?"

"Crazy. Where...is this?"

Emma had to lean in to catch her words. "Organon. In Kentucky. You just showed up here, outside on the grass. The Abba Paulos sent you here is what we imagine. You knew him?"

"Yes, the cave..."

"He sent you here so that we could take care of you. I'm a nurse, just like you. I'll bet you were busy seeing all the patients. From where I came, we, Reece and I, would sometimes see a hundred patients a day, most with worms or eye infections.”

“Me too.” Emma stifled a yawn, but then smiled.

In room ten, Timera Scocpol’s EEG shifted to alpha waves, and her eyes opened. Claire from the nursing station alerted Jim, her nurse, and he trotted that way.

“Timera?” Jim raised the head of her bed to forty-five degrees and checked her blood pressure, which was very high. He went to the nursing stations to retrieve Procardia and punctured the gel capsule. “Timera, I’m going to squirt some medicine under your tongue. Your blood pressure is too high.”

Timera followed him with her eyes and stuck out her tongue.

“Okay, great,” said Jim. He washed his hands at the sink. “Can you talk?”

Timera blinked, exhausted from seizing. “Hey, I found her...” Little beads of sweat lined her eyes.

Jim perked up. “You found who?”

“My Lucinda, on an island, Lake Tana. She was living with the monks in a little hut. I...I need to get back and quick.”

“That’s great,” said Jim. “Is she okay?”

“Yeah, but she look thin.”

“Super,” said Jim. “I’ll let Dr. Markush know. Are you hungry, thirsty?”

“I need a drink.”

Jim poured some water into a cup and held it with a straw to her lips.

Timera drained the cup. “Need some more.”

After drinking three cups of water and smacking her lips, she became more alert and stretched her arms. "So stiff. She called me Mama and was crying. I was just holding her in my lap. It was dark in the hut, and some incense was burning. I need to bring her home, but don't know how."

"Is there an Abba Paulos there?" asked Jim.

"I don't rightly know."

"He may be able to help. He's helped others in your situation."

Timera's IV pump beeped, and the bag was about empty. "Hold on," said Jim, and he went to fetch another bag of saline mixed with dextrose. While in the nursing station, he called Markush and left an urgent message.

Markush looked stunned as he gazed at Dahlia. He fumbled in his pocket for the tape recorder. Dahlia sat with her legs under her on the couch as if posing.

"Hello, Clyde," said Dahlia. "It's nice to meet you. Mommy, come and sit by me."

Kristin looked at Clyde, her eyes wide. "She just appeared out of thin air, in the bedroom."

"Mommy!"

Kristin sat beside Dahlia, and Dahlia took her hand.

Markush sat in the chair closest to the couch and put the recorder on the coffee table. "Dahlia. You are Dahlia?" He leaned forward.

"Yes, who else could I be? Kristin is my mommy, and she loves me very much, don't you, Mommy?" She brought Kristin's hand to her lips and kissed it.

"Where did you come from?" asked Markush.

"Oh, you know very well," said Dahlia. "You call it the Pinch, but it's where I used to live."

Markush had a million questions. The air felt rarefied. "Now that you have a mommy, how will that change the way you see the world, the universe?" He wanted to throw her under a microscope and take a very close look at this being.

"I'm so happy! I don't have to stay all squashed up in the Pinch, but I still need to keep an eye on things. I'm going to let my sister Julia take my place there for now."

"Wow," said Markush. "Will Julia want to kidnap little girls?"

Dahlia laughed and pulled down her golden skirt over her ankles. "I doubt it. She's too kind. She even likes bugs."

Kristin could feel a genuine warmth emanating from Dahlia through her hand. Dahlia had a hardened expression as if having long dealt with pain. "Are you going to stay here?" asked Kristin.

"I need you. I have to stay here, but I may leave now and then."

"What happened to Mia?" asked Markush.

"I don't need her anymore. She's back in the Pinch with everything else, all the ideas and such."

"Dahlia," said Kristin. "You took my Mia and hid her somewhere. Can you bring her back?" Her voice trembled. She withdrew her hand, and Dahlia moved in closer, touching shoulders.

"Yes, I hid her, but look what happened. I found you!"

"You have to bring Mia back," said Markush. "Right?"

"Maybe," said Dahlia. "Unless Mommy tells me to bring her back."

"Please, yes, bring her back as soon as possible," said Kristin.

"But Reece Myers is looking for her. I think he's having a blast with Beo."

"Not really," said Markush. "He's anxious about Mia and wants her back, too. He loves her. Kristin loves her."

"I love you, Mommy." Dahlia put her head in Kristin's lap. "Can you run your fingers through my hair?"

Kristin did as asked and marveled at the softness of Dahlia's golden hair. "We love you, Dahlia, just like you love me, see? Bring her back so that we can all be together."

"Oh, Mommy. You might love Mia more than me, and that would make me sad. Will you promise to love me the most?"

"I promise to love you both just the same. I have to be fair, right?" Kristin could feel the warmth of Dahlia. She was real.

"Just give me a little while," said Dahlia.

"What about all the other little girls you abducted?" asked Markush. "Can they go back home? They need to go back home."

"There are so many," said Dahlia. "Here, there, and everywhere."

"In just this universe?" asked Markush.

"Oh no, lots and lots. I've been busy. I think Julia should send them all back. That's right up her alley." She giggled. "So many mommies and daddies without their little girls."

"That would make so many people happy," said Kristin. She brushed Dahlia's cheek with her fingers.

"Can you visit Julia soon and have her return everyone?" asked Markush.

"Not right now. Mommy's hands feel so good. Would you take me for a walk in the woods, mommy?"

"Sure, of course," said Kristin. "Want to go now?"

"Maybe in a minute. I'm so happy. I've never been happy before. There are more bad ideas than good ideas, and I just got stuck with them."

"Is the Pinch just ideas?" asked Markush.

"Pretty much," said Dahlia. "I can make them come and go. It's like a gigantic puzzle."

"Wow," said Markush. "You're being very helpful."

"That's a new one," said Dahlia. "Most people don't like

me, especially the ones in Dogtown. I guess I need to let them go. But they were thinking mean things about me."

"Yes, absolutely. You can make them happy again as well. How many are there?" asked Markush.

"About a zillion, I guess. I don't count them."

"Dahlia, are there more than one of you and Julia? I mean, do you watch over all the existing universes?"

"That would be me," said Dahlia. "I just wanted a mommy. I was getting tired."

"Fascinating," said Markush. "What will the world do now?"

Without thinking, Reece withdrew the two hundred firkins he had left and presented them to the Abba. With a deft motion, the Abba took the bills and secreted them into his robe. "Nah," he said and motioned for them to follow him through yet another passage into another chamber, the walls smoothed and debris carted away. The tiny kerosene lantern sent forth a red glow, illuminating the chamber in a sickly light. In the middle of the chamber stood a wooden bier similar to others Reece had seen in those other places. On the bier stood the golden Ark of the Covenant, deadly still.

"Damn, he wants to ship us off to another realm," said Reece. "Mia's not here."

"If we must," said Beo. "I am ready."

"I'm kinda scared," said Lila. "It's so spooky in here, and I'm cold. My hair is wet."

"Don't be scared," said Reece. "We're going to take you home, but we have to travel to another place. There'll be a bright light and a loud noise. Just hold my hand."

The Abba motioned for them to kneel in front of the bier. He began the familiar chant in the ancient language of Ge'ez, his voice coming louder and louder. A faint glow emanated from the Ark. The Abba paused, waiting, and then began his chant once again, this time louder, but the light faded, and there was no wind.

"Dahlia!" said the Abba, followed by nothing.

"My knees hurt," said Lila.

"Nothing happened," said Reece. "The world is my will

and representation!" he said. Nothing happened. "Damn, the system's broke."

The Abba shook his head. "Rise," he said. "No one listens, and all hope is lost."

Beo roughly interpreted for Reece. They stood and shivered as the Abba led them back into the main living chamber, where his pot of lentil stew bubbled.

"What do we do?" asked Reece. "Dahlia is mute today."

"I'm hungry," said Lila.

The Abba spoke, and Beo said he was inviting them to dinner. The Abba pointed to large biscuit tins and bade them to sit. He produced a large metal platter and placed two layers of enjera on it. In the middle, he placed a steaming mound of lentils, then put the platter on top of three biscuit tins as a table. "Be-low," he said. "Eat."

They ate in relative silence, Reece showing Lila how to tear a flap of enjera and use it to pinch some lentils.

"This is spicy," said Lila.

"Yeah," said Reece. "But we have to fill our bellies. I'm out of money."

"Okay," said Lila.

When they finished, the Abba brought out a tall bottle of birzz, the sweet honey drink. He poured equal amounts into four purple plastic cups. Lila sipped hers at first and then gulped it down.

"Amenseganolo," said Reece, meaning thank you.

"Yiqirta," said the Abba. "No problem."

"I wonder why the Ark is not working," said Beo.

"Maybe Dahlia is busy in another universe," said Reece.

"The Abba says this has never happened before, and he is worried," said Beo.

"Am I going home?" Lila licked her fingers, drawing a look from the Abba.

"We'll figure it out," said Reece. "We can't go back to Gordian, having set free some tough meat, as they say."

"They will punish us," said Beo.

The Abba cleared his throat and stood. "Great things are coming."

Beo interpreted.

"I wonder..." and Reece slumped forward.

Markush had notified Glenelle Lock of the fresh development, the appearance of Dahlia, and she had briefed the others, including Sherri Loveless, who was on tour with Arthur. How would she be able to spin the idea of "Dahlia among us," the young God come to Earth? After Arthur appeared on a TV morning show in Dallas, she and Arthur traveled to Birmingham, Alabama, for a show at the Jemison Concert Hall, which held thirteen hundred seats. Loveless had told Glenelle she would like to introduce Dahlia to the world at the show.

Markush and Dr. Mumford were with Timera, who had returned from Lake Tana, getting the details of finding her daughter, Lucinda. Pumped, they reiterated the importance of finding the Abba Paulos to see if he could send them back.

Carletta popped into Timera's room. "Got a call for you, Dr. Markush, from next door. Come, hurry!"

Markush trotted to the nursing station and grabbed the phone beside Claire, who was at her station watching the monitors. "Markush."

"Hey, Doc," said Shelby. "Reece Myers is back, thought you would like to know."

"That's great, thanks, and I'll be right over." Markush entered the long-term unit through the connecting door, entered the nursing station where Sheila was charting, and then out the door into the hall and room eleven. "Hey, buddy!"

"Hey." Reece looked whipped, his eyes glassy. An empty Coke can sat on his overbed table. "Beo and I still have Lila, and we've found the Abba Paulos. He tried to transport us to God knows where, but the Ark didn't work. I don't know what we'll do. We can't go back to the house we were staying in. We let one boy we were watching escape."

"Wow," said Markush. "So much has happened. I think I know why the Ark didn't work for you. Are you ready for this?"

Shelby left the room to check on the other Reece.

"Good Lord, what?" asked Reece. "So damn weak."

"Yeah, the traveling is taking a toll on you. So, the news. Dahlia is here, at the guest house, with Kristin."

Reece frowned. "Dahlia? Here? With Kristin? How the hell did that happen? How do you know it's her?"

"She just magically appeared, and she sent Mia, the replacement Mia, away, back to the Pinch. It's her for sure. Brown skin, soft yellow hair, perfect features, arrogant. She's in love with Kristin." He then explained how Kristin had become Dahlia's mother.

"Jesus, Kristin is Dahlia's mother. That's brilliant. But how will we get Mia home?"

"I don't know, but we have Dahlia, or rather Kristin has Dahlia. I have to get back over there. Try and will yourself to stay here for a while to see what happens, if you can do that."

"I'll try, but I need to get back and help take care of Lila."

"Right, look, let me go. I'll check back in soon." With that, Markush exited the building, noting that it was two o'clock. He ran across the parking lot to Kristin's apartment and saw Emma's door. He needed to let her know as well, but she was on the medical unit, no doubt working with Emma.

Markush didn't bother to knock and entered Kristin's apartment, the warm air enveloping him. He looked left and saw Kristin and Dahlia in the kitchen, Dahlia seated at the small dining table, eating chicken noodle soup, Kristin sitting beside her. Kristin's curls fell over her eyes, giving her a weary look.

"Hello, Clyde," said Dahlia. She was so perfect—she almost looked like a cartoon.

Clyde was astounded and searched for words. "Hey, what's going on? Everything okay? Eating?"

"Mommy made me some soup! We're gonna make cookies tomorrow, right, Mommy?"

Kristin managed a smile. "Yes, cookies, tomorrow. She has quite an appetite."

Markush leaned against the fridge. "That's great. Maybe we could talk some more."

"I think you like Mommy," said Dahlia.

Markush blinked. "You could say that, very much in fact."

"So, will you be my daddy or will Reece be my daddy?"

Kristin broke in. "I don't think you have a daddy right now, but Clyde can fill in if you would like that."

"Fine by me," said Clyde. "But we need to talk."

He then told her about Reece looking for Mia in Gordian and how the Abba had failed with the Ark, while marveling at Dahlia. Dahlia laughed and said that she was too busy being loved by Kristin to be concerned with the likes of Mia, just another little girl to her.

"But I need Mia back, very badly," said Kristin. A few

tears formed.

"I'm putting Julia in charge," said Dahlia. "She likes to be nice. But you may not love me as much if Mia comes back." She put on a pouty face.

"No, she will," said Clyde.

"Dahlia, I love you very much. I'm your mommy. Nothing will make me love you less. You just have to trust me, okay?" She ran her hand through Dahlia's shoulder-length hair. "You are quite the looker, gorgeous even. I can't believe that you run a universe or universes."

"I've been wasting time with all those worlds and people, always asking me for stuff. I just want to be with my mommy." She picked up her bowl of soup and drank the rest. "That was yummy. Are you going to give me a vitamin, so I'll be big and strong?"

Kristin laughed. "If you want vitamins, I can buy some vitamins."

"Flintstones vitamins, the fruity ones."

Markush fidgeted, wanting to get down to business. "So, what about Julia, putting her in charge of bringing all the little girls back home?"

"Hold on," said Dahlia. She spent nearly a minute looking thoughtful.

Finally free, Julia skipped along to find the edge of the Cylinder. In every direction was a blank distance without a breath of air. She saw specks in the distance and soon arrived at the edge of a group of thirty-two souls, all with blank faces.

"Dahlia," said a tall, thin woman.

"No, I'm Julia, her sister."

A man with sad eyes walked forward. "You're Dahlia. You don't have a sister. You look the same, though."

"Don't be angry. We're twins, but now that she's so busy with her new mommy, I'm going to the Pinch."

"Yeah, right," said another gaunt figure. "Can you please just let us go to find our daughters? This is cruel and unbearable. It's not fair to keep us here."

"I don't want you to be here. Dahlia wants that, and I'm Julia." She smiled.

A general murmur emerged. "Maybe she's not Dahlia," said one. "That would be a miracle," said another.

"I'm Julia, and I want to help you, but first I have to get to the Pinch. Trust me."

The group had pressed together, all with wondering eyes.

"My daughter, Sheila," said one. The others began speaking the names of their daughters and pleading their cases. A woman with brown hair and blue eyes dropped to her knees, crying.

Julia approached and touched the woman's bowed head. "It's okay. But I have to hurry. Dahlia may change her mind. I can't help you here." She passed through the group, some reaching to touch her hair, still murmuring the names of their daughters.

Julia pressed forward, leaving them behind, saddened by the sadness. For weeks, months, and years, she walked and skipped and ran until the light grew brighter, and then she was at the edge of the Cylinder, into which she slipped on her way to the Pinch.

On the medical unit, the phone was ringing off the hook. Debbie called Markush and told him to hurry back. His chest bursting, Markush made his way to the nursing station. The first call had been from Helmut Grayson's wife. Her daughter Lila was back, sound asleep on her bed. And then Clark Peters' ex-wife with the same news. An exceptional event was unfolding: the return of girls abducted by Dahlia.

"Julia," said Markush.

"Julia?" said Debbie.

"I'll explain later. Everything changes from here on out." His cell phone rang. "Hey."

"My God, Mia is back, the real Mia! My daughter," said Kristin. Her voice seemed to come from a well.

"Wow!" said Markush. "Julia is on the move. Is Mia okay? Wait, I'll be right over." He hurried off the unit, even though he needed to tell the patients that their daughters were being returned.

Kristin's door locked, Markush knocked three times. He looked up at the clear, cold sky and said a thank you.

"Clyde, in here," said Kristin. "She's back."

"Where?"

"On the bed."

Markush went to the bedroom door, and his jaw dropped. Mia slept on the bed, with Dahlia beside her.

"Hi, Clyde. I've got a sister. How about them apples?"

Markush took it all in, as if in a dream.

"She's out like a light," said Kristin. "My baby. I'm afraid she'll disappear again." She pushed past Markush and stood over Mia, her expression one of bewilderment.

"No worries, Mommy," said Dahlia. "I won't send her back unless you stop loving me." She laughed.

"We have to let Reece know she's back before he seizes again. I feel like I'm inside a washing machine. So many people to call. Make sure you preserve her clothes. Don't wash them. We'll want to scrape under her fingernails too, so don't give her a bath anytime soon."

Kristin leaned over and brushed Mia's cheek with her fingers. Mia breathed as if sleeping like the dead. "Thank you, Dahlia, for being so nice."

"Yeah," said Dahlia. She wiggled her toes inside her red socks. "We're still making cookies tomorrow? Snickerdoodles?"

"Absolutely. Clyde, when will she wake up?"

"In another case like this, in Cedar City, Utah, the girl slept for nearly a day. When she woke up, it was slow."

"Old Julia is on the job," said Dahlia. "Undoing my handiwork. You know, I had to go to a lot of trouble, hiding all the girls? But now that I have a mommy, I can just be a little girl."

Markush's phone rang, and it was Debbie. "I have to get back. So much is happening. This is great news. What's to come? I can only imagine." He hugged Kristin and kissed her cheek.

"Watch it, Clyde," said Dahlia. "That's my mommy."

"Yes, yes, she is," and he was out the door and jogging across the parking lot to Organon.

Within two hours, Markush verified the return of ten of

the eleven girls abducted from patients on the medical unit. The only one missing was Granny D's little girl, Kisha, but Kisha was a granddaughter. Markush kept his fingers crossed and left the nursing station to inform the patients of the impossible news. He started with Helmut Grayson. Reece had found Lila in Gordian, but now Lila was back home in St Louis, Missouri, with Grayson's wife, asleep but alive and well.

Grayson sat in bed with his wrists loosely restrained, staring at the TV. "Hey, Doc, what's shaking? Get me out of this goddamned bed."

Markush washed his hands out of habit, disbelieving what he was about to say. He stood at the foot of the bed. "I've got some great news, my friend."

"Really? Gonna give me some of that Scotch? Sure could use a slug."

The unit was a beehive of activity, with Jim, Debbie, and Carletta popping in and out of rooms. Three of four patients who had been traveling were back. Only Granny D remained in travel mode.

"This calls for a celebration, for you, me, and the entire planet."

"Spill the beans, Doc. Did I win the lottery?"

"Better than the lottery. Lila, your daughter, is back home with your wife. She's—"

"The hell you say? Maybe old Gandhi found her and sent her home. I need to see her, Doc. Are you shittin' me? You better not be shittin' me."

"No, it's true. She's asleep on her bed. Your wife is extremely confused but overjoyed. I spoke to her. It's true. We have to figure out what to do next. We have to get you home, but we need some time. The public still thinks you killed Lila."

"Goddamn the public. I did what I had to do. My Lila is back." Grayson's face and chest flushed with pure joy.

"Okay, that's the news, but I have the same news for the others. All the girls have been returned except for one. So, I have to go for now. Congratulations, Mr. Grayson."

"Hey, Doc, untie my hands," but Markush left on his way to the next patient. He bumped into Emma in the hall.

"Is it true?" asked Emma.

"Yes, true as true can be."

Glenelle Lock picked up the phone, having returned from a smoke break. Her lips were a dark red to match her pumps. "Hey, Markush. Getting late in the day for a call."

"Where do I start? Two things, and hold on to your teeth. Dahlia is in Kristin's apartment at the guest house."

"What the hell, Markush? Dahlia, the puppet master of the universe? How do you know?"

"Glenelle, this is big. Dahlia bought the ruse that Kristin is her mother. That's what she has always wanted, a mother to love her."

"Is she not smart enough to know that she's being tricked?" Glenelle rubbed a knee, aching from the cold. "And how do you know it's Dahlia, the one and only?"

"She has the mind of a seven-year-old. She's desperate for a mother. She came out of nowhere, and she made the fake Mia disappear. It's her, a little brown girl with golden hair and perfect features."

"Have you told anyone else?"

"No, can you let the team know? I wonder what plan Loveless will devise. If we're being transparent, we have to let the public know."

"I'll pass along the development and get back to you."

"And there's more news. You won't believe this either."

"Give it to me, Markush."

"The patients at Organon, the abducted daughters, they've all returned except for one, Mia included."

"Jesus Christ, that's huge. You've verified this?"

"I've spoken with the moms and dads around the country. Their girls are back, all of them in a deep sleep. I may have jumped the gun, but I let the patients know that their daughters have been returned." Markush drew a cylinder on his desktop calendar.

"But how are they suddenly back? Dahlia just let them go?"

"Julia, it's Julia, I think. I told you that Dahlia has a twin sister. Julia is the good one of the pair. She's undoing the evil deeds of her sister."

"You told me about Julia, but I didn't buy it. How do you know this is the work of Julia?"

"I just do. Once Dahlia had Kristin as her mom, Dahlia set Julia free from Dogtown. Julia's in charge now. Dahlia is acting like a helpless kitten, letting Kristin pamper her."

"The ramifications are huge. Will this make Organon obsolete? You may be out of a job, Markush."

"I thought of that, but there's still the mystery of time, of those gifted with the music that drew in Dahlia. I would like to keep Organon going as a research organization. There are still the questionable cases of murders that have yet to be solved. All around the world, little girls are being returned. Imagine the surprise to the uninitiated."

"This changes everything, Markush. All the funding we receive may go away. I suppose that Griffiss Air Force Base is no longer needed to house families. There will be an uproar surrounding the returned girls, but this notion of Dahlia on Earth and her sister, Julia, running the universes is what the long term holds. The focus will go there. You may have to abandon forensic psychiatry and take up religion."

"You may be right. The past, present, and future of God

are at stake. Will you contact the others right away, especially Loveless? I want to protect Dahlia, but the game has changed. She may like the publicity. We'll just have to see."

"Will do, Markush. Hang in there."

Glenelle then called Sherri Loveless at her home base near Stanford University. She told Sherri about Dahlia and the return of the abducted girls. Sherri took the information with ease, being used to surprises, and got to work with her assistant on a new wave of publicity. In her head, she framed an idea and called it "Meet Dahlia: Savior or Sorceress?"

Sitting on 600 acres of hilly pasture lands, Truth Ranch consisted of eleven houses, three barns, a staid two-story office, a few rough outbuildings, and a large church built of cement, stained a light green, with redwood rafters. Led by Simon Klinefelter, a polygamist from Utah, Truth Ranch existed in a whirl of change, spurred by the stories of Dahlia. The group's primary source of income came from a slaughterhouse in nearby Bakersfield and the mining of a special clay used for cat litter.

A Monday, Simon's senior wife, Xenia, placed a bundle of newspapers on a coffee table. "She's come," she said. A trio of young girls sat knitting in a corner. The boys were out feeding the chickens and gathering eggs.

Simon went to *The New York Times* Sunday edition first. On the front page ran the headline, "Dahlia finds a new home and mother," followed by a story written by Jeremy Sims. "Astounding," said Simon. He read the entire piece as the kitchen phone rang in the background. Simon was an awkward man with narrow, sloped shoulders and very neat blond hair, his face smooth and devoid of emotion. His blue eyes loomed behind thick lenses. "Cut these out for me," he said.

"Let Clarissa do it," said Xenia. Clarissa was the youngest wife, on the second floor.

"Damn, don't be pulling your weight. This is important." Simon looked like a large little boy in his soft blue jeans and plaid shirt. "We have to make contact. Dahlia belongs to us."

Xenia clicked her tongue and grabbed the remote, *CNN* with breaking news. The very professional anchorwoman, Alicia Ostrik, dressed in burgundy, told the story of Dahlia's return, switching to a live feed outside Fort Knox's main gate. The reporter, Ron Simin, rehashed the press release from Sherri Loveless, stating that photos and possibly video of the young God would become available.

"Ron, a lot of people have been speculating about what Dahlia looks like. Many want to know if she favors a particular race or ethnicity."

"That's right, Alicia. From what we've gleaned from a private source, she appears to have brown skin with golden hair. What that ultimately means is hard to say, but it will be mighty interesting to see what the master of the universe looks like."

The story continued with conjectures and second-guessing, ending with an urgent plea by Ron for more information from Organon.

"She has to be white, but with a tan," said Simon.

"Now why does she have to be white?" asked Xenia. "Because you're white?"

"Hell, Frieda is black."

"Oh, so you're above racism because wife four, or maybe five, is half black. You're as racist as a redneck on Robert E. Lee's birthday."

"Okay, what does it matter? It means nothing to me. What's important is that Dahlia has come to Earth, although I need some real proof. Get me another cup of Joe...please?"

"For Christ's sake," said Xenia.

"Mommy, that's bad," said the oldest girl, sitting on a

huge blue cushion in a rattan chair.

"I think we've had a change of heart since Dahlia came along," said Xenia.

"I have to get working on the sermon for tonight. Did you forget the coffee?"

"Get it yourself, prophet of Dahlia. How can you be a prophet if you've never met this Dahlia?"

"This is what we, you, me, and the entire Truth family believe." The news switched to a breaking story of a car plowing into a gas pump. Simon turned off the TV.

"This is what *you* believe, and the rest are just dumb enough to go along with it." Xenia grabbed a dishtowel and wrung it in her hands.

"Dahlia...is...God. I am her prophet. She commands the Ark of the Covenant and time travel. Dahlia is what I, we, have been waiting for. A seven-year-old girl imbued with all-knowing power. It's brilliant."

"I'm a seven-year-old girl," said Tess, the middle girl.

"Criminy," said Simon, standing. "There can only be one Dahlia. And only one prophet."

"Good to know the prophet," said Xenia. "Have you even thought of making payroll at the slaughterhouse? Dahlia can just take a back seat for all I care."

"Have you forgotten the meaning of obey?"

"Yeah, but it's in the dictionary if I need to know."

Simon coughed, got his coffee, and went outside, faced with piles of lumber and mounds of sand.

The news was out, and Markush felt like a bullseye with requests for interviews pouring in. His personal cell phone number had been leaked. Some good news was that Granny D's granddaughter had been returned to Tempe, Arizona. There was no one in Granny D's house, where she had been raising Kisha, and she had arrived unannounced in an empty hospital bed.

Markush's cell beeped. It was Kristin.

Markush trotted down the hall, headed to the guest house. "It's definitely Julia. She's in control and reversing the wrongs of Dahlia. This is great. All the patients' abducted girls have been accounted for. As soon as she's able, we need to let Reece see Mia and stop his travels." He panted across the parking lot, Kristin waiting at the door.

Markush walked into the living room as if through mud. First, he saw Dahlia standing at attention next to the window, and then Mia asleep on the couch, covered with a plush green blanket.

"Mommy, I don't like Mia hogging the couch," said Dahlia. "Can we just drag her to the bed?" She preened her golden hair, giving a faint frown. "Hi, Clyde Markush. Are you going to love Mia as much as me?"

Markush took it in. "I play no favorites." He gazed from Dahlia to Mia, utterly amazed and overwhelmed.

"Dahlia, let's just let Mia rest. She's so tired from her ordeal." Kristin stood beside Markush with her arms folded. And then she said it. "Don't you think it's your fault that Mia—"

"Kristin—"

Dahlia took the wing-back chair. "So, I'm a bad girl? I just wanted to find you, Mommy. I had to make her disappear. You don't really love me?" Her eyes blinked as if tears wanted to flow.

Kristin remembered her script. "Dahlia, I'm your mommy, and I love you very much. But I love Mia too. Thank you for letting her come back." Kristin kneeled and took Dahlia's hand. "Can I get you anything? I want to make you happy."

Markush stared, trying to fathom the implications.

"Yes, Mommy, I want some orange juice."

Mia's foot jerked on the couch. Markush sat there just beyond her feet. "Did you let Mia come back?"

"I suppose you could say that, but it's Julia. She's a do-gooder. I just might have to go back and rip her a new one. I don't like Mia."

"Wow," said Markush. "But you haven't really met Mia. She'll be a great sister."

Kristin handed Dahlia a plastic cup of orange juice.

"Thank you, Mommy." Dahlia scooted from the chair and, with a single motion, poured the juice over Mia's face. "Uh oh!"

"Dahlia!" said Markush and Kristin.

Mia's head turned, and her eyes opened, but then closed again.

"I was just trying to wake her up. I'm sorry." Dahlia put the cup on the coffee table and resumed her seat.

Kristin hurried to the bathroom and returned with a warm washcloth to clean Mia's face.

"Mommy, let's take a walk to the lake and see the ducks."

"I can't leave Mia. You know that."

"She'll be fine. She'll sleep for a long time. Mia was in the circus in a cage."

"Really? You put her in a cage?" asked Kristin, clenching the wet rag.

"Reece mentioned a circus with little girls in cages when he was in Gadam." Markush had stood but resumed his seat on the couch. "This is crazy."

Kristin seemed to have aged ten years in the past hour, her happiness clouded by Dahlia. "A cage. That's nice. Clyde, what are we gonna do now? I'm at my limit."

Markush told her they would just wait and watch as Mia slept, waiting until she awoke, and that everything would be fine. He took in the scene once again and headed back to Organon.

Markush spoke with Sherri Loveless on speaker phone. He had read the headlines regarding Dahlia and watched bits of coverage and knew that a storm was brewing. Loveless told him of her plan to make Dahlia available to the public. She would make her debut with Arthur at his speaking engagement at the Jemison Theater in Birmingham.

"That's insane," said Markush, playing with the phone cord. A mess of letters, files, and unopened mail littered his desk. "She's not just a little girl. She has godly powers."

"We have to stick with our plan. People have to see for themselves and believe or otherwise," said Loveless.

"I'm really worried about security with Dahlia," said Markush.

"There will be security. Through General Watkins, we've arranged for Secret Service presence at the event with local law enforcement at the perimeter. Maybe God, a god, doesn't need security."

Markush laughed and coughed. "I've thought of testing her to see if she can do anything spectacular, like make an ashtray float."

"Yeah, she'll need to feed the masses with two fish and a loaf of bread."

"What are we releasing regarding Julia?"

"I figure we'll wait a couple of days and then spill those beans along with more information about the returned girls. The two are connected. It's too much to fathom, really, but no one can accuse us of a cover-up. We remain naked and see-through."

The call soon ended, and Markush put his feet on his desk, knocking off a coffee cup. His mind whirled with the impossibilities, and he remembered his lunch date with Arthur. In reality, his dream was coming true. He had at his fingertips the sentient being who ran, or who had run, the universes. The mystery of the replaced girls was over. Plus, his relationship with Kristin was going well, although he knew she was highly stressed, having dealt with Mia's replacement and now Dahlia, plus the return of the real Mia. He hoped she would not crash.

"What next?" he said to himself and thought about how Organon would be emptied of patients, as they no longer needed to travel and were essentially exonerated of the murders. He imagined Organon empty and wondered what was next. There was the issue of the original Reece, who remained in a persistent vegetative state. He picked up a copy of *The Washington Post* and read a story about dozens of comatose individuals coming back to life. He conjectured that Julia had emptied Dogtown, sending back the damned to their various universes. Thanks to Kristin being Dahlia's mom, he thought of the world as a different place.

"Dear Julia, make this earth a better place...and give me a new job. Amen."

The sounds of endless cries inundated the Pinch, with a hum of glad tidings running just beneath. The infinite universes inherited by Julia cried out for justice. Dahlia had taken a hands-off approach, allowing the tendency toward evil and disorganization to propagate. Julia infiltrated the dreams of the many and created images of things good and fruitful. She understood the parity of wealth as a guiding factor in relieving the vast majority of hate and resultant crime. People needed to get along, help one another, and care for the worlds they inhabited. The sheer volume of nastiness that Dahlia had fostered staggered and humbled her. She heard the pleas of the endless Dr. Markushes and set about to make things right, but with an eye on Dahlia and her romance with Kristin.

Kristin drowsed in the chair next to the couch, where Mia slept. When Mia awoke around six a.m., she rolled to her back and stared at the ceiling, realizing she was in a new place. She turned her head and saw Kristin, slumped and dozing, and a muted TV.

Mia tried to speak, but her voice caught, and she cleared her throat. "Mom? Mommy?"

Kristin's mind waded through a haze and then clicked. She saw Mia propped on an elbow. She had somehow expected music and lights, but all was silent. "Mia," and Kristin went to her knees beside the couch. "My baby. Oh, Mia, you're okay. I was so worried. Are you really okay?" She draped her body over Mia, tears wetting her cheeks.

"Mommy, I'm okay. I was in that same cage with mean people in a circus. There was that poor old whale hooked up to a machine. Dahlia said Daddy would never find me. Mommy, I can't breathe."

"Well, well, well, look at who popped out of a rabbit hole." Dahlia, wearing panties and dragging a blanket around her shoulders, marched into the room. "I hope you're happy, Mommy. She's been on quite an adventure."

"Mommy?" Mia's eyes widened.

Kristin kissed Mia's cheek and stood. "Mia, this may be a surprise, but this is Dahlia. I'm her mommy, and she's your new sister."

"Dahlia. You stole me and locked me up."

"And plenty more like you. Can you forgive me?" Dahlia flashed a cupid smile.

"Okay, girls, we have to get along. What's important is that Mia is safe. She's back. Mia, I missed you—"

"Hey, what about me? You never said you missed me?" Dahlia put on a serious pout, staring at Kristin.

"You leave her alone!" said Mia, sitting up straight.

"Bitch, you shut your pie hole!" Dahlia let the blanket fall from her perfect shoulders.

"No! Dahlia, no!" said Kristin. "What is—"

"What is wrong with me? You were gonna say it. I know it. You're *my* mommy!"

Mia looked as if mightily confused. The heaviness of her recent captivity and sudden return tired her. She took a deep breath, her chin trembling, and she broke into a cry. She crawled off the couch and went to Kristin, hugging her waist.

"Mia, all is well. Things are just a little different now." Kristin kissed her reddened cheek.

"Buddy, here we go," said Dahlia. "I didn't come to Earth to be treated like a second-class citizen." She marched right up and joined in the hug, pushing Mia with her elbow.

"Mommy!" Mia hugged Kristin even tighter. "Where's Daddy? He'll beat her up."

Kristin stood like a statue, wondering what to do. "Girls, let's sit on the couch. One on each side. Now, that's much better. Dahlia, Mia is my little girl, just like you are my little girl. We have to get along."

"Yeah, but she's your favorite," said Dahlia. "I'm fucking cold."

"Dahlia? Go put on some clothes if you're cold." Kristin put a hand on each girl's thigh.

"This sucks." Dahlia went to the bedroom and found a flannel shirt of Kristin's. "She's not being a good mommy." She returned and sat on Kristin's lap, giving Mia a solid look.

Back at Organon, a week of chaos ensued. One by one, the patients were discharged and sent home to start anew. Only Clark Peters and Emma remained on the medical unit. Peters' wife had divorced him and wanted nothing to do with him, despite having her little girl back. On the long-term unit, both of the Reeces were still in the house. Markush was at a loss as to what to do with his employees. Nearly $400,000 remained in his budget, and he gave the nurses and the techs a month off with pay, except for four nurses, Jim, Debbie, Sheila, and Shelby, who would alternate day and night shifts. Emma, the Returnee, stayed as well, venturing back and forth between the units to visit Reece and her double.

Emma, the patient, sat in the bedside recliner with a cup of ice in her hand. With the dedicated care of Emma, the Returnee, Emma looked great and had begun to practice standing.

"You okay for now?" asked Emma. "I'm going to visit with Reece for a few minutes."

"Yes," said Emma. Her speech was slow but distinct. With the remote, she could change the TV channels.

Emma passed over to the other unit, glanced at the comatose Reece, and made her way to room eleven. "Looking good, my friend."

"Feel pretty good. Markush is releasing me tomorrow to the guest house. I'll get to see Mia and even Dahlia. Can you believe it?" The lights were off in the room, just the glow from the TV and light from the hall.

"So, you haven't had any seizures for a couple of days?" Emma sat on the corner of his bed.

"None, but my job is done. Mia is safe. I feel sorry for poor Beo, stuck in Gordian. But the girl, Lila, made it back safe, thanks to Julia, or so says Markush."

Reece gave her the rundown of Gordian again, how the inhabitants practiced cannibalism of their own flesh and blood. Emma shook her head, gazing at Reece's thin face, the frequent seizure activity depleting his body.

"You know what?" asked Reece.

"What?"

"Well, first I want you to come and meet Mia. Then maybe we could go out for lunch or some such." Reece smoothed his mahogany hair to the side.

Emma smiled. "Damn, we have so much to talk about, especially our Ethiopia connections, plus we're just a stone's throw from the former leader of the universe. Yeah, I would love to get lunch."

"Okay, deal."

"What about Kristin?" she said.

"Doesn't look like we'll get back together again," he said. "I'm pretty sure she has a thing with Markush, which is fine, I suppose. I just need to spend time with Mia."

"Right."

"There was a Reece at the clinic you worked at," said Reece..

"Just like you worked with an Emma, I worked with a Reece. We worked so well in the clinic together. I was sort of falling in love with him, and I think he was the same way. But he was engaged. When we returned, he was left behind, I think. He just never arrived with us." She sat in the recliner.

"When I was in Godo, I was engaged as well. Kristin sent letters, begging me to come home."

"Yeah. I felt like I had fucked up her life and mine. I was becoming a different person. Amid all the suffering, one night, I just gave up the idea of God. I mean, I was a missionary, for Christ's sake. How was your relationship with your Emma?"

"We were pretty tight. The night the village administrator shot me, I was at her house, giving her a neck massage. The bullet came through a chink in the wall." He pointed to the scars on his temples. "Passed right through."

"That's terrifying."

"Emma saved my life that night, and then the real adventure started."

"All of that led you to be here."

"And with an Emma."

The event to eclipse all events rolled forth under its own steam. Arthur would be speaking, but it was Dahlia's appearance that had the nation electrified. Clarity Stillwell and the Christian Instinct Network had mobilized followers to protest in thirty-two states, proclaiming Dahlia a fraud and a tool of Satan. There had been talk of moving the event from Birmingham to a larger venue, such as Madison Square Garden, but Loveless decided that the spectacle would generate the most presence and suspense by being held in the heart of the Bible Belt.

A primary issue with the sold-out event would be parking, and the city convinced the university to open up parking lots to the general public. The show, as Stillwell called it, took place on a Saturday night, but news crews from far and wide had set up shop outside the university's performing arts center days in advance.

Accompanied by two military policemen on special duty, Markush, Arthur, Reece, Afewerki, and Emma, with her majesty Dahlia in the middle, walked as a pack into the Sheraton, pushing through a group of journalists who shouted questions, one asking, "Can we see the face of God?" The group convened in Markush's executive suite, where he would stay with Dahlia and Emma, who was serving as her caretaker. The group stood in a circle, with Dahlia running to look out the window. The MPs stood guard in the hall.

"Wow," said Markush. "We made it."

Afewerki was the first to sit on the bright white furniture. "The people have come to see her. They frighten me." He looked preppy in his EKU sweater over a button-down.

"Yes, quite the crush of humanity," said Arthur. "I fear someone will get their hands on the little one."

Emma walked over and stood by Dahlia. "What do you see?" Emma touched Dahlia's golden hair.

"Not much. This place is pretty yucky." Below, the street clogged with traffic.

"Are you excited to speak tomorrow night?"

"No. People bore me. All they want is a new car or a new boyfriend. But now Julia can deal with it. She thinks she's so nice and all, but she'll see the light."

"You talk so much like an adult sometimes."

"Well, I am a billion zillion years old." Dahlia looked dead serious.

Meanwhile, Markush had an MP walk Arthur and Afewerki to their suite. Dahlia roamed from room to room but soon settled on a white recliner. Markush tried to engage her in a conversation about what she would say to the expectant audience, but all Dahlia would say was "You'll see."

Saturday inched along with room-service meals for everyone. At two p.m., Markush, Afewerki, and Arthur held a press conference in a large room with select media chosen by Sherri Loveless. The trio sat in rolling chairs behind a long folding table. The dull gray room had no windows and seemed short of oxygen. With an armed MP standing guard at the door, the event started amid a general buzz. Seven cameras crowded the back of the room, with sound booms reaching.

"Welcome!" said Markush, and the buzz died down. "So many events have taken place in the past two weeks, primarily the return of the abducted daughters and, of course, the appearance of Dahlia. With us today are Arthur Schopenhauer and Afewerki Nigussie, both of whom are Returnees that you are familiar with. We have about half an hour, and we can start taking questions." He smoothed back his long gray hair.

A dozen voices called out, and Markush pointed.

"How godlike can we expect Dahlia to be?" asked a man sweating in a blue suit.

"She is not God," said Afewerki, a frown on his face and his voice rising. "But she is practicing magic, which is of the devil."

"Arthur, what do you think?" asked a woman with chopsticks through her chignon.

"Well, my good friend Afewerki comes from a religious background where beings such as Dahlia are impossible, it seems. She is capable of omniscience, knowing all. But her presence on Earth has taken her from her seat of power, where she rules as if God. As with Christ, God, my pardons to Afewerki, has come to us in flesh and blood."

The heat in the room from the bodies, equipment, and lights warmed the atmosphere. Markush pointed to a woman waving a clipboard, his armpits beginning to stain.

"If we have Dahlia with us, then who's minding the universe?" That brought a few laughs.

"I can address that," said Markush. "By now, you have heard of Dahlia's sister, Julia..." Hands shot up. "Bear with me. By vacating the Pinch, which some compare to heaven, Dahlia has allowed Julia to more or less take charge. Instead of Dear Dahlia, now it's Dear Julia—"

"Although many see this as fantastical, what's the difference between a Dahlia or a Julia?

Markush spoke. "I've yet to say this publicly, but the fate of our universe is forever changed. From what I know, Julia represents goodness, whereas Dahlia was indifferent and took little interest in the fate of humanity, only being concerned about who her mother was."

"So, to the panel, has Dahlia done anything godlike since her arrival? Has she raised the dead? People, most people, want proof."

"She has not," said Afewerki. "She is a girl with magic."

"She has not moved a mountain nor parted the seas, as of yet." Arthur smacked his dry lips. "But she *magically* appeared from thin air and caused the disappearance of the replacement Mia. I would say her powers remain unknown at present."

The reporters murmured.

"We can't ask her to do tricks to appease the masses," said Markush, "but I have a feeling that she will make her powers known as time goes by, perhaps out of necessity."

Dahlia wanted Emma to help her bathe and wash her hair, which Emma did. Emma found her body curious, with not a freckle or mole in sight, just pure, smooth brown skin.

"Comb my hair." Dahlia sat on the couch, her feet just shy of the floor. A hospitality tray of crackers, nuts, and cheese rested on the coffee table. "You know I don't need to eat, being God and all."

"Can you say please when you ask for something?" asked Emma. "Then why do you eat?"

"Maybe to fit in. My mommy likes to cook for me. I miss her. She stayed home to be with that Mia girl."

"Well, that's her daughter, too." Emma combed Dahlia's luxurious golden hair, tackling a tangle.

"Ow, watch it, bitch!" Dahlia jerked her head away.

Emma stopped. "That wasn't very nice. Be more polite and thankful. Geez."

"Whatever, talk to the hand." She held her hand up to Emma's face. "I learned that one in Dogtown."

Emma sighed and asked Dahlia to get dressed in clothes that belonged to Mia.

"You're not going to help?"

"You can dress yourself. I have to get ready." Emma entered the bathroom and closed the door.

Dahlia kicked her feet back and forth. She gazed around the large room that looked brand-new and had a plan. She put on a pair of panties and tennis shoes, walked to the door, and opened it. The MP gawped at her. He wore his greens with a billy stick, pepper spray, radio, and handcuffs. His black boots glistened.

"Hello, Stinson." Dahlia stood with her hands on her hips.

"Hey, you can't be out of the room, back inside, okay?" He was young with a smooth face but a hard chin.

"Look, soldier boy, I'm Dahlia. I can do what I want." At that, she took off, running down the plush carpeted hallway.

"Fuck! No!" Stinson pursued.

Laughing, Dahlia reached the end of the hall and took the stairs, flying down two steps at a time with Stinson in hot pursuit. At floor seven, she stopped and waited. When she saw Stinson's feet, she wished for there to be a steel door, and there was a steel door. Stinson tripped and fell headlong into the door, cursing. Dahlia resumed her descent at a more leisurely pace until she reached the lobby. Before entering, she wished to be with Kristin and was then standing in the guest house apartment. Kristin and Mia sat on the couch.

"Hi, Mommy! Just popped in for a visit. Why are you sitting so close to Mia?"

Kristin nearly jumped out of her skin. "Dahlia! How?"

"I'm different. You know that." She walked over and squeezed herself between them. "Oh, hi, Mia, or should I address you as Sister?"

"Mom, she's hurting me," said Mia.

Kristin stood, and Dahlia stood with her, giving her a big hug. "I missed my mommy. Dear sweet Mommy."

"Mia, you're supposed to be with Clyde. How, oh, well, never mind how. Go back, if you can."

"Do you love me, Mommy?"

"I love you *and* Mia."

"Okay, that's all I needed. Bye!"

Dahlia pushed through the door into the lobby, noticing the nicely buffed floor.

Stinson had alerted the other MP, Bailey, who was with Markush, by radio that Dahlia had escaped. Bailey, not knowing what to do, barged into the press conference and whispered into Markush's ear.

"Damn," said Markush. "Find her. I'm coming. Ladies and gentlemen, I will have to be excused, but you may continue your questions." He gave Arthur and Afewerki a serious look and hurried from the room. A reporter from ABC News, sensing adventure, left right behind, followed by a camerawoman.

Markush spoke with Bailey. Bailey and Stinson would do a floor-by-floor search. Markush would take the lobby and alert hotel security. The ABC reporter, Demetrius Jackson, followed Markush, asking questions, but Markush waved him off.

In the lobby, amid a crush of people, Dahlia ran. Just for kicks, she conjured an elephant that floated above the crowd. All eyes went there, and Dahlia scooted through the bodies and made it outside onto the crowded street, where there were protestors with signs: "Dahlia, go home!" Dahlia laughed, and the posters went up in flames. She spotted two men in coveralls carrying a large pane of glass. She willed them to trip and fall, and the glass came crashing down. She grinned and noticed a woman alone in a crosswalk and willed her to be naked. The startled woman tried to cover her body and ran into a small park.

Dahlia put her hands on her hips, bored. She thought of Kristin and longed to be with her mother.

Traffic poured into Birmingham, cars and trucks parked in every available space. Police in cruisers and on bikes did their best to corral the crush. On Tenth Avenue South, which had been blocked off in front of the Jemison Concert Hall, protestors shouted and pumped their signs. News crews had camped out along Thirteenth Street South near the library, but had infiltrated the protesters. A blonde woman with ABC News, Sharon Bodine, interviewed Simon Klinefelter of the Truth Ranch in McKittrick, California. Around him, his followers, many of them his wives, held signs that read "Dahlia, We Worship You!" and "Dahlia, the True Savior!"

"Mr. Klinefelter, why are you here?" She moved in closer to Simon, the noise around her near deafening.

Klinefelter looked innocent with his thick glasses and narrow shoulders. "We have traveled to see the miracle of Dahlia. We have been waiting for her all our lives."

"What is it that Dahlia can do for us? She seems to lean toward evil, abducting little girls."

"We do not understand the motives of Dahlia. We must have faith in her as knowing what is best for us. Anyone can learn more about the Truth Ranch by visiting our website—"

"Before you promote your affiliation, does Dahlia care about us?"

His followers, twenty-eight present with him, crowded him, shouting "Dahlia, Dahlia!" Simon cleared his throat. "Of course, she cares about us, but she is the source and needs an intermediary. I believe that Dahlia has chosen us to be her portal with this universe. My name is Simon Klinefelter."

"Yes, right. Well, thank you, Mr. Klinefelter." She turned away and wriggled into a clear spot. "Next, we have some insight into the detractors of Dahlia with Demetrius Claudell. Demetrius?"

The feed shifted to Demetrius, standing in front of a large oak. He stood short and wide with a toothy smile. He was being jostled and attempted to get some space between himself and his subject, the Reverend Clarity Stillwell, who had flooded the event with his nationwide flock of believers.

"Yes, Sharon, there are many here who support this Dahlia, but they do seem to be outnumbered by those who call Dahlia a sham. I'm here with Reverend Stillwell of the Christian Instinct Network." The camera zoomed out, and Clarity beamed, but with concern. He seemed somewhat plain, average height, with a paunch underneath his light-blue suit coat. "Tell us, Reverend, what is going on today, and why are you here?"

Clarity licked his dry lips. "God is furious, and the devil is having a play day. A seven-year-old girl named Dahlia is not God. America is being brought to the brink of insanity, like a yellow Cadillac on fire. Yes, we are to meet this Dahlia tonight. We will see that Dahlia paints the bucket but refuses to carry milk in it. The blind can now see, and what we have is a brown girl with the teeth of a shark." Several "Amens" rose above the din.

Demetrius seemed puzzled. "Will your God allow humanity to worship this Dahlia?"

Clarity, being pressed from behind, stepped on Demetrius's foot. The microphone jabbed Clarity in the chin.

"We worship Christ, the risen One. There are no other gods before us! It's outrageous that this troupe of supposed Returnees and now Dahlia are being allowed to take the stage and burn holes in the fabric of our society!"

"Dahlia! Dahlia!" Supporters of Dahlia moved in. "Stillwell, go to hell!"

Pushing and shoving, and the cameraman fell, sending the feed back to the anchor desk after a glimpse of the sky. For February, the temperature was quite warm, in the seventies, and the moving crowds glistened with sweat, as if releasing poison.

As a parting shot, Dahlia let loose a hailstorm around the Sheraton, sending pelting balls of ice onto the crowds. People screamed and scattered like buckshot, seeking overhangs and crushing into the hotel's main entrance. Dahlia hovered above it all and giggled, humming a tune off-key. Somewhere far away, she heard Julia chastising her.

For kicks, Dahlia spanned the universe and entered Dogtown. The sheer quiet and endless whiteness calmed her. She walked for days and saw no one; no groups of worried parents gathered in knots, waiting and waiting, as the Dogtown captives had been sent home by Julia. "Well dang," said Dahlia. "All of my hard work undone." She skipped along, nearing the edge of the Cylinder and its shocking blue light. She missed her mommy and did a spin.

"Hi, everybody!"

The hotel suite buzzed with law enforcement.

"She's back!" said Emma.

Dahlia hugged Emma's leg. "I'm so sorry I was a bad girl, but I was bored."

Markush rushed from the window. "Dahlia, you have to stay with us, please. We only have two hours before the event. Where have you been?"

Emma frowned and held Dahlia close to her. "Baby, you have to be good. We must be careful."

Markush maneuvered to the hallway and spotted an Army MP. "We got her back. Call off the search."

"Are you sure? How did she get back in the room?" asked the MP equipped with an AR-15.

"Just take my word. She's Dahlia." Markush rushed back into the room, afraid that Dahlia would disappear again.

"Group hug!" said Dahlia

Having battled through traffic and throngs of demonstrators, a military escort consisting of four armed cops stationed themselves outside the green room as the premiere of Dahlia approached. Sherri Loveless had managed to be there when they arrived, full of the same advice to be open and honest.

"Arthur, you take the stage first and prepare the audience for Dahlia." Sherri squatted in front of Dahlia. "You have to tell your story to the people. They are very curious about you. Can you do that? Do you need Dr. Markush to be on stage with you?" "Aww, hell no, I want my Mommy to sit in a chair beside me. She spends too much time with Mia."

"Okay." Loveless checked her watch. Just then, a talent minder popped into the room.

"Everybody ready? There are chairs in the wings."

"Quite ready," said Arthur.

"Great, follow me."

They made it backstage and found their seats. A rumble of voices greeted them from the other side of the curtain. The minder showed Arthur where to stand beside the microphone. A theater director stood ready to introduce Arthur and Dahlia. The lights dimmed, and the rush of noise seemed to silence like a wool blanket.

Arthur watched the curtain rise and the humanity appeared before him. He stood with clasped hands and a serious look. There was a boo and then a volley of boos.

The spotlight shone on the microphone. "Welcome to the Jemison Theater!" The director waited for the noise to die down. He gave Arthur's biography, and then "As promised, Arthur Schopenhauer!" He stepped aside amid a drone of voices and hisses.

Arthur walked into the spotlight, dressed in all black, including his tennis shoes. "We have good news to share tonight." He spoke of his work to help find Reece's daughter, Mia, and blamed the debacle on Dahlia. "She is omnipotent and everlasting, but can be, how do you say, a pain in one's ass." He was being transparent as instructed.

"Satan! Satan!" yelled a plump woman.

Arthur conjured a smile. The people in their seats looked like toys. "Dahlia, Satan, if you please, emerged long ago. In her role as what we can call God, she has visited trouble here on our tiny Earth. She has the cares of a seven-year-old girl, yet she holds great power. Precocious but stunted, she has allowed life in our universe to reach a dizzying despair."

"Liar! Lies!" a man with red hair yelled.

"Very hard to believe, I assure you, but I have been the victim of her unhinged ways."

Jeers and hoots, and then "Dahlia is our savior!" The ruckus grew, and Arthur stepped away from the microphone. He let the din die. "Dahlia's primary concern for an eternity has been to have a mother. You have heard that the mother has been found. I would like to introduce Dahlia, if not God, then the mistempered queen of this universe and others."

Behind the curtain, Markush, Arthur, Emma, Mia, and Dahlia had been sitting, fidgeting. Poof, Dahlia was gone.

"Oh, hell and high water," said Emma. All stood, peering into corners.

Arthur watched the curtain. Suddenly, there were kettle drums and a bright, fuzzy light hovering high above. People stood and shouted, and a few cowered. Followers from the Truth Ranch set up a chant of "Dahlia! Dahlia!"

The glowing ball drifted to the stage, sending out golden sparks. The ball split, and Dahlia stepped forward, unfurling a huge set of wings, giving her the look of a demented angel. The ball of light dissolved. All went quiet.

Dahlia flexed her wings and relaxed them. "Hello, you bags of blood and poop." The wings drooped to the stage. "For ages and ages, I've been listening to you gripe and complain. You need to put on your big-boy pants and quit bothering me. You're lucky, though; my sister Julia is in the hot seat, and she's weak like you are. I'm just a little girl with a brand-new mommy, but I have eyes in the back of my head. I hope you like me, but don't need you to."

The crowd sizzled like bacon. Dahlia rose from the stage, extending her wings, her dress like a triangle. And then, pop! She was gone. Arthur looked amazed but annoyed at Dahlia's theatrics. Behind the curtain, Dahlia landed on Emma's lap.

Arthur glanced around, looking for something, anything. The crowd mumbled and whispered. The confused announcer appeared and asked if the show was over. He had expected more from Dahlia, even a question-and-answer period.

Loveless was no nonsense in her tights and cashmere sweater. A vein popped on her temple. "Dahlia, get back out there and do your part. The people are very curious. Tell them your story. They do not need to fear you."

"Huh, they want a show? I can do that for sure." She smiled a perfect smile and snuggled into Emma.

"What a hell," said Afewerki.

"You can do it, Dahlia," said Markush.

"Go and do a good job," said Emma. "Your mommy wants you to be nice."

Dahlia slid off Emma's lap. The crowd beyond booed and hissed, many standing and clapping.

The lights cut, and the darkness elicited cries of alarm. Arthur nearly fell and worked his way to the curtain. A bright spotlight that seemed to be of the moon hit the stage. Dahlia appeared as a cartoon character in a black dress with roughly cut edges.

"You want more! I'll give you more!" Dahlia grew and grew, soon standing twenty feet tall. There were screams, and many clawed their way to the aisles. A toy piano played a simple song. The cartoon hand reached out and, with ease, plucked a woman from her chair, levitating her above the horrified audience. She seemed to be lying on a cloud of see-through cotton and writhed like a snake.

Markush stepped from behind the curtain. "Dahlia! No! Please!" Dahlia simply turned, and Markush found himself inside a steel cage. Dahlia laughed a wicked laugh.

A fire appeared, floating in the darkness. The red flames drifted toward the suspended woman named Jenny, an acolyte of the Reverend Clarity Stillwell. She rose farther, and the fire slid beneath her. Jenny screamed. Everyone was standing, transfixed. Jenny's polyester aqua pants smoked and melted. A smell of burning flesh wafted. No one knew what to do. Jenny writhed like a burning insect.

"Dahlia!" came a booming voice. There was a flash, and the ball of fire went up in smoke.

"No!" shouted Dahlia. "Damn you!" She was again her normal size.

A large hand materialized and enveloped Jenny. The crowd went silent. A wind of peace seemed to flow and fill the auditorium. Dahlia transformed back to her little-girl self, standing amid a pool of her own urine. The hand unfurled, and Jenny was lowered back to the aisle unhurt.

"Julia!" cried Dahlia. "Go home!"

A flash of blue light saturated the auditorium, leaving a scent of lavender. The crowd, many in the aisles, understood that the show was over. As if having waged a great battle and now exhausted, the crowd dispersed and began to exit. The group backstage converged on stage and surrounded Dahlia, who was weeping.

Clyde Markush sat in his office, stupefied. All hell had broken loose after the Birmingham performance. The entire nation and the world were following the story. Demonstrations, primarily against Dahlia, popped up around the country. The demand for interviews was overwhelming, and Sherri Loveless worked overtime to supply the media with information. Markush wearily checked his personal cell phone, and his message box was full. He had several messages from Jeremy Sims at *The New York Times*.

"Jeremy, it's Markush."

"Oh, hey! Thank you so much for responding. I'm at the Ritz Motel."

"So, tell me what you need to know."

"Oh my God, where to begin. Since the Birmingham event, people have gone nuts, the press has gone nuts, wanting to know about Dahlia and now Julia. Julia is Dahlia's twin?"

"That's correct. I've never met Julia, but she is the antithesis of Dahlia. Julia has taken Dahlia's place in the Pinch. Julia has been busy, returning parents from Dog Town and returning the abducted girls. If Julia had been God all along, the universe would be a much kinder place."

"Wow, I love the good versus evil aspect. How is Dahlia doing right now?"

"She's in the guesthouse with Kristin, soaking up mother love. Dahlia is not the nicest to Mia...competition for sure."

"My editor is foaming at the mouth for more information about Julia. Have you had contact with her? Can you have contact with her?"

"I'm working with the D.C. folks on a strategy to communicate with her. It seems, though, in typical God fashion, that Julia is omniscient and aware of what people want and need. She, in effect, hears prayers and pleas and cares, unlike Dahlia, who just lets the masses maim and kill. Julia is the real hope for humankind. The world seems to be a calmer place in some way, except in the vicinity of Dahlia. Julia saved that woman from burning alive at the Birmingham event. After Julia's appearance, everything calmed. The crowds dispersed peacefully, and no one was hurt. Julia is like a balm for the masses."

"Ooh, a balm for the masses. I like that." Jeremy tapped at his laptop, the special of the day from the restaurant next door sitting heavy in his stomach.

Markush doodled on his desktop calendar. "Yep, if anyone can save us, it's Julia."

"Can you keep me informed of any updates with Julia and Dahlia?"

"Sure thing, Jeremy. I'm partial to *The Times*. Listen, the long-term unit is calling me, and I should go. Looking forward to your next story."

"Got it. I appreciate it. Call me any time."

Markush hung up and called the long-term unit. "Shelby?"

"Hey, Dr. Markush, big news. Reece Myers in room three is back. He's opening his eyes and moving a bit, but isn't talking yet."

"I'll be right over, thanks." He hurried that way and arrived at room three.

"EEG looks normal," said Shelby.

Markush checked Reece's pupils, normal and reactive to light. "Reece, can you hear me?"

Reece moved a leg and pursed his lips. "So...weak."

"Great! You're talking. We'll let you rest, but we need to get you up in a chair. Shelby will help you do that. Where have you been? Your EEG went completely flat for nearly two months. Let me raise your head a bit."

"Can't...talk. In the Pinch. Julia." Reece's face looked tight and oily. His sharp nose stood in relief. He had lost fifteen pounds while seizing.

"You're good, Reece. Back at Organon. You've been through an ordeal. Everyone is safe," said Markush.

"Mia?"

Markush brightened. "She's back and safe with Kristin. I'll let you rest, but will be back later. I hear laughter and need to check it out. There is the other Reece, and we have two Emmas. Okay? Just stepping out. Shelby is here to take care of you."

"Water?" asked Reece. His gown lay flat around him.

"Will do," said Shelby.

Markush walked around to the other hallway, which was dimly lit, and saw Emma, along with the other Emma, in a wheelchair. They were visiting Reece.

"You gals doing okay?" asked Markush. "Reece?"

"Yeah, just visiting Reece here. It seems his traveling days are over, thank God."

"Catching up with these gorgeous gals," said Reece. "We heard that the other Reece is back. I'm dying to talk with him."

"Yes, and you can talk soon. He's wiped out right now,

weak. How are the Emmas?" He put his hand on wheelchair-Emma's thin shoulder.

"Good," said wheelchair-Emma. She cracked a half-smile. She raised a hand and pushed back her dirty-blonde bangs.

They talked for forty-five minutes, Markush telling them all about the Birmingham fiasco, although all had ended peacefully. He left them with the news that Dahlia and Mia would be enrolled in school soon. The replacement Mia was gone, and the real Mia would take her place in Ms. Butterworth's class. Markush bid them a good day and went to check on the other Reece again, then Clark Peters, the only patient left on the medical unit, along with wheelchair-bound Emma. Although his daughter had been returned, Peters' wife did not want him back, and he was too unstable to be discharged. He was scheduled to be transferred to Walter Reed National Military Medical Center and included in Glenelle Lock's late-onset schizophrenia study.

Kristin tossed back her curly locks. She regretted being Dahlia's mother as she gathered dirty clothes to take to a base laundromat. Mia and Dahlia sat on the couch, each perusing a magazine.

Dahlia yawned. "I'm so bored, and you're a terrible sister, worse than Julia."

"Stop it," said Mia.

"Do you like cats, dear sister?" Her head swiveled in a complete circle.

"Mom!"

"I think you like cats."

And then there was a tiger in the room, dark yellow and black with a slobbery gaping mouth. It turned and knocked over the TV, pacing, jumping, wild with excitement. Dahlia laughed as Mia screamed.

Kristin ran from the bedroom. "Oh! Dahlia, no!" She leaped to the couch and cowered over Mia. The tiger roared. "Make it go away! Please!"

"Sure," said a giggling Dahlia. "Come here, kitty."

The tiger kneeled, and Dahlia grabbed him by the whiskers and led him to the front door.

"Bye, kitty." The tiger exited and halted as if afraid of the cold. "All better now."

Kristin ran to the door. "Dahlia, please, send it away! They'll have to kill it!"

"I don't care, really. Let's read a book, Mommy."

Kristin slammed the door and called Markush, who called the military police, then rushed over to the guest house. He saw the tiger slinking away toward the main road into the complex and rushed into the apartment.

Inside was chaos; Mia was crying, and Kristin scolding Dahlia.

"You guys, okay?" asked Markush. "Dahlia, make that tiger disappear right now!"

"You're not my daddy," said Dahlia.

"No, I'm not, but I'm responsible for you. That tiger can hurt people, and then they will hurt the tiger."

"Don't hurt the tiger!" said Mia.

"She's a monster," said Kristin, one tennis shoe on.

"A monster?" Dahlia turned into a large wolf with red eyes. "Like this?"

Mia screamed and tumbled off the couch.

"Dear God, Mia," said Markush.

Dahlia became a little girl again. She laughed a wicked laugh.

A tiny dot of blue light appeared and hovered in the room. All went quiet. A voice as if from a well.

"Dahlia," said the voice. "Stop being a brat. I'm watching you, sister."

"Julia, I hate you!" said Dahlia.

"No need to hate me. Just be a good girl. I'm always watching." The blue dot faded, followed by silence.

"Wow, no time to process that," said Markush. He hugged Kristin and gave her a cheek kiss. "Mia, you okay?"

"No."

"Are you hurt?"

"No."

There was commotion from outside. The military police had arrived on scene. Markush filled them in, but they could not understand how a tiger had gotten into the apartment and questioned Markush as if he were a crazy man. No tiger was found.

Unaware of the chaos at the guest house, Emma took wheelchair-Emma back to her room on the medical unit. Debbie, the only nurse on shift, was bored, just having Peters to look after. He was no longer seizing or traveling but still hallucinating. Emma helped Emma into a clean bed and brought her two cups of cranberry juice.

"You okay for a while?" asked Emma.

"Yeah, just tired."

"I'll let you take a nap." She didn't want to say that she was going back to visit with the Reece in eleven.

Emma entered Emma's bathroom and looked in the mirror. She needed to wash her face, and did that. She wore no makeup and had that natural-beauty look. Butterflies filled her stomach as she made her way to the long-term unit. She waved at Shelby upon entering and headed to eleven, a trapezoid of light spilling from the room.

"Hey!"

"Hey! You're back to keep me company." Reece lay in bed with the head up. He turned down the TV volume with the remote.

"I guess so." Emma blushed. "When will Dr. Markush move you out of here?"

"Well, maybe the guest house. Ideally, I would go there. He's working on a solution."

"What if you slept on my couch? I only have one bedroom." She sat in the recliner, her eyes a foot below his.

"Huh. That could work. Hadn't thought about that. But it would be a major issue having me around. I would just be in the way."

"Are you kidding. I would love to have you. I spend most of the day with Emma."

"Yeah. I would like it."

Emma shot off a half-smile. A little shiver went down his spine, and there was awkward silence.

"So, tell me about the Emma you worked with in Ethiopia."

Reece laughed. "She was the best. She saved my life. Looked and talked just like you do."

"I know the basics, but what happened?" She gripped the armrests. The overhead light dispelled shadows from the room.

Reece cleared his throat. "We worked together in the clinic, some hard days together. All of the suffering seemed to push us together."

"I get it. It was the same with the Reece I worked with, but he was engaged."

"I was engaged, too, but that life disappeared. In Ethiopia, I felt like I was on another planet and that my previous life was just a wash of color, if that makes sense."

"Were you attracted to her, the Emma you worked with?" She put her hands between her knees.

"Ha. How could I not be? She was so cute and spunky, a real fire eater. Nothing could stop her."

"So, what happened? The night she saved your life."

"A man came to us, and the meat of his lower leg was missing. He'd been shot in the leg, and a terrible infection had set in. His foot was just this gelid mass of gray skin. I felt so bad for him that I gave him my room and bed for a night before he could be airlifted with the copter."

Reece told her about his plans to sleep on the floor of Emma's tiny house that night. One thing led to another, and he was standing behind Emma, who was sitting, massaging her shoulders. His hands slipped lower, and then the bullets crashed through the wall. One went through a chink and passed from right to left through his head.

"And then she saved my life and had me evacuated to Addis Ababa. Then a medical jet to UAB Hospitals. The Hyena shot me, but it was my fault. I shouldn't have been doing what I was doing and standing where I was standing."

Emma nodded. "And she's back in Alabama? Your Alabama?"

"Yeah, as far as I know. I wasn't allowed by Kristin to have any contact with her. I somehow felt that Emma was the love of my life and that I had made a bad mistake. I'm pretty sure she's married. I guess I was a bad boy."

"Hey, it was stressful. You two were shoulder to shoulder, healing the sick. There's no way you couldn't have gotten close."

"Did I tell you about the helicopter?" Reece looked pained.

"What about it?"

"After I was shot, she tried to jump out of the helicopter. Terry saved her with some wild helicopter acrobatics."

"Jesus. And we had a Terry too."

"I felt so terrible when I heard that." Tears came to his eyes. "She was just super stressed. It was my fault."

Emma reassured him that it wasn't his fault. Reece nodded, and there was a brief silence.

"So, about me sleeping on your couch?" said Reece.

Helmut Grayson, the unruly and sometimes violent patient at Organon, had been returned home by ambulance to be reunited with his wife and daughter, Lila. He had drowned Lila's impostor in the bathtub and luckily been picked up by Organon after Markush learned of the crime. One of the articles Markush read mentioned that Grayson had served a year as a civil engineer in rural Ethiopia, building bridges. While traveling, Reece had found Lila while looking for his daughter Mia in the nightmarish city of Gordian, where children were meat. At Organon, Grayson traveled via seizures to a version of Ethiopia, searching for Lila. All of the Organon patients had been helped by a variety of characters. Arthur Schopenhauer had helped Reece. Grayson had the service of the great Gandhi. Ultimately, it was Julia who had sent all the abducted girls back home, undoing the wrongs of Dahlia.

Grayson arrived home in Novelty to find news crews camped along his street. The news of Lila's return, along with the story of Dahlia and her antics, had the quiet town in an uproar. A lone man with a sign that read "Child Killer Free!" paced the road. Grayson was still weak from the extended seizures and moved around the three-bedroom rancher with a cane. Lila had not been out of the house since her return, her mother fearful for her life.

Around the globe, thousands of impostors disappeared, their places taken by the original abducted girls. All the worried parents held captive in Dogtown had also been returned by Julia, reinhabiting their unconscious bodies.

Families rejoiced at daughters being returned and loved ones awaking from their deep sleeps.

It was noon, but Grayson steeled himself for another shot of Johnny Walker Red. His large hand gripped the tumbler as he peered through the living room curtains at the small crowd of reporters outside.

"Damn idiots," said Grayson. "They want to take Lila, the bastards." Even though taking an antipsychotic, Grayson retained his baseline paranoia.

"Honey, they're just wanting our story, that's all," said Helen. She wore a print dress with house shoes. "We should talk with them and then maybe they'll go away."

"Hell no! Lila! Where are you?" He downed the whiskey.

"Honey, she's in the kitchen, making a sandwich."

"Where's my pistol? It's not in the dresser."

"No, honey, I got rid of it while you were at that place, Orgonio?"

"Goddamn." He stared through a space in the curtains."

"Can I go out and talk with them, Honey?" Helen stood a foot shorter than Grayson and kept her brown hair in a bun. She twisted her wedding ring.

"No! I guess I'll do it myself if it will make them go away. Get my coat, the green one, and gloves too."

Lila had been listening from the kitchen. Grayson's booming voice filled every nook. She finished making her cheese and mayonnaise sandwich and took a bite, thinking back to being held in a cage at a circus that featured a giant whale.

Grayson bundled up and opened the door slowly, expecting perhaps gunfire. With his cane, he walked onto the narrow front porch and stepped onto the sidewalk. The cold was biting, and he wished he had worn a cap. A woman in a red parka hurried toward him, followed by a cameraman. He met her halfway to the mailbox.

"Mr. Grayson, Talia Hebco with NBC News. Are you able to talk?" Her face looked tight and cold with bright red lipstick.

"You all need to leave us be and get scarce. Who do you think you are, anyway? Probably a tool of Dahlia." He spit on the cold ground and looked up into the dirty-white sky toward the hidden sun.

"Is Lila doing well? Where was she held captive?"

"Lila's fucking fine. She went through hell, could've been eaten for God's sake."

"Yes, we're hearing the story second-hand. Was it you who told Dr. Markush that Dahlia has a sister? Julia made her presence known at the recent event in Birmingham. How did you know about her?"

"Dahlia let it slip for sure. Dahlia hates Julia, but Julia's the good egg. So, why don't you and your bunch just mosey along?"

Three other cameramen had moved in closer, standing in the yard, their respective reporters creeping in as well.

"This is so valuable, Mr. Grayson. What do you know about Julia?" She glanced back.

"I said mosey along. Julia is Dahlia's twin sister, and that's all I've got, so you and your kind get your asses off my property." He turned and limped onto the porch. A volley of questions hit him.

"Who is God here, Julia or Dahlia?"

Grayson turned. "You figure that out yourself."

Arthur enjoyed his walks around the nearby lake as he contemplated the universes. He longed to return to his true home, but no one knew how to accomplish that. In all his writings, he had never embraced the idea of a divine being, but was now faced with the reality of Dahlia and Julia. He walked with his gloved hands behind his back, wearing a long black coat that had been tailored for his appearances. An MP in a jeep pulled alongside him.

"Hey, Mr. Arthur!" said the MP, Glen. He looked tidy in his olive drabs and fur-lined hat.

"Well, hello, my dear friend. Have you found anything unusual on this crisp day?"

"Nothing much, just a shoplifter at the PX is all. Tried to steal a calculator, but he confessed and even said he was sorry."

"I see. A calculator, you say? I believe I have seen one, to be held in the hand. Quite amazing."

"I saw you on the news yesterday. You were talking about Julia." A plume of exhaust streamed from the muffler, pooling then twisting away in the cold breeze.

"Yes, Julia, the good sister. Since Dahlia now has a mother and has claimed her place on this Earth and perhaps other Earths, she relinquished her grip on the universes. Julia, a bright and shining star, is now in control, despite Dahlia's uncouth behavior."

"Mr. Arthur, I believe in God. How can a little girl be God?" He revved the engine.

"We have to rethink God. Dahlia was cruel and allowed

us to misbehave, commit murders, rob, and wage war. The universes, infinite, I believe, are now being looked after by Julia."

"Do we pray to Julia?"

"I think you can, but she seems capable of pre-empting evil, which is most exciting."

"I'll keep watching the news, Mr. Arthur. Have a good one."

"Yes, you as well. I predict that your job will become obsolete, but I'm sure there are plenty of jobs that can be provided."

"Okay, see you soon." The jeep crawled away.

Outside of his ESL classes, Afewerki spent most of his time in his dorm room, afraid of the reporters and questions. He had been shocked and troubled by Dahlia's acts at the Birmingham event. A woman had been roasted alive, but saved by Julia. His God was the God of the Bible and not a little girl, but Dahlia and Julia possessed powers he did not understand or want to understand. He wanted to speak with the Abba Paulos, who had assisted in Mia's return, but that was impossible. He could envision the Abba digging his church into the rock near his home village of Godo.

From the top bunk, he watched the door open, and Maurice, his roommate from Senegal, entered the room, shouldering a black backpack. Maurice feared Afewerki as a Returnee and treated him with caution.

"Hello, how is it?" asked Afewerki. He pretended to be interested in a book, a copy of *Of Mice and Men*.

"It is good. There are some people in the front with recorders, asking for you. I told them you are sick." He sat in the single wooden chair. "What can it be? A circus?"

"Oh, that is bad," said Afewerki. "They are asking about Dahlia and Julia always." He slumped a bit and took off his Exxon cap.

"Julia is the good person. I like her. Did you meet her?"

"No."

"She is doing good things?"

Afewerki sighed. "My eyes tell me it is true, but I cannot believe."

"Where do they come from? I do not understand." Maurice leaned back in the chair. He was stocky and tall with deep black skin.

"Oh my. I must speak in riddles, perhaps lies. I am told that there is a Cylinder that has been pinched in the middle. Dahlia was living in the Pinch. She has left because she found her mother. Julia has been re-leas-ed and takes her place." Afewerki shook his head. "So hard to believe. I just want to go home."

"No, no, you must study. Forget this trouble."

"Yes, thank you. This Pinch is very strange. It is minimal but contains all things. Dr. Markush said that what is there are ideas of all things. I do not understand, but that is where Julia lives. Dr. Markush says that we can pray to her for many things, but I cannot pray to her."

"This is sounding like voodoo from my country. I wear the gris-gris to protect." He pulled a small leather amulet from within his shirt and coat.

"May it protect you, I wish."

"Yes, it will." Maurice put on a serious look. "You should go and speak with the reporters, to speak against evil. They are waiting."

"No, I cannot." Afewerki stretched, still wearing his heavy, blue coat.

"You should. I am useless as I do not have your experience."

Afewerki slid down from the bunk and peered through the blinds. He could see the hollow of the amphitheater beyond and two news vans on the road in front.

Afewerki reached for the ceiling, stretching. "Okay, I will go and talk with them." He traded his cap for a knit hat.

"It is good, man," said Maurice. "You cannot be a prisoner."

Afewerki took a deep breath and entered the hallway. Most of the room doors were decorated with photos and marker boards. He trotted down the stairs, looking at his feet, and then pushed out into the cold air.

"Afewerki, Mr. Nigussie!"

Markush worked frantically to keep up with the reports of abducted daughters returning home. There were thousands, most from the United States, but also from around the world. Dr. Mumford assisted him in gathering data and brainstorming future possibilities. Markush and Mumford also had to worry about the welfare of their released patients. All of them faced threats from the public, having murdered their daughters' replacements. A week after her return to Tempe, Arizona, Granny D, the grandmother of Kisha, had a psychotic break after being assaulted in a grocery store parking lot and had to be hospitalized.

"Dahlia?" said Kristin. "Give Mia some space." Dahlia crowded against Mia on the sofa.

"Yeah, move!" said Mia.

It was a March Saturday, and Markush had promised them lunch. Kristin was at her wits' end dealing with Dahlia.

"Poopy!" said Dahlia.

Kristin stared at a tiny hovering blue dot that seemed to have a silver aura. "What the hell is that?" The dot passed through her hand.

Dahlia threw off a blanket and stood. "That's Julia, stupid. She's watching me."

"What? And don't call me or anyone stupid. Got it?" She wore a plaid dress with fur-lined boots and was ready to eat.

"Yes, Mommy, I'm so sorry." Dahlia did a little dance around Kristin. "Watch this, Mommy."

A miniature whale on a wooden platform hooked up to a gasoline engine that pumped air into its blowhole filled the room. The engine puttered and clanked. The poor whale's eyes strained for mercy.

"Dahlia!"

Mia pulled her legs back to keep from touching the whale. "Oh, that's like the whale at the circus I was at. Dahlia had me in a cage so people could look at me."

"Very good, sister," said Dahlia.

There was a slight brightening of the blue dot, and the whale disappeared.

"See! She's watching, that little slut of a sister. She thinks she's a fixer."

A rap on the door and Markush entered, wiping his feet on the indoor welcome mat. "Hello!"

"Clyde, there was a whale in here, a real whale, and it was so sad," said Mia.

Kristin filled him in on the story. She sat in the wing-back chair, and Dahlia hopped onto her lap. "I promise to be good, Mommy. Can you kiss me?"

Kristin pecked her on the cheek.

"A whale?" asked Markush. "Reece told me about a whale that he and Arthur saw at a circus in Ethiopia. Just a giant whale hooked up to machines. He found Mia there in a cage."

"This is making me crazy," said Kristin. "Can we just go eat? And Dahlia, no tricks." She smoothed Dahlia's perfect golden hair.

"Yeah, Volvo's outside," said Markush. "We'll have to watch for reporters, so be prepared."

They exited the base, headed for Radcliff. Dahlia sang

an off-tune children's song. Markush pulled into a shopping center complex, and they walked to a restaurant that was attached to a department store, low budget and no frills. The place was packed, and they had to wait for a few minutes, but then were seated in a maroon vinyl booth. Heads had been turning, and there were whispers.

"I'm Agatha. What can I get y'all to drink?" Agatha stood tall and gaunt with pendulous breasts and no bra.

"Do you have buster?" asked Dahlia.

Markush laughed.

"Buster?" asked Agatha. She leveled her notepad, suspecting foul play.

"Dahlia, no buster. The menu is in front of you," said Markush.

They all ordered sweet tea. Markush ordered the clam strip plate. Both Dahlia and Mia chose the chicken fingers with fries, and Kristin had the BLT.

While waiting for their food, Dahlia became restless. Without anyone at the table noticing, she switched the brown floor tiles into a bright yellow shag carpet. Right away, someone fell, and there were shouts of confusion from the staff. The blue dot appeared in a far corner, and the tiles reappeared, but not before Agatha stumbled and caught herself on a chair. The staff gathered in a group, staring at the floor and mumbling. Markush knew that whatever was happening was Dahlia's doing. It took a minute, but their food arrived, Agatha limping from her near fall.

"I don't like to eat," said Dahlia. She looked extra brown in her white sweater. "I don't like pooping. There's no pooping in the Pinch." She doodled a chicken finger in ketchup.

"That's gross," said Mia.

"Do you have to eat?" asked Markush.

"Of course, now I have to eat, otherwise I might die, dummy. I'm one of you now. It's worth it to have my mommy." She scooted closer to Kristin and kicked Mia under the table.

"Hey!"

Kristin felt she should tell Dahlia that she loved her, but held back. "Everyone, eat. We don't have a lot of food at the apartment. We need to go to the commissary, Clyde."

"Ha, we need a lot of things," said Markush. "So, Kristin, what do you think about Reece moving in with Emma?"

"Very strange, but he can do what he wants. We're done. He always had a thing for the Emma in Ethiopia, in Godo. Yeah, she saved his life when he was shot, but she's the reason he got shot in the first place."

"But it's a different Emma, younger."

"She looks the same, acts the same."

"I'm bored," said Dahlia. "I wish it would snow." She slumped in the booth.

"Have you actually spoken with her yet?" asked Markush.

Kristin wiped her mouth, a bit of mayonnaise there. "Aside from meeting her when she was returned with Reece, Mia, and the others, we haven't talked. She doesn't know me from Adam, which is good."

"She has some strange ideas about healthcare, which she brought from her world. There are priests who oversee the care of patients like the Priest of Digestion."

"You mentioned that. Bizarre."

"Look, snow!" said Mia.

Curtains of large flakes fell outside, quickly covering parked vehicles.

"Dahlia, did you do that?" asked Markush. The blue light still hovered in the corner.

"Do what, dear Clyde?"

"Make it snow."

"I'm just a little girl, Clyde, but a very special little girl, right?" She crammed a fry into her mouth.

In Building 205 of the Army Research Laboratory, focus shifted from evaluating materials related to the Returnees to gathering data on the flood of returned daughters and granddaughters. The forensic specialists, led by Colonel Ignatius Lawrence, found themselves reduced to creating spreadsheets and making phone calls. The idea of using a decommissioned base as a refuge for Returnees was scrapped, and a more decentralized approach was implemented.

Lawrence gathered his staff of six in an empty boardroom. He looked dashing with his black mustache, silver hair, and full Army dress.

Dr. Lily Nashburn spoke first. "We've created records for 1,982 returned girls and 1,876 returned parents, always parents of the abducted girls, released from what is called Dogtown. That is the United States only. All fifty states and territories are involved. International data is proving hard to obtain and verify. It's a case-by-case basis."

"We need to treat this as a global issue," said Lawrence. "But priority goes to US cases, considering national security. We will visit every last one of these returned individuals and get their narratives, along with a battery of clinical tests. I appreciate the work that you've done thus far and your flexibility."

"What about the materials research?" asked Dr. Nathan Wells, an expert in taxonomy. "As you know, I was working on the analysis of the mesh retrieved from Mia that contained thallium cuprate. If we can decipher how that mesh works and the information it may contain, we may be on to the coup of the century. The military applications could be astounding."

Lawrence looked thoughtful. "We are winging it to be sure, as changes occur, and I think what you say is important. I've discussed this with Markush and Glenelle, and both are very curious that the research continue. I like it, so make it your priority. Obtain whatever equipment you may need. Blank slate, as it were." The group mumbled their approval.

"What I find fascinating," said yet another PhD, Maury Blankstone, "is the relationship between Dahlia and Julia. If we could, in a controlled environment, observe the interactions, we may be able to revolutionize communications."

"A great idea that we have discussed before. Put that on your to-do list and create a timeline along with objectives and a budget. If we can get Dahlia and Julia in the same room, as at the event in Birmingham, sparks will fly," said Lawrence. He touched his mustache. He liked to get things done.

Rory Green, a former munitions expert, swiveled in his chair. "Has anyone noticed the papers and news reporting less crime? I watched the ten o'clock news last night, and there was not a single story about crime. It was all good news. I was shocked."

"That is strange," said Dr. Nashburn. She shifted her heavy hips.

"Well, we have a new God in place," said Lawrence. "So, wow, let's keep an eye on that. Start a daily check of national crime stats and look for trends. I like it." He smiled.

"Has anyone converted to Julianism? Maybe said a short

prayer?" asked Green.

No one answered. Lawrence grinned.

"Just checking," said Green. "I'm a good Jewish boy, but things have gotten out of focus with Dahlia and now Julia. "I feel like we're at a crossroads of some sort. That things will never be the same."

After only two days of deciding to move in with Emma, Reece was ready. He had nothing to pack, just his toothbrush, which he placed in his pocket.

"Goodbye, room eleven," said Reece.

Markush stood ready to catch Reece if he fell. Shelby gathered the sheets from the bed and walked to the laundry bin.

"Bye, Shelby."

"Bye, Reece. Come back when you can't stay so long."

Reece braced himself in the doorway. He wore clothes that Kristin had brought from home, jeans and a plaid long-sleeve beneath a down jacket. Reece hobbled along, still weak from his travels. Markush buzzed them off the unit and into the hallway. Emma was with wheelchair-Emma on the medical unit, talking nonstop about Reece moving in. They walked past the kitchen and buzzed into the lobby, where Denise sat. She looked up and smiled.

Outside was brisk and cold with three inches of snow. Reece shivered and watched his breath blow smoke. Markush held his arm as they walked across the parking lot to the guest apartments.

"You can use the phone to call me anytime," said Markush. He opened the unlocked door.

"Cool, Emma's place," said Reece. "Smells girly."

"Yeah, she's a lady for sure. A good one."

The floor plan matched Kristin's apartment, except there was only one bedroom. Reece surveyed the brown carpet, the floral print couch, chair, and TV. There was a bottle of lotion on the coffee table along with a fat Stephen King novel, *Insomnia.*

"And Arthur's next door?" asked Reece.

"Yes, I'll let him know you're here. He likes to take walks."

"Neat." He sat on the couch and gazed around at his new environs. "Beats the hell out of an ICU room."

"It's two o'clock and Emma will be off around three. I have to go, but like I said, call if you need anything."

"Wait, and Kristin is to the right with Mia and Dahlia?"

"That's correct, everyone in one place, except for Afewerki."

"Right. First, I want to see Mia. I suppose Kristin won't mind." Reece felt his head, the hair growing back.

Markush glanced at his watch. "Sure, I'll go with you. Should be interesting. I guess technically you're Dahlia's stepfather."

"She's a bitch for sure."

Markush walked with him next door and knocked. Dahlia answered.

"Look who's here!" said Dahlia. "Clyde and that deadbeat dad, Reece Myers. Come in! Welcome to our world!" She danced back into the apartment, arms flailing.

Kristin made eye contact with Reece. "Hey. Hey, Clyde."

"Hey—"

"Daddy!" Mia ran from the bedroom, still in pajamas. Her ginger hair looked dark in the light.

"Mia, my girl!" He grabbed her and hugged her. "Sit on the couch with me."

"I guess I am the stepchild," said Mia. She did a twirl.

"Daddy, Dahlia won't stop bothering me. She talks in

her sleep and uses my toothpaste."

"Bad Dahlia. Julia's keeping an eye on her, I'm sure."

"It's chaos," said Kristin. She sat in the chair.

"Got to go, guys," said Markush, and he left.

Mia snuggled against Reece. "I missed you so much, Daddy. I love you."

"Mommy loves me best," said Dahlia, pouting, still standing as if in charge,

Kristin yawned. "I hear you're moving in with Emma, your life dream, I suppose. You always had a thing for her. You basically cheated on me with her in Ethiopia."

Mia looked concerned. "Cheat? What is that?"

"Your daddy wanted to sleep with another woman."

Reece folded his arms. "Look, I'm sorry about what happened. You have no idea how stressful it was. We just clicked. It just happened. Her couch is the only spot for me right now unless I stay at Organon. She's just doing me a favor."

"Yeah, right," said Kristin. "Whatever."

"So, you can divorce me and shack up with Markush, but I'm in the wrong?"

"We haven't shacked up!"

"Then what?"

"Don't try and put this on me! You cheated and you paid for it, dammit, getting shot in the head. What a nightmare."

"Let's go outside to the lake," said Mia. "I don't like this."

"I'll go with you. Mommy, I can go, right?" asked Dahlia.

Kristin agreed to take Dahlia and Mia to the lake after a few more choice words for Reece. She was genuinely hurt that Reece was moving in with Emma. Too weak for the walk, Reece headed back to wait for Emma. A large group of chimpanzees was suddenly scampering across the parking lot, but they disappeared within seconds. Reece did a double-take.

An hour later, the door opened, and in walked Emma. She looked fresh in her aqua scrubs with cheeks red from the cold. Reece waited on the couch, his heart in his throat.

"Hey!" Emma stood with hands on hips, as if looking at ice cream.

"Well, hey," said Reece. "Looking good as always."

"Ha, and you look like you've been dragged down a dirt road." She sat on the couch with space between them. She gave him a killer half-smile.

"Thank you kindly."

"Does Kristin know about this? She shouldn't care, right?"

Reece laughed. "She knows. I can tell she's not happy with it, though."

She stared at him. "Damn, if you don't look just like the Reece I worked with. It's flat amazing."

"He must have been good-looking."

"We'll let a mirror decide that, good sir." Her natural look glowed in the light from the window.

"We'll have to figure out groceries. Are you on a stipend?"

"Yeah, all of us are, and it's enough to stay pretty well fed."

"I guess I didn't know I was on a stipend."

"Just talk to Markush. There's big money behind Organon."

"I can't shake the feeling that Markush is getting rich off of us and the others." He scratched his head.

"I'm sure he's paid well, but I doubt if he's directly profiting. He'll make sure we're taken care of. I'm pretty dang sure Organon would buy me a house if I asked."

"Does he have you lined up for any appearances? I know Arthur has been staying busy."

"Yeah, a morning show for a station in Louisville, next Wednesday. I've done a couple of email interviews at Organon. I'm sure the questions will be about Julia and Dahlia. They're quite the pair."

"Yep, God, or what was God, lives next door with my daughter." He laughed and caught another of her smiles.

"And your ex-wife is the mother of Dahlia, formerly God, as you say." She laughed. It just seemed so ridiculous and unlikely.

Reece laughed more, leaning forward. Emma stayed with him, laughing, tears coming to her eyes.

"You...you..." She took a deep breath. "You went looking for Mia and found Arthur Schopenhauer. Oh!"

Reece reeled it in for a moment. "I traveled to a world where children...were...meat!"

Emma lost it. "My God, the Ark of the freaking Covenant!"

"The Abba...the Abba Paulos. Oh wow, the Abba Paulos."

A sudden magic seemed to descend and cut the laughter. Emma had the hiccups.

"Well, Reece, you can't say that we're just skating. This is real and we're in it."

"It's all just so preposterous, but like you say, real. I

think this all started because I truly love Mia and can hear her music. The replacement Dahlia sent looked like Mia, but the music was all wrong. Without thinking, I strangled the impostor. I think there have been abductions that have gone unnoticed because the parents didn't pay close attention. I'm sure some girls have been returned who were never suspected of being missing."

Something like tension settled. Someone politely knocked on the door.

"I'll bet that's Arthur. He likes to pop in and talk about buster, the crazy stuff that you guys drank in a place called Gadam. And other things." She went to the door. "Hello! Come in and visit. We got company."

"Good day, my beautiful lady. How is your world?" Arthur looked relaxed in his stretch jeans, pullover, and fleece jacket.

"Arthur!" said Reece. He tried to stand, but fell back onto the couch. "Damn."

"Ah, just a fellow gentleman from another world," said Arthur. "My, it's warm, Emma." He plopped onto the sofa with Reece.

"Yeah, I like it hot."

"For sure," said Reece. "What's your day like, Arthur?"

"I've had my walk by the lake. I saw a lone goose, as if it were lost. I felt an affinity with that gray beast. Reece, I was also reminiscing about that troublesome woman whom I pushed and caused to fall outside my apartment in Berlin."

"Caroline? The crazy lady we met in Gadam who followed us around."

"Yes, her. In retrospect, I think she did us a great service in finding Mia, employing her womanly charms at key moments. For the first time, I've begun to sympathize with her. All those years ago, I did push her, but she threw herself to the ground and claimed injury for which I was sued. I do think that my temper was at fault after all. We lost her transitioning from world to world. I do hope that she is safe and that Julia has sent her home. A pretty woman." Arthur looked wistful, his eyes crinkling. He had hated her with a passion, having been forced to pay reparations."

"So, you lost her?" asked Emma.

"Yes, Reece and I were traveling from world to world with the help of the Abba Paulos, looking for Mia, and we became separated. I've never before felt such remorse. I wrote on her obituary, for she died, 'Obit anus, abit onus,' meaning in my temper that the old hag has departed. I regret my actions and only wish her well."

"You know, I've been feeling remorseful lately about several things," said Reece. "In high school, I kicked a boy with a learning disability. He was helpless. There was no reason for kicking him. I would like to find him and apologize."

Emma then told a story about how she had bullied a girl at a bar into taking too many shots of whiskey. The girl had vomited, passed out, and been hospitalized. Reece and Arthur continued talking about their travels, filling in Emma on the details. She laughed at the story of Arthur dancing on a bar in a buster establishment to earn money to pay the Abba Paulos for his services. She wanted to know more about the Abba. There had been an Abba Paulos in her village, but she had not experienced his mystical side.

"He is a monk of the Orthodox Christian faith," said Arthur. "He spends his time digging with a pick into a rockface to create a church. He communicated with Dahlia through the Ark of the Covenant and transported us through its powers as well. He may be my only hope of returning to my home, another universe it seems."

"He was very useful," said Reece, "but he must be paid for his services, which created problems because we had no—"

The room blackened, and Emma yelled.

"Hey folks!" said Dahlia. "I've been listening. Watch me." She stood to the side of the TV on the wall. As if grain by grain, an object materialized, crowding the room.

"The Ark," said Arthur.

The gold-plated Ark sat on a heavy wooden platform, topped by two cherubim with wings spread.

"The Abba Paulos is just a tool," said Dahlia. "Every universe has one."

The Ark began to glow, and the space between the wings flickered silver.

"What are you doing, Dahlia?" Reece stood.

"Oh, just being a little curious monkey, I suppose."

The front door opened, and Kristin, followed by Mia, stormed in.

"Reece! Dahlia's gone." She stopped short in the gloom, seeing the Ark and Dahlia. "Dahlia, you can't just disappear, for God's sake. What the hell's going on?"

"She's bad," said Mia.

"Mommy, you're interrupting!"

"Dahlia, dear, could you send me home with the Ark?"

asked Arthur.

"Hold your horses, old man. Hocus pocus, Julia!"

There was blue light, and the face of Julia hovered between the wings.

"Julia," said everyone. Mia clasped her hands in prayer.

"Hello," said Julia. "How may I help? Dahlia, you need to listen to your mommy and be a good girl."

"Shut your pie hole, loser," said Dahlia.

"I wish to return home," said Arthur. "Can you assist, dearest Julia?"

"I'm sorry, Arthur, but you are needed here to spread my word. In due time, you may return home. I promise you that."

Kristin and Emma looked shaken, eyes wide.

"I see," said Arthur. "I place my fate in your hands, but I have one request. Will you find Caroline Marquet, the fair lady who assisted Reece and me, and send her home? We are very worried about her well-being."

Static crackled between the wings, and Dahlia's face flickered. "Unfortunately, Caroline lives in Dogtown with just a handful of others. If I send her back home, she will have died, and I feel bad about doing that."

"Oh, mighty sister, you think you're so important now," said Dahlia.

Reece wanted to take advantage of Julia's presence. He knew that Markush would be pissed if he didn't ask questions. "Julia, a change of subject. Where do we go when we die? Is there a heaven and hell?"

Julia's image wavered. She looked so innocent. "They do not exist. When you die, your idea returns to the Pinch and modifies the perfect idea of you for possible redeployment to another viable world. Your body decays to dust. But you live on as a perfect idea, communing with me to run the universes."

Dahlia decided to do jumping jacks, counting loudly.

"Julia, my queen, if I may call you that, why did young Reece experience seizures in order to traverse worlds?" Arthur looked thoughtful.

"Dahlia mapped his brain with the mesh. She gathered information and controlled the seizures with the mesh, which enabled universal travel. I'm not here to answer questions, dear people. I have to go now. There are tons of cruel stuff to fix. Dahlia, be nice, please." Her face faded, and the Ark was gone.

With Reece's help, Emma made a dinner of fried chicken thighs with oven-baked potatoes and steamed broccoli. It was their first night together, and both fought the impulse to grab one another and go for the gold. They sat at the kitchen table, looking dreamy.

"Great job with the chicken," said Reece. "I was getting tired of Organon sandwiches." He speared a chunk of broccoli with potato.

"Thank God you have the same food here as in my world."

"You're from Atlanta?" asked Reece.

She sipped her lemon water. "Yeah, but a small version of the Atlanta here. We had about 2,500 residents or so. My mother lives there with two of my sisters. I miss them so much."

"I get it. I miss my grandparents. I have to see them soon."

"They sound pretty important to you. Want to watch a movie? There's a VCR and some old movies under the TV."

"Sure. Love to." He walked over to the TV and scanned the tapes. "Oh, hell no, here's *Green Acres,* the best of. I love *Green Acres,* especially Mr. Kimball and Fred Ziffle."

"And Arnold the pig? Help me do the dishes?"

He rolled up his sleeves to clear the table. He stood side-by-side with Emma, noting that she was about a foot shorter than he was. The small window over the sink looked over the parking lot. She washed, and he rinsed, their hands touching.

Emma had beer, and they each took a can. Reece slid in the tape and rewound until he hit opening credits. "Okay, let's watch this one. What time is it?"

"Little after seven." Noises of shouting came from Kristin's apartment. "I hope they're not killing each other over there." She settled into the corner of the couch with a blanket. "Onward!"

Reece hit play. After a couple of minutes, he knew this was the episode where Lisa finds square eggs and Oliver is dumbfounded. He sat on the couch with Emma's feet hitting his thigh. He felt awkward and tried to watch the video, but kept looking at her. She had neck-length dirty-blonde hair and a serious look that cracked wide open when she smiled. They sat, somewhat uncomfortably, for a few minutes, the tension rising.

"Heck, get over here under the blanket," said Emma. "No time to be shy."

Reece felt a great pulse of energy flood his brain. Like a careful cat, he nudged into her, but the position was awkward. As if choreographed, Emma stood, and Reece eased into the corner with his legs on the couch. She sat between his legs and leaned back so that he was her support. His right arm draped over her. She drew the blanket over them and felt that anything was possible. After a few minor adjustments, they settled and paid not one bit of attention to the TV.

"I can't believe we spoke with Julia," said Emma.

"I know. I had a million questions, but she left in a hurry."

"Julia is God, and Dahlia used to be God, right?"

"More or less. Dahlia vacated the Pinch, and Julia moved in, just like that, all because Dahlia wanted a mother. Dahlia had somehow trapped Julia in Dogtown, but now she's free."

Emma sighed. "I really want to go back to my village and work with the people. They still need help."

"Hmm, there is a Reece there, the one you worked with."

"Yeah, he's all alone, and that's sad unless I was replaced."

On the TV, Lisa explained to Oliver the square eggs. They relaxed into each other and let happen what may.

Back on the medical unit, all was quiet. Only two patients remained, Emma and Clark Peters. Peters was asleep. Jim, the nurse, sat in the empty nursing station, reading a novel. Emma slowly sat up on the edge of her bed. She was gaining strength each day, but still had weakness on her right side, as if she had had a stroke. The wheelchair was bedside, and Emma transitioned. She hit the call button.

"Hey, Emma," said Jim. He looked very tan, as usual, and built.

"Jim...Can I...visit Reece?"

"I'll be right there." Jim went to her room. "Hey, you got in the wheelchair by yourself. Great." He tidied up the bed.

"Reece. I...want to visit." She had lost some twenty pounds, her face thin.

"Well, he's awake and talking, but still kind of out of it. I'll take you over and leave you for fifteen minutes. Will that work?"

"Yes. Thank you. Need to comb my hair."

"No problem. I can help." He grabbed a brush from the bedside table.

"I can do it." She took the brush.

"Yeah, that's good."

It took a minute, but she finished. "Ready, Freddy?"

Jim wheeled her through the nursing station into the long-term unit nursing station, which was brightly lit. Sheila, with her cat-eye glasses, was on duty. She looked tired but smiled. Jim explained the purpose of their visit and pushed Emma into the hall to number three. The room was dim. Reece lay on his back, his head at forty-five degrees. Jim stood by his head. Reece's eyes were closed.

"Hey, Reece, got a visitor," said Jim. He rubbed his knuckle on Reece's sternum.

Reece opened his eyes. "Hey."

"Emma from next door is here to visit. I'm going to leave her here for a few minutes, okay?"

Reece leaned his head forward and saw Emma. "Hi, Emma."

Jim parked Emma next to the bed and left.

"Good...to see you." Emma smiled and tugged at her gown.

"You too. What's up? I'm so lonely in here. Dr. Markush said he was going to move me over to your unit."

"That's good...to hear. I just wanted...to talk. You worked in Ethiopia, right?"

"Many years ago, yes. I worked with an Emma, just like you. She saved my life when I was shot." To see Emma better, he raised the head of his bed with the button.

"I worked with another Reece. Younger than you,

though."

Reece laughed, then coughed. "It's a ball of confusion, I know. Dr. Markush has explained it to me, although I don't quite understand. I killed Mia's impostor and became a patient here. I suffered seizures that took me to other places, all in Ethiopias of one sort or another. During an attack by a horde of little Dahlia's, I uttered a few choice words, and we returned to this world. There are two of me here."

"Oh...hard to believe. The other Emma came back with the other Reece, Arthur, and Afewerki. I was shot in Gajjo, and the Abba Paulos sent me here. The Vulture shot me."

"So, we've both been shot. I was shot by the Hyena, the same guy, basically the village administrator. Emma saved my life."

"Yes, both of us. But you're of this world...and I'm not."

"We're back together." He smiled.

"Well...sort of." Emma laughed and smoothed back her bouncy hair. "Were you close...with the Emma at your clinic?"

Reece sipped some water from a pitcher with a straw. "Definitely. I had only been there a couple of months when I was shot, but we worked so hard together in the clinic. You, she, was great. You can't help but grow close. But I was engaged to Kristin at the time, and I was very confused about my feelings for her."

"My Reece was engaged too. Same...thing. I was upset that he was engaged."

"Yeah, complicated for sure."

"The other...Reece and Emma, Emma told me that he was moving in with her."

"Markush told me. That Reece spoke to me once after

my return, but he hasn't been back, even though I asked Markush. I want to see me and talk to me. I have a twin now."

"Me too," said Emma.

Jim and Sheila came to the room.

"Ready to go back?" asked Jim.

"Not...not really...but my voice is getting weak. He's a trooper." She pointed at Reece.

"I think you're a trooper as well," said Jim. "Debbie can bring you back over tomorrow for certain."

"Jim, I'd like to be moved to the medical unit. Markush said it would be okay. Can you ask him?" said Reece.

"Yeah, I'll call him in a few minutes. Maybe we'll plan to move you tomorrow. We'd be glad to have you. Not sure what is going to happen to the unit, but we'll see."

"Bye, Reece." Emma put her feet back in the chair rests and caught a bit of drool with her hand. "Oops...sorry."

"Ha, you look good when you drool."

The next day, Markush called Glenelle Lock to check in. On the call with him was Letitia Mumford. Glenelle sat in her subterranean DC office, wearing a sharp, dark green sweater dress that hit just below her knees. She was fresh off a cigarette break and craving another.

Markush wanted to check his number of returned parents with hers and ask about DNA results. Markush's numbers were off by more than a thousand, and Glenelle convinced him to let her keep tabs on the numbers, as she had access to sources unknown to him, and that data was being filtered through the Army Research Laboratory. Contact was being made with all the returnee cases and evaluated for authenticity. The typical scenario was that a returnee from Dogtown just popped home magically, and the other parent was dumbfounded, having watched their spouse exist in a comatose state for years. The revivals and the ensuing conflict made great local news. She also noted that the returned abducted girls simply replaced the impostors, and there was no duplication. The impostors just vanished.

Lock elaborated on the DNA results, saying that Arthur had twenty-eight pairs of chromosomes, as Markush already knew, and that Emma and Afewerki had twenty-five pairs. DNA from the returned girls thus far showed normal results, with twenty-three pairs, and the returned parents as well.

Mumford asked about the phenomenon of crime reduction occurring nationally. General Tom Watkins, their

Pentagon contact, had taken a special interest in the numbers. In the past two weeks, there had not been a single murder in the entire country. Watkins also was working with the physicist Dr. Desmond Ory on establishing communications with Julia and deep diving her role as God. National security was a number one priority, and Julia could be an ultimate deterrent to aggression from other countries. Would Julia choose sides? What was the role of Dahlia now that Julia had taken control?

Markush asked Lock about the rising tide of action being taken for and against Dahlia and Julia by the masses. Talk and news were all about them. Clarity Stillwell was the touchstone of resistance to Dahlia, but the appearance of Julia posed an even greater threat. Dahlia represented the past, pain and suffering, and Julia symbolized the future, love and joy. How could the Gods of humans compete with a generous and cute little girl? Stillwell's Christian Instinct Network buzzed with all the latest news and gossip, fueling a national campaign designed to discredit the twins. Stillwell prayed and called for prayer. He filled his daily televised shows with speculation about the evil nature of the twins, even though Julia was proving to be rational and kind. She was a wolf in sheep's clothing, according to Stillwell.

Lock said that Sherri Loveless, the gaunt publicity guru, was working overtime, feeding the media with updates and setting up interviews. A White House task force had invited her to assist them with a strategy to incorporate the bona fide existence of the twins into American society.

On a more practical note, the Army Research Laboratory had prioritized the evaluation of the mesh found beneath the scalps of returnees. The sophisticated web-like structure facilitated travel via seizures and gathered and stored data that Dahlia wanted, but which no longer seemed of interest to her after she found her mother. So far, dozens of returnees had come on board to basically have their heads examined. They were seeking answers, as well as the government.

Markush ended by asking what would happen to Organon? His role, and Mumford's, as caretakers of parents who had murdered replacements, no longer seemed necessary. Lock said that their positions were secure for now, but that changes at Organon were necessary. The returned parents were clamoring for support and insight, said Lock. She imagined Organon as a hotel for the returnees, including the little girls, where they could debrief in a safe environment and be evaluated for mental health problems that may have resulted. Markush and Mumford agreed that it sounded like a plan and promised to remain flexible.

"Clyde, you've got a lot on your plate," said Lock.

Kristin needed help. "You girls settle, please." She was trying to put on eyeliner in the bathroom.

"I don't want to go to school," said Dahlia. "I know everything." She stood in the hall.

"You don't know everything," said Mia. "You can't read."

"I don't need to read, dummy."

The tiny blue dot floated near the ceiling.

"Mommy, why are we dressed the same? I don't want to look like her," said Mia. Both she and Dahlia wore checked trapeze dresses.

"They're different colors!" said Kristin. "Just go with it!"

Kristin managed to get them in coats and out the door to Emma's Corolla, which she was sharing. A sheet of off-white clouds blanketed Fort Knox, and a steady breeze blew. She pulled into the parking lot at Van Voorhis Elementary School. Both girls would be in Ms. Butterworth's second-grade class, the same teacher who had handled Mia's replacement.

They walked the pristine halls, the walls covered with art, and arrived at the classroom. Ms. Butterworth was expecting them and felt that anything could happen. The replacement Mia had given her fits. Mia and Dahlia shuffled into the classroom.

"Hi, girls!" said Butterworth. She was slim with long, black hair and had apple cheeks.

"Hi, Diane Butterworth," said Dahlia. "What's for lunch?"

"Girls," said Kristin from the doorway, "be good. I'll be

back at three." She still worried that Dahlia would make Mia disappear, send her off to some other world.

"Yeah, go snuggle up with Clyde," said Dahlia. She resembled a cartoon character with her brown skin and golden hair. "We'll be just fine."

Butterworth introduced them to the wide-eyed class, who had seen them on TV, and asked them to take an empty desk. Mia took a seat close to the front, and Dahlia sat in the back. Butterworth gave them textbooks.

"Today we're going to start by talking about the president and what a president does," said Butterworth.

Dahlia took an interest in the boy next to her. "Hi, William. I used to run the world. What do you do?"

William looked terrified.

"Dahlia, no speaking unless you raise your hand," said Butterworth.

"That's great," said Dahlia. She caught Mia's eye and stuck out her tongue.

"We live in the United States and have a president. Who is our president?" asked Butterworth.

The class was frozen, but Dahlia was in her groove. "Harry Sheets," said Dahlia. "He has a mole on his butt that he scratches and makes bleed."

"Um, yes, Dahlia, very good. Harry Sheets is our president. The American people, your parents, voted for him to be president. Does anyone know where President Sheets lives?"

"Duh, the White House," said Dahlia. She reached and pinched William's arm.

"Hey!"

"Dahlia, please do not bother William."

Dahlia smirked. "How about Billy then? The kid over there with red hair and freckles. He touches his pee pee in bed."

The blue dot hovered just above the teacher's head.

"Oh, hell," said Dahlia.

Billy lifted from his seat, his butt rising into the air. He grabbed his desk and wailed, lifting higher.

"No! Dahlia, what are you doing?"

Billy was released and fell back into his chair, tears flowing. A flash of a dragon filled the room, and everyone screamed, except Dahlia.

"Darn you, Julia!" said Dahlia.

Butterworth tried to calm the class. She hit the intercom button. "Can you send the principal right away? Room 112."

It took about five minutes for Principal Humphries to arrive. He walked in as if about to be shot. "What's going on, Diane?"

"Ooh, the bossman," said Dahlia.

"She's making things happen. Dahlia, the new girl, is. I can't teach with her in the class. She made Billy float. I saw it."

Humphries surveyed the room and noted both Mia, looking cross, and Dahlia, looking quite bored.

Terrified, Humphries asked Dahlia to meet him in the hall. She smirked and followed him. "So, what's the game plan, Dexter?" Dexter was Humphries' wife's pet name for him.

"What? How do you know about Dexter?"

"I just do." Dahlia yawned.

"Listen, Dahlia, we have agreed to welcome you to the

school, but you must behave and follow the rules. We can't have any…uh…magic tricks."

"Right on, brother. I'll do my best to toe the line. Just kind of slow around here is all." She gazed up and over Humphries' belly. "You need to wash your hair, sir."

"Right. Well, go back in and listen to Ms. Butterworth. I don't want to send you home."

Dahlia returned to her desk and began drawing in a textbook.

"Okay, class, Dahlia was right when she said the president lives in the White House. The president helps to pass laws. What is a law? Anybody know?"

Dahlia spoke. "Let's just ask him."

"Ask who, Dahlia?"

"Harry Sheets. Right there."

Butterworth screeched. President Sheets stood beside her with a bewildered look. Before he could say anything, Julia returned him to a press conference.

"Dahlia?" Butterworth's hands trembled as well as her voice. She didn't notice the piece of chalk, writing on the board.

F-U-C-

Cecily raised her hand and spoke. "Ms. Butterworth, the chalk is writing a word."

"Dahlia, no, please!" She slapped the chalk from the air and watched it skitter like a bug.

A flash of blue light, and Julia's face hovered above the chalkboard. There were shrieks, then silence.

"What the hell?" said Butterworth.

"Hello, children. I'm Julia. You should ignore Dahlia's pranks and listen to your teacher. If you ever need help, you can call my name, but I'm always watching. There's another planet with a world war, and I'm dealing with that, among a zillion other things."

"Boo!" said Dahlia. "Go away! Bad sister! You're such a dried-up stick. And you don't have a mommy, so there."

The children sat petrified. A few squeezed their eyes shut. Ms. Butterworth was speechless, holding her hand over her mouth.

"Dahlia, please be kind," and Julia vanished.

The day for Emma's appearance on "Good Morning Sunshine" arrived. Reece had agreed to go with her and drove the Corolla. She had to be at the NBC affiliate by seven a.m. with her appearance at close to eight a.m. They exited the base on Dixie Boulevard and were immediately followed by a Honda minivan.

"I guess we're being followed," said Reece.

"Yep," said Emma.

Reece found a fuzzy rock station and turned the volume low. He told her about his grandparents, Horace and Dora, and how they had raised him after his parents were shot in Texas. They had lived on a lake north of Birmingham in an expanded cabin that Reece had loved. They had taken him in after he was shot in Ethiopia, after being discharged from the hospital, following a tornado, and cared for him.

"Tell me about the tornado," said Emma.

"Oh God, it was about two weeks after I had been flown back from Ethiopia. I was in a room at UAB Hospitals, in Spain-Wallace Tower. Kristin, I remember, was there. I was still pretty immobile and could barely lift my hand or move my eyes. The tornado came from the west, Tuscaloosa, I think, and followed the interstate to Birmingham. I just remember loud roars, glass breaking, and water slashing. I had no idea what was going on. The top floor of the building was ripped off. My poor nursing assistant Debbie Dee had her face crushed, but she survived. She always had cold sores in the corners of her mouth."

"Holy cow." Emma sat snug in a lavender sweater and corduroy pants. "But I thought you went to Kristin's house after the tornado."

"I did. Her mother put me in the basement in a sewing room. That's where I started to move around and began to walk. Her parents got tired of me, and I decided to go and stay with Horace and Dora. Her parents never really liked me, and I can't blame them."

Emma then told him about how she had lived with her mother in Atlanta before going to Ethiopia. Her mother worked at a barbecue, long divorced from an abusive father. She had five sisters, all older, and a younger brother.

"What about when we were returned from Gwar? The Reece I worked with didn't return with us. I wonder what happened to him?" Emma slunk in her seat, watching the road signs go by.

"I have no idea," said Reece. "There are two of us here, and maybe that's the limit. Dahlia might know."

After an hour of driving, they found the news station. The minivan continued to follow. They had been instructed to park in a gated lot, found it, and entered. The minivan did a U-turn and double-parked in the street. A man exited with a tape recorder and ran toward them, shouting, "Emma, Reece!" Two policemen stationed at the entrance of the two-story building took note and walked forward.

The driver of the minivan caught them, out of breath. "Hey, guys, Jeremy Sims with *The New York Times*. We've talked before."

Reece and Emma kept walking, and Sims followed. "Tell me about contact with Julia. How is Dahlia doing?"

The cops intervened, expecting Emma but not Reece.

Emma explained who Reece was, and the cops looked very interested. They told Sims to leave and escorted Emma and Reece into the building. They were quickly taken care of and placed in a dressing room for makeup. The host of "Good Morning Sunshine," named Tiny T, found out that Reece was there and insisted that he be on the show with Emma. Tiny T had light brown skin, a short, straightened afro, and stood about four feet eleven. Within forty-five minutes, Reece and Emma walked onto the set, their eyes wide. Reece had not planned to be on the show and wore blue jeans with an old flannel shirt. On the semicircular set were a leather chair for Tiny T and two swivel chairs. The light was bright. A small coffee table was empty. Behind them, in large letters, was the show's title on curved polycarbonate, featuring a bright yellow sun. The camera zoomed in on Tiny T., who wore a red polo dress with white sleeves.

"Good morning, Louisville, and good morning Sunshine!" Tiny T sat stiffly as if she had a neck injury. "The world is abuzz with the stories of what we now call the Returnees and the truth behind Dahlia and Julia." The camera zoomed out. "Today, we are privileged to have two of the Returnees, Emma Smith and Reece Myers. How are you guys doing today?"

Emma and Reece looked somewhat like a deer in headlights. They both said they were doing fine, and Reece added that he was getting bored at Fort Knox.

"You were both somehow transported from an Ethiopia in another universe?" Tiny T looked pleased with herself.

"That's right, but hard to believe," said Emma. "I was in a village called Gwar where I worked as a nurse."

"Fascinating," said Tiny T. "How is Dahlia doing with her new mother, Kristin, Reece's wife? That was quite a surprise."

"Actually, ex-wife. She divorced me while I was a patient at Organon. Dahlia is doing the best she can, considering her bad behavior at times." Reece squinted at the bright light. "She still possesses powers and likes to play pranks."

"And her sister, Julia. Give us an update on what you know."

Emma spoke. "It's hard to say, but Julia is always watching out for Dahlia's antics. I don't fully believe it yet, but Julia is God somehow. Since she's been in control, crime has decreased around the world. There has to be a connection."

"That's right," said Tiny T. "Here in our own city, police have been stymied by the quiet in the streets, as if a magic dust has been sprinkled on us. How could Julia possibly be a part of that?" She painted a look of amazement on her face.

Reece raised his hand and glanced at Emma. "Julia is the good twin. She only has our best interest in mind. She has the power to influence bad actors, turn them into rabbits."

"Is Julia here, now, with us?" asked Tiny T. She looked toward the ceiling.

"Who knows?" asked Emma.

"Do we pray to her if we have a problem?" Tiny T widened her eyes and smiled.

"Well, if you believe in prayer, then I would say give it a shot," said Reece. He spoke slow and without an accent, having lived around the world.

"There are a lot of folks out there who denounce Julia and Dahlia as fakes, such as Clarity Stillwell and his movement," said Tiny T.

"I've seen it with my own eyes, their power. I'm from another planet. How do you explain that?" Emma looked at Reece with a smile.

Camera 2 zoomed in, and the cameraman reached into his waistband. No one noticed. A tiny blue light appeared and hovered.

"How do we know you're from another planet, though? It's hard to believe, right?"

"Well—"

Two shots rang out. Screams. Reece threw himself over Emma and tackled her to the floor. Two more shots fired. Tiny T sat transfixed, then stood. The cameraman fired one last shot into the ceiling and ran for it. No one tried to stop him. There was a cut to commercial, and Tiny T yelled for 911.

An armored Humvee was sent on orders of the office of General Tom Watkins to collect Emma and Reece, after interviews with the police, and return them to Fort Knox. Emma's Corolla was towed home. The news was abuzz with the shooting. The nation was torn between seeing Reece or the shooter as a hero. Everyone with Organon had by now witnessed the footage, and Sherri Loveless, along with General Watkins, Glenelle Lock, Colonel Ignatius Lawrence, Jacob Jacobi, and Dr. Markush met quickly that night by phone. They developed new security measures, and Watkins authorized armed military escorts of the Organon Returnees whenever they were off the base. They had expected violence concerning Dahlia herself, but not the Returnees. The day after the shooting, Reece and Emma holed up in her apartment. They sat together on the floral couch, watching the news, covered with a blanket.

"He zoomed in on us and then shot," said Reece. "I swear I felt a bullet hit my chest." He wore gray sweatpants and a Roll Tide sweatshirt.

"You were on me like bark on a tree," said Emma. "You're definitely the hero, at least my hero." She squeezed his thigh.

"Just a reflex, I guess. They caught him quick."

The TV displayed the shooter, Baker Kidd, being driven away in a squad car with bystanders cheering and booing.

"Damn, he wanted to kill us," said Reece. "Father of two and a follower of Dahlia for Christ's sake."

The reporter, wearing a blue blazer and standing in bright sunshine outside the Louisville news studio, squinted and explained that Kidd had begun to "place faith" in Dahlia and resented her sister Julia for taking the spotlight. His wife said he had quit church and become obsessed with Dahlia. Despite Dahlia's evil nature, increasing numbers of followers found one another, many being led nationally by Simon Klinefelter of the Truth Ranch in California, who had a profile for his group on Five Degrees, a new social media site.

Reece gazed at Emma, their faces close. He admired her clear skin and bright eyes, which bore an ounce of pain.

"What are you looking at?" Emma looked serious.

"I'm looking at Emma."

"Which one?"

"This one?"

"Dummy, I'm the Emma from Gwar. I returned with you." She touched his nose.

"Right. But I can't stop thinking that it was you who saved my life in Godo."

"But I didn't. That was the other Emma. Do you like me less?"

"Hell no. I'm liking you quite a bit. You just look the same." He touched her nose.

"They're talking about Julia, listen," said Emma.

An anchorwoman spoke with a reporter.

"That's the Sims guy from *The New York Times*," said Reece. "Remember, he followed us to Louisville in the minivan."

"Hush."

The anchorwoman, a Leslie, asked Sims if there was

proof that Julia existed. Sims replied that Dahlia affirmed the existence of Julia. Dahlia, for an eternity, had overpowered Julia and banished her. But upon finding her mother, Kristin Myers, Dahlia had come to Earth and relinquished control of the universes to Julia. Sims cited the dramatic decrease in crime and the return of thousands of abducted parents and little girls. This was all the work of Julia, as hard as it was to believe. Sims spoke with conviction. He said that Earth would never be the same, that this was the most important development in the history of this Earth and undoubtedly others. Leslie asked why there were so many followers of Dahlia if Julia was so good. Sims, wearing his tinted glasses, replied that he was not sure other than Dahlia represented the status quo. She had shaped human history and led us to our current condition. Humanity was used to murder and famine, and a world of good seemed impossible in the hands of just a seven-year-old girl.

"Do you think he's right?" asked Emma.

"I hope so. But Dahlia has a 4.5 billion–year head start. People don't like change."

From Kristin's apartment next door came shouting and the distinct voice of Mia and Dahlia. They looked at each other with slight smiles.

"That reminds me, I'm having dinner with Kristin and Mia. I feel bad for Kristin, but that was a brilliant move by Markush to give Dahlia a mother. Changes everything."

"Yeah, I really like this Julia. She's real, and good." She snuggled into Reece.

"You're so damn soft. Drives me crazy."

Emma gave him a half-smile. "I have to get back with

Emma tomorrow. I feel bad about taking a day off." She pecked him on the cheek.

"She's keeping herself busy, though, visiting with the other Reece." He turned his head and kissed her on the lips.

She followed through, and they wound up side by side, Reece barely hanging on.

Bored and needing exercise, Reece suggested they take a walk around Tobacco Leaf Lake, a 0.6-mile walk. The lake sat just across Gander Branch Loop. Emma suggested they take the other Emma and Reece in wheelchairs. Markush was not excited about the idea but gave his blessing.

Twenty minutes later, Emma pushed Reece, and Reece pushed Emma, looking like two sets of identical twins. Due to the time travel, the Reeces were twenty years older than the Emmas. Both Reece and Emma could stand, but they were still weak. At the last minute, Arthur joined them. He'd had a bowl of minestrone for lunch and a glass of white wine. He was bored, too.

The temperature hovered in the forties without wind, and a bright blue sky enveloped the scene. A large round film of ice floated in the middle of the lake. Both in wheelchairs, Reece and Emma wore double gowns and socks with house shoes and knit hats provided by Kristin.

Arthur stood straight as a rail, his cheeks rosy. "Such a lovely day."

Everyone agreed as they crossed the road and accessed the trail that circled the lake, which was surrounded by a mixed hardwood forest.

"Kinda bumpy here," said Reece.

"I'll be glad when my hair grows back," said Reece. "Cold."

"Me too," said Reece.

They walked slowly, gazing at the greeny, icy water.

"Are we...safe?" asked Emma.

Arthur spoke. "The MPs, as they call the police, travel through here almost on the hour. They are quite polite. One lad told me a filthy joke that I regret I cannot pass on to such young ears." His eyes twinkled, belying his gruff facial features. "A turtle of some sort," and he paused. They all got a good look at the tortoise and moved it off the trail. No one noticed the bright blue dot following above them.

"Maybe in a few days," said Reece, "we can all go out and eat together. I hate being pushed around, no offense. I know I can walk in a couple of days, and maybe Emma too. Kristin told me about a greasy spoon in Muldraugh next to a motel. Maybe we could go there? Sounds like it should be interesting."

"Reece...what do you think about being shot twice?" asked Emma.

"God, I was sure I had been shot. I felt it, but there was no bullet hole and not even a bruise. It had to be Julia protecting us."

"You...saved Emma."

"Well, once upon a time, an Emma saved me."

Emma blushed. "My hero! But it wasn't me who saved you. That was another Emma."

They strolled along, Reece and Emma straining to push the wheelchairs over the gravelly path. They seemed to be a family, embracing the chill and sunshine. They looped briefly into the woods, then came to a sandy area. It was impossible to push the wheelchairs farther, and they turned around, cursing and laughing.

Reece spoke to Reece. "You were essentially brain-dead for a month. Where were you? Were you traveling to other places? Were you in Dogtown?"

Reece shook his head. "My memory tells me that I was in the Pinch with Dahlia. I was the perfect idea of me for a while. Julia released me."

"What was that experience like?" asked Arthur. "Everything crushed to a point is what I understand." He noticed Emma struggling with the wheelchair and took over for her.

"It was just black and floating. I was everywhere at once, surrounded by brief strikes of light, as if atoms were crashing together. That's the best I can describe."

They returned to the paved road and took it north for a short jaunt to an area of sandy roads. Talk returned to the news and the increasing uproar across the nation and world. The primary opposition to Dahlia and Julia was the Christian community led by Clarity Stillwell, followed by the Islamic faithful. Crime was still down and dwindling by the day, although protests were rampant since the Birmingham battle between Dahlia and Julia. Fort Knox was being painted as a Sodom and Gomorrah and the likely center of the end times. It seemed that anything could happen.

Dahlia looked so perfect and uncanny with her brown skin and golden hair. She wore PX jeans and a pink sweater over a flannel shirt.

"I love you, Mommy." She held Kristin's hand.

Kristin smiled at her as they entered the base commissary. She had left Mia with Reece and Emma, trying to avoid any public fighting between Dahlia and Mia. Dahlia was a challenge, but Kristin found her motherly instincts kicking in, growing quite fond of her. Dahlia liked pranks, but she could be very loving toward Kristin, too loving at times, which caused Mia to be jealous. Mia found Dahlia to be noisy, always out of tune, and bothersome. Plus, Dahlia had been the one to abduct Mia and replace her with a near-twin, not once but twice. She knew that Dahlia held special powers, but could not understand her as a God or a past God.

Kristin pushed a buggy with a squeaky wheel. A woman idled in front of the apples with her own little girl in the buggy seat. Kristin spotted a problem. The little girl wore a Julia t-shirt that showed a little girl's face as if it were the sun. Dahlia and Julia t-shirts, along with posters and even jewelry, were becoming mainstream in a short amount of time. The woman looked back, noticed Dahlia, and put her hand to her mouth.

"Look, Mom, it's Julia!" said the little girl. She wore designer overalls and was too big to sit in the buggy.

Dahlia stomped her foot. "I'm not Julia, you little brat. I'm fucking Dahlia!"

"Dahlia, no!" said Kristin. "You apologize right now."

The color drained from both the girl's and mother's faces.

"I'm so sorry," said the woman. Her eyes strained at Dahlia.

"No, I meant Dahlia," said Kristin.

"Julia's a pussy! You got that!" Briefly, Julia transformed into a towering giraffe, but she had meant to become a werewolf.

A small, dumbstruck crowd gathered in the produce section, whispering. Everyone on base knew about the Returnees and Julia and Dahlia. Kristin ordered Dahlia to come along and resumed shopping as if all was well. She needed potatoes and broccoli, pork chops, canned green beans, a frozen pizza, orange juice, milk, and something sweet. Dahlia liked the chocolate Ho Hos.

"You have to behave, please," said Kristin.

"Yes, Mommy." She seemed to be a drawing that moved.

Dahlia made eye contact with everyone they met, looking for weakness. Down a canned goods aisle, like the aisle of a large airplane, came a mother with her teenage son, who wore his brown hair long. Both could not help staring. They were passing Kristin, the mother of a former God, and that God herself.

"Just a damn girl is all," said the teen.

Dahlia smirked, and then the teen was wearing a red triangle dress.

"Mom!" the teen shrieked. He touched the dress and his knees.

Kristin grabbed Dahlia's arm. "Put his clothes back on, right now."

"Yes, Mommy," and the teen's jeans and hooded sweatshirt reappeared.

"Have a nice day," said Dahlia.

The woman and her son remained transfixed as Kristin and Dahlia walked away.

The produce section curved left and led into the meat aisle, which was perpendicular to the grocery aisles. Shoppers gave them wide eyes. Kristin focused, exploring each aisle: Pop-Tarts, chicken noodle soup, Gatorade, soap, and her favorite, sweet tea. With the buggy half full, Kristin entered the check-out line and placed items on the belt.

"Hello, little girl," said the cashier. She wore a red apron.

"Hello, yourself, and don't mind me more than you would a wart on your butt." Dahlia did a tippy-toe dance and sang a snatch of song off-key.

The cashier frowned and looked to Kristin, as if expecting Kristin to punish Dahlia.

Dahlia spoke. "I know you think my mommy should spank me, but she loves me too much."

A sacker swung into action, popping open paper bags and carefully packing like items together. He looked wary with eyebrows raised and mouth pursed.

"You're a honey," said Dahlia. She patted her golden hair with both hands. "I'm patting my golden hair with both hands. The doofus writing this all down is smoking a stinky cigar. You know, I'd like to see your resume. Blah, blah, blah."

"Oh, interesting," The sacker packed items with alacrity, seeming unfazed. "I heard you can do magic."

"No, she can't," said Kristin. "She's not allowed."

"Oh, Mommy, just a teensy-weensy trick for our friend

here who still wets the bed."

"What?"

A full-size mattress appeared near the ceiling and descended behind the sacker. The mattress showed several large pee stains. The image lasted about twenty seconds. Everyone in the lines gawked and whispered. The sacker finished and said nothing, a pained look on his face. His father whipped him when he wet the bed.

Kristin paid, warned Dahlia once more, and began to exit, but was stopped at the automatic sliding doors. A woman, Cindy, in military fatigues, grimaced at them, as if trying out a kayak in whitewater for the first time.

"Ma'am, you and your daughter need to come with me," said Cindy. She held out her arms as a barrier.

"What's happening?" asked Kristin.

"Got you a little thief there," said Cindy. She led them to a back room off a short hallway.

"Yeah, I loaded up while you weren't looking," said Dahlia.

The three stood in a small room that smelled of chili with CCTV monitors lining one wall. Dahlia toed the tight carpet.

"Little girl, can you empty your pockets for me? Right here on this table. You have to pay for everything, right?"

"Not where I come from, sister." Dahlia scrounged in her pockets and pulled out a pack of gum, a PayDay candy bar, a tube of sun-dried tomato paste, and a toothbrush. "There you go, Chesterton."

"Dahlia, why in the world would you steal? I would have bought those things for you. I'm so sorry." Kristin looked at Cindy with tired eyes. "What do we do now?"

The MP filled out a form and had Kristen sign it. "Y'all are free to go, but if she does it again, we may have to trespass her from the store. Got it?"

Dahlia made a weak promise, and Kristin reinforced it. As soon as they left, Cindy got on the horn with Darryl Hicks of the base newspaper, *The Gold Standard.*

Markush okayed Reece's transfer from the long-term unit to a room beside Emma in the medical unit. Emma and Reece sat in wheelchairs in the bright dayroom, the TV on mute, facing each other. They were helping each other stand and shuffle with a walker. Reece was the stronger of the two and encouraged Emma mightily. Debbie, the nurse, watched and cheered them as well.

"Hey, Dr. Markush," said Debbie. "What'cha got?"

Markush entered the dayroom, wearing a long, black coat. His long, gray hair glistened from the light rain. He held two large plastic bags. "Hi guys! I had Denise buy some street clothes for you two, a bag for each, tennis shoes included."

"I'll put those in their rooms," said Debbie.

Markush held a newspaper, *The Gold Standard.* "Check this out." He held up the front page with the headline "Dahlia caught stealing at base commissary." "Can you believe that? The national press will be all over it."

"Hey, Dahlia is mean *and* a thief," said Reece.

Emma laughed.

"Not what one would expect," said Markush. "We have a somewhat safe haven here on base, but still have plenty of folks who pose a risk to you. If you need to go out and want an escort, just let me know. But you're restricted to Fort Knox for the time being. For your safety."

"I think Julia is watching over us," said Reece. "I can't get her glowing image out of my mind. She looks like Dahlia, but her energy is totally different."

"Well, crime is down, and so are the hateful letters. There are still those stirring up trouble, of course, questioning the reality of Julia and Dahlia. I want Julia to be the all-knowing, purely good deity that humanity deserves, but who knows what will happen? Will Dahlia get bored and want to be in charge again?"

"I hope not," said Emma. "I've seen Julia...in my dreams."

Markush perked up. "Any seizure activity?"

Debbie returned. "None that we've captured."

"In the dream, Julia was in a zoo...releasing the animals." Emma tugged at the neck of her gown.

"Yeah, the opposite of Dahlia. She put Mia in a cage at a circus, after she was abducted," said Reece.

They talked for a few minutes longer, and Markush left for a phone call with Glenelle Lock.

"Emma, stand up, and I'll hold the walker in the front and move it toward me. Got to get you stronger, my dear." He stood over Emma like a concerned father.

"Okay." Emma grabbed the walker and took a deep breath. Reece held the walker steady as she hoisted herself vertical. "Not...too fast." She smiled a half-smile.

"You got it," said Debbie. She folded her arms across her chest, feeling she should be helping.

"Oh...brother." Emma took a step forward, then another.

"Doing great," said Reece.

Emma looked Reece in the face, taking him in. This Reece was an older version of the Reece she had worked with in Gajjo, but looked the same. She took another step, and Reece moved backward. The strain of standing felt good.

There was a brain zap, a brief loss of equilibrium, and she jerked forward. Reece lost his balance, and then Emma fell into him, laughing. Debbie jumped up to help, but Emma and Reece went to the floor, both laughing. Their faces were in kissing range, but nothing happened despite the tension that both felt.

"Got to get you guys off the floor," said Debbie.

"We're fine," said Reece, catching his breath. "So damn cold in here."

"You're warm, though," said Emma. She continued to laugh.

It took some work, but soon they were back in their wheelchairs, looking a bit sheepish in the large, airy day-room.

"Hey, Afewerki!" Reece pointed to the TV. He grabbed the remote and turned up the volume. A man in a black suit, without a tie, was stalking Afewerki outside the library at Eastern Kentucky University. Afewerki wore his Exxon cap. The reporter stopped, and the camera followed Afewerki as he hurried away. The coverage returned to the sleek studio with a Charlotte and Jim.

Charlotte spoke. She looked like a doll sitting behind the large, curved desk. "So, Mr. Nigussie has verified the existence of Julia, saying that she has visited him in his dorm room, encouraging him in his studies."

"That's right, Charlotte, but he does not see Julia as God, saying there is only one true God." Jim tapped a pen on the desk.

"I'm with him there, but can understand the appeal of a kind God. Julia has gained quite the following nation-wide."

"Next," said Charlotte, "we have the Reverend Clarity Stillwell. He appeared earlier today at a press conference from his offices in Colorado Springs."

Both Jim and Charlotte gave stellar smiles as the feed shifted to Stillwell sitting at a narrow table with his lovely wife Patricia to his left. She wore a blue slimming dress with a white sweater. Clarity wore a light peach suit with a red and blue tie. A prominent Christian Instinct Network logo in blue and gold hung on the wall behind them. To his right sat Dr. Newton Frasier, CIN's very own physicist and a member of the Pilgrim Sanctorum. No matter how much makeup and attention to his unruly black hair, Frasier still looked somewhat homeless. Cameras and reporters filled the room amid a bustle and low roar.

Clarity cleared his throat and began speaking, sending the room into a hush. "Woe is upon us, my dear friends and neighbors. The prophet Isaiah says, 'Woe to the wicked; disaster is upon them!'" He looked side to side to make sure his compatriots were with him. His face registered sincere distress, his mouth forming words as if straining for sense. "First, we had Dahlia and her shenanigans, and now we have this Julia, supposedly her sister, with a twist of goodness. There is only one true God, the God that hard-working Americans worship. God is Almighty, and He does not suffer fools! I'm calling for the American people and the world to face the music and pull this demon from the shelf!"

"Amen!" said Patricia, holding a Bible in her lap for comfort.

Debbie, Reece, and Emma watched with amusement. Dahlia was real. Julia was real. They knew it in their hearts.

"The Father God sent his only Son, Jesus Christ, to this Earth to save us from our iniquities. He did not send twin sisters who look like little brown dolls. Dahlia and Julia are tools of Satan sent to mystify us. They want to pose as saints and unbalance the seesaw." He looked to Frasier for moral support, but Frasier looked glassy and bored. "Can I get an Amen?"

"Amen, Brother," said Patricia.

Clarity found himself at a loss for words and asked for prayer, which he duly provided. "Dear Lord, You are watching as this joke of sanctity plays out before You. You have the power to stop this tomfoolery in its tracks, but have chosen to test your people. Give us the strength we need to tackle these harlequins and remove the mayonnaise from their chicken salad. In Jesus' name, Amen."

"Amen," said Patricia.

Frasier looked dreamy.

Two months later, crime continued to decrease at home and around the world, with many attributing the change to Julia. In contrast, there were others who saw the perfectness of Julia as repulsive and oppressive. For them, Dahlia represented the development of human history, which necessitated the battle between good and evil. There was no end in homes and offices to the heated conversation of who was in charge. For many, the opportunity to recognize a benevolent God seemed impossible.

In India and other countries where there were many Gods to choose from, Julia and Dahlia were simply added to the pantheon. Shintoism alone accounted for some four million sacred deities, and two more were not a problem. However, in countries that generally recognized a single God, the people were divided, such as the United States and Europe.

While Dahlia lived out her fantasy of having a mother, she became used to the idea of being human, but did miss the power that she had relinquished to Julia. She knew Julia watched her every move, and this cut into her enjoyment of the occasional prank, like setting a girl's hair on fire at school. Julia had quickly corrected the situation with no harm done.

Julia cared for the infinite universes with diligence, fairness, and quick action. Dahlia's reign of uncountable years had been one of disinterest. She simply did not care if a baby died from diarrhea or if a man beat a child. She did not find violence, disease, or accidents repulsive, but rather somewhat entertaining, like watching a woman feed her toilet paper addiction.

Julia heightened her presence on this Earth, navigating yet another transition from bad to good. Around the globe, she interrupted TV broadcasts with brief messages. She knew that she had to get her face out there to have a chance of defeating the past neglect of Dahlia. One such interruption occurred in Osaka, Japan, during a game show. Her brown face and golden hair played against a dull white background. She spoke in Japanese of humans as reservoirs of kindness and urged people to consider the well-being of others in deference to self-interest. These appearances multiplied, hundreds being logged and tracked by Glenelle Lock's team.

The number of deaths globally had dropped sharply, as noted by the Centers for Disease Control and Prevention. The only people dying were in excess of one hundred years old. No cars hit children in the street. No one mugged old ladies walking in parks. Those who hit their thumbs with hammers felt immediate relief.

In grocery stores, less meat was being sold by the week. Fast-food restaurants were experiencing neglect by the masses and were being forced to come up with plant-based options to chicken and burgers. McDonald's executives, seeing the writing on the wall, decided on a plan to convert their restaurants' service to pesto dishes and French fries.

With stubbornness, the White House finally decided to take a stance on Dahlia and Julia. The president noted the impossibility of developments but, due to unrest and division, tried to quell fears and navigate a peaceful resolution. Dahlia was categorized as a being of unknown origin with limited powers. Julia was given the beatific title "power of goodness." Urban areas tended to be more accepting than rural areas. California, New Hampshire, and Vermont passed legislation recognizing Dahlia as a divine being, but other states remained divided, with the Southeast being the least interested in a new God.

At Organon, plans were underway for the medical and long-term unit rooms to be converted into suites, replacing the hospital beds with twin beds and the sliding glass doors with a wall and lockable doors. Dr. Mumford and Markush planned to have the returned parents and abducted girls stay at Organon for a few days and debrief while undergoing lab testing, including DNA analysis and a head X-ray to check for the mesh, in which the Pentagon was very interested. Sherri Loveless worked overtime to keep the public aware of developments, but had curtailed off-base interviews, although Arthur was clamoring for more speaking engagements.

Both Emma and Reece made great progress. Both could walk, although Emma used an aluminum cane. The other Reece and Emma continued to live together, Reece having moved from the couch to the bedroom with Emma. Against the orders of Markush, the four planned an outing to the Ritz Diner with Reece driving Emma's Toyota.

Reece pulled into the lot, tires crunching gravel. Inside, they grabbed a booth overlooking the parking lot. The large window was milky around the edges with a dead fly on the sill. The orange setting sun sent bulky shadows through the diner, which smelled of grease and perhaps a soupçon of lemon.

The waitress, Sandy, took about five minutes before bringing them water and taking their orders. "Special's beefless hash with two vegetables: corn, green beans, collard greens, and squash casserole." Sandy wore a dirty-white apron that flared over her ample hips. She knew who they were but didn't care. A fortyish man with a cowlick, eating at the counter, turned and stared, knocking a tater tot onto the sticky floor. Sandy scribbled their orders and left.

"We're here at the famous Ritz," said Reece. "Want to play a song?" A miniature jukebox sat at the end of the table near the window. He flipped through the songs. "Need a dime."

Emma pulled a dime from her small purse and handed it to Reece. "Play 'Little Willie.'"

Reece slid in the dime, and the song started. All four

bobbed their heads to the music, smiling at one another.

Emma brought up the topic of the clinics in Ethiopia. "Did you guys...work with a Barra? He was a terrific singer."

"Oh yeah," said Reece. "I always thought he was in cahoots with the village administrator that everyone called the Hyena."

"The Hyena shot me, or I guess us," said Reece. Both he and Reece had the same scars on their temples.

"I'll never get used to talking with myself," said Reece.

"Yeah, right," said Emma.

"If we were mixed up in the dark, how would we know who is who?" asked Reece, making them laugh.

Reece's cell phone chirped. All of them had been given cell phones. "Hello? Dr. Markush? I know you told us not to leave the base. We're sorry. It was all my idea." He listened. "We're at the Ritz diner, having us some beefless hash and tall glasses of sweet tea. No, we're fine. We'll come straight back, I promise. Give us an hour." He folded the phone. "He's pissed."

Emma spoke. "We can't be corralled like animals. He's asking a lot."

Sandy arrived with heavy white plates covered in food. "Y'all are famous, you know. Why the hell are you eating here?"

"We're just regular people," said Reece.

Sandy took that as the last word and went about her business.

"What's in the hash?" asked Emma.

"Probably soybean meat," said Reece.

"Kind of good," said Emma.

"Just have to feed the horse," said Reece. "Keep the motor running. What's the latest on Dahlia?" He was Mia's father as well as the other Reece, and he had begun to drop by Kristin's apartment to visit with Mia. He recognized the situation for what it was and had given Reece the lead in terms of being Mia's father. "I saw Mia today and Dahlia as well. She's driving Kristin crazy as expected, but she gets a break when Dahlia is in school. Kristin is the constant entertainer, and the little blue dot follows them everywhere. Julia's on her case."

The guy at the counter, Jerome, picked at his food, glancing back every minute or so. A battle within was raging. The Returnees were in league with the devil. He slapped the counter and stood.

"Uh oh," said Emma.

Jerome walked with a slight limp, as if he had a thorn in his foot. "I know you...I know you well," he said. "Do you deny the existence of the one true God?" His voice trembled, his fists clenching.

There was a moment of silence before Reece spoke. "Do you want something? We're just trying to have dinner here."

"You are blaspheming God with those two girls. There are no other Gods before me."

"Where do they get their powers?" asked Reece.

"From Satan, of course," said Jerome. "You guys had better just accept that you're being duped and follow the true God." He wore a Kentucky basketball jersey.

"If you could be in my shoes, you'd believe in Julia. She saved me," said Reece. "Saved all of us. But Dahlia, for now, is just a sideshow."

"You must give your life to the Lord and be redeemed," said Jerome. He was wringing his hands.

Just then, the blue dot appeared above and to the side of Jerome. The dot expanded and filled with the face of Julia. "Jerome, how can I help you?" Julia looked weary but managed a smile. Jerome took a huge step sideways. Others in the diner were looking.

"It's Julia," said Emma, a spoon of mashed potatoes coming toward her mouth.

"What is this? said Jerome. "Some kind of joke. You can't fool me with your smoke and mirrors. God will punish you for sure."

Julia looked a bit sad at that. "Jerome, I want the best for you. The only God that would be doing any punishing is Dahlia, but I've got her pulse. I promise you that I don't see myself as God, but I have always or almost always been around. There is no God like the God you worship. Your prayers all come to me. If that makes me God, then we all just have to live with that. I hope you understand, Jerome." Dahlia returned to a blue dot and then disappeared.

Jerome looked perplexed, his mouth opening and closing. "Very funny, ha-ha. God will make you pay for your sins, AKA hell!" Backing away, he felt the pistol in his waistband. "Satan is throwing you to the dogs, I tell you!" He spoke to the whole restaurant, but no one responded. He threw his hands into the air and headed toward the exit, needing a serious smoke and fast.

Sandy came over with the check and handed it to Reece. "Sorry about all that. He's normally a nice guy. Might be a tad religious." She laughed and left.

Reece nudged Reece under the table. They had a plan,

and now it was time.

"Need to go to the bathroom," said Reece.

"Me too," said Reece.

"Don't get too rowdy in there," said Emma.

"Come back soon," said Emma.

The Reeces stepped into the bathroom for one. The light switch was blackened and covered with fuzz. A rust stain shaped like a sword adorned the old sink, hanging lower on one side. They reviewed the general plan and prepared themselves. Reece splashed some water on his face. "Ready?" he said. "Ready." Each held a small box. They arrived back at the table, the Emmas chatting.

The Reeces glanced at one another, then went to a single knee. At once they said, "Will you marry me?" The Emmas put their hands to their faces, one laughing and one crying.